Heaven in YOUR EYES

La Fleur de Love: Book Four

By
LORI LEGER

CAJUNFLAIR
PUBLISHING

DEDICATION

To my wonderful husband, Michael…you will always be the love of my life.

My beautiful mother, Diana Guidry Hebert, who taught me everything I know about being a good wife, mother and grandmother. Your legacy of love will outlast us all.

Special thanks also to the two tiny book stores with big hearts who carried my books long before anyone else did:
Sean and James Gayle of **Patti's Book Nook** in
My old home town of Gueydan, La.
www.pattisbooknook.com

and

Christy Lepretre of **Java Joltz** in Jennings, La.
http://www.Facebook.com/JavaJoltz

ACKNOWLEDGMENTS

In light of ending my eighteen year career as an Engineering Technician for LA DOTD, I'd like to thank my *other* family. The Designing Women: Roxanne, Joan, Tina, Barbara, Catherine and most recently, Leigh. The guys: Dale, John, Jerome (J.C.), Douglas, DeWayne, Jake, Cody, Shane, Chuck, David, Jules, Clayton, Patrick, Chris and Kevin. My *other* brother, John Faulk, a man I've worked closely with over the years—who has taught me the value of being meticulous in my work. Years of mark ups from you have turned me into a pretty good editor. Outside our office, there are too many to name…the DA's and ADA's over the years, area engineers (Ronnie Dupont, thanks for everything), all the secretaries, accounting, the lab, real estate, maintenance, all the techs in permits, utilities and bridge (big shout outs to Tammy Pryor and Cindy Holden), all of Lake Charles headquarters, District 07, and Baton Rouge. ALL you smokers and jokers, it's been a pleasure for the most part…and when it wasn't, it was always interesting!

To my mom, Diana Hebert, or 'Princess Di' as we've taken to calling her…whose recent illness has slowly, painfully, *grudgingly* forced her to turn over the caregiver reins to us kids. I love you so much, Mom but for God's sake, wear that damn bracelet to bed, would you?

To my own children—blood, step, and in-laws—both Mike and I love you all dearly. To our crown jewels, our grandchildren—we are so blessed to have all of you to enjoy, and thank your parents for bringing you all into our lives.

Thank you to my soul sister, Arlene Trahan Vincent, whom I can always count on for good advice and a place to vent. To my old friends from elementary through high school, and afterward, throughout two marriages. My new friends—critique partners, book clubbers, Bayou Writers' Group, Ottomaniacs, the notorious Ass Cheek Angels, fellow authors, Facebookers, Tweeters, Goodreaders and the other multitude of media friends I've met through my writing or their reading.

Update: We lost mom in August of 2013, but she's still with me when I write, urging me to "keep it clean whenever possible." Miss you, Mom.

Map of South Louisiana
Real and *Fictional* towns in book

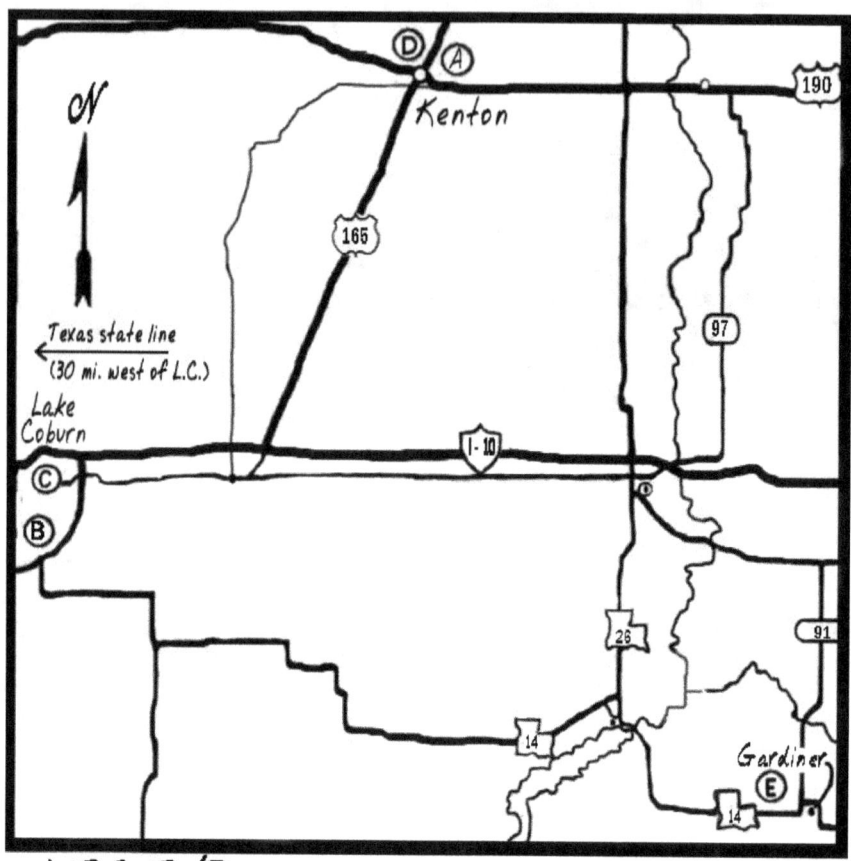

LEGEND:
- Ⓐ Annie's home
- Ⓑ Drake's place
- Ⓒ Red's new L.C. Club
- Ⓓ Annie's practice
- Ⓔ Vivi & Pete McAllister's home

Houston, TX is *140* miles west of Lake Coburn

Chapter One

New Year's Eve

Annie sensed his presence the moment his masculine-as-all-hell profile filled the doorway of her brother's club. He drew her attention like a mosquito to a fresh supply of B-positive. She targeted him within seconds. Once again, she questioned God's wisdom in gifting Drake LeBlanc with more than his fair share of All-American-southeast-Texan-*buffitude*. The man's drool-worthy qualities: six-foot-plus of sinewy muscle, broad shoulders tapering down to a narrow waist—she could only imagine what he looked like under that shirt—packaged with a strong jaw, chiseled features, and heavenly brown eyes. Male babies all over the world must have cried "Foul!" the millisecond he was born.

She sipped on her drink, able to admit the one thing eating at her. Despite his annoying habit of pissing her off in ways no other man could, the s-o-b was hotness personified. *Why* must he show up just in time to ruin her night? And *why* must he always look so damned good doing it? She groaned inwardly at how good he filled out his sexy attire of dark grey slacks paired with a burgundy shirt. As usual, tailored to torso-hugging perfection.

He turned in her direction, as though homing in on her presence. Annie ducked behind a column, hoping she'd purchased a bit more relief from the intolerable cockiness he flaunted like a Friday afternoon paycheck.

Drake inched his way through the crowd. The place was ass-to-ass people, great news for his brother-in-law and club owner, Red McAllister. It turned out New Year's Eve made for a hell of a grand opening for the brand new club named, simply, *Red's*.

Partiers on the packed dance floor moved rhythmically as the latest country chart-buster blasted from the sound system. Gorgeous women, dozens of them, swayed and gyrated in step to the pulse-pounding beats.

He scanned them in a quick, practiced search for the one face, the one particular shape in the crowd. He thought he spotted her but the vision vanished just as quickly. A familiar voice at his shoulder cut into his concentration.

"Hey, bro! We were beginning to wonder if you'd be able to make it."

Drake grabbed Red's outstretched hand and gave it a firm shake. "I'm late, I know!" He had to yell to make himself heard over the sound system. "But I'm working my ass off trying to get settled in. I unpack at the office until seven, go home, eat a little take-out, and unpack there until ten."

Red gave him an understanding nod. "It gets easier." He pointed to a corner of the club's huge, open room. "Everyone is over there."

It took a few minutes to get to the far side of the room, where the rest of their group had taken up three rectangular tables in the VIP section.

Tiffany McAllister jumped out of her chair at his approach. "There's my little brother!" She hugged him tightly then pointed at a chair next to her.

Drake exchanged greetings with all the familiar faces at the tables then seated himself. "Great crowd, Sis. I'd say this has all the makings of a successful dance club." He scanned the room. "Is all the family here?"

Tiffany grinned at Drake. "Annie's on the dance floor."

Drake nodded, trying to look nonchalant. "Did she come with anyone in particular?"

Tiffany leaned closer to him. "You mean is she alone, or with a date?"

He gave her a cocky smile. "Whether or not she's got a date is of no concern."

"I call bullshit, little brother. We all know how you feel about her."

"I know how I feel about her, too. All I'm saying is I'm not worried." The music stopped suddenly. He straightened his collar and cleared his throat. "It'll just make her realize how dim the competition is when compared to me," he drawled. A feminine voice cut through his calm composure like a machete through rice paper.

"Someone got an early start on the pompous-ass-act tonight."

He turned, focused on the crystalline blue eyes of Annie McAllister. His stomach knotted with excitement, despite the angry glare she flashed. He dropped his gaze to encompass shapely, stocking-clad legs in stiletto heels. As usual, trying to add a few inches to her just-under-five-foot frame. Her short, black leather skirt hugged her hips enticingly, torturing him further. A modestly cut, cream colored sweater clung tightly to her tiny waist. Once again, he marveled at this tightly packed little body. Thoughts of the sight before him kept him awake nights. If he fell asleep long enough, most times he woke drenched with sweat from dreaming about her. Drake leaned forward to catch her fragrance, a soft scent, uniquely hers and appealing as all get out. "Annie, you always bring to mind the old phrase 'dynamite comes in small packages,'" he drawled, while nodding appreciatively.

"You bring one to mind as well. 'An ounce of pretension is worth a pound of manure.'" She turned to sit in the one remaining chair across from him and shook her head in disgust. "You're so pretentious it doesn't even bother you that I think you're pretentious."

"I'm not pretentious, Annie. I'm just sure of myself, that's all."

"See? That's pretentious," she accused.

"It's confidence."

"In what?"

"In the knowledge that there's not another man out there who can make you feel the things I *will* one day."

"It'll never happen, Drake."

He leaned across the table and placed a light touch on the inside of her wrist. "I don't know why you keep fighting this, Annie. I was there, I know what you felt that night."

She pulled her hand out of his reach, trying to ignore the jolt of sensation his touch created. "That was a combination of exhaustion and too much alcohol." *One beer? Liar.*

Drake pushed his chair back slowly and rose, making his way to her side of the table. "You are so dead set against giving yourself the chance to be happy." He leaned closer. "I could completely satisfy you, in more ways than you can count."

She shivered at his Texas-sexy drawl.

"Come on, Annie. Dance with me. They're playing our song." He held his hand out to her. "You remember this one, don't you . . . Nicole?"

She caught the introductory piano melody to the tune she'd only played a hundred times since that fateful night at Red's club in Lafayette a month earlier. Three dances. Three dances with a complete stranger had changed everything—and not for the better. Especially when she finally discovered said stranger was younger brother to her future sister in law, Tiffany. Why hadn't she given him her real name that night? Why hadn't she put it together earlier—like before she'd practically had vertical sex with him on the dance floor?

She couldn't risk getting that close to him again. The man was dangerous. She turned away from his outstretched hand. "No. And if you ask again, the answer will still be no." She rose from the table, and in a desperate effort not to throw herself shamefully at him, she ran like hell. She pushed open the powder room door and plopped down with an agitated huff on the couch situated against one wall. She looked up, catching her sister-in-law's curious gaze via the floor to ceiling wall of mirror.

Jules popped open her compact and began applying lipstick. "What's wrong with you?"

Julia's daughter, Miranda, grinned slyly. "I'd bet it has something to do with that hunky Texas attorney sitting at our table."

Annie rolled her eyes in frustration. "Having him around is going to ruin every family function for me for the rest of my life. Gawd, but he's arrogant."

"Maybe you ought to just drop your defenses and see if there's something worth looking into. Drake is an absolute doll," Miranda purred, as her mother nodded in agreement.

"Don't defend Beelzebub's progeny to me," Annie spat, before covering her head with both hands and groaning. "This is it. I'm in hell."

Julia threw her compact and lipstick into her clutch purse and snapped it shut. "You're upset because he makes you feel things you don't want to. You have to admit he's a nice guy, and he sure is easy on the eyes. With that sexy Texas accent of his, those big brown eyes, cleft chin, and thick, wavy hair—don't be surprised if other women try to climb that cowboy."

Miranda nodded. "Mom's right, Aunt Annie. That's a good-looking man. He runs a few times a week and I'd be willing to bet he visits a gym regularly. I saw him at Uncle Red's a couple of days ago, and he was wearing jeans—you know the kind, worn in all the right places, and just tight enough to make you want to know what that faded denim was covering up." She shook her head slowly. "And let me tell you, there was some serious definition going on under that ab-hugging tee shirt of his."

Annie massaged her temples. "Oh God, I hope he doesn't join Billie's gym on Ryan Street. I signed a two year contract and I don't need him screwing up my workout time."

Drake kept a close eye on the bathroom door in case Annie tried to slip out on him again. He'd waited all week for this night, determined to get her to dance with him again. Barring that, he'd be satisfied with conversation—anything to get her to loosen up around him. He'd screwed up royally by not revealing his identity to her until Christmas lunch at Red's a week earlier. Crappy luck had it happening in front of the entire McAllister family—over two dozen of them. Miranda left the ladies room, and he smiled as she sat beside him.

She gave him a light tap to his shoulder. "Have you had time to join a gym yet by any chance, Drake?"

He frowned. "No, but I think my feelings are hurt. Does it look like I need to?"

"Absolutely not, but Annie recently signed a two year contract with Billie's Gym on Ryan Street." She twirled her hair and batted her eyelashes innocently.

"Well, that's a mighty helpful tidbit of info, Miranda. Thanks, I owe you one."

"Just doing my Christian duty to help you get settled in." She sent him a wink before reclaiming her seat a few spots over.

Julia returned to the table next, making a quick stop at Drake's chair. "Mondays, Wednesdays, and Fridays, from five to seven." She took the seat next to her daughter.

"Excuse me?" Drake asked.

"That's when Annie works out at Billie's Gym."

Drake beamed down the table at the two women. "I love this family."

By the time Annie left the powder room, Drake was out on the dance floor with Julia. She watched them doing a Texas two-step and remembered how it had felt to dance with him. She closed her eyes...could still see his smile, his penetrating gaze, and the kiss. Oh God. That kiss.

If she could just go back and erase those fifteen minutes of her life, she would do it in a heartbeat. Those three dances had ruined everything. Annie shook her head in frustration. Why hadn't she put it together sooner? The strong family resemblance...that east Texas accent...the fact that they were waiting on Tiffany and her brother from Houston to walk in the club any minute? The worst part of all of this? She had no one to blame but herself. If she'd only given her real name, she wouldn't be slap dab in the middle of this mess...drooling...lusting over a man she could never have. Check that. A man she would never choose to have. Lord knows all she had to do was say the word and he'd come running. *Don't think about it.*

She turned her attention to the dance floor, watched him move Jules smoothly around the room, and let herself mourn the fact that she'd never experience that with him again. She couldn't let him that close to her. He was too dangerous—just one of many pitfalls she'd so carefully avoided over the years. She'd let herself care for someone once, a long time ago, and it had very nearly cost her everything.

The flash in front of her eyes was the first sign of the debilitating migraine. The dizziness was the second. She put one hand over her closed eyes and tried to breathe deeply, praying the pain wouldn't come. Knowing time was of the essence, she grabbed her purse and leaned over to tell Miranda she was leaving.

Miranda gave her aunt a look of concern. "Do you need me to drive you home?"

"No, I think I can make it. Tell everyone I said Happy New Year, and I'll see them tomorrow at Red's and Tiffany's." Annie stood, gripping the table in an attempt to steady herself. She took a deep breath and began the walk to the exit. As soon as she reached the cool air outside, the pain hit her, along with the nausea. She leaned against the brick column to rest. The door opened behind her and she was too sick to worry if it was Drake.

"What do we have here? You okay, honey?"

Annie focused on the owner of the masculine voice, stared into the face of a stranger. He wasn't quite six foot tall, but was seriously built, like steroids built. But he didn't particularly look like a nice guy. Alarm bells went off in her head, but the pain caused her to make the first stupid mistake of the night.

"I-I've got to get to my car. I'm sick."

"Why don't you let me help you, sweetheart? Here, lean on me."

The pain blinded her momentarily and she knew this was one of those rare migraines that wouldn't let up easily. "Have a migraine. I can't see," she mumbled, making her second mistake.

The stranger chuckled deep in his chest. "Can't see, huh? This night's gettin' better and better."

A chill ran down Annie's spine as she realized the implications of the man's statement. Even in debilitating pain, she knew she was in trouble. "I think I better go back inside and get my brother, he owns this club."

"Sure he does, baby—and I'm the Prince of Persia."

"No, really. Red is my brother and...wh..wha...what are you doing?" Suddenly the breath left her in a whoosh as the man picked her up and threw her over his shoulder like a sack of potatoes.

"Honey, you don't weigh nothin', do you? You're as light as a bird. This won't take long at all."

Annie tried to scream, but couldn't catch her breath. The pain from the rush of blood to her head was unbearable. "Put me down," she pleaded, weakly.

"As soon as I get you where I want you, hon."

Annie stiffened when his hand went up under her skirt. "Put me down! Somebody help me!" she screamed, even as her head throbbed with the effort.

"Ain't nobody out here but you and me, hon. I do like a lady in leather and high heels, and you're just the right size," he drawled. "We don't grow 'em this pretty in Arkansas."

Truly terrified now, Annie tried to scream again, but her abductor bounced her roughly on his shoulder, and it momentarily knocked the wind out of her. Pain sliced through her head, and she groaned loudly.

"Oh, yeah. I like the sound of that." He reached a pickup truck behind the club. "I think this spot'll do just fine. Ain't nobody gonna find any evidence on *my* truck this time." He lowered the tailgate and dropped her roughly on the truck bed, making her head bounce painfully on the surface.

"Stop it! Help me!" She screamed loudly, ignoring the pain, and scratched at his face and eyes.

"Shut the hell up, would you honey? You know you want this, dressed like you are. Hell, you're just asking for it."

Annie grabbed both sides of her head in an attempt to stop the throbbing. She forced herself to open her eyes and look her attacker in the face, knowing she'd need to be able to pick him out of a line up if she ever got the chance. She stared at two faces, thinking for a second she was seeing double, until Drake's voice came out of one.

"Son of a bitch! What did you do to her?"

Annie heard a surprised yelp then several thuds, like fists hitting flesh. She heard someone else groan, another series of thuds, then silence.

"Annie, are you alright? What did he do to you? I'll kill the son of a bitch if he hurt you!"

"Drake?"

"Yeah. Where'd he hurt you?"

"My head...Migraine...Bad one. I'm going to be sick." Drake helped her to sit up.

"Move," she managed to say. He supported her weight as she became violently ill. Afterward, she clutched her head with both hands. "Oh God. Oh God. I need to get home. Just get me to my truck."

"You're shittin' me, right? There's no way you could drive home, besides, I need to go report this son of a bitch to someone. He was about to—he nearly . . ." Drake's voice trailed off, then he swore loudly, kicked the unconscious man in the side once more for good measure before releasing a fairly creative conglomeration of curse words.

Drake forced himself to calm down. "You can't drive. Wait here and I'll get Red."

"No." She groaned then leaned over to throw up again. She pitched forward, obviously too weak to keep herself in an upright position.

He grabbed her. "Hold on, Annie girl, I have you." He held her hair away from her face with one hand as he supported her with another. "Damn, you really do have bad migraines, don't you?"

She answered in a weak, shaky voice. "Yeah...need to go home...medicine's at home."

"You don't carry it with you?" he asked, incredulously.

"Forgot...different purse." She groaned and grabbed her head again. "Please, Drake. Get me home."

"Okay, okay, Annie. I'll get you home." When she tried to walk, she stumbled, so Drake gently scooped her up into his arms and carried her to his Denali truck.

"Purse?" The single word came out in a hoarse whisper.

"I have it. I found it on the ground just outside the door. That must have been where he got to you. I should have taken his I.D. from his wallet. I need to go back and get it, Annie."

"No. Please. Home."

"Okay—shhh—okay, I'm bringing you home. You live in Kenton, right? What's your address?"

"One twenty-two, White Oak Drive," she mumbled.

Once he got her buckled in he started the truck and spoke the address into his On Star navigation system. It began to give him directions to Annie's house as he pulled his cell phone out of his pocket to call Red.

"Don't tell Red, please."

Drake swung around to look at her. Her head was turned in his direction, but her eyes were closed. He caught his breath when he saw a single tear run down her cheek. "Why not, Annie?"

"Don't want anyone to know. Won't let me be after this."

"I need him to go see if that guy is still out there. He needs to be thrown in jail for what he tried to do."

"Please. Don't talk. Please."

Another tear trailed down her cheek and he didn't have the heart to deny her. He closed his phone and kept driving in silence. He had to stop once because she was sick and didn't want to throw up in his truck. When they arrived at the destination thirty minutes later, Annie had fallen into a fitful sleep, sometimes moaning in pain as she grabbed her head.

"Annie, is this your place?" Drake gently roused her. She opened her eyes, looked around and nodded. Drake got her keys out of her purse and found the one marked 'house-front door'. He stepped down from the truck then scooped her up into his arms. "Do you have a roommate?"

"Martin and Lewis...pets."

"Martin and Lewis?" He stopped in front of her door. "Is either of those a bull mastiff, or pit bull, or something?"

"Harmless," she murmured.

He nodded and unlocked her front door. She'd left the under cabinet lighting on in her kitchen, so there was enough dim light for him to see without turning on anything extra. He knew her eyes would be sensitive to light.

Drake jumped as a shrill voice yelled, "Hey lady! I'm home!" He turned to see a large grey bird in a huge cage.

"Aaannie...Aaannie...is that you? Hey la-dy! *Squawk...*"

"Let me guess, that's Lewis, right?" he commented. "Where's Martin?"

"Probably in bed," she murmured. "I can walk."

"Hell no, where's your bedroom?" She pointed and he started down the hallway. There was a nightlight on and Drake placed her gently on the side of the bed. "Where's your medicine, Annie? I'll get it for you."

"Bathroom." She pointed to a door. "Medicine cabinet...injection."

Drake walked through a door into a small, but immaculately clean bathroom. He found the medicine cabinet and opened it, scanning the contents. He picked up a case with a prescription tag on it, saw that it was for severe migraines and brought it quickly to her.

Drake watched as she opened the case and loaded a cartridge into the injector. Her hands shook as she tried to tear open a packet containing an alcohol pad. Drake took it from her, tore it open easily.

"Where do you want the injection?" When she pointed to her upper left arm, Drake swabbed it with the alcohol pad and scanned the instructions before injecting the medication.

"Now, lay down." He helped her into bed and tucked her in. She looked miserable with her eyes closed, and hands clutched to both sides of her head. Drake leaned over to check on her. "Are you still nauseous?" When she nodded, he brought the empty trash can from the bathroom and set it on the floor directly in front of her. He leaned over, about to ask if she needed anything else, when something large and heavy jumped on his back. "What the...Ho..o..ly sh..ii..it!" Drake jerked up and turned in one quick movement so that the 'thing' fell onto the floor with a heavy thump. "A cat? You have an attack cat? Son-of-a-bitch!"

"Martin," she murmured.

Drake stared at the huge yellow cat, its amber eyes glowing in the near darkness of the room. The cat stared back at him, emitting a strange growl from its throat.

"De-clawed front paws...harmless," Annie whispered.

"Hmph...he might be de-clawed, but I'd be willing to bet he isn't de-toothed, and that makes him far from harmless. That's the biggest friggin domestic cat I've ever seen in my life. A veritable walking lawsuit!"

"Must not like you."

"Well, hell—what'd I do to him?" Drake backed slowly toward the door, away from the growling cat.

"He's old—protective."

"And territorial as hell, obviously." He leaned against the door jamb, relaxing a little once the cat jumped up on the bed with Annie. Drake watched in amazement, as the huge animal walked softly to her and stretched out a paw to touch her gently on the head, almost as if checking her for a temperature. He nuzzled her hair then settled right up against her shoulders and head, and immediately began to purr loudly.

"Annie..." He didn't know what to make of the scene before him.

Her whispered reply shocked him into silence. "Shhh—he knows it helps me."

Drake stood for several minutes watching the scene before him, listening, as Annie's breathing evened out and she fell into a deep, hopefully painless sleep. The cat's purring lowered in volume as well, and Drake pulled the door closed except for a small crack.

He walked into the living room then reached over to turn on a lamp, perusing the tidy room and its contents. One word came to mind—cozy. Although the well-worn leather sofa and loveseat were both beginning to show their age, they were high quality, the end tables, solid wood and holding weighty brass lamps with bell-shaped shades. The walls and trim work of the room had been painted in shades that brought to mind scenes of Tuscany—in deep gold, muted green, and terra cotta.

The smell of leather bound books lining the shelves, all well-worn and looking as if they'd been handled repeatedly over the years, permeated his senses. He surveyed the room, checked out the various family portraits and framed pictures of Annie as an adorable child, posing for the camera and wearing big cheesy grins.

Drake made his way into the kitchen and saw what seemed to be professional grade cookware hanging on a rack above the flat surfaced island range. Large glass canisters containing sugar, flour, and pasta lined the counter top, while smaller ones contained coffee and various types of teabags. The kitchen looked as homey and cozy as the living room. More importantly, the room looked as if it was used on a regular basis, unlike his. He lifted his nose, trying to identify the source of some luscious aroma, and found it, a plate of homemade chocolate chip cookies covered in plastic wrap. He took one and bit into it, savoring the crunchy goodness as a multitude of flavors hit his tongue. *God, I hope she baked these.*

Drake walked back into the living room and relaxed on the soft, broken-in leather sofa. He popped the rest of the cookie into his mouth and leaned forward to browse through a stack of magazines on the coffee table. Good Housekeeping, a fitness magazine, tropical birds, and a trade magazine for physical therapists. Exhausted and heavy eyed, he checked his watch—just before ten. Enough time to stretch out on the sofa for a short nap. He'd be back at Red's club well before midnight . . .

Subconsciously, he picked up another presence. Sounds, foreign to him—a light fluttering, and tapping against metal. He breathed deeply, inhaling the aroma of something sinfully luscious and tantalizing, pre-empted by the hint of brewed coffee, rich and robust, tickling his senses— daring him to wake and open his eyes. He didn't remember setting the timer on his coffee maker, but he must have. Trying to emerge from the asleep-awake state he lingered in, Drake heard a light snap at his mid-section. Before he could open his eyes to investigate, a solid weight landed on his chest.

"*Hu...humph!*" The breath left him in a rush as he jerked upright, cursing, and swatting the muscular pile of feline fluff from his body until it hit the floor with a solid *thump.* Only then did he hear the distinctive feminine giggle. Drake's eyes flew open, staring into the highly amused face of Annie McAllister.

He jumped to a standing position, glaring at the cat's owner. "That thing's a menace." He growled low in his throat before dropping back onto the sofa. He breathed deeply, trying to regain his composure and slow the pounding of his heart. He blew out noisily, puffing his cheeks. "What time is it?"

"Four a.m."

He jerked back up, shocked that he'd slept for six hours. "Jesus, Annie! Your family must be worried sick about you."

She waved him off. "I called Red. He'd left a message on my phone asking where we were. Apparently, the fact that we disappeared at the same time was food for gossip and speculation all night long. I had to explain to him about the migraine. I hope he believed me."

Drake cocked an eyebrow. "Do you normally give your brother reason to doubt you?"

"Only when you're around, it seems," she snapped.

He gave her a wink. "That's because everyone but you can see what's between us."

"You mean the endless supply of annoying animosity?"

"Ah, now don't forget the arrogance and pompousness." He smiled, sending her a wink to go along with it.

"As if –I—could."

He couldn't help but notice the catch in her breath—the tell-tale falter in her indignant reply as her gaze locked onto his grinning mouth. Not quite as impenetrable as she likes to think she is. Then he saw it. The stiffening of her spine, the steel resolve and careless one-shouldered shrug perfected by years of practice, no doubt. If she only knew how bad he got off on a challenge. It took some effort to keep the laughter at bay. This was going to be so much damn fun. Bring it on, Annie Girl.

"Seriously, Drake. I'm happy alone. I'm independent for the first time in my life, and accountable to no one but God and myself."

"Yeah, I know. Your freedom, to do what you want, with whomever you want, at any time it's convenient for *you*. Blah, blah, blah. You are woman, hear you roar." His eyes sparkled with unhidden humor.

"I'm glad you find me wanting to live my life free of complications so damn funny."

"About as funny as you making your cat scare the crap out of me a few minutes ago."

"Martin has a mind of his own."

"Bullshit. I heard you snapping your fingers. You *made* that mangy animal jump on me."

Annie bent down to pick up the cat and brought its face up to hers. "Martin is not mangy, are you fat boy? You're a handsome devil, aren't you? Yes, you are."

Drake watched, in disbelief, as the cat reached his paws up to touch both sides of her face softly, then rubbed his head affectionately under her chin. Whatever else he was, he was clearly fond of his mistress. "Honestly, that's the biggest cat I've ever seen. What do you feed him, small children?"

She grinned up at Drake before leaning over to place Martin gently on the floor. "Nah, I used to feed him attorneys, but there wasn't enough nutritional value. Turns out they're all just a bunch of hot air. Now I just feed him the cat food his vet recommends."

Drake pointed a finger at her. "Good one, Ms. McAllister. I take it you're feeling better?"

"Yes, I am. Want some coffee, or is it too early for you?" She headed for the kitchen.

Drake watched her retreat, marveling again at the tightly toned little body, clad in a long sleeved, fitted tee-shirt she'd tucked in to her belted jeans. Her light auburn hair was pulled back in a damp ponytail. "Coffee would be good, thanks. I'm always up at this time, anyway. Did you shower already?"

Annie pulled two cups from the cabinet. "Yeah."

Something in her murmured reply made him think about the situation he'd found her in last night. After being raped, a woman's first instinct was to scrub all traces of the attacker from her body. "Annie, are you all right? I mean, that guy—he didn't, did he? I got there before he had a chance to—hurt you, right?"

"I'm okay." She spoke quietly. "Just angry at myself."

"Why?"

"Because I knew better, that's why. As soon as that guy made an appearance, I should have gone back into the club. The migraine progressed so suddenly. Usually I have time to get home."

"Can you talk about it?"

She took a deep breath before plunging headlong into the story, talking at a brisk pace, as though she'd lose momentum if she spoke too slowly. "After he threw me in that truck bed, I made myself take a good look at him, in case I got the chance to identify him. When I looked up, I saw you next to him. That's when you—"

"Proceeded to beat the living hell out of him," Drake seethed. "God, I can't believe I left without getting his ID out of his wallet." He reached out to touch a long tendril of her hair. "I just wanted you pain-free."

Annie turned slowly toward him. "And I thank you for that, but I'm asking you again not to breathe a word of this to Red."

Drake took her gently by the arms and turned her to face him. "Why, Annie? Somebody needs to do something about that guy. What if he tries that with someone else and succeeds?"

Annie pulled away from him then froze, as though remembering something. "Or what if he already has? Oh, God, what have I done?"

Drake frowned at the despair in her voice. "What's wrong?"

"I think he's done it before and got caught. Something he said—something about them not finding any evidence on his truck *this* time. In Arkansas. The scum-bag is from Arkansas. Oh God, he'll keep on doing that. We might have been able to put him away." She stared at him, her eyes glazed with tears. "If he does it again, it'll be my fault. I was selfish. I didn't want Red to know because he would have told dad, and they never would have left me alone because of—because I'm the youngest."

Drake's people reading skills were too sharp to miss her confession's obvious change in direction. "What happened to make them over-protective of you?"

She pivoted to walk away. "I'll need to pick up my vehicle. Can you drop me off at the club on your way home?"

He followed her into the kitchen. "I'll just ask Red—he'll tell me, you know."

Annie swung around to face him. "He might, but if you're trying to score points with me that sure as hell won't do it."

Her tone said she wasn't fooling around.

Well, hell. His dad always told him he had the patience and diplomacy of a jack-ass caught in a hail storm. It looked like he'd have to work on that. He sighed, temporarily accepting defeat before he approached her. "I'm sorry, I shouldn't have said that. I know it's none of my business, but maybe it'll help to talk about it and get it off your chest."

"Trust me when I tell you it won't."

"Trust is a two way street, Annie."

Annie's blue eyes pinned him in place. "Will you take me to pick up my truck, or not?"

He nodded slowly. "Could I have that cup of coffee first? I'm seriously addicted to caffeine."

She seemed to relax as she turned toward the coffee maker. "I was about to cook myself some bacon and eggs. I can cook extra if you're hungry."

"I'm starving. So, you really do cook in that kitchen?"

She pulled a carton of eggs from the fridge. "What's the matter, Drake? Don't people cook where you come from?"

"I used my kitchen in Houston. I cooked eggs—baked pizzas occasionally, that sort of thing."

"How about the women you dated? Didn't any of them ever cook a meal for you?" She placed several thin slices of bacon in a preheated pan.

Drake snorted before bursting out into laughter. "Honey, the women I dated survived on green salads, fat free Greek yogurt, and Evian. They probably use their ovens for storage."

Annie shook her head. "That is so sad."

He grinned. "I can't argue with you, there. It *is* sad, I don't know how they survive."

She frowned at him. "I mean, it's sad that you're actually attracted to those women. Says a lot about your tastes."

He shrugged. "Tastes change, obviously. Even before I met you, I'd gotten bored with that type."

"Why?" She reached into a cabinet and produced two coffee mugs, both emblazoned with the LSU logo. "Pick one."

He studied the mugs for a moment, almost said something but the smirk on her face stopped him. He took the one without the picture of the LSU stadium plastered across it. As a season ticket holder for Texas A&M, the thought of drinking out of a "Death Valley" mug irked the ever loving shit out of him. He waited until she turned her attention to the sizzling bacon, and opened the same cabinet door—traded the offensive mug for one from a set of plain dark blue stoneware mugs. By the time he poured his coffee and turned to face her, she was standing there, arms crossed and one eyebrow quirked in amusement.

"Something wrong with the mug I gave you?"

He leaned against the cabinet and took a sip of hot coffee. "This one seems to suit me better."

She clucked her tongue. "What are you, a Longhorn fan?"

"God no! Aggies all the way."

Her face scrunched in distaste. "Worse! Much worse. Like, I said. It says a lot for your tastes."

He shrugged. "It was local for me, and I'm a season ticket holder. I could probably be lured to the dark side—by the right girl."

"If you're looking for a girl, you might want to hit up Kenton High. Besides, A&M *is* the dark side. You need to come over to the light. Start bleeding purple and gold like the rest of the good people of Louisiana. Either that, or go back to Aggie Land." She turned around. "It's where you belong anyway."

"I'm thinking more and more, that I belong right here with you."

She ignored his comment. "How do you like your eggs?"

"Scrambled is fine, thanks."

"You know it won't happen with me, don't you?"

"What I know is that I'll die trying, because you're worth it."

"Yet, you're willing to incur my wrath by insulting my entire family's team? You're off to a hell of a start, counselor." She cracked five eggs into a bowl and started whisking them.

He shot for a quick, but favorable change of subject, one to steer them away from rival college football teams. "How'd you learn to cook, Annie? Did you take lessons?"

She stopped, turned to stare at him, her mouth pulled tight. "Seriously?" She shook her head. "Wow. Your privileged upbringing is showing, Drake. I learned from watching my mom. You know—cooking, cleaning, doing chores around the house. Those quaint little things people who aren't filthy rich do to pass their terribly mundane days."

He took a couple of sips of his coffee to fuel himself before forming a reply. "It's not like we had butlers or anything, Annie. Tiffany and I had Melinda to take care of us. She cooked for us, washed our clothes, got us to practices and school events. A housekeeper came in a couple of times a week to take care of the rest of the place. Catering services came in when our mother entertained. Other than that, our parents ate most of their meals in restaurants."

"You had a nanny, Drake—"

"And *you*—" his voice took on the sharp edged tone she seemed to bring out it him, "—had two parents who were actively involved in your life, who showed you affection. You really think Tiffany and I wouldn't have given our eye teeth to live like that?" He shook his head, tired of her judgmental attitude. "So, which one of us here grew up more *privileged*?" Annie's eyes widened at his reprimand and she backed down immediately.

"I'm sorry. You're right." Without another word, she turned her attention to their meal.

He kept himself from gloating over the fact that she'd actually apologized to him for something—admitted to being wrong.

In minutes they were eating their morning meal. Only slightly sorry for snapping at her, Drake looked up at the fresh-faced beauty seated across from him. "Happy New Year, Annie."

She nodded. "You too."

"You know," he drawled. "It's customary to kiss whe—"

"Forget it." She bit into a slice of bacon.

He sighed. "You can't blame a guy for trying."

"I can do anything I want to. I am woman, hear me roar, remember? I am strong . . . I am invincible." She put her fork down and flexed both her arms.

He reached out and squeezed her tightly packed biceps. "That's impressive. You've got serious muscle definition for as tiny as you are. Do you lift weights?"

"Some, but my work is my real strength training."

"Speaking of strength training, I find myself without a gym membership. Do you have any suggestions?"

She pointed her fork at him. "You'll need a hair stylist. I've noticed your hair's longer than you used to wear it."

He laughed at her attempt to change the subject. "Haven't had time for a haircut, besides, I'm not at the firm anymore. I can be a little less strict about it. My main concern is a gym. Can you recommend one?"

Annie stared at the sexy dimple in his chin, then moved on to his full lips. When she saw one side of his mouth curve up seductively, she forced herself to look away. "Did you say something?"

"Suggestions—on a gym I could join?"

"Guys on Enterprise is supposed to be pretty good."

"Is that where you work out?"

She cleared her throat, got up quickly from the table, and placed her dishes in the dishwasher. "You finished?"

"Yep." He met her at the appliance with his dishes.

Annie grabbed the plate and fork from his hands and dropped them with a clatter into the dishwasher before closing the door. "Are you done, or do you need more coffee?"

"I could use another cup."

"No problem. Grab yourself a travel mug." She walked to her bathroom to ready herself for the trip back to Lake Coburn. Her first priority of the day—get this man the hell out of her home.

Ready for the trip, Annie draped her purse over her shoulder as she entered the living room several minutes later. She stood watching Drake at the birdcage, trying to converse with Lewis—without much success.

"He doesn't like strangers, do you Lewis?" she called out.

"Stranger Danger! Aaa-nnie!"

"Yes, Lewis?" She approached the cage.

"I lo-ove Annie!"

"I love you too, Lewis." She stuck her face to the bars so Lewis could smooch her lips.

"Ugh! That's disgusting." Drake's face twisted with disapproval. "You don't know where that beak has been! He could give you some kind of bird disease."

"Sshh, he's sensitive. You'll hurt his feelings," she whispered.

Drake frowned. "Oh, stop."

"Aaa-nnie!" cried the bird.

"Yes, Lewis?" she asked.

"Who's the prick?" Lewis asked, with a flutter of wings.

Annie snorted with laughter. "Oh, oh. Too late."

Drake turned to her. "That is so wrong. Why would you teach him something like that?"

Annie laughed. "I didn't. He heard one of my brothers ask that once and he picked it up immediately. He's a very intelligent bird, aren't you Lewis?"

"Lew-is...Sharp as a tack!" the bird replied.

Drake put his head back and laughed. "That's amazing! How old is he?"

"Chad gave him to me for my fourteenth birthday, and he was about a year old when I got him, so around seventeen years old. African Grey Parrots live to be around fifty and are very intelligent."

"Aaa-nnie!"

"What Lewis?"

"Lewis wants a cook-kie!"

"Okay, baby." Annie went to get a cookie from the plate covered with plastic wrap.

"Hey, I ate one of those last night. They're damn good."

She turned to Drake, open mouthed, and held up the plate. "You ate one of these?"

"Yeah, I'm sorry, were you saving them for something else?"

She shook her head, couldn't keep the grin off her face. "I make these for Lewis. There's bird seed in them. And, ah—other things."

Drake's eye narrowed suspiciously. "What other things?"

Annie's low laughter carried through the room. "Okay, Drake. This is one of those times when you really need to trust me. You don't want to know."

Drake placed a hand on his stomach and shook his head slowly. "One question...were those really chocolate chips?"

"No." She laughed at the look on his face and took pity on him. "They were carob chips, which is completely fine."

He breathed a sigh of relief then narrowed his eyes again as he seemed to remember something else. "Okay, bird seed I can handle, but those *other* crunchy things were nuts of some kind, right?"

She bit her lip and tried to keep a straight face. "Sure they were, Drake. I hear dehydrated crickets are chock full of protein."

He closed his eyes, cringing. "Oh, crap."

"I'm kidding."

His shoulders drooped in relief. Her impish smile had him holding his breath again.

She gave one delicate shrug of her shoulder. "Or maybe I'm not."

He cursed under his breath, knowing she wouldn't make this easy. As in nothing. Ever. A sudden thought had his shoulders relaxing, had him settling down, ready to take her on. He'd had easy. In life, in women, in career—stepping into his father's footsteps, walking in his shadow. He'd left Texas for a change, for something more challenging.

He grinned and gave her a nod. Annie McAllister was more than a challenge. She was epic—life altering—she was forever.

And he was up for forever.

Chapter Two

By the time Drake arrived at Red and Tiffany's place at eleven, Annie had already told Red about the attack. Red greeted him at the door with a firm handshake. "We owe you one, Drake. That could have turned out so much worse than it did. Did you leave him hurting?"

"I left him unconscious. If Annie hadn't been so sick I'd have let you know."

"If you had, the bastard would be jailed by now."

"I know, and I've been kicking myself in the ass all morning. Annie was so damn sick—she begged me not to call you. And she cried, man."

Red raised a hand to stop him. "Say no more. If there's one thing I've learned about myself, it's that I'm a pushover for the waterworks." He pulled a chair out at the snack bar, motioning for Drake to sit.

"I'm not usually. But, when I think about how he took advantage of the pain she was in . . ." Drake struggled to get a hold of his anger. "I've never come so close to wanting to kill somebody with my bare hands. Wherever that son of a bitch is, he's not in nearly enough pain this morning."

Red lifted a lid to stir the contents of a pot. "We called the hospitals with the description she gave me. Nobody checked in with injuries to the face or cracked ribs. Either he crawled off on his own or someone else helped him to his vehicle. I also gave a description to the police department. They called Annie over there to work with a sketch artist. That's where she is. Do you think you could help with that?"

Drake stood quickly. "I can do better than that. What's the address to the station?"

Drake was lead into a room where Annie leaned over a monitor.

"No. His eyes were further apart than that." She frowned, clearly frustrated.

"I can help with that."

She whipped her head around. "What are you doing here?"

"The same thing you are. I can sketch the guy if someone finds me a pencil and pad."

Someone handed him what he asked for, and within five minutes, Drake had sketched an amazingly accurate image of the man as well as every tattoo he'd seen on him. He held it up for Annie's inspection.

"Oh, God!" She took a step back. "That's him. Down to the last detail, even the pierced ears and scar over his right eyebrow." She clutched a hand to her stomach. "Jesus, Mary, and Joseph—I'm going to be sick."

Drake watched the color drain out of her face as she ran to the women's restroom. He stood at the door, waiting for her. She came out, still pale, with both hands placed gingerly over her stomach. "Are you okay?"

She nodded. "Sorry, but it took me by surprise. I wasn't ready for that perfect of an image. You must have excellent night vision."

"There was a full moon that night, and I wasn't suffering from a debilitating migraine." He turned to the officer. "Are we finished here?"

"No sir, I believe Detective Manuel wants to speak to you. Come with me, please."

Drake spent the next fifteen minutes giving a statement, and trying to defend his actions to a smug-faced detective. "So, the fact of the matter is, instead of calling us to pick him up and get him off the streets, you took it upon yourself to beat the hell out of him."

Drake glared at the man who, in his opinion, had been rude and obnoxious since they'd entered his office. "Look, when I saw Annie in the back of that truck she was clutching her head and in agony. I thought he'd hurt her already."

"Had he?" the detective asked him.

Drake nodded. "Miss McAllister suffers from severe migraines that she has to take injections for. It came on fast, causing nausea and excruciating pain. When he threw her over his shoulders, like a sack of potatoes it caused the pain to worsen dramatically. Then he dropped her on the bed of a pickup truck and her head hit pretty hard, causing *more* severe pain. So, I'd say yes, he had hurt her."

The detective looked over at Annie and almost sneered. "These— *injections*—you give yourself, Miss McAllister. Would you, by any chance, have a prescription for them?"

"Yes sir, I do. If you have any doubts, my doctor's name is Alex Bertrand and he practices in Kenton."

"And how long have you seen Dr. Bertrand for this—*condition*—of yours, Miss McAllister?"

"Six months, or so, but that's because I just moved to Kenton from Gardiner six months ago. My family doctor, Dr. Williams, has treated me for migraines for twelve years."

The detective wrote everything down then looked her directly in the eye. "Miss McAllister, what were you wearing the night of the attack?"

Drake stood suddenly. "Oh hold the hell up, now. What she was wearing the night of the incident has nothing to do with any of this."

The detective pursed his lips, looking amused. "Sometimes it helps us to get a better understanding of the, ah, situation."

Tightlipped, Annie answered Drake without meeting his gaze. "I'll answer his question, Drake. I was wearing a black leather skirt, with a cream short sleeved sweater, black hose and high heels. It was chili that night, so

I'd worn my black leather jacket, also."

"Was it a mini-skirt?"

"Yes."

"In your opinion, were you dressed suggestively?"

"I wouldn't s—" Annie began.

"What?" Drake demanded. "Annie don't you say one more word to this asshole!"

"Drake, I want to gi—" she began again.

Drake cut her off and turned to the detective. "And you—" He stuck his finger in the detective's face. "I want to speak to your supervisor, right damn *now!*"

"Now, hold on, don't get your knickers in a knot, Mr. LeBlanc." The detective's voice oozed condescension.

Annie began again. "Detective, I don't think my—"

Drake stood up angrily, grabbed Annie's hand to pull her up from the chair. "We'll find someone else to speak to."

"Hey!" Annie raised her voice in a bid for his attention.

The detective tried once more to speak. "Mr. LeBlanc—"

Drake placed a hand on the small of Annie's back as he led her to the door and turned to look at the officer. "This isn't the last you've seen of me, officer. I'm not done with you by a long shot. You've just screwed with the wrong man."

Annie turned to block his path to the door. "Drake!"

"What?" He yelled, staring down at her.

She glared up at him, her mouth set in a stubborn line. "Maybe you're finished with this guy for right now, but I'm not. I've got something to say to him."

"I don't think that's a good idea. Let's just go find his superior officer."

Annie took a deep breath then stepped around him. She pushed him roughly through the door. "Get out, Drake. I want to speak to him in private." She grabbed the handle of the door and went to close it in his face.

Drake reached out with one long arm to stop the door. "This isn't a good idea, Annie."

"I don't need you to fight my battles for me. Despite what you and my brother think, I'm an adult. Now go, because I've got something to say to this—gentleman," she said, turning her glare on the officer.

Drake remembered what Red had told him once about Annie's temper. He let go of the door reluctantly and left to find the unfortunate man's boss.

Ten minutes later, a sheepish looking detective opened the door to his office and stepped aside to let Annie pass through first. "After you, ma'am."

"Thank you. Is there anything else you need from me, detective?" She spoke quietly, with no sign of anything other than sugary sweet politeness.

"No, ma'am. I believe you've given me all the information I need to set this into motion. I'll let you know the second I receive any more information on this matter."

"I'd appreciate that, Officer Manuel. Thank you."

Drake, who'd been sitting at a table speaking to Captain Woodard, stared in amazement at the exchange.

The Captain strode to Annie's side. "Has everything been handled to your satisfaction?"

"Yes sir, I believe it has. I'm Annie McAllister. And you are?"

"It's a pleasure, ma'am. I'm Captain John Woodard. Your friend made a complaint against Officer Manuel, here."

"My friend spoke prematurely, Captain Woodard. The gentleman and I have come to an understanding, haven't we, officer?"

"Yes ma'am, we have. I apologize again for my behavior earlier. I assure you, it won't happen again—ever," he added.

Annie gave him a brilliant smile. "I'm positive it won't." She turned toward the door, barely sparing a glance at Drake before heading out. "I'm done here."

He snapped his mouth closed and followed her through the exit.

They stepped into the lobby after a particularly quiet elevator ride. Drake got to the door first and held it open for her, watching her closely. The tight lips and clenched jaw were both indications that she was still pissed.

"Just try not to think about that guy." He walked her to her black SUV in silence, then reached over and pulled her to a stop a few feet from her vehicle. "Are you still upset?"

She turned slowly to face him. "Why would I be upset, Drake? It couldn't possibly be because you treated me like a child in that station, could it?"

"What are you talking about?"

"You constantly interrupted me, completely ignored me, and finally pulled me up out of the chair and tried to push me out of that office."

"He insulted you!"

"Yes, he did. He insulted *me,* not you! And it was up to *me* to put him in his place. It was not for you to go running to his 'superior officer'." She mimicked the tone he'd used with the detective. "I'm far more upset at your treatment of me than his."

"I can't believe this. I can't do a damn thing right where you're concerned, can I?"

"Apparently not." Her tone dry and unimpressed. "So stop trying, already."

He looked down at her furious eyes. "I won't apologize for defending you."

"What am I, a damsel in distress?"

"Last night you were."

Annie took a step toward him. "Last night I had the worst migraine I've ever had at the most inopportune moment of my life. If it hadn't been for that, I could have handled myself, I assure you."

"You're not serious, are you?"

She placed her hands on her hips. "Of course I'm serious."

Drake smiled out of one side of his mouth. "Annie, you're too tiny to be a threat to somebody that size."

Her eyes narrowed dangerously. "Attack me."

"What?"

"You heard me. Attack me."

"Annie, I can't."

"Do it, you big pussy!"

"Hey, now." He frowned at her. "No need for name calling."

She shoved hard at him. "Go on, attack me."

"All right." He stood for a moment then made a half-hearted attempt at rushing her.

She laughed at his effort. "Forget it, Drake. I should have known not to expect much from a sissy lawyer. You're just a bully with a law degree." She turned her back on him and began to walk to her truck.

Drake decided to teach her a lesson. He rushed at her from behind, as if he really meant it this time. The next thing he knew, he was on his back, and she was standing over him with her foot on his trachea. Well, shit.

She glared down at him then stepped away. "Get up and try it again from a different angle. Surprise me, this time."

"I'd just as soon not do this on the concrete, if you don't mind. You could get hurt."

She snorted then turned and walked toward a patch of grass. Drake got up and charged at her again, this time taking her totally by surprise—or so he thought. Again, he ended up on his back, this time with her knee on his groin.

"Got enough?" She rose quickly. "I didn't hurt you, did I?"

"No," he grunted. He pushed himself to his feet and turned toward her. "But how are you at frontal attacks?"

She lifted both hands, gave him a classic come on over and try wave. "Show me what you got, big boy."

Drake mentally prepared himself then rushed her in full frontal attack mode. This time he ended up on his stomach, with one arm twisted at a dangerous angle behind his back, and her knee braced against it.

She let him up. "Give up?"

He got to his knees slowly, then rose, with some difficulty, to his feet. "Did your brothers teach you that?"

"No, but they sure motivated me to learn everything I could. I took self-defense classes religiously for a year. I still go once a month to keep in practice. Satisfied?"

He nodded and rubbed the back of his head. "I guess so. But that still doesn't mean I was wrong in there. You couldn't have done that to a cop without getting thrown in jail. You'd have needed some pussy lawyer to get your ass out of trouble."

She shook her head. "If you hadn't been in that room, it never would have gone that far. I'd have made sure the officer and I understood each other a lot sooner, without your interference. You made it worse by going all 'He-man' on me."

"I don't see it that way."

"Of course you don't." She shook her head while buckling herself into her truck.

He grabbed hold of her door. "I guess I'll see you back at Red and Tiff's?"

"I'm not going back."

"Why not?"

"I'm tired of you ruining every family function for me, so I'll give you today and I'm going home. Tell Red and Tiffany I'm still feeling drained from last night's migraine."

"Are you serious? You're going to skip New Year's Day with your family because I'll be there?" Drake felt about as small as a tadpole in a pond full of bullfrogs.

She spoke, and her smile belied the tone dripping with sarcasm. "I've had enough of your little games for the day. Happy New Year."

Drake watched her drive away, totally disappointed in the direction this day had taken.

Chapter Three

He pulled the pillow over his head to block out the ringing. Someone was ringing that damn doorbell, long enough to make him want to put a bullet through the damn thing. He rolled to a seated position on his bed, rubbed the sleep from his eyes and glanced at his alarm clock. Midnight. Exhausted and unsteady, he shuffled to the front door passing his hands through his hair in an effort to tame his bed head.

"This better be damned good!" he growled, throwing open the door. "Annie?" he barely had time to ask before she threw herself at him, wrapping her arms tightly around his neck.

"When I got home I saw a strange truck parked in my driveway. I think it's him, Drake," she screeched, sounding near hysteria. "He's back and he's waiting for me."

"Did you call the cops?"

"No!" Wild-eyed and shivering with fear, or cold, or both, her voice quavered as she spoke again. "I didn't know what to do, so I came straight here."

He pulled her close. "It's all right now, I've got you." He locked and dead-bolted the door then led her to the sofa. "You're freezing." He wrapped her in a couple of throws draped over the back of the couch. He turned to get his bottle of Gentleman Jack and a glass. "Let me get you a shot of whiskey to warm you up."

"I'd rather you warm me up."

Drake came to a screeching halt halfway to the bar, certain he must have misheard. "What did you say?"

"I said, I'd rather have you warm me up. Would you mind?"

He turned slowly, afraid if he moved too quickly, he'd scare her away. Turned out it was a needless concern.

Annie stood, dropped the blanket and walked slowly to meet him. "Warm me up, Drake."

"Wait, is this a set-up?"

"No set up. I want you to heat me up—from the inside out."

He studied her, saw all the signals of a woman who wanted him. Wet, parted lips, pebbled nipples showing through the skin-tight Aggie button down shirt she had to have worn just for him. "You know what'll happen if we start something like that, right?"

She gave her head a slow nod. "I know what I hope will happen." Annie undid the top button of her shirt, then another, and a third. "You know, skin to skin contact is the quickest way to get warm."

He swallowed hard, as she progressed. "It's the quickest way to get something else, too." He heard a low growl, realized suddenly it had come from him.

Her shirt dropped from her arms, baring the flimsiest piece of lace and elastic he'd ever seen in a chic's bra—and he'd seen plenty. She stepped toward him, reached her hands under his white tee until she'd lifted it over and off of his head.

"Oh . . ." she breathed. "I've dreamed of seeing you like this."

Drake sucked in his breath as her hands placed feather light touches on his chest and abs.

He pulled her close, running his hands along her back, searching for the clasp to her bra.

"Nooo..."

He lifted his hands. "This is a set-up, isn't it?"

She chuckled, a low, seductive sound. "No, Drake, it's a front closure." She jiggled her breasts in his face.

He slipped the metal hook free from the loop and gasped as she spilled out before him, pale, nearly glowing in the moonlight streaming in from his windows. Before he could touch them she ran down the hall to his bedroom. They both slipped out of their jeans and met on the bed, where she forcefully pushed him back to straddle him. Clasping his hands in hers, she leaned forward in an agonizingly slow motion that had her petal soft nipples lapping gently at his chest.

Drake closed his eyes, groaning at the touch of Annie's soft mouth against his neck. He didn't know how or why this was happening, but who the hell was he to question this sudden change of luck? Nope, this Texas transplant was more than willing to sit back and enjoy the ride—in the purely sexual sense of the word.

She turned loose of his hands and lifted her breasts, pushing them together for his perusal.

Filled with searing heat, he reached out to touch—to grasp the perfectly shaped globes—his mouth watering for a taste of them. The doorbell rang again.

"God! I don't want to answer that," he groaned.

Annie pulled her mouth away from his neck just long enough to whisper in his ear. "Then don't." Her mouth returned to his neck.

It rang again.

"I have to."

"Why?"

"Hell, I don't know."

It rang again, this time sounding more like a cell phone than a doorbell.

She pulled away. "You have to answer that."

He groaned at the loss of her mouth against his skin. "Why?"

"Because I'm not here, and neither are you.

"Don't say that, Annie." He reached for her. She faded before his eyes, transforming into a translucent, ethereal glow. "No. Don't go. No. Arrgghh!" Drake bolted to a sitting position on the couch, the roar of frustration still on his lips, hands outstretched, grasping for what wasn't there.

He grabbed his cell phone, wanted nothing better than to hurl it at the wall. He came to his senses in time to save himself the cost of another phone. Red's number flash across the screen, he raised the phone and growled into the mouthpiece. "I could—kick. Your. Ass."

"Bro. What the hell?"

"Sheee-it."

"What'd I interrupt, or do I even want to know?"

"You don't." Drake winced, put one of the throw pillows from Tiffany's couch over his painful erection.

"Uh, okay, I was hoping to get the scoop from you about what happened at the station, but you bowed out. You, ah, sound kind of—are you in pain?"

"You have no idea," Drake grunted, praying for something to loosen up. The sound of Red's amused chortle reached him, adding fuel to the fire. "Not cool to laugh, bro. Not cool at all."

"Says you," Red snorted. "I lived through my dry spell, buddy. This one's on you."

Drake took three deep, cleansing breaths and promptly yawned into the phone. "What's up, McAllister? I'm wrung out, and you're keeping me from my beauty sleep." *Not to mention some damned sweet dreams.*

"That's Annie, man. You'd just as soon get used to it."

Drake dropped his head back on the couch and closed his eyes. "Lay off your sister, man. She's not that bad."

"You'll figure it out. Mom always says she can suck the energy right out of a person like a thousand watt light bulb. Anyway, Annie told us all during lunch about her interview with the detective, but I wanted to get your spin on it."

Drake sat up straight. "Did you say during lunch?"

"Yeah, we had all the traditional fixings—black eyed peas, cabbage, pork roast, and a huge green salad. Tiffany even made a batch of pralines. She saved some for you."

"Annie was there—today?" Drake teetered somewhere between anger, disbelief, and where-the-hell-else-would-she-be?

"Well, yeah. She showed up just after you called to say you couldn't make it."

Drake passed a hand roughly through his hair while chuckling into the phone. "Sneaky little shit."

"For future reference, she doesn't like guys handling her problems for her. She likes to take care of herself."

"Yeah, I got the impression my interference wasn't welcome."

"So, you decided to give her some space to let her cool off today? That was a pretty smart move."

Drake drew in a deep breath and released it slowly. "That's right." He'd skin her alive when he saw her. "Hey, give me her number so I can call to see if she's okay."

Annie put down her mug of cocoa to answer the ringing phone. When Drake's name flashed across her caller I.D., she drew in a deep breath and released it. "What can I do for you, Mr. LeBlanc?"

"I wanted to see how your afternoon went. You feeling okay? Did you get any rest?"

"Sure did. I had a nap and woke up a few minutes ago."

"That's strange. Red just told me you were at his and Tiff's place for lunch."

She smiled at the irritation in his voice. "I was. Stuffed myself with all that good food and took a nap as soon as I got home. I seem to get my appetite back when you're not around."

"Was it your intention to guilt me into skipping lunch?"

"I said I wouldn't go, and I simply changed my mind—woman's prerogative and all."

"Bullshit. You played me."

Annie shrugged on her end of the phone. "All's fair—"

"In love and war? Is that what this is all about? You ready to admit you have feelings for me?"

She chuckled. "I have so many feelings where you're concerned, Drake. Annoyance, extreme aggravation, bordering on loathing. None of them flattering."

"You could never loathe me, Annie."

Annie blew out her breath in exasperation. "Don't bet your annuity on it, counselor." She waited, while he seemed to consider her answer.

"What happened to turn you off of all men and relationships?"

"Don't put words in my mouth, Drake, and don't lump all men together. That gigantic ego of yours may have to accept the fact that maybe I'm just not that in to you. It's obvious that you're spoiled rotten and used to getting your own way."

"I'm not spoiled, and you can lie to yourself honey, but not to me. I was there on that dance floor, remember? We were mutually in to each other."

Annie squeezed her eyes shut, wishing for the billionth time she could take back that night. "Look, I can take you in small doses, but I don't want to have to see you at every family function. They're my family."

"Tiffany is my family."

"You are so seriously outnumbered when it comes to actual body counts, it's ridiculous."

"Why don't you answer my question?"

"What question?"

"About the guy."

"What guy?'

"The reason you don't want to commit to anyone now. Who was it? Some kid in high school that broke your heart?"

"That's none of your business, and it has zilch to do with you. The fact is, you have to control every situation you're in, and I don't like that."

"Whoa—spoken by little Miss Mission Control herself."

"I admit I like being in control of my own life, but I don't try to control everyone else around me, as you do." Slow building anger coursed through her.

"Oh, stop exaggerating. That officer had no right to ask how you'd dressed last night, and the attorney in me came out."

"Which would have been all well and fine, had I asked you to be my legal counsel, but I didn't. You just showed up on your own and tried to take over the entire situation."

"I wanted to give them an accurate description of that maniac."

"And you did." A chill came over her as she remembered how accurate it had been. "But, once you were done, you should have left. I know how to handle people like that detective." She heard him sigh in surrender and slightly relaxed her guard. "Just so you know, I do appreciate what you did for me. Everything from beating that animal unconscious to the sketch."

"You're right," he finally admitted, sounding reluctant at first. "You obviously found a way to bring him to heel. What did you tell that guy when you were alone with him?"

"That I have the right to dress however the hell I want in a public dance club, as long as I'm not breaking any dress code, whether it was 'suggestive' to someone or not. I told him I'd never laid eyes on the guy before he followed me outside, where, despite my protests, he threw me over his shoulder like he was auditioning for Clan of the Cave Bear."

"Was he more sympathetic after that?"

"No, but then I noticed of couple of snapshots of him with his teenage daughters, both showing a lot more skin than I ever have, this side of a bikini. I pointed out if I was 'asking for it' that some other guy could easily say the same for his girls. Then I told him if he didn't adjust his attitude toward female victims, he was begging karma to come back and bite him on the ass. He was the perfect gentleman after our little talk."

"I gotta admit, I'm impressed. You handled that with finesse, and I apologize for underestimating you. It won't happen again."

"I don't plan on spending enough time with you to let it happen again."

"Annie, don't spit up in the air—it's liable to fall back on your nose."

Lewis began to make a loud ruckus in his cage. "Aaa-nnie! Aaa-nnie! Aaa-nnie!"

Annie turned her attention to her bird. "What, Lewis? You feeling neglected, my love?"

"Lewis is bored! Squawk! Where's the prick?"

Annie giggled as Drake's groan carried over the line.

"He's not still talking about me, is he?"

"Afraid so; he has a very good memory. Did I mention how intelligent he is? He's an excellent judge of character."

"Aaa-nnie, where's the prick?" Lewis squawked.

"The prick's on the phone, Lewis."

"Prick's on the phone. Prick's on the phone. Squawk!"

"Aw, you've gotta make him stop. Please!"

Annie erupted into uncontrollable snorts of laughter.

Lewis switched to channeling Pete McAllister. "Annie Nicole! Get off that damn phone!"

Annie wiped tears of laughter from her eyes as she tried to catch her breath. "Lewis, my love, that's the smartest thing you've said to me all day."

"Lew-is, sharp as a tack!"

"Yes, you are, baby. Goodbye, Drake."

Drake barely had to time to say goodbye before he heard the line go dead. "Damn bird," he grumbled. "I wonder how he'd taste in a gumbo." As he rose from the couch his phone rang again.

"Hello?"

"Well, hey there. We missed you at Tiffany and Red's today."

"Hey Melinda. Yeah, sorry about that."

"I wanted to let you know that we'll be at Giselle and Jackson's in Kenton this evening. They said to have you come over since you passed on lunch. Greg and I are leaving in the morning and we'd love to get in another visit with you. Tiffany and Red will be here too."

"There's food, you say?"

"Oh Lord, yes. A traditional southern New Year's Day feast."

His stomach growled. "I'm on my way."

It was right at five o'clock when Drake pulled into Jackson and Giselle's driveway. The ominously dark sky brewed with the undercurrents of a winter storm. Drake stepped from his Denali truck, pulling his leather jacket closer to his body. Jackson met him at the door, and ushered him inside.

"It looks like we've got a bad one coming our way."

Melinda approached, arms outstretched. "Thanks for driving over, Drake. I'd have been upset if I had to go back without seeing you again."

"Me too, Melin. Thanks for calling. What time's your flight?"

"We're flying out of the Lake Coburn airport at eight a.m. It breaks my heart to leave here."

Greg walked up and hugged his wife tightly. "It won't be for long, though, just until we get some things squared away."

Drake smiled as he watched his former nanny cuddle with her husband. "You two are really going to leave Washington to live here permanently?"

"Absolutely!" Greg answered.

"Nothing's more important than being with our child and grandchildren," Melinda added, watching Giselle's two girls help their mom in the kitchen.

"So, it's official? You got the DNA test results?"

Melin nodded, her eyes brimming with tears. "Giselle's our daughter—and Mac, Lexie, and the twins . . ."

Greg's face nearly split from the grin he wore. "We have grandchildren."

Drake hugged Melinda again. "Damn, I'm glad y'all found each other. It's good to see you happy."

She nodded and wiped at a tear. "Are you hungry?"

"I'm starving." He rubbed his stomach in anticipation.

Luckily, the storm gave them just enough time to finish supper before moving furiously into their community. The lights flickered once, twice, before going out completely.

Drake pushed himself up from the table. "Damn that was some good grub, ladies. You need help finding flashlights, Jackson?"

"Nope, they're right here in the utility room." Jackson opened a door off of the kitchen while Giselle, Tiffany, and Melinda calmed the panicking children. Within minutes, the living area glowed with the soft lighting of oil lamps and candles.

Drake surveyed the cozy atmosphere, watching as the three women sat with cups of tea or coffee on the sofa while Mac and Lexie cuddled with their newly found grandmother. He smiled to himself, amazed at how quickly their lives had changed. He nodded at Melinda as she pulled Lexie on her lap. God sure had his own way of making things happen.

He slipped into his coat before joining the other men out under the covered patio. "Looks like the whole town's out." Drake stared out at the all-engulfing pitch blackness. "I wonder how Annie's handling this."

Red grunted, reaching for his phone. "Little sis always hated being in the dark. I'd better check on her."

Annie hauled the last of the boxed ornaments and Christmas decorations into the storage room off the garage. The end of the Christmas season always left her feeling empty and depressed. She made a mental note to pick up a few Mardi Gras decorations for her door, knowing the bright purple, green, and gold colors would lift her spirits.

After dragging her dying noble fir tree to the curb for recycling, she disposed of the needles and stood at the door, gazing out at the threatening sky. The lights flickered twice, then went out, throwing her home as well as the entire neighborhood into an eerie, early-evening darkness.

Great.

Annie stood in the dark, still clutching the broom and dust pan. "Oh crap!" Lewis began to chatter. "Oh, crap! Aaa-nnie! Who turned out the lights? Aaa-nnie!"

"Hush, Lewis, it's okay. Or it will be once I remember where I put the flashlights." She made her way to the kitchen and found a lighter. She carried it with her to the utility room where she found the flashlights she'd purchased. She gave triumphant yell, until she remembered she hadn't bought batteries. She saw the brand new oil lantern she'd purchased, still in its box, knowing good and damn-well she'd neglected to buy a container of lamp oil. The only type of candles she had were a box of birthday candles, and a couple of scented ones, if she was lucky.

"Way to go, Annie. I think you take the title for being most unprepared home-owner." She moved to the bathroom with the lighter to fire up her one scented jar candle before carrying it back into the kitchen. As soon as she placed it on her table, her cell phone rang, jarring her nerves. She reached for it, thrilled to see Red's number flash across the screen. "Your timing is impeccable, big brother."

"Hey, Sis. You in the dark over there? You want to come over and meet us at Giselle and Jackson's place?"

"It's out here, too." She squashed her first instinct to jump at the offer. "And it depends. Who else is there?"

"Tiffany and I came by to see Melinda and Greg before they leave tomorrow morning to catch their flight . . ."

His pause told her there was more to the guest list. "And?"

"And Drake."

Just as she thought. "No thanks. I think I'll take my chances here."

"You got supplies?"

She touched the jar candle on the counter top. "This place is a prepper's worse nightmare. I've got a couple of candles. Plenty of flashlights with no batteries, and lamps with no oil.

Red's chuckle reached her, doing little to calm her. "Jackson says he has plenty of extra lamp oil and some emergency candles. I'll be there in a few minutes."

"Thanks, Red. I appreciate it."

Annie disconnected and thought about stepping outside to wait for him. A vivid image of the sketch she'd seen earlier had her dead bolting the door instead. She waited by the door, her chest tight with uneasiness. She forced herself to keep Lewis company, to quit staring out the window. She didn't breathe easily until a truck's headlights shined into her carport. She opened the door and sucked in her breath as Drake stood there, illuminating his face with a flashlight.

"I come bearing gifts."

"I was expecting Red."

"I volunteered."

"Of course you did."

"Braving the storm to, once again, rescue my damsel in distress. I thought you'd be happier to see me."

She stepped aside to let him in. "Sure you did. You're so full of yourself, you can't imagine why everyone else wouldn't feel the same way."

"Hardly, sweetheart—Jackson and Giselle invited me to supper with Red, Tiffany, Melinda, and Greg. Melin wanted to see me again." He leaned in close. "You know, since they didn't get to see me at Red and Tiffany's place today."

Annie shrugged, deciding her best defense was silence.

Drake grinned out of one side of his mouth. "You should be ashamed. I may have to tell your mom, you know. Ms. Vivienne would never approve of that kind of behavior."

She clucked her tongue. "Yet *another* way to score zero points with me. And thank you again for reminding me why I don't feel the slightest bit guilty. I actually had one holiday meal in peace."

"You better be careful or that karma will come back to bite *you* on the ass, Annie Girl."

"Karma! Karma! Bite you on the ass!" Lewis repeated.

Drake put his head back and laughed then shined his flashlight on the bird. "That's right, Lewis. Karma! You *are* a smart bird, aren't you?"

"Lew-is! Sharp as a tack!"

Annie sent Lewis a sour glare. "Traitor."

Lewis hid his head under his wing, as if in shame.

Drake shook his head. "You hurt his feelings Annie."

"Shut up, Drake. Did you bring batteries?"

Drake dug into the bag. "Let's see what we have here—emergency candles, matches, lamp oil, and an extra hurricane lamp. Oh, and enough C batteries to keep you in business for a good while. Good enough?"

She nodded. "That's perfect. Thanks, and now you can leave."

"Hold on, now. Not until I've made sure everything works and you've battened down the hatches. Where are your flashlights, Annie Girl?"

"Don't call me that."

"Why not?"

"Do you need another reason, other than I don't like it?"

"I might."

She handed him the flashlights and he began to put batteries in them while she filled her lamp with the oil and lit the wick. She found a couple of candle holders and placed the emergency candles in them. By the time she was done, the kitchen and living room glowed with the cozy warmth of candles and lamp light.

"That's better," he murmured.

"Yes it is, and thanks. Now, please leave so I can lock up for the night."

"I can hang around for a few minutes."

She turned to stare out the window over her kitchen sink. "I think-I-I'd rather you didn't." She braced herself, keeping her eye on his reflection as he approached from behind.

"It's because you don't trust yourself when I'm around."

"It's you I don't trust."

Drake positioned his arms on either side of her, caging her in against her kitchen cabinet. He leaned in, bringing his mouth near her ear. "Are you afraid of me, Annie Girl?"

"Don't call me that." T.J. called her that, and she didn't need to revisit any part of the T.J. incident. A particularly awful time, with even more awful memories.

"I'll stop if you tell me why."

His response, whispered softly next to her ear, had her fighting off the urge to turn to him.

"Because it's a silly nickname and I don't like it." She turned, pushed him away with both hands. She faced him, chin lowered, staring into his chest. "Satisfied now?"

"Not in the least." He reached out to lift her chin. "I wish you'd quit pushing me away. You've got to feel the same attraction I do. Every time we're near each other, the air practically crackles."

"Maybe it's that Karma you talked about getting ready to bite us both on the ass. We'd be at each other's throats the entire time, and we'd never agree on anything."

"We only do that because you can't see what's in front of your face."

She saw it, but kept it to herself. How could she admit her darkest fear to him? How could she tell him that once she let him in her life, into her heart, she'd never be able to say no to him. She'd lose herself. Just as she had with T.J. She shivered at the thought of what else she'd nearly lost.

He placed a gentle kiss on her brow. "I'm, crazy about you, Annie." He lowered his mouth, lightly brushed his lips against hers.

Before he could deepen the kiss Annie slipped out from under his arms.

"Thanks for bringing everything. Thank Jackson and Giselle for me." She held the door open for him, struggling to keep her composure.

He brushed his hand softly along her waist. "Think about the possibilities."

She avoided his gaze, focused instead on the third button of his tailored shirt instead. "I have, and that's why it can't happen. Good night."

Drake cupped her face. "Good night, Annie. Sweet dreams." When she turned away from his second attempt to kiss her, he sighed and pressed another kiss onto her forehead. He stepped through the door opening and headed to his truck.

Annie showered by the light of two candles and went to bed early, snuggling with Martin. She tried to read a book in order to settle her nerves. An hour later, she was still distracted. She lay there, on the edge of tears. *It's the darkness.* It unsettled her. It always made her feel vulnerable, and she hated feeling vulnerable.

She groaned when her cell phone rang, knowing damn well she'd left it in the kitchen. She ran, taking a flashlight with her, and answered with a flustered "Hello."

"Just passing by your place on my way home to see if you're okay."

Her pulse quickened at the sound of Drake's voice. "I'm fine." She cringed at the edginess in her voice, shivered at the darkness of the room. "Why wouldn't I be?" She used a lighter to re-light one of the emergency candles.

"Because." He spoke softly, as though calming an agitated animal or child. "You looked like a scared little girl in the dark, Annie Girl. Are you afraid of the dark?"

Annie walked to the window, lifted the edge of a drape in order to see the truck parked on the street in front of her home. "No, of course not."

"I see no evidence to support that claim. Are you sure you don't want some company? I'd be glad to keep the boogeyman away for you."

"Sometimes I think you are the boogeyman." Her reply had been barely more than a whisper, more for her benefit than his.

He was quiet for several seconds. "You would never have to be afraid of me, Annie. Let me in, and I'll prove it to you."

She squeezed her eyes shut, wished for once, she could. Just for tonight, so she wouldn't be afraid in the dark. She reached for the deadbolt, turned it slowly, and moved her hand over the knob. She paused, her fingers trembling as she fought not to throw the door open. Struggled not to invite him in. He couldn't possibly know the discipline it took to stop herself.

He was wrong about one thing. She did feel their connection. Enough to know that if she let him in, her life would change. She didn't want that. Her life was finally the way she wanted it.

"Goodnight Drake."

She heard his sigh of disappointment, could practically see his head falling back on the seat of his truck.

"You're killing me, Annie. A slow, gradual death, but painful as hell."

"I doubt that."

"You don't know what I'm willing to do for you, hon."

"Don't say that. I don't want to know."

Drake stared at the shadow behind the curtain, longing for the feel of her in his arms, the touch of her sweet mouth against his. "You need to know, Annie. You need to know that I'd give up everything for you." He heard a click, recognized dead air space. Drake stared at the phone in his hand and smiled sadly.

"I already have."

Chapter Four

Drake slid the new gym membership card into his wallet, locked it up with the rest of his things before pocketing the key. He entered the machine room, found her on one of several treadmills. He stopped to watch her run, admiring her athletic gait. Damn if she didn't look sexy as hell in a pair of work out pants and a plain white tee shirt.

"Hey, Annie."

She barely faltered as she sent him a glare. "You are stalking me, aren't you?"

"I'm here to work off all that good Cajun cooking I've eaten way too much of. Frankly, I'm surprised to see you here. I thought you went to Guy's gym."

Annie seemed to ignore the comment as she stepped up the pace on the treadmill. Drake started off at a slow trot then quickly picked it up so that they were jogging at the same pace.

"You here as somebody's guest?"

He glanced down at the top of her head, repressing a laugh at her last bit of hope he was about to shred. "Just signed a contract, binding and legal. I should know."

Annie sent him an angry frown before popping in her ear buds. She worked out furiously, all the while seeming outwardly to ignore the hell out of him. Unfortunately for her, he had excellent peripheral vision and it only took one surreptitious glance for him to see her checking him out. He'd have to work hard to make up for that pitiful performance of his outside the police station the other day. Granted, he wasn't trying all that seriously to attack her, but she'd surprised the hell out of him, none the less.

He couldn't help but be proud that she'd learned to defend herself, but he could still see her in the truck bed with that animal standing over her. He shook his head, angry at himself all over again, wishing for a do-over with that son of a bitch. He'd make damn sure he never touched another woman. Thank God that creep had no idea who she was.

Annie tried not to look at him, tried not to notice the powerful strength in his legs as they pumped up and down on the machine, the muscular calves and thighs as they bunched and knotted. She passed a quick glance over his chiseled biceps and triceps, and wondered if that upper torso looked as good as it felt the first night she'd met him. She forced herself to look away, feeling the heat beginning to build low in her abdomen. Looking away couldn't quell the memory of those sexy as hell pads of oblique muscles under her hands. Dear God, how she remembered latching on to them for those dances. Regardless of her emotional turmoil, she couldn't deny the truth. That night had been the biggest, baddest turn-on of her entire adult life.

She watched as he lowered the speed of his treadmill before stepping off, his brow furrowed. "What's wrong? Had enough, already?" She was barely winded.

Drake shook his head. "No, but I just thought of something. The attack at the club. There's no way that guy could possibly know who you are, is there?"

Annie shook her head, jogging for several more seconds before the sliver of a thought finally developed into a full-fledged memory. She slowed the treadmill to a gradual stop and stepped down beside him. "Oh God. Oh my God." She stared straight ahead, her breath hitching as dread, rather than oxygen, filled her lungs.

Drake released a low hiss as he pushed his hair back from his forehead with both hands. "What?"

"I-I told him Red was my brother. I thought somehow if he knew, it would stop him, but he didn't believe me." She could hear herself speaking faster as she became more flustered. "He didn't. He didn't believe me, I mean. That's good, right?"

Drake's face seemed to register several emotions at one time, as though he was torn between lying just to reassure her, or telling her the truth in order to keep her safe.

"Yeah, it would be good, if you knew for sure that he didn't believe you. But, if he ever lays eyes on Red, he'd put it together." His eyes softened suddenly as he reached out to touch her hair, then brushed a knuckle gently across her brow. "In case you forgot, the McAllister family has some very dominant traits."

She snorted and pulled away from him. "Tell me about it. I couldn't get away with a damn thing the whole time I was in Gardiner. From Kindergarten until I was thirty years old, all I ever heard was, 'You must be Pete and Vivi's daughter,' or 'You're *so and so's* baby sister, aren't you?' This is the first time I've *ever* had a life of my own." She rested her hands on her hips and concentrated, chewing on her bottom lip. "And now I have to worry about some asshole trying to ruin it for me." She shook her head as she headed to the stair climber. "This is just great."

"Maybe we could see about getting you some protection."

She had to check to make sure he wasn't wearing that infuriating smug look he seemed to be so fond of. For a change, he wasn't. "For a second I thought you were serious."

"I'm serious as shit, Annie. I could have someone tail you for a while— for your own protection, of course."

"Oh absolutely. My fantasy has always been to have you know my every move."

"It works for me." He shrugged nonchalantly.

She sent him a dry, humorless smile. "No doubt, but it's out of the question."

"Look, Annie girl, I only want to make sure you're okay."

She glared at him while adjusting the stair climber. "Didn't I ask you to quit calling me that?"

"You did, but it rolls off my tongue too easily."

"Look, I'm trying to work out here and this building is humongous," she huffed. "Can't you do your own thing in another corner?"

He chuckled. "I will, but one day you're going to tell me everything there is to know about you."

"Don't hold your breath." She thought better of it and smiled up at him. "Or better yet—do."

He grinned then walked away from her—but not too far away. Now that he'd thought about that animal being able to find her somehow, he'd never be able to relax. He wasn't about to take any chances with her safety. He needed to speak to Red about this, and he needed to know he wasn't being paranoid.

Drake spent the next hour watching Annie work out, majorly impressed that someone so tiny could have so much strength and stamina. She worked at the stair climber until she was drenched with sweat, then moved on to the upper body machine. When she came out of the locker room dressed in her regular clothes, he was waiting for her at the exit.

She released an exasperated sigh. "I don't need you following me around like a puppy."

"I'm going to walk you to your truck." Her glare prompted an unapologetic, one-shouldered shrug from him. "Hey, I can't help it if I'm the only one here with enough sense to be worried about you."

"You're not going to tell Red and the rest of my family about this, are you?"

"Not if you do it first."

"Oh, come on, Drake. I'm sure he's long gone. He's from Arkansas, for God's sake. He probably ran home with his tail between his legs."

"Annie, I'm from Texas, but I live *here* now. Just because he's from Arkansas doesn't mean he's not here, too. He could be working here, living here. He could be running from the law in Arkansas. You need to be smart about this."

Annie walked to her black Escape and hit the unlock button. She opened the door and threw her gym bag into the passenger seat. "You need to mind your own business for a change. I do not want Red knowing about this. He'll overreact like he always has where I'm concerned."

"That would be a damned sight better than you underreacting." He rested a forearm on her door. "Can't you see how potentially dangerous this situation could be?"

"It could be, but it's unlikely. I'm not going to let you use scare tactics to control me or my life."

"Scare tactics? God, Annie, you sneeze at a gnat, but yet you'll swallow a camel in a second."

"Oh what*ever*. I don't even know what the hell that's supposed to mean." She slid the seatbelt across the front of her body.

He reached inside to grab the belt. "It means you're too worried about losing your independence when you should be worrying about losing your life."

She jerked the seatbelt out of his hand and snapped it. "You wouldn't understand. Now move your arm, please, I need to go home. I have responsibilities."

"God forbid you get home ten minutes late. Martin and Lewis might have a shit fit."

"Say what you want but Martin and Lewis have both been there for me without fail."

He leaned down so that his face was even with hers. "I'd be there for you too, if you'd let me."

She stared silently, as though studying his features, before looking away.

"How about it, Annie, won't you let me be there for you?"

"I've gotta go." She reached for her door handle again.

"You know, if you keep pushing me away, one day I might just decide to leave you alone. Then how would you feel?"

Annie put a finger to her head, pretending to concentrate. "Hmm, let me see. At peace?"

The slam of her car door preceded the rev of its engine. As she pulled away, he waved, catching one last glimpse of her in her side view mirror. Her frown had him wishing he had Mel Gibson's gift in that movie where he could read women's minds. What he wouldn't give to know what Annie McAllister was thinking right now. Would she miss him if he did stop paying attention to her one day? That was something to think about for another time, when he was sure she wasn't in danger.

Tiffany greeted Drake at the front door with a hug. "Hey, little brother, who's on your mind these days?" She grinned at him. "As if I don't already know."

He stepped inside and gave his sister a frown. "It's the same little firecracker pain in the butt, all right, but not for the usual reason. Where's Red?"

Red entered from the hallway. "I'm right here, what's going on?"

"I'm thinking Annie may need some kind of protection. She told the guy her brother owned the club. Now, supposedly he didn't believe her when she told him, but—"

"All he has to do is get a glimpse of me to figure it out. Hell, I'm all over the damn internet."

From the looks of it, Red was obviously ready to jump on the better-safe-than-sorry band wagon with Drake. "I know I hurt him too bad to act on it the last few days, but he's sure as hell had time to think."

Red nodded. "If he's as mean as he sounds, he could be pissed you kicked his ass rather than scared. Not that I wouldn't have done the same thing," he was quick to add.

"Maybe he was just passing through and he'll run home to Arkansas, but I can't see taking the chance, Red."

"Me either. I agree with you, Drake. I'll need to get her some protection."

Tiffany walked over and laid a comforting hand on her husband's chest. "Are you thinking of having someone tail her? Because she's going to hate that—Annie is funny about her privacy and independence."

"Babe, A little bit of investigating on his part, a few questions here and there, and he'd find her easily. If anything happened to her and I could have done something to prevent it, I'd never forgive myself. She'll have to be inconvenienced until this guy is caught."

Tiffany stood and rubbed her hands up and down her arms briskly, as though to ward off a chill. "You two are really scaring me."

Drake paced the kitchen floor. "This is my fault. I'm responsible. If I'd called you, he'd be behind bars."

Red rested his hand heavily on Drake's shoulder. "I won't blame you for taking care of my sister when she was suffering. She told me once that a migraine was like having a tank running around in her brain."

Drake frowned as he remembered how she'd looked when she was in so much pain. "Even then she didn't want me to call you."

"She's stubborn as hell, something you'll have to get used to—if you're serious about her, that is."

"Annie Girl has no idea how serious I am about her." Drake cocked his head at the look Red gave him. "What's wrong?"

"You don't call her that, do you?"

"She's not fond of it, but I usually can't help myself."

"We don't call her that since T.J."

"T.J.?"

"Tommy Boudreaux, an ex-boyfriend. It was a high school thing, but pretty serious."

Curious about his earliest competition, Drake wanted to know more. "Did it end badly?"

"Not badly, as in a big fight, or anything. He got a scholarship to UCLA for football. She planned to go to LSU, but applied to UCLA too, just to see if she could get in. When they both offered her full scholarships, she was forced to choose one. T.J. assumed she'd follow him to UCLA, but Annie chose LSU."

"Pressure at home from your parents?" Tiffany asked, slipping an arm around her husband's waist.

"Nah, if she'd have chosen UCLA the folks would have backed her. Hell, we *all* figured they'd get married eventually. T.J. was like a member of the family—the only guy she ever dated."

"Dated seriously, you mean?" No way had a girl as hot as Annie McAllister spent many weekends without a date.

Red gave his head an adamant shake. "I mean dated, period. She pretty much stayed away from guys. Always said she didn't want to end up like mom—with a passel of kids, no college education, and no career."

Drake couldn't picture it. "Was she one of those reclusive book geek type or something?"

"No, she was smart. But she was popular, too. Cheerleader all four years in high school, homecoming court all four years, homecoming queen her senior year, Senior class president, class favorites, Beta club, FFA Sweetheart, Ms. GHS . . . you name it, she was it. Look up the word 'extrovert' in Funk and Wagnall's or Webster's dictionary and it'll say 'Annie McAllister'."

"I figured that. It's why I'm having a difficult time believing she only had the one relationship."

"She made a choice, man," Red told him. "Until Tommy came along, nobody made her second guess that choice. They'd always been close friends, even before they became a couple. We liked him, and his family was crazy about her. It shocked the hell out of everyone when she turned down UCLA and they broke it off."

"It was mutual?"

"Yeah, but he forced the issue. He said he couldn't manage a long distance relationship, and wanted her by his side, not thousands of miles away from him. He forced her to make a choice, and she chose not to follow him. I don't know exactly how it all came down. She's never spoken about it to any of us."

"I had no idea," Tiffany groaned, wiping at her eyes. "That is so sad!"

Red pulled his wife close for a hug. "It's okay, sweetie—it was a long time ago."

Drake watched his sister retreat to her bedroom in tears. He turned to Red. "What the hell's up with that?"

"Hormonal fluctuation," Red explained. "If Dad and Jackson hadn't both warned me about this, I'd be a wreck by now."

Drake allowed himself a chuckle at the thought of his always collected sister breaking down into tears over something so trivial. "So what are we going to do about Annie?"

"I'll get Sidney Graske, my P.I., on it. If she can't do it herself, she'll give me the name of the best in the business."

Drake shook his head. "I won't feel better about this unless I know she's safe. I know she won't like it, but she'll be seeing a lot more of my mug for a while. By the time they catch that guy, Martin and Lewis may think I'm a permanent fixture in that household."

"You've met the family pets?"

Drake's reply came in the form of a low growl. "That damn cat attacked me. Twice. And the bird ain't happy unless he's calling me a prick."

Red burst into laughter. "You've got me to blame for that one."

Drake sent him a glare. "I gotta tell you, man, there's something fundamentally wrong with being verbally abused by a parrot. Then I went and ate one of his damn birdseed and bug cookies by mistake."

Red finally caught his breath long enough to explain. "When Annie was a freshman in high school, her date for the homecoming dance sat out in his car and blew the horn for her to go meet him. I asked who the prick was and Lewis picked it up. What would *you* have done in that situation?"

"I would have gone out there and said it to his face."

"Unnecessary. He'd already pissed her off by having her corsage delivered earlier that day. He was too cool to go inside and take pictures for Mom, or meet Dad. Annie met him at the car, threw the corsage in his face, and told him her bird had more sense than he did. She went by herself."

"Doesn't surprise me." Drake shook his head and got serious again. "Man, I hope that guy had enough sense to haul his ass outta here, Red. I can't stand the thought of her being in danger."

Red slapped him on the back. "I'm with you." He cocked one brow at a curious angle. "Little sister got you in a bind?"

"She's the first thing I think about when I open my eyes, the last thing I think about before I close them at night—and I dream about her, too."

Red's shoulders shook with laughter. "No mercy! I'd still be one miserable son of a bitch if Doc hadn't married me when she did." His expression sobered as he turned to Drake. "Tell me the truth, though. Do you love her?"

Drake was quiet for a minute as he weighed the question in his mind. "When I see any kind of future for myself, I see her in it, and the thought of her in any kind of danger makes me crazy."

He squeezed his eyes shut. "In my mind, I can still *see* that creep standing over her when she's in so much pain." He stopped to take a deep, steadying breath. "I believe I could kill him if he ever tried to hurt her again."

Red grinned and nodded in understanding. "Yeah. You love her."

Chapter Five

Annie and Tiffany were perusing the mall's food court when they heard someone calling their names. "Look who's here!" Annie caught sight of Julia and Miranda several yards away.

Julia rushed up and gave her sisters-in-law a couple of hugs. "If we had known you two would be at the mall today, we could have come together."

"We didn't know until this morning. Besides, I thought your flight left at noon," Annie exclaimed.

"The powers that be gave me another few days with my daughter." Julia beamed at Miranda. "But we're starving. Have y'all eaten lunch yet?"

"Nope, I'm trying to decide whether to have a slice of pizza or Chinese," Annie said.

"I may have both. I'm eating for two, remember?" Tiffany said, at the look Annie gave her.

Annie shrugged. "I couldn't care less if you order from every restaurant in this place. *I'm* not the one who'll have to squeeze that butt into a pair of too tight jeans after your kid's born."

Tiffany waved her off. "I'm gonna keep running, just slow it down a bit. My doctor said I could, as long as I promise to stop if I'm not gaining enough weight."

Within a few minutes the four women sat at a table in the center of the food court, each with a meal from a different restaurant.

Tiffany closed her eyes as she took her first bite of food. "Mmmm. This pizza is so good!"

"Are you having any cravings, yet?" Julia asked.

Tiffany pointed at the slice of supreme in her hands. "You're looking at it, honey. I could eat pizza for breakfast, lunch, and dinner. Red's worried about the baby being born with an Italian accent and smelling like a pepperoni."

Julia laughed as Tiffany stuffed her mouth with another bite. "Enjoy it while you can. In a few more months, you won't even be able to think the word, much less eat it—hellacious indigestion."

Tiffany nodded. "I'll get my fill of it before then."

"Any morning sickness?" Annie asked her.

"Not yet, I'm hoping I'll bypass that part of it, but I'm prepared, just in case. Red keeps buying boxes of saltines and bottles of ginger ale. Vivienne told me that would help when it started up."

Annie snorted. "Well, if anyone should know, she should. I can't even imagine being pregnant eight times. What was she thinking?"

Miranda looked at her youngest aunt in amazement. "I don't know, but if she hadn't thought what she thought at the time she thought it, you wouldn't be here, little Miss Baby of the Family."

"Here! Here!" Julia cried.

Annie waved her off. "Sure I would—I probably would have been born with a golden spoon in my mouth to some fabulously wealthy family."

Tiffany beamed at her. "But you wouldn't be nearly as beautiful."

"Or loved," Miranda added.

Julia grinned at Annie. "And speaking of love—how's Tiffany's delectable, hunk of a brother doing lately?"

Annie's forkful of stir fry stopped in mid-air. "Don't talk about love, there is no love! The man is a thorn in my side—no offense, Tiff."

Tiffany swallowed another mouthful of pizza. "None taken, but you two would make a great couple. Drake has never acted this way about anyone else. You'd make your sister-in-law ecstatic by re-considering."

Annie shook her head in disgust. "You should be ashamed. I never thought you'd sink so low as to use emotional blackmail."

Tiffany grinned at her. "I can fight just as dirty as the next girl when the outcome is important to me. Your happiness, as well as my brother's, is very important to me." She jutted out her lower lip and placed a hand on her belly. "It would make your unborn niece or nephew so happy, Aunt Annie."

Annie laughed and used her hand to shield her face. "Stop. That won't work with me."

Tiffany shrugged then stuffed another bite of pizza in her mouth.

Annie's gaze landed on her other sister-in-law. "Okay Jules, since you're the one who brought up the subject of love, how are the peace talks progressing between you and Chad, a.k.a. my idiot brother?"

Julia sobered immediately. "I haven't spoken to him since the Christmas fiasco."

After several moments of quiet, Annie placed her hand over Julia's. "You do know he loves you, don't you, Jules? He just has a hard time putting into words what he's feeling."

Julia looked into Annie's eyes. "I, more than anyone, know that, hon. It's not about love, I know he loves me. It's about sacrifice. He's never been willing to sacrifice a thing for me. I've done all the bending, and giving in, and sacrificing that I'm going to do. It's his turn, and if he can't find it in his heart, then I'll sacrifice one last time, and I'll let him go."

Annie covered her mouth with one hand. "Oh Jules, is it that serious?"

Julia's eyes filled up with tears. "He filed for a legal separation without saying one word to me, Annie. Those papers were delivered to me in the middle of a business meeting. Do you have any idea what that did to me? Do you have any idea how betrayed I felt? He couldn't have hurt me more if he'd slept with another woman in our bed."

The other three women remained silent as Julia wiped a tear from the corner of her eye.

Annie spoke again. "Look, I know he hurt you, I know he's a selfish jerk, I know he can act like a Neanderthal on occasion. But I also know that you're the best thing that has ever happened to him. You can't blame the rest of us for wanting to see the two of you back together." She grabbed Julia's hand in both of hers. "We miss you, and we miss having the both of you around as a couple. You two were so great."

Julia sniffed loudly and dabbed at her eyes. "I know we were, and it breaks my heart that it has to be this way. But I'm telling you, I won't be the one to give in. It's up to him. I've got a little over a year left to my original post in London. I haven't told anyone yet, but I've been offered a permanent position there after the year is up."

"Oh, Mom!" Miranda gasped, obviously hearing this for the first time.

Julia reached out for her daughter's face. "Sweetie, I don't expect you to understand this now, but one day, when you meet someone special, you will. If your father lets the year go by without sacrificing a little of himself, then I can't see how I'll be able to come back here and pick up the pieces to our marriage. It would break my heart to see him on a regular basis. If our marriage ends, I'll take the permanent position in London."

Miranda wiped at her mother's tear-streaked face. "He's a fool, Mom."

Julia nodded. "I know, but I haven't given up on him completely."

"He's adopted, he must be," Annie exclaimed, hoping to lighten the mood. "No one else in our family is as stubborn as he is."

Both Julia and Miranda turned to stare at her.

"What?" she asked.

Her niece snorted. "You and Dad run a close race, you know."

Annie pushed her plate away. "Give it a rest, will ya?"

Drake approached the group just as they rose from the table. "How are all you lovely ladies doing today?"

"Hey, little brother, I'm surprised to see you here. I know how much you hate to shop."

He gave his sister a grunt of distaste. "I put it off as long as I could."

"Do all guys hate to shop?" Miranda asked.

"Red doesn't mind it," Tiffany said. "But, he always knows exactly what he's looking for. He's in and out of those places in under an hour."

Annie cringed. "I hate the crowds, especially around the holidays. I'd do all my shopping online if I could."

"One of many things we agree upon, Annie Girl," Drake drawled.

"What brought you out of your man-cave to brave the mall? The promise of seeing someone special, maybe?" Miranda sent him a wink.

"Put a plug in it, little girl," Annie hissed, her jaw tight with annoyance.

Drake faced Annie. "I needed a few things, but I can't say I'm disappointed. How are *you* doing today?"

Annie shivered at the seductive lilt of his voice. She caught a whiff of something delicious. Something—Armani. Allowed herself the luxury of one deep breath. Acqua di Gio, definitely, along with the purely masculine scent of one Drake LeBlanc. She knew the smell, remembered it from *that* night, the night that turned her life into a dread fest of tortured longing for a man who wasn't good for the future she'd planned for herself.

She shook herself out of the pheromone induced trance long enough to speak without sounding like a dim-witted groupie. "I'm okay. Are you sure you aren't in stalking mode again?"

"No, but if you're going to accuse me of it anyway, I could always start. It may not be such a bad idea, considering your current situation."

"What current situation?" Julia asked.

"No situation. What do you have in that bag? Listening devices for my phone, cameras to spy on me?" Annie asked, hoping to change the subject.

"I picked up a few Polo shirts, socks, tee shirts, jeans, things like that, oh, and several new pair of undershorts. You want to see?"

Miranda turned to her aunt wearing a smug look. "Maybe she'd like to set up a modeling sess—"

"Shut up, Miranda, and no, I don't want to see. All I want is to attend family functions and go shopping without having to see you every time I turn around."

"What's the situation?" Julia asked again.

"Polo shirts and jeans?" Annie continued. "I figured you for the stuffy three thousand dollar suit kind of guy, like most *arrogant* lawyer types."

"I find the suits I have aren't getting much wear these days. I did purchase a couple of sport coats though. They're being altered for me. I'm leaning for casual." He leaned toward her and smiled. "If I'd known you were so interested in my wardrobe, I'd have asked you to come along with me. I could have used a pretty lady's opinion."

"Hey!" Julia's voice rose insistently. "What current situation are you talking about?"

Annie bit her bottom lip and looked from Jules, to Drake, and back to Jules. "That guy that attacked me—I sort of told him Red was my brother. Drake thinks that if he decides to come back and ask around, he might be able to find me."

"Oh shit!"

Jules spun around to face her daughter. "That mouth, Miranda."

"Oh, sorry, Mom, it slipped out. But, that can't be good—what are you going to do?"

Annie stood and hung her purse on her shoulder. "I don't know. Be on the lookout, I guess. I know self-defense—it's not that big of a deal."

Julia grabbed her arm, and pulled her to a stop. "You knew self-defense the night he nearly raped you. That's not good enough. You have to be smart about this."

Annie closed her eyes and dropped her head back. "I'm trying to be, but what the hell do you want me to do about it, Jules? Move back in with mom and dad? I have a business in Kenton."

"No, but you need some kind of protection."

"Red suggested hiring someone to tail her," Tiffany volunteered.

Rubbing at the steadily increasing throbbing at her temples, Annie took small comfort in knowing that at least it wasn't a crippling migraine. "That's just what I need—to have someone know my every move. This is frustrating." She turned to Tiffany. "Now that I'm good and depressed, are you about ready to go?"

Tiffany pointed to a bench. "I've got a couple more errands to run. Wait here and I'll meet you in fifteen?"

Both angry and on the verge of tears, Annie wanted to be anywhere but in the middle of a crowded mall.

"You know what, let's just go," Tiffany said. "I can run those errands another day. I'll bring you to the ranch to get your car."

Drake stepped up. "Actually, I'm leaving right now. Let me take you to your car and Tiffany can get the rest of her shopping done."

Annie stole a glance in his direction and decided she didn't want him thinking she couldn't trust herself alone with him for a few minutes. "Only if you promise to keep your hands to yourself."

"Absolutely. I'm ready when you are."

She turned to Jules. "I guess this is it before you leave."

Jules nodded and pulled her close for a hug. "Don't be afraid to take a chance every now and then, Annie. Just not with your life. Let others help take care of you. You mean too much to everyone."

Annie stepped away, nodding. "I'll be fine. And tell my stupid brother it's time to straighten up and fly right." She reached for her bag, and when Drake tried to take it, she jerked it away. "I've got it," she snapped.

They walked silently to the opposite end of the mall, had just cleared the exit when someone called out to Annie. Already in protective mode, Drake pivoted to check out its owner, a man, a tad over six feet and of medium build. The guy stood staring at Annie as if he couldn't believe she was real. Drake turned at the sound of Annie's barely audible gasp. She also stood frozen in place, but pale-faced, and staring at the man as if he'd returned from the dead. It only took an instant for Drake to know he didn't like him.

"Annie, I can't believe it's you."

"T.J. What are you doing here?"

Drake snapped to attention at the title.

"My fiancé's family lives here and we're down for the holidays. How are you?"

"I'm fine. Your fiancé?"

"Yeah, I moved all the way to California and ended up meeting someone from here in Lake Coburn, ain't that a kick? We're getting married next month. Her name's Britt Holland."

Drake watched Annie's face as she attempted to absorb the news. He could see how she struggled to keep her composure, but then, she'd been doing that before this new bombshell had fallen into her lap.

She finally seemed to collect herself enough to speak. "Congratulations. I wish you the best."

The man turned to Drake, who made the first move and extended his hand. "Drake LeBlanc." He reveled in the opportunity to squeeze the crap out of T.J.'s hand. "Congratulations on the upcoming nuptials. I hope it all works out for you." *Buddy, I hope you have eons of wedded bliss.*

"Thank you. Tom Boudreaux. Nobody's called me T.J. in years. I'm an old—friend—of Annie's from Gardiner." He looked back and forth between Drake and Annie. "Are you two—"

"No!" The word burst forth from Annie's mouth as her face flushed pink. "Drake is just the brother of my new sister-in-law. Red got married the day after Christmas."

"Red is married? Mom usually keeps me well informed on everything that goes on in Gardiner, but I hadn't heard that. How are your parents, Annie?"

"They're good. We-we were just leaving," she stammered.

"Oh, well then, I'm holding you up. It was good to see you Annie." He took a step forward and placed both hands on her shoulders before leaning in to kiss her on the cheek.

Annie's barely noticeable flinch at the contact had Drake offering no more than a silent nod at the blast from her past. He placed a hand possessively on Annie's lower back, and turned her toward the parking lot. Surprisingly enough, she allowed it and they walked to his truck in silence. Drake opened the door for her, took her bags, and placed them in the rear seat. Once they were strapped in, he glanced at the passenger, who sat staring straight ahead and stone faced.

"Are you all right?"

She nodded. "And before you ask, no, I don't want to talk about it."

"Is he..." he began.

"I don't want to talk about it."

Drake waited a good ten minutes before attempting to speak to her again. He'd just turned down the long stretch of roadway that led to Red and Tiffany's ranch when he glanced over at her. She continued to stare blindly ahead, as if she were deep in thought.

"Hon, we need to discuss what we're going to do with you."

She blinked several times and finally turned toward him. "We? What is this, *we*? You're not a member of my family. Red will obsess about this enough for everyone."

"I want to do something. I feel responsible."

Annie shook her head. "That doesn't make any sense. You stopped him and brought me home. Why should you feel responsible?"

He slapped his hand on the steering wheel. "Because I listened to you, dammit! I pushed aside every instinct I had, and I walked away from that asshole. I don't know *why* I listened to you, but I did. I should have called Red."

"Red would have over reacted, as usual."

"Like we're over reacting now? He'd have done what needed to be done with him. Can't you see what's going on here? Don't you understand that he could still come after you—*find* you? That he could . . ." Drake let his voice trail off as he rubbed his hand roughly over his face, feeling about as ineffective as a gelding on a stud ranch.

"I do understand. Now. If I hadn't been in such pain that night, I would have understood then. But it didn't happen that way. When I have those migraines, I get irrational. I didn't want to lose my independence, but by stopping you from acting on it then, I have done exactly that. But, it's not your fault. It's mine."

Drake watched her as she stared out of her side window. He touched her shoulder, urging her to face him. "Look, Annie, we could play the blame game all day long, but the cold, hard fact is that we need to make some decisions. We need to insure your safety, and I won't be satisfied unless I'm an active participant. You can fight me on this all you want, but I can promise you, this time I won't listen. Do you understand what I'm saying?"

She sent him a glassy-eyed look, nodded slowly as she turned away from him.

Forty-five minutes later, Annie and Drake sat with Red and Tiffany, still trying to decide how best to handle the situation. Red had contacted his P.I., Sydney Graske, only to discover she was recovering from an emergency appendectomy. When that fell through, Drake tried to obtain his old friend, Travis Blood, to do some investigating and tail Annie. Unfortunately, he was on another case for the law firm Drake had recently left.

Red stood and walked around to his sister. "There's no hope for it, Annie, either you move in here with Tiffany and me for a while or we'll go stay with you at your place."

Annie gaped open-mouthed at her brother. "You can't be serious. I am not about to put Tiffany and the baby in danger, as well as you." She was bordering hysteria. "I'd never be able to live with myself if something happened to either of you because of this. You'd better damn-well come up with something else."

Red sat in front of her and took both her hands in his. "Annie, I don't know what else to do. It's either that or hire you a bodyguard, and you've said you don't want a stranger in your house."

"I've got a solution," Drake broke in. Red and Annie faced him, simultaneously. "I can move in with her."

"Oh, hell no!" Annie's wild-eyed glare should have been enough to scare off a normal man. One who wasn't crazy about her.

Drake met his brother-in-law's gaze long enough to recognize acceptance in Red's facial expression. The next step: to see that same look on Annie's face. Drake stood and paced the floor, weighing the arguments in his mind, considering how best to plead his case. He finally stopped an acceptable distance from Annie and faced her.

"Look, this would be strictly for practicality's sake. It would keep you from having a full time body guard that's a stranger to you, and it would keep from involving Red, Tiffany, and our un-born niece or nephew in a potentially dangerous situation. I'm sure it won't be for long. I'll leave as soon as we know this guy isn't a threat."

"What if that doesn't happen for a while? What then, huh, Mr. Mastermind?"

"Don't blame him, Annie—he's just trying to ke—" Red began.

"No, it's okay, Red. I know where she's coming from, and she has every right to be upset about this." He turned toward the tiny woman, whose body practically vibrated with tension. "Hear me out, Annie. If I move in for a while, we'd work out a schedule for work, shopping, work-outs at the gym—everything. But we have to keep you safe. What do you think?"

She stood suddenly. Her glare hard, her voice shaking with anger and frustration. "I think you're enjoying this way too much."

Red reached out to her. "Annie—"

She turned on her brother, her angry eyes flashing. "Put a sock in it, Red! This is *my* life that's being turned upside down, and if I can't be pissed off about it at least for a little, I'll lose my mind." She pivoted, marched angrily up to Drake, and shoved a finger in his chest. "I swear to God, Drake LeBlanc, if I didn't know better, I'd think you had arranged this whole mess, just so you could take advantage of the situation." Her eyes narrowed to two angry slits at the grin he was trying his best to hide, but couldn't. "You think this is funny? Laugh at *this!*" She reared back, punched him in the belly.

"Ooo-omph!" Drake doubled over, the air whooshing from his mouth at the surprise hit.

"Jesus, Mary, and Joseph!" Red turned on his sister. "Have you lost your mind?"

Drake coughed a couple of times to catch his breath, then straightened, recovering quickly. He leaned in low, meeting the tiny little powerhouse nose to nose. "This is your one warning, lady," he growled. "I've never in my life raised a hand to a woman, but I swear before God and your brother—if you *ever* do anything like that again, I won't think twice about turning you over my knee and paddling that spoiled little ass of yours. You'd better find some other fool to take your temper out on, you got that?"

Wide-eyed with shock, Annie retreated until her back hit the wall.

"I said, you got that?" he repeated, louder this time.

Annie lifted her chin, keeping her stubborn silence. His single, angry step closer had her raising her hand to stop him. "I got it."

Drake took a couple of deep breaths and finally backed down. "Do we have a deal, or do I let this guy get a hold of you and finish what he started New Year's Eve?" He hated to do it. Hated the coldness in his voice that caused her to shudder visibly.

She shut her eyes, finally gave him a reluctant nod. She headed for the guest bathroom, slamming the door behind her.

Drake shook his head in exasperation then frowned as he put a hand to his belly. He felt his brother-in-law's gaze on him. Finally faced him, fully prepared to defend his words. "What?"

"Nothing. I'm-I'm so damn impressed with you."

Drake frowned, confused by the guilt he felt at Red's grin of admiration. "Don't be. I didn't want to humiliate her. I shouldn't have lost my temper."

"Man, I'm telling you, I have *never* seen her back down like that from anyone, except Mom and Dad, of course. I believe you can handle her, bro."

Drake shook his head. "No, seriously, don't be too impressed. She's a little off kilter right now because of something that happened at the mall. Good old T.J. showed up."

"She spoke to T.J.?"

"Yeah, except he's *Tom* now, nobody's called him T.J. in years," Drake corrected, not even trying to hide his disgust.

Red shrugged. "Tough shit, he'll always be T.J. to me. What brought him around here?"

"His fiancée's parents live here. He said he went all the way to California to meet a girl from Lake Coburn."

Red's eyes widened at the information. "His fiancée—was she there? Was Annie upset?"

"He was alone. She seemed upset, but she didn't want to talk about it. Maybe once I'm there, I can get her to open up. Find out if there's anything else behind that story."

Red cocked one eyebrow. "She hasn't mentioned a word to anyone in our family about the breakup since it happened. Good luck with that."

Chapter Six

Drake parked his Denali truck next to Annie's Ford Escape, dwarfing the smaller vehicle. She unlocked her door and walked inside, leaving him to unload his own suitcases and duffle bags. He met her in the kitchen, loaded down with bags. "Where do you want me?"

She didn't even look up from slicing a large apple. "China would be nice, but since that won't happen, second door on the left."

Drake glanced at the assortment of fruits and vegetables she'd laid out on the counter top. "Is that supper?" He had to yell over the various cries and squawking of Lewis the bird.

She jerked her head at the bird. "It's past his supper time. If I'm thirty minutes late he pitches a fit."

Drake made his way to the bedroom. He deposited his suitcases, then went out to get a load of books and file folders. A third trip was for his laptop, briefcase, and various other items from his truck. He made short work out of getting everything put in its right and proper place then stuffed the empty suitcases into the closet.

He plopped down on the bed to try it out. The bed was comfortable enough, but his feet hung off the edge unless he lay diagonally across the mattress. He got up and took a long look at his new digs, however temporary they may be. He'd planned on buying a new bed anyway; he supposed he could just have it delivered here instead. He may as well be as comfortable as he could while he was here. He grabbed his phone and his laptop and walked back into the living room to meet Annie. She attempted to feed Lewis, but the bird's distressed squawking seemed to take precedence over his hunger.

"Aaa-nnie! Stranger danger! Oh oh—brawk!"

Annie motioned Drake to approach the cage. "You may as well introduce yourself and get to know him. It's necessary now."

Drake sent her a heated look. "Thanks hon, I didn't know I mattered that much to you."

She rolled her eyes. "You don't, but he does. If he doesn't warm up to you he'll get really upset and start pulling his feathers out. You're a sensitive boy, aren't you Lewis?"

"Lew-is is a fox."

"Yes, you are, you're a handsome boy."

"Aaa-nnie! Who's the prick?" Lewis asked.

Drake shook his head. "I was waiting for that. I hear Red's to blame."

Annie gave him a tight smile, as though she was holding back something more substantial.

"Oh Re-ed! Where's Red?" Lewis called.

"Red's not here, baby. But Drake is here. Can you say Drake?"

Drake stepped up closer to the cage. "Hey Lewis, remember me?"

Lewis turned his head to the left and squawked. "Prick's on the phone!"

Annie giggled. "Yeah, he remembers you, alright."

Drake held up his hands. "Come on Lewis, I'm a good guy! Can you say 'Drake's a good guy'?"

Lewis flapped his wings. "Stranger danger!"

"I guess his phrases are pretty limited."

Annie smiled smugly. "Actually, he's got the intellectual capacity of a five year old child. You've only heard a tiny bit of what he knows." She turned to the bird. "Lewis, you ready to show off?"

"Let's get it on!"

For the next fifteen minutes Annie treated Drake to a small show of Lewis's vocabulary skills. He sang the alphabet song, counted, danced, whistled the theme to *The Good, The Bad, and The Ugly,* and mimicked several perfectly executed imitations of quotes from movies. The bird's Terminator impersonations, "I'll be back" and "Hasta La vista, baby", had Drake doubled over with laughter.

"That's fantastic!" Drake tried to catch his breath. "Do some more."

"Lewis, what's your favorite movie?" Annie asked.

"Steel Magnolias!"

"What's your favorite quote?"

"Wheeza, you know I love ya more'n my luggage."

"Who's your favorite R&B singer, Lewis?"

"Ray Charles! Ray Charles!" Then he started swaying his head from side to side in imitation of the famous singer as he sang a line from *Georgia on My Mind.*

"Who's you favorite girl country singer?" she asked him.

"Shania! Man, I feel like a woman!" the bird sang.

Annie continued with the line of questioning. "Who's your favorite guy country singer?"

"Trace Adkins. Turn it up boys." He bobbed his head and sang, "Honky Tonk, Badonkadonk—Whoo-ee, shut my mouth, slap your grandma!"

"That's amazing. Lewis you are amazing." Drake gave him a piece of fruit.

Lewis puffed out his chest at the compliment. "Thank you. Mm Mm good."

Annie beamed at her bird. "Take a bow, my man."

Lewis bowed several times as Drake applauded. "I'm really impressed—I had no idea parrots had that much capacity for learning."

She leaned over to whisper in his ear. "He also knows fart noises—courtesy of my dad, but I'm hoping he'll forget that one of these days." Annie smiled at Drakes guffaw of laughter and continued. "African Grey's are very intelligent. Of the three different kinds of Grey's, TAG's have the best temperament, I believe."

"TAG's? What's a tag?"

"Timneh African Grey. There are also Congo and Ghana African Grey's; different sub-species for different areas of the continent."

"He's a handsome bird, and he looks healthy. You must take wonderful care of him. That's the biggest single bird cage I've ever seen."

"I bought it when I moved in this place. He was in a two foot by three foot cage before, but I always wanted him to have more room. This one is five by five. It took him awhile to get used to it. He has to ease into changes."

"Kind of like his mistress?"

She turned abruptly away from him. "Don't start picking on me. I'm not in the mood today."

Drake shoved his hands in the back pockets of his jeans. "I'm sorry. I didn't mean to offend you."

Annie waved him off. "What do you want for supper? I guess the least I can do is feed you."

"You don't even have to do that. I was thinking of ordering a pizza; is there a place here that delivers?"

Annie opened up a drawer and pulled out a flyer. "The Pizza Palace opened up a couple of months ago and they're good."

"What do you like on yours? My treat tonight," Drake said.

"Oh, you don't have to do that. I can eat something else."

"It's a pizza, Annie. Not a lifetime commitment."

"Okay then, I like mine loaded. Seeing as I'm stuck with you for a while, I may as well make the best of it," she said.

"Me too, except..."

"Except anchovies," she added.

He grinned. "You took the words right out of my mouth."

She smiled, and added, "But I love jalapenos."

He nodded. "I do too, the hotter, the better. Just like my women." He froze as Annie's mouth fell open. "I'm sorry. I-uh-really didn't mean to say that out loud."

She snorted then turned away from him.

"I'll-I'll order from back there." He pointed to the hallway before skulking off to his room.

Drake placed the pizza box on a small table set with plates and napkins. "Got milk?" he asked, staring into Annie's fridge.

"Yes, but milk with pizza? I've got tea and water."

Drake pulled out a carton of two percent. "I like milk." He took the glass she offered.

As soon as they'd seated themselves, Martin, the cat showed up to rub on Annie's leg, meowing loudly.

Drake eyed the beast warily. "He acts like he hasn't eaten in weeks."

"Pizza is literally his favorite food." Annie leaned over and placed a thick slice of the loaded pizza in his food dish on the floor. Martin attacked it hungrily, growling as he chomped and chewed.

"Jesus, remind never to bother him while he's eating." Drake stared at the cat, still somewhat intimidated.

Annie chuckled as they watched the huge feline gnaw on the pizza. "Fat boy does enjoy his food. He's on a diet, but he cheats every chance he gets."

Drake cocked an eyebrow and looked at her. "How can he cheat? You're the one that feeds him."

She grinned secretively. "You'll see. By the way, don't give him anything else for the rest of the night. That's all he's allowed, and *never* leave your plate unattended."

When Annie was done eating she put her plate in the dishwasher and put the remaining pizza in a plastic container. Drake got up to get himself another glass of milk to go with his last slice. He turned back to see Martin standing over his plate and chowing down.

"Oh crap!" He groaned as Annie's laughter rang out. He turned to face her, grinning sheepishly. "He does cheat. I can't say you didn't warn me."

"*Never* leave your plate unattended. He's fast for a fat boy, aren't you, Martin?" She took the pizza away from him, grinning as she offered it back to Drake.

He made a face at her. "No thanks, he can have it."

She laughed and shook her head. "Nope. It'll have to go." She put it down the garbage disposal then shook her finger disapprovingly at Martin. "Bad cat!"

"Baaad Cat! Martin's a fat boy!" Lewis cried.

Drake sipped at his milk while he checked out various items on display in the living room, then ended up at her computer. He noticed the nice set up, and the surround sound wireless speaker system placed strategically around the room.

"Do you mind if I check out your sound system?"

She plopped herself down on the sofa and picked up the cable program guide. "Go right ahead." Martin jumped up on her lap and she began to rub him behind the ears.

Drake pulled up an extensive list of artists from hard rock to classical and everything in between. He opened up a playlist that was dated a week after Thanksgiving and discovered one of the songs they'd danced to at the top of the list. Actually, it was *the* song...the one that he'd kissed her to. *Interesting,* he thought, continuing the search. He found Trace Adkins and grinned as he chose a song. He swiveled around and walked up to Lewis's bird cage.

"Here you go Lewis! In your honor." Drake laughed as the bird immediately started swaying from side to side and bobbing its head to

Honkytonk Badonkadonk.

Drake interacted with the parrot, singing along at parts and shaking his hips to the beat of the music. He heard Annie's laughter as he and Lewis sang a line or two from the chorus together. At the end of the song, Drake praised the bird and gave him a small piece of apple.

"Thank you vee-rry much. Mmmm...good!" Lewis told Drake.

Drake laughed. "You're such a smart bird."

"Sharp as a tack!" Lewis cried.

"Yes, you certainly are." Drake gave him a small chunk of mango and watched the bird eat it.

Lewis looked up at Drake and cocked his head to the side. "No stranger danger. What's your handle?"

Drake looked at Annie, who was staring at the bird with a frown on her face. "What's that supposed to mean?"

"That's his way of saying he wants to be friends. He wants to know your name."

"Really?" He turned back toward Lewis. After only five more minutes of working with him, Lewis was saying his name like he'd known him for years.

⚜

Annie shook her head, amazed and feeling more than a little betrayed that Drake had befriended her bird in such a short period of time. She wasn't about to tell him that no one, not even she, had won Lewis over this quickly. It had taken a week or more for Lewis to warm up to her when she first got him.

Drake walked over to the computer again. "I'm really impressed with him."

"Yeah, he's something, all right," Annie murmured as she thumbed through the program guide. *Damn traitor bird.*

Drake chose a country station to play from her computer and Jimmy Wayne's *I Will* blasted from the speakers. He walked over to Annie and held his hand out to her. "Dance with me, Annie?"

She looked at his hand and for a moment considered taking it, but then looked up into his intense brown eyes and couldn't make herself move. With her heart pounding in her chest, she tore her gaze away, pretending to be interested in her magazine.

Drake's voice lowered to a seductive growl. "Come on Annie, I don't bite."

She purposely avoided looking in his direction. "But I do, and I'm beginning to wonder if any of this is really necessary."

He withdrew his hand. "We just went over this at Red's; this is how it's got to be for a while, so you'd just as soon get used to it."

She looked at him accusingly. "Then don't try anything stupid with me, like try to get me to dance with you."

Drake dropped down beside her on the couch. "Is there anything good on the tube tonight?"

She jumped to her feet and practically slapped him with the magazine. "Here, check it out for yourself. I've got bills to pay online." Seating herself at her computer, she stopped the music to scan her mail when the phone rang. She answered the phone, then turned toward Drake. "Yes, Captain Woodard, this is Annie McAllister. Do you have any more information on the man who attacked me?"

"Yes, ma'am, I do, and I'm afraid it's not good news."

"Captain, Drake LeBlanc is here also, and I'm going to put you on the speaker phone so he can hear this, too." She pressed the button and cradled the handset.

"It seems you were right about him being from Arkansas, although just barely. His name is James Bradley Montgomery and he's from some little nowhere town in Columbia County, just north of the Louisiana state line. The Columbia Sheriff's department has a warrant out for his arrest."

"What for?" Drake asked.

"He's a suspect in the murder of a young woman in Magnolia, Arkansas, also in Columbia County. It wasn't pretty, from what they told me. She was beaten and raped repeatedly. The sheriff said she put up a fight, but it didn't do her any good. She was strangled, and thrown in a lake."

Drake kept his watchful eye on Annie. "Do they have DNA evidence from the rape?"

"Yes, but her body wasn't found until after he'd skipped town, and that was after they'd impounded his truck to check it for evidence, and they found plenty. Someone called in with an anonymous tip that they saw him man-handling the woman earlier. The caller worried that if J.B.—that's what they call him over there—found out it was him who tipped off the law, he'd kill him for sure. They still don't know who called it in."

Annie turned away to keep Drake from seeing how upset she was. She flinched and twisted away from the touch of his hand on her shoulder.

"Thank you Captain," Drake said. "Is there anything else we should know?"

"Only that Miss McAllister needs to be very careful. She got a good look at him, and she's the one who can testify about what he said and what he was planning to do. I'm sorry, but that's the way it is. He doesn't know who she is or where to find her, but I'd say she shouldn't go back to that same club until we catch him."

"Uh, captain, Annie remembered something later that we think may make the situation even more dangerous for her. She told him the club owner was her brother in the hopes that he'd leave her alone."

"Oh." Several seconds passed before he spoke again. "Miss McAllister, are you there?"

"Y-yes Captain," she stammered.

"Is there a place you could go until this blows over? Somewhere he wouldn't be able to track you?"

Annie dropped her face in both her hands. "That's really not an option for me right now, Captain Woodard."

Drake cleared his throat. "Sir, we've come up with a solution to secure her safety. I've temporarily moved in with her. I'll drive her to her office in the mornings and pick her up in the afternoons when it's time for her to leave."

"You're staying in her home?"

"Yes sir, I am. We all thought that was the best possible solution for now. Are you going to notify the Kenton P.D. to make sure they're on the lookout for this guy?"

"We already have, since we knew she was a resident of Kenton. I've spoken to the chief about sending regular patrols by her place. Miss McAllister?"

"Yes sir?" Her voice sounded shaky, even to her own ears.

"It's important that you don't give this guy the opportunity to catch you unprotected—do you understand what I'm saying?"

Annie nodded then remembered he couldn't see her. "I understand. Thank you, Captain Woodard."

"Keep your chin up, Miss McAllister, we'll get him. Just be aware that he may alter his appearance by letting his hair and facial hair grow. The picture we're broadcasting shows both his head and face clean shaven."

Annie squeezed her eyes shut, thinking the phrase 'clean shaven' was a deceptive description for a filthy animal like that. She held herself tightly as the Captain told them he'd let them know if they learned anything else. Once he'd disconnected, she stood listening to the hum of the dial tone over the speaker phone, nearly deafening in the otherwise stillness and silence of the room. Even Lewis had ceased making any of his usual noises.

Drake hit the speaker button to stop the buzz of the dial tone, filling the room with an eerie silence. He placed both hands on Annie's shoulders, turning her gently to face him. "I promise I won't let anything happen to you." She didn't meet his gaze, but pulled away, retreating behind her bedroom door.

Drake lowered himself onto the overstuffed rocker near the bird cage. When Martin approached to sit at his feet, man and beast stared silently at each other, and Drake got the strangest feeling they'd established a mutual truce for Annie's sake. He snapped his fingers over his thighs. Surprisingly, Martin jumped heavily onto his lap, then settled down with loud purring. Drake rubbed behind his ears while Lewis the bird looked on in silence.

"Okay, guys, we need to do whatever we can to protect our Annie girl, because all three of us have one thing in common." He released a heavy sigh as he spoke. "We all love her."

Chapter Seven

January 4th

Drake was on his third cup of coffee when Annie dragged-ass into the kitchen at six-thirty the next morning. He took one look at her pale, drawn face and grimaced. "Didn't get much sleep, huh?"

She bypassed all the pretty coffee cups to grab her oversized LSU mug and half-filled it with the strong coffee. After topping it off with cold milk, Annie stood staring outside the window over her sink as she gulped the mug's contents. She finished and refilled the mug with coffee, this time adding a little creamer. She sat at the table to sip it slowly. Looking dazed and exhausted, she finally faced her houseguest.

He sent her a sympathetic smile. "Sometimes you need it too quick to allow for cooling."

"If there was a way I could inject it intravenously, I would." She stifled a yawn, and looked at the open paper on the table. "Were you able to rescue the paper before the neighbor's dog peed on it?"

Drake nodded and grinned at her. "He was just lifting his leg when I opened the door. I scared him so bad he peed all the way back to his yard, but at least he missed the paper."

Annie attempted a smile that didn't quite reach her eyes. She rolled her head, rubbing the back of her neck.

"Did you wake up with a crick this morning?"

"Yep. Just what I needed to top off this perfect week."

He rose to put his plate in the dishwasher. "I would have cooked you some breakfast, but you're out of eggs and bacon. You want toast?"

"I can do it."

"Hey, I'm up already." He reached for the bread under the cabinet. "Two slices?"

She nodded, and thanked him.

While waiting for the bread to toast, he walked over to where she was slumped over with her head resting on the table surface. She flinched at his initial touch to her shoulders, but stilled when he began to knead the tension from her tight muscles. She emitted a low moan of obvious approval.

Drake smiled as he continued the gentle manipulations. "Feels good, huh?"

"Heavenly. You may prove your worth around here after all," she said, her voice muffled.

"I've been told I'm very good with my hands. Maybe one day I'll get to show you some other tricks I've become quite accomplished at over the years."

"Don't ruin this for me, Drake. Physical therapists very rarely get to have any kind of physical therapy performed on them." She sighed. "You don't realize how much of a treat this is."

"Okay, hon. I'll leave you alone—just close your eyes and relax." He continued the massage, working his way up her neck as he rubbed in soft, circular motions.

Annie sat up and dropped her head forward as another low moan escaped from her. "Let me guess, you slept with a massage therapist and she taught you everything she knew."

Drake laughed. "Nope, but I know what feels good to me. The trick is to use just the right amount of pressure. If it's too firm it's painful, and if it's not firm enough, it's ineffective."

As soon as the words were out of his mouth Drake recognized the possibility of a double entendre. Annie did also, judging by the soft shaking of her shoulders. The circular motion of his hands slowed as he waited for her inevitable comeback. Stumped by her unexpected silence, he finally spoke. "Well hell, go ahead. I left it wide open for you."

"I think I'll leave it alone, if it's okay with you."

"Really? I didn't think you had it in you." He paused before continuing. "Shockingly, I'm disappointed." He waited, wondering what she'd come up with, hoping she'd reconsider. Eventually, she did.

"One man's ineffectiveness is another man's impotence."

"*There* it is! I knew you wouldn't let me down this morning."

Martin chose that moment to enter the room. Annie put her hand down and made smooching noises. "Good morning, baby! How's my fat boy this morning?" She stared, wide-eyed, as the feline walked past her to rub on Drake's leg. "What the hell?"

Drake beamed and halted the massage long enough to cuddle the huge cat, rubbing under his chin. "Hey buddy, did you sleep well?" Martin purred loudly as Annie watched, open mouthed.

"How the hell did you do that?" she asked.

"Do what?"

"How'd you win over my cat so fast? He usually doesn't take to strangers that quickly."

Drake raised the cat so that he was face to face with him and grinned. "We have an understanding, don't we buddy? As well as a mutual interest in keeping you safe. Martin and Lewis have agreed to do their parts."

"And just what would those parts be?" Her voice thick with sarcasm.

He shrugged. "I don't know. Whatever they feel is necessary, I guess. The important thing is *they* understand that, as the three males in the household, it's our duty to keep you safe."

Annie snorted and shook her head. "Are you done with the paper?"

"I just glanced through the headlines." He handed it over to her then watched, amused, as she turned straight to the colorful section of the Sunday comics. She spread it out on the table in front of her and began to scan the cartoon strips.

After a few minutes of trying to avoid his attentive perusal, she turned on him. "What?"

He shrugged. "I expected you to dive right into the headline news. I figured you were the type to be up to date on world politics and issues."

She shook out the paper and turned it to the next page. "Sorry to disappoint you. I've got enough on my plate. I only subscribe to the Sunday paper for the comics, the sales inserts, and the Entertainment section. You're quite welcome to the rest of it."

"Can I have the Sports Section?"

She turned to the back, pulled the section out, and handed it over to him.

"Thanks." The two of them sat there, each perusing his or her section of the paper while sipping their coffee and eating breakfast. Lewis woke up and began making various noises from his cage.

"I'll get your breakfast in a little bit, Lewis." Annie spoke without looking up from her paper.

Drake put the paper aside and stood. "I'm done here. Tell me what you normally give him for breakfast, and I'll do it."

By the time he'd prepared the various fruits and vegetables, Lewis had amped up the noise level. Drake hand fed Lewis and began to work with him. Within thirty minutes he'd taught Lewis to repeat "Drake" when asked, "Who's the man?"

Annie shook her head disgustedly. "You're contaminating my bird. You know, when you leave this place, he'll drive me crazy asking for you."

"Then I'll have to come visit him often, won't I?"

She frowned. "That may not be an option."

He begged to differ, but kept it to himself. "So, what do you have planned for today?"

"Actually, I had planned to go to my parent's, but I guess that's out of the question."

He looked at her curiously. "Why?"

"I don't want to get them involved in any of this."

"They don't know what happened?"

She shook her head. "If they do, it's not by me. Dad would move me and my menagerie of pets back home in two hours flat." She scowled at Drake's laughter. "He's been known to do things like that."

"Well, if you really wanted to go for a visit, I don't have anything to do today. I could go with you."

"Now, why would I want to bring you along with me?"

"Well, because then, you could let your parents know what's going on while, at the same time, assure your father that your welfare is being seen to.

We both know that'll be his main concern. He may not be as worried if he knows I'm in your presence any time you're not at your office."

Annie closed her eyes and rubbed the back of her neck. "You don't know my dad very well."

Drake smiled at her. "I can be very persuasive when I want to be. Just give me a few minutes alone with him when we get there, and I promise he'll be fine with it."

"You mean alone, as in you and I with him, right?"

"Actually, I mean alone, as in just he and I."

Annie turned a suspicious eye toward him. "And why is that necessary?"

He shrugged. "Just for a man to man talk; nothing for you to be worried about."

"Yeah." Her tone was icy. "Why don't you just come out and say it like they did two centuries ago, Drake? As in, 'It's nothing to worry your pretty little female head about. Just leave it up to the superior males of the species.' It ain't happening, big boy."

Drake repressed the grin he knew would just piss her off, and changed the subject. "So, how about it? You want to take a trip to see your folks today? It'll do you some good to get out of this town for a while."

Her brow furrowed. "I normally go early enough to attend ten o'clock mass with them. What'll you do for an hour?"

He jerked back a little, surprised at her question. "I was baptized and confirmed in the Catholic church, Annie. Grant it, I haven't been in a few years, but I hardly think the Vatican has changed the mass so much I won't recognize it."

"I should have realized that, since Tiff is Catholic. I never connected you with religion. I guess I thought you were—just . . ."

What?" He gave her a wicked grin. "A heathen?"

Her reply was dry and unamused. "I was going to say non-religious, but heathen fits perfectly."

"I'm neither so if you're up for parental visitation, it's fine by me."

She thought about it for a moment then nodded. "Okay, let me call my mom and warn her."

"Your mom's crazy about me, Annie. You don't need to warn her."

Annie snorted with laughter. "If I showed up with an extra mouth to feed, and she doesn't have enough prepared, she'll be mortified."

"Why don't we give her the day off? I could take you all out to a restaurant."

Annie waved off his suggestion as she picked up the phone. "That would be an even bigger insult to her, trust me."

They pulled into the St. Peter's Catholic Church parking lot at nine-thirty. The two of them entered the quiet church, joining her parents who were already seated in a pew.

After sharing several quiet hugs and handshakes, Drake positioned himself next to Annie on the cushioned kneeler. He said a few prayers he remembered from childhood, threw in an extra thank you for helping him get to her on time New Year's Eve then sat back in the cushioned pew.

Annie removed a rosary from her pocket and remained kneeling next to her mother. He studied the two women, noting their similarities in build, mannerisms, profiles, even the way they held themselves.

He caught Pete's curious gaze on him and nodded as Annie's dad cocked his head toward the side door. Drake rose from the pew and followed him outside, unlocking his truck so they could get out of the cold and speak in peace.

Pete McAllister got settled in then turned to Drake. "Is there something we need to discuss?"

"Yes sir, I think there is. Annie didn't want you and her mother involved in this, but I think you have a right to know if your daughter has been threatened in any way." He proceeded to tell him about the events of New Year's Eve and how it had all turned out. "I can't help but feel partly responsible because he's still out there."

Pete placed his hand on Drake's shoulder. "Don't do that to yourself. She got those migraines from me and I know what it's like. When you're in the middle of a bad one, all you can think about is how to stop the pain. Mine finally stopped when I hit my mid-forties but it's not something you forget. I'm thankful you were there. Have they identified her attacker?"

"Yes sir, but it's not much of a comfort." Pete's face turned progressively more ashen as Drake revealed more details.

"Do the local police in Kenton know about this?"

"The Kenton P.D. has been alerted, sir, just in case he comes snooping around."

"I'd feel a hell of a lot better if she were home with me and her mother."

"She doesn't want to put any of her family at risk. I haven't opened my new practice yet, so it's easier for me to bend my schedule around Annie's right now. I've moved in with her, sir."

Pete's jaw popped ominously as he fixed him with a stern glare. "You've *what*?"

"It's just to make sure she's safe. Red and I agreed it's too risky to leave her alone right now. As I said, the local police have been notified, they don't have the man power to camp out on her doorstep." When Pete's glare didn't abate, Drake added to his statement. "Of course, I'm staying in the guest room."

Pete McAllister's posture relaxed somewhat. "Next time, you might want to lead with the statement that won't get you an ass-whipping. I don't imagine my daughter was too thrilled with the idea of sharing her space."

Drake grinned. "No sir, she damned near accused me of having something to do with it just so I could situate myself in her home—just before she punched me in the gut."

Pete's eyes sparkled with laughter. "You know, out of all eight of my children, she's the one that's tried the hardest not to be like her mother, but Lord Almighty if she isn't her clone."

"I was just noticing the resemblances inside the church, Mr. Pete."

"Oh, it's more than just looks, Drake. Vivi's got a way of getting people to respect her, whether they want to or not."

"Annie's tough, but she seems a little spoiled," Drake admitted.

Pete grunted. "You think so? Well, when you have babies of your own one day, I'll remind you to raise them without spoiling them. Annie was the last of eight children and stayed longer than most, probably because we weren't in a hurry to see the last one leave the nest. She was a good kid, too. Never gave us a moment of worrying, until some business with an old boyfriend." He shook his head. "I have to admit, I worried about her for a while. It changed her."

Drake's brow furrowed. "I've met T.J., you know."

Pete's brow rose curiously. "Where?"

"We met up with him at the mall yesterday. By the way, nobody's called him T.J. in years, Mr. Pete. He's *Tom* now."

Pete snorted like a bull seeing red. "He'll be damned lucky if I don't call him something worse. So what's old *Tom* been up to?"

He listened quietly as Drake explained T.J.'s reason for being in Lake Coburn. "So, he's got a fiancée." Adding under his breath, "Better someone else's daughter than mine. Once somebody hurts my little girl like that, I don't care to have him around. California is a good place for him."

"She didn't want to talk about it, so I don't know what went on. Is there anything you'd feel comfortable telling me about that time in her life?" .

Pete's gaze intensified. "That's kind of personal, don't you think? Is there any reason you feel I should do that?"

"Yes sir, there is. There's a very good reason, and it's kind of personal, too." He sent the older man a look, hoping to convey, without words, the message that his intentions toward Annie were honorable.

Pete studied him long and hard before nodding slowly. "Will you keep my daughter safe until that animal is caught and behind bars?"

Drake smiled. "For longer than that, once I convince her how crazy she is about me."

"I see." Pete glanced at his watch. "We'd better be getting back inside now, or Vivi will be upset. Trust me, you don't want Vivi upset with you. Despite what my wife would like people to believe, Annie didn't get her temper entirely from me. She may be slow to fire up but she's got a hell of a burn time, and a memory that never fades."

Drake followed him back inside to take their respective seats alongside the two women.

The end of mass had everyone bottle necked at the exit an hour later.

"Hello Annie, we meet again."

Drake and Annie turned simultaneously at the sound of T.J.'s voice. After hearing what Pete McAllister had to say about him, Drake found it difficult to hide his disdain for the man.

Annie acknowledged him with a nod and a somewhat low-key "Hello, T.J."

Drake ignored him completely, instead studied the tall blonde beside him. The woman could have been any one of the women Drake had dated over the last several years—gorgeous, high maintenance, totally unremarkable, and nowhere near Annie's caliber of natural beauty.

T.J. gave Annie a grim smile and spoke in a disapproving tone. "It's Tom now." He turned toward the woman beside him. "I'd like to introduce you to someone, sweetheart. This is an old friend of mine from high school, Annie McAllister. Annie, this is my fiancée, Britt Holland."

Drake placed his hand at the small of Annie's back, bristling as the busty blonde looked down her nose at Annie.

"McAllister? Why does that name sound familiar to me?" Britt oozed, stiff-jawed and looking bored to tears.

Annie's spine stiffened to ram-rod straight under Drake's hand. She must be every bit as annoyed with this bimbo as he was.

"I'm sure I have no idea. I know we've never met before," Annie said.

"No. I'd have remembered meeting someone from this God forsaken place. I'll bet there isn't even an ATM here."

Annie stepped over to a woman who stared at the blonde with obvious disapproval. "Mrs. Pat, how are you?"

"Annie, sweetie, I'm wonderful. How are you?" She embraced Annie in a warm, heartfelt hug and whispered just loud enough for Drake to hear, "My son's a fool, and don't think we don't know it." Pat smiled as her perusal extended to Drake. "And just who is this handsome young man?"

T.J. spoke up. "He's just Red's new brother-in-law—his wife's brother."

The woman turned on her son, sent him a glare that had him taking a step back from her. Seeming to be satisfied at his retreat, she turned back toward Drake and Annie again. "I'm Patricia Boudreaux—and you are?"

Drake flashed the woman a brilliant smile, liking her instantly. "Drake LeBlanc, ma'am, and, although I *am* Red's new brother-in-law, that's not to say I couldn't be something else, as well." He flashed a grin over in T.J.'s direction. "Things happen." He gave him a sly wink.

T.J.'s mom touched Drake's arm gently. "It's wonderful to meet you, Drake. I know you're not from around here with that lovely Texas drawl."

"No, ma'am. I'm from Houston originally, but I just relocated to Lake Coburn to start my own law firm."

T.J. snorted. "You hate lawyers, don't you, Annie?"

Annie turned to her ex wearing a brilliant smile of her own. "Well, that was true enough eons ago, *T.J.,* but that was before Drake. I guess I just needed the right lawyer to come along to change my opinion." She finished by looping her arm around Drake's.

Drake never had been the sort of man to waste a golden opportunity, He pulled her in front of him and wrapped both arms around her, grabbing both her hands in his. He bent low to place an affectionate kiss on the side of her head. For whatever reason, Annie decided to play along by laying her head back against Drake's chest.

Patricia Boudreaux smiled. "Well you two certainly are the perfect couple, I must say."

Britt looped her arm through T.J.'s. "Actually, I think *we're* the perfect couple." She looked at her future mother-in-law, her glare challenging.

"Yes, you two are quite lovely also. But Annie has had a special place in my heart for years. She's such a beautiful, *polite* young lady." The woman was half a head shorter than Britt, but still stared her down, as though daring her to say another word.

"Well, sweetheart, are you ready to go?" T.J. interjected. "We're driving to Houston after church to catch a flight back to L.A."

"Have a nice flight." Drake nodded as he turned Annie away and began to walk with her toward Vivienne and Pete, who'd apparently observed the scene from a distance.

Their group had nearly escaped through the door before T.J. caught up with them.

"Mr. Pete! Mrs. Vivienne! It's been a long time, hasn't it?"

Pete stared at the outstretched hand with disgust before seeming to reconsider. Drake stifled his laughter as Pete took the man's hand in a knee-buckling squeeze that had poor old Teej wincing.

"Not long enough, T.J.," Pete growled, before finally releasing his hand. Vivienne nodded politely and the two of them headed outside.

Annie caught up to her parents. "We'll meet you at the house, Mom. Do you need us to pick up anything?"

"I'm low on soft drinks, and your father would like a six pack of beer."

Annie nodded. "We'll get it, you two go on home. I have my phone if you can think of anything else."

The older couple departed and Drake and Annie made a bee line for the grocery store. Once there, Drake pulled out a shopping basket and loaded up a couple of containers of soft drinks for Vivi, and the beer of choice for Pete. "As long as we're here, I may as well stock up on a few things for your place," Drake added. "I'm sure I eat a lot more than you do. I need sustenance."

Annie nodded quietly and followed along as Drake began to fill the basket with snack cakes, chips, pretzels and two different kinds of beer as well as two decent bottles of wine. He pushed the basket, sending a sidelong glance at Annie. "You okay?"

"I don't want to talk about it." Her reply sounded somewhat hard and clipped.

Drake stopped the buggy. "Hold on. Are you upset with me for implying we're a couple?"

She turned on him. "Implying? You couldn't have been more blatant if you'd put it on a billboard."

"Well, you went along with it."

"You didn't leave me much choice. What was I going to do, call you a liar in church, right in front of my parents?" She checked out an older woman watching them from the other end of the aisle, lowered her voice accordingly. "We can't discuss this here. My parents do still live in this town, you know."

Drake paid for their purchases and loaded them in the truck. En route to the McAllister homestead, Drake picked up the precious conversation.

"I'm sorry, Annie, but *Tom* is a real prick. I know it was wrong, but I couldn't let him off the hook that easily. And that girlfriend of his—ugh!"

Annie grinned reluctantly. "She obviously thinks highly of herself. I have to admit she is gorgeous."

Drake huffed in disgust. "That woman is about as real as a plastic doll. A total fabrication. I guaran-damn-tee she's been botoxed, liposuctioned, lip-plumped, lasered, and silicone-enhanced, until there's not a square inch of her left the way God intended. Believe me, honey. I've been around enough plastic-surgery-enhanced Houston females to recognize a pair of fake hooters when I see them."

Annie shook her head. "You couldn't possibly know that without actually *seeing* them. Take this road." She pointed to the highway leading south of town.

"I sure as hell can. Hers are way too high for someone her cup size."

Annie covered her eyes with one hand and laughed. "I cannot believe I'm even having this conversation with you."

After a momentary awkward silence, they faced each other and both burst into laughter.

Annie quieted enough to continue. "Maybe she's just wearing a really good support bra."

Drake sent her a serious look. "Annie, she wasn't *wearing* a bra."

Her eyes widened in shock. "For real?"

He nodded, and they got in a second round of snickering at the Barbie doll's expense. Drake sobered before continuing. "I told you, I know what

I'm talking about. Britt doesn't possess true beauty . . . but you do."

Annie's mouth twisted in a cynical grin. "If you're just saying that to get me to fall into bed with you, it won't work."

He tweaked her nose and chuckled. "Not that I wouldn't welcome you falling into bed with me, but no. I recognized that the moment I first saw you. It's the truth, whether you believe me, or not. Those eyes are enough to stop a man in his tracks, but that perfectly proportioned body of yours . . ." He sucked in his breath. "That would drive any man insane."

She stared at him. "Perfectly proportioned?"

He nodded. "Absolutely—as in appropriate dimensions—a harmonious arrangement of parts. Your parts are all in perfect harmony with each other."

She smiled. "Well, thank you, but it still won't get me to fall in bed with you."

Drake sent her a wink. "We'll see."

Chapter Eight

"It's the last house, all the way at the end of this road."

Drake approved of the location. "It's nice out here, all the perks of country but with conveniences of city life."

Annie laughed at his word choice. "Town life, you mean. By no stretch of the imagination would I call Gardiner a city. It was nice growing up out here, though. I could ride horses out the back door, and ride my bike to school from the front; the best of both worlds."

He pulled up into the driveway and parked his truck. Drake grabbed the drinks and followed Annie to the side door of the large two-story house. The exterior was clean, sharp, and looked freshly painted and well-kept. The yard and outbuildings were all neat and trimmed, as well.

The second he stepped inside the pleasant space, Drake's senses flooded with delicious smells and mouth-watering sights.

"Man, it smells awesome in here," he whispered, his stomach growling in anticipation.

Annie grinned. "It always does. If any of my friends were dieting, they refused to come here."

Vivienne walked into the kitchen. "Oh, you got drinks. *Merci, ma petite fille.*"

Annie hung her purse on the coat rack. "Don't thank me, *ma mere.* Drake insisted on paying for everything."

"*Merci beaucoup*, Drake. You're such a sweetie," Vivienne said, giving his arm a pat.

Drake turned to her. "You're welcome, Ms. Vivi. By the smells coming out of that kitchen, I know I'll be well compensated." He set the drinks on the counter top and turned to embrace her in a bear hug. "And have I told you how much I love that photo album you designed for me as a Christmas gift? I can't tell you how many times I've sat and looked through it. I still can't believe you did it."

Pete McAllister chose that moment to walk in the room. "Hey now, should I be worried?"

"Sorry, sir." Drake grinned and released her. "I was just thanking her again for my photo album."

"I could lie and say you'll get used to her thoughtfulness, but she still amazes me, even after forty-six years." He embraced his wife gently and gave her a tender kiss. They turned simultaneously toward Annie, clearly expecting a scathing comment from her.

Annie surprised them with a tender smile. "Obviously, I'm totally desensitized to you two."

Drake cleared his throat. "Or maybe something happened to make you feel a little more empathetic?"

Annie walked past him, issuing a sharp command. "Don't you start with me, LeBlanc." Just as quickly, she dismissed him. She lifted the lid on the huge pot on the stove and stirred it. "Shrimp and okra gumbo, for us?"

"Actually, Julia requested it. She and the children will be here, too," Vivienne admitted. "Julia and Jacob are leaving for England in the morning, so it's even more perfect that you and Drake could be here with us."

"I'll be glad to see Jules and the kids again," Annie added. She turned toward Drake. "You do eat shrimp and okra gumbo, don't you?"

Drake shrugged. "Honestly, I've never had it before. I eat shrimp and okra in any other form, so I don't see why not."

"You're in for a treat, because Mom's is the best."

Drake held up the drinks. "Where do you want me to put these Ms. Vivienne?"

"There should be room in the bottom of the fridge."

Drake did as he was told then made his way over to the cabinet to stare at one of the most beautiful cakes he'd ever seen in his life. "Is this coconut?"

Vivienne nodded. "You've met Carrie and Sam, haven't you, Drake?"

"I did, at Tiffany and Red's wedding. Isn't Carrie also from here?"

Vivienne nodded. "She and I are cousins, actually. That recipe comes from Sam's mother, who used to sell her baked goods around Kenton. That coconut cake was her specialty. The filling is a boiled custard type that we Cajuns call *bouille* which means simply 'boil' in French."

"Vivi!" Pete called from the living room. "What'd you do with my glasses? I can't find them, and yes, I already checked to see if they weren't sitting on my head."

"That man." She left the kitchen muttering under her breath.

Drake wrenched his gaze from the luscious frosted concoction as Annie spoke from just behind him.

"That cake is made from scratch and has four layers, with that pudding between each layer. Do you like coconut?"

"It's my favorite cake in the world. Coconut cake and pecan pralines, that's my idea of heaven." He looked down at Annie, couldn't help but come up with a vision to top that. This woman . . . wearing his ring on her finger, and carrying his child . . . Yeah, that would easily make it to the top of his idea of heaven. He smiled as he caught her curious gaze on him. "What's wrong?"

Her brow wrinkled. "You didn't seem as though you were thinking only of cakes and pralines."

"Maybe I wasn't. All you have to do is ask, and I'd be happy to tell you what else is included in my idea of heaven." He leaned in low to speak softly into her ear. "I'd be happier to show you."

Annie struggled for calm, tried to keep her breath from hitching—no easy feat with her heart thudding furiously. Drake's eyes, sexy and deep, chocolaty brown. Her dad's noisy, grumbling entry jarred her comparison of his eyes to chocolate M&M's again.

"If people would leave my damn glasses where I put them, I'd be able to find the damn things when I need 'em."

Her mom swept into the room, wearing her classic I'm-about-to-put-you-in-your-place look. Annie elbowed Drake's side. "Watch this. She's so good at it."

"Oh, I know, sweetie," Vivienne gushed. "Just yesterday I left them in *your* shop out in the back yard. The day before, I laid them down on *your* barbeque pit out on the back patio. This morning I managed to place them next to the book *you* fell asleep reading last night. One of these days, I'll learn to tell the difference between your glasses and mine." With that, she held up her own tiny pair of reading glasses next to his own considerably larger ones, before handing them over to him.

Pete reached for them and grunted at her obvious victory. "No need to gloat." He leaned to kiss her lightly on the mouth. "Thanks, hon."

She gave him an indulgent smile. "You're welcome, Dear."

Pete turned to Drake, wearing a smug expression. "Nag, nag, nag! Sometimes there's no living with this woman."

Vivi's tinkle of laughter drifted across the room. "Take a few minutes to show Drake around the place, Annie. Your dad and I have everything under control in here, don't we, Pete?"

"Sure, sure," Pete grumbled.

Annie shoved Drake through the doorway into the living room. "Hurry. That's code for they want to make out in the kitchen."

"Annie Nicole!"

She chuckled at her mom's mortified reply, while pushing Drake ahead of her into the huge family room. He stopped in the center of the room, staring at the conglomeration of McAllister family portraits—a visual display of their family history, open to anyone who cared to look.

"What a great place to live." His comment sounded sincere. "If you could see the house where Tiff and I were raised, you'd realize how little it means to have money. Our house never felt comfortable. It still doesn't. This place says *home* without having to utter a single word."

She studied him. He studied the room, seeming to absorb every detail of the place she'd always taken for granted. She suspected he meant every word. "Money can't replace being loved and wanted."

He scanned his surroundings and nodded slowly. "You've got that right." Then he smiled. "I love the way your mom gets Mr. Pete to eat out of her hand without raising her voice. He knows he's being played and it doesn't bother him a bit. Your folks are something."

She walked over to the mantle and touched the most recent family portrait they'd taken. "Yeah, they are. We always knew we were lucky. I'd go to spend the night at the homes of some of my friends, and sometimes it was like being in a war zone. We never had to worry about things like that."

Drake snorted. "Ours was more like a refrigerator. Cold as ice."

"Did your parents argue a lot?"

"My parents tried never to be in the same room at the same time. It worked for them, but Tiff and I would have been seriously warped if it hadn't been for Melinda."

"Who says you aren't?"

"Be nice, Annie Girl."

She sighed. "God, I wish you wouldn't call me that."

Drake turned her shoulders gently so that she had no choice but to face him. "What did he do to you? I wish you'd talk to me about it, so I could understand why you put up this wall."

"It's ancient history, Drake. Leave it alone." The sudden, noisy arrival of Julia, Miranda, and Jacob saved her from having to dodge any more of his questions.

Annie intercepted the look Julia and Miranda passed each other when they saw Drake accompanying her. She held up one hand. "Don't get any ideas. This is a girl and her bodyguard, taking a road trip. That's all."

"Oooh…" Miranda teased. "Is that *bodyguard* prepared to perform any extra services?"

"Stop, brat." But Drake's deep chuckle had Annie's gaze locked onto his mouth.

His lip curled in a sexy invitation. "Fully prepared. I just haven't been asked . . . yet."

Drake stretched out on one recliner next to Pete McAllister and yawned. He rubbed his belly, still full even hours after that delicious lunch.

Vivienne and Annie walked in with two trays bearing coffee and slices of coconut cake.

"Who has room for cake?" Vivienne asked.

Drake snapped to attention in the chair. "I'd have to be crazy to pass that up, Ms. Vivienne."

Annie eyed his belly. "You sure you can handle that right now? I told you to pass on that second bowl of gumbo."

Drake reached out for a dessert plate containing the slices. "I'll make room. That cake has been calling to me since I got here." He took a bite and closed his eyes in blissful appreciation. "Man, the filling is out of this world." He took another bite then got up to hug the baker. "Please adopt me.

I'll be the perfect son, I swear."

Vivienne laughed. "I told you for Christmas you're already a part of this family, Drake, but if it'll make you feel better to call me Mom, you go right ahead. One more in our brood won't make much difference."

Julia laughed and added, "Why not? The hard part is taken care of already."

Annie turned to Drake. "You *are* potty trained, right?" The room's occupants burst into laughter.

"I was referring to college, but potty training is a plus, too," Julia commented.

"You two stop teasing my new baby boy, now," Vivienne fussed. "Drake, you're welcome here anytime."

"Thanks Mom," he drawled before giving Annie a gentle nudge with his elbow. "More and more stuck with me," he whispered just before a deep voice called from the back door.

"Anybody home?"

Chapter Nine

Julia & Chad

Julia

Julia felt the color drain from her face as her husband entered the room.

"Chad." Vivienne rose from her chair to meet her eldest son. "I thought you had a flight this morning."

"I did, but it got cancelled. That winter storm up north sure has plugged things up." His McAllister blue gaze landed on Julia.

She sucked in, trying to catch her breath as the atmosphere in the room suddenly thickened, like the deadly calm before a category five hurricane moves in.

"Jules."

She nodded. "Chad."

Chad looked over at their son. "I'm glad I get to see you one last time before you left for London."

"Yeah, it's been a good visit, but I'm anxious to get home, I've got some studying to do," Jacob admitted.

Chad stiffened noticeably. "Your home's here, Son."

"Come on, Dad, you know what I meant."

Chad pulled the teenager close for a brief hug. "Yeah, I do. Sorry, but I wouldn't count on that flight leaving tomorrow morning. Things are pretty bogged down for connecting flights up north."

"We've got a direct flight from Houston at six a.m.," Julia countered.

"Oh." He nodded. "You should be okay, then. When are you leaving?"

Julia glanced at her watch. "Actually, we should be going now. This was our last stop before we leave town. Miranda's driving and spending the night with us in Houston."

Chad headed for the side door. "I'll check out her car."

"You be careful in that Houston traffic, you hear me?" Pete McAllister said in that classically gruff 'real men don't cry' tone of his. Jules got one smile in before her father-in-law enveloped her tightly in his arms.

"I will, Pop." She turned to her mother-in-law and braced herself. "It's always so hard to leave you, Vivi." She fought to control the quaver in her voice.

Vivienne placed a hand on Julia's cheek and smiled through her own tears. "It's not forever, Julia. I know you'll be back and things will be fine."

After a few more minutes of goodbyes, Chad stuck his head in the door. "Hey Houston, we have a problem. Come check this out, Jules."

Julia wiped her eyes and met him outside, praying this wasn't an excuse to get her alone. "What is it?"

"Her tires are bad, hon. Look at this. I don't think you should take this car to Houston."

Julia checked out the tires and swung around to face her approaching daughter. "Miranda Gail, why are you driving around on bad tires?" She faced her husband. "And why have you allowed it?"

He raised his palms in the air. "I gave her seven hundred dollars two months ago to get four new tires and pay for balancing and realignment. She promised me she'd take care of it, as soon as possible."

Julia's glare pivoted from Chad to their daughter.

Miranda's face fell. "He did, Mom. I was in the middle of a project for school at the time. I forgot all about it. I'm sorry, Dad."

Chad crossed his arms, gave his daughter a stern look. "Did you spend that money on something else?"

"No. It's still in the emergency fund in my bank. I haven't touched it."

He sighed, seeming to accept her excuse. "Well, you sure as hell can't drive to Houston on those tires."

"We have to go today." Julia glanced over at his brand new Yukon. "Would you consider letting her drive us there in your truck?"

He shook his head. "It's out of the question. It's only a month old, and *nobody's* putting the first scratch or dent on it, but me. There's no choice but for me to drive you there myself."

"The hell you are." The last thing she wanted was to be in an enclosed vehicle with her estranged husband for three hours. "Mr. Pete will let us borrow one of their vehicles." She turned to walk back into the house to ask her in-laws, but Chad grabbed her arm.

"Look, you're always telling me I'm not willing to sacrifice for you. Here I am, attempting to do something and you won't let me."

She pulled away from him, and spun around, truly annoyed at his suggestion.

"Come on, Mom," Jacob pleaded. "I'd like to get some more time in with Dad and Miranda. Please, let him drive us there. It'll be nice."

Overcome with guilt at her son's pleading, Julia took a deep breath and turned to her husband. "All right, but if you can't get a room in the airport hotel, you can stay with Chad, and Miranda will stay with me. Understood?"

Chad

Chad nodded, trying not to grin like a six year old boy with a toad in his pocket. "You go tell Mom and Dad what's going on and Jacob and I will transfer the luggage. Please ask Mom to get the change of clothes I left here the last time I came for a visit. I don't have anything else with me."

Julia and the others came out a few minutes later. Vivi went straight to her son, with his clothes hung on a hanger, while Pete went to check out the tires on Miranda's vehicle.

He clucked his tongue at his granddaughter. "Honey, you're lucky they've lasted this long. Chad, I can bring it in first thing tomorrow morning and have new tires put on here in town. By the time you get back it'll be taken care of."

Miranda handed her grandfather a card. "Here gramps, use this to pay for them. It's the debit card for my emergency fund and there's nearly a thousand dollars in it. The PIN is my birthday, April 1, or 0401. Can you remember that?"

Pete's eyes narrowed. "Look here, Missy—*I'm* not the one driving around on bald tires. Of course, I remember the birth date of my oldest grandchild. It's the younger ones I can't seem to retain. Your grandma keeps telling me I need more RAM, whatever the hell that means."

"Are you okay, Jules? Need me to stop for a bathroom break or water or anything?"

Chad's voice sliced into her quiet thoughts like the screech of an owl in the woods at midnight. She didn't look up from the book she'd remembered to place in her purse, thankful for a reason to avoid conversation. "I'm fine."

"Let me know if you need me to stop at any time."

She kept her eyes on the book. "I will."

"You know, you might want to be careful with that. Reading in a vehicle makes you sick sometimes."

Her jaw tightened. "If I start to get sick, I'll stop." She prayed for him to keep silent.

"How's Jacob doing in school?"

She sighed at the waste of a good prayer. "He's doing well—the top two percentile in all of his subjects, except for one."

"Let me guess. Speech?"

She nodded, lifting the corners of her mouth just a bit.

Chad snorted. "Poor kid—he gets it from me. I'd die if I had to do any public speaking."

Julia nodded, choosing to remain silent.

"Miranda made the Dean's list again last semester. Did she tell you?"

"Yes, she told me."

Chad nodded. "Yeah, I guess you two talk quite a bit, huh? Probably more than she and I do."

Julia made a big show of turning a page she hadn't read yet. "We talk at least three or four times a week."

Chad nodded. "That's good, then. How's your brother and his family?"

"I didn't get to see them for Christmas. They'd had a ski vacation planned over the holidays for months." She turned another page she hadn't read. Dammit! The man hadn't called her in three months. You'd think he could keep quiet for a little longer.

He reached out slowly and placed his hand on hers. "Do you think we could use this time to talk?"

She pulled her hand out from under his. "I'd rather not."

"Come on Jules. This is serious. This is our future. We've got two more hours on the road. Maybe we could get some things out in the open."

Julia gave her head an emphatic shake.

"Are you telling me you don't want to try to save our marriage?" His tone was deflated.

She measured her words before speaking in a quiet voice. "Are you telling me you do? Because the papers you had delivered to me several months ago told a different story."

"I was mistaken in sending those papers. I was thinking that if I . . . if you . . ." He ran his hand nervously through his hair.

Julia finally faced him. "You were trying to use emotional blackmail on me. You thought if you gave me an ultimatum, I'd run back home to you?"

"I don't know what I was thinking. I guess I wasn't thinking at all. But, I know two things, Jules. I love you and I don't want a divorce."

"I love you too, Chad, but it doesn't change anything. We're at an impasse, and neither of us will give an inch."

"Jules, please . . ."

"I don't want to talk about this right now." She reopened her book and pretended to read again. Thankfully, Chad ended his efforts to converse. Her eyes grew heavy with the effort to read, and she finally closed the book and reclined the seat to take a nap.

Chad glanced over occasionally to watch his wife sleep in the passenger seat. She wore a pair of black jeans that fit her hips snugly, paired with a two piece sweater set in a deep burgundy color. The sweater had a scooped neckline that complimented the flawless, creamy skin of her neck and upper chest area.

Sleeping soundly now, she raised her left arm above her head, causing the hem of her sweater to rise and expose her bare midriff and belly button to his view. He glanced at the roadway, then back down to the expanse of smooth skin. His sex starved brain immediately sent a message to his groin area, and soon Chad was in a significant amount of discomfort.

Checking in the mirror to make sure both kids were still asleep, he slowly reached out his hand and placed it on her bare belly, and held his breath. When she didn't waken, he slowly began to move his thumb with a feather light touch in a circular motion. Julia moaned in her sleep. His groin tightened significantly. He softly caressed her waist and belly, aching with need for his wife. As she stretched and arched in her sleep the waistband of her jeans gaped slightly and he couldn't resist slipping his hands just under the snap to caress the velvety softness of her skin. Another moan escaped Julia's lips and this time her hands came down to cover and caress his own as she spoke his name softly in her sleep.

His hand froze inside her jeans as he stared down at the sleeping beauty he'd been married to for twenty-one years. God, he'd missed her. After all this time she was still as beautiful as the day they had wed. He gazed at her lovely face, her fair complexion, set off by the coal black of her hair. Her gorgeous lips were formed in a pout as she slept, making him ache to kiss her. He tore his gaze back to the I-10 Westbound roadway. When he looked back at her his gaze locked onto her startled blue eyes.

Julia blinked twice, and her eyes widened before she pushed his hands roughly away and pulled her sweater down. She raised the seat back to the sitting position and cleared her throat, all the while blushing furiously.

"Jules. I'm sorry. I just—It's been so long . . ." He squirmed uncomfortably in his seat, trying to adjust himself so he wasn't in such a bind. He checked the roadway before glancing back at her, but his hand froze in place at the sight before him. Julia's embarrassed staring at his significantly bulged crotch area, as though totally mesmerized. The sight of her licking her lips caused another, somewhat painful, stiffening in his jeans and Chad sucked in his breath sharply.

The sound seemed to wake her from her sexually induced trance and she tore her gaze from his crotch to his face. Mortified at being caught staring, she tore her gaze and faced frontward.

Chad did the same and clasped both hands on the steering wheel in a vice grip that had his knuckles turning white. "I'm sorry, Jules. Like I said. It-it's been a long time for me."

Julia turned to stare out of the passenger window, stiff and unyielding.

Neither of them spoke for the remainder of the drive.

Chapter Ten

Drake's gaze followed Annie through the kitchen door after her mother, before turning to face Pete. "I guess she'll want to be heading home soon. She hates leaving Martin and Lewis alone too long on the weekends."

Pete's face broke into a big grin. "How are those two?"

"They seem to be doing fine."

Pete picked up his glass of iced tea and sipped at it. "I never was too fond of cats in the house, but Martin never bothered me much." He chuckled. "That damn bird about drove me crazy sometimes, but I swear, after she left with him, it got too damn quiet in this house." Vivi bought those to replace some of the noise he used to make around here." He pointed to a set of large wind chimes hanging in the patio. "I'm kind of partial to that old bird." A grin suddenly spread across his face. "Taught him few sounds of my own over the years."

Drake didn't bother hiding his amusement. "Yeah, Annie told me she's hoping he forgets all about the fart noises. I have to admit, I like him a whole lot better now that he calls me by my real name."

"What was he calling you before?"

"Prick mostly, as in 'Who's the prick?', 'Where's the prick?', and 'Prick's on the phone.'"

Pete's eyes sparkled with laughter. "The real *prick* was Annie's date. Sitting out in that car, blowing the horn for his homecoming date. Can you imagine? He's lucky she dumped his ass and went without him. If he'd set foot in this house after that incident, it wouldn't have been pretty."

"Yeah, Red told me she handled it."

"Annie's always been full of sass and brass, except for the time . . ." He swallowed. "Except for the first couple of months after she and T.J. split up." His mouth tightened in a frown. "Let me tell you, when you have a daughter as full of spirit as Annie was, and have her close herself off like she did for two months . . ." He shook his head. "It wasn't an easy thing for her mother and I to watch."

Drake turned serious. "Can you tell me about it, sir? Please?"

Pete sighed and nodded. "How about a beer while we talk?"

Drake went inside and returned with two beers, handing one to Pete as they made their way to his shop.

Annie's dad pulled up two chairs and seemed to contemplate, to choose his opening words with care.

"T.J.'s dad is one of my closest friends, and our families have always been close, so we were fine with our kids dating for two years in high school. Everything was fine until it was time to choose a college. Long story short, he forced her to choose. She chose LSU and T.J. chose to make a clean break."

Pete set his beer bottle on a nearby table and leaned forward with his hands clasped tightly.

"Annie didn't seem as outwardly upset as she was withdrawn. I never saw her shed a tear, but she stayed to herself for the next two months. She lost her appetite, must have dropped fifteen pounds. For someone as tiny as she is, that's a significant loss."

He popped his knuckles nervously and got really quiet for several moments before continuing in a low drone.

"Vivi and I finally sat her down for a talk. We discussed depression, whether or not she needed counseling, or anti-depressants. She asked us to leave her alone in her room for the rest of the day, and promised us she'd be fine. We trusted her, so we did as she asked. She came out of her room around nine that night, and it seemed as if she was over it."

Pete sat back in his chair. "She started eating again and went back to being outwardly sociable. It seemed forced, at first, as if she avoided being alone at all costs after that night. It got easier, and by the time she left for college she seemed to be back to her old self, or almost—"

"Except for the wall she put up to stop anyone from getting too close," Drake added. "The night I met her we had this instant attraction. I'm telling you, no woman has ever had that kind of effect on me before, or since. I know she felt it too, because it scared the hell out of her and she ran. Introduced herself as Nicole, but as soon as I met Red, Melissa, and Bailey I knew she had to be one of them.

A wave of understanding flashed over Pete's face. "So, you knew, but she didn't. *That's* why she was so upset at Christmas."

"I figured Red would have told you about that before now. I'm sorry."

Pete waived his hands in front of his face. "Hell, no! If they don't offer, I try not to ask. Keeps me sane." He drank from his beer and sighed. "It's hard enough handling the things you need to know."

Drake sensed a distinct in his words. "Does it have anything to do with Annie, Mr. Pete? Is it anything you could share with me to help me to understand her better?"

Pete took a deep breath, his face paled, his expression turned somber enough to cause Drake's stomach to turn.

"A month after Annie left for LSU, I came home from work and found my wife in tears. The kind of crying that scares the hell out of a man, you know? Hysterical, heartbroken sobs that took ten years off my life, I swear. She couldn't speak, just handed me a letter she'd found while cleaning out Annie's closet."

He pulled a handkerchief from his pocket to wipe his eyes, and sniffed loudly. "Now, I know you'll hate me for this, but it's not my place to tell you the contents of that letter. I will tell you this much, though. Her fear of being alone at the time was justified. It also explains her unwillingness to let anyone too close."

He sat forward, grasped his beer bottle in both hands. "Maybe one day you'll be able to tear down that wall enough for her to tell you about it herself. If that day ever comes, you just might have a chance with her."

"When," Drake added.

"Excuse me?" Pete asked.

"When that day comes," Drake said. "I'll have that chance, and I don't squander chances."

Pete's chuckle turned into full blown laughter. "I'm looking forward to it, Drake. You look like you can carry your weight in hay bales, and by God, I can always use the free labor."

Annie sat in the quiet kitchen with her mother, staring out at the workshop the two men had disappeared into. "I wonder what they're talking about out there."

"Oh, your dad's probably going to show him his new cordless drill. I think at last count he had four of them."

"Well he needs that many when the damn things grow legs and walk away," Annie interjected as her mom snorted with laughter.

"My husband is seriously obsessed with power tools. I may need to arrange an intervention." Vivienne poured herself another cup of coffee and turned to her daughter. "Okay, Annie love. We're alone now, so what's going on?"

Annie swiveled back and forth in her chair, stealing cautious looks at her mother. "Nothing's going on, Mom."

The older woman cocked her head to the side. "Can it, baby girl, you always were a bad liar. Now, why are you here with a man you've been trying to avoid?"

Annie took a deep breath and released it slowly. "Okay, but don't freak out."

Vivienne frowned at her daughter. "I was awarded that God-given prerogative the day you were conceived, but I'll try to hold back." She sat down beside Annie. "Talk to me, Annie Nicole."

Several minutes later, Vivienne sat there, in utter shock. "Oh, my God! He's a murder suspect?"

"Yes, of a woman in Arkansas, and rather than put anyone important to me in danger, Drake offered to move in just until they catch this guy."

Vivienne stood suddenly, staring at nothing, open mouthed, hand on her chest. She finally managed to speak, her voice shaky with nervous tension. "Drake is staying with you? In *your* house, as a bodyguard?"

Annie nodded. "In the guest room."

Vivienne turned her wide eyes on her daughter. "In the guest room?" Her voice squeaked, tinged with hysteria. "Do you think that's wise, Annie?"

"Mom, nothing's going on between us. He's in the *guest room.*"

"I know sweetie, but think about it. If you are asleep in your bedroom, and he's in the guest room, how can he protect you?"

Annie stared, dumbfounded as her mother continued in a hysterical rant.

"What if that man crawls in through your bedroom window and Drake doesn't hear, or doesn't wake up? Is he a light sleeper? Your father can sleep through a hurricane! What good is Drake if he's in the guest room?"

Annie stared at her mother. "What do you want me to do, Mom? Let him sleep in my bed?" Her question seemed to take her mother by surprise.

"Not in your bed, but in the same room. He could make a bed on the floor—no wait! I'll send you home with our inflatable air mattress. He doesn't have to be in your bed. Oh my God, Annie. I think your father and I should go stay with you. There's safety in numbers, right?"

"Mom, stop. You're not supposed to freak out, remember?"

"Annie Nicole, the man is suspected of murder. Don't you dare ask me not to worry about something like that. You're my baby girl!" Vivienne stood quickly, spun around to clutch at the rim of the kitchen sink. "Oh dear Lord, first it was that awful business with Red, Tiffany, and Benji, and now *this*? What the hell is going on with my family?"

"Mom, please." Annie breathed deeply, steadying her voice, attempting to project calm to her mother. A classic reversal, for sure. "Drake has everything under control. We have it worked out so that when I'm not at the office, he's always with me. He won't let anything happen to me. He . . ." She paused, thinking anything was allowable if it helped to calm her mother, who was clearly nearing a hysterical breakdown. "He cares about me."

"He *cares* about you?" Vivienne's voice quavered.

Annie stepped close to her mother, placed her hands on her face. "Yeah, he does. He won't let anything happen to me. I don't know how I know that, but I do. I'm not afraid with him around, honestly."

Her mother stared at her for several seconds as the info seemed to sink in. "Annie, is he in love with you?"

"I-I don't know, Mom. I doubt if his feelings are that strong. He's just very attracted to me, and I know he cares about me."

"And how do you feel about him?"

"I don't feel anything about him. As soon as the cops catch this guy, *if* he's even still around, Drake will be out of my house. I'll be able to get back to my nice, normal life." She fidgeted under her mother's perusal. "What?"

"One of these days you're going to have to let someone into your life."

Annie picked up a dishcloth, and began to wipe down the spotless countertop. "Martin and Lewis are enough for me right now."

"They're pets, love. They can't fulfill your life. You need to find your partner, your match to be happy. But in order to do that, you need to let your guard down a little. How will you know if a man is the one or not, if you don't let him get close enough?"

"I can't do that, Mom. I won't."

This time Vivienne placed her hands on Annie's face. "You're *stronger* than you were back then. If you could fight your way back from that, anything you face now will be a walk in the park for you. Please, don't close yourself off to love because of something that happened twelve years ago."

Annie squeezed her eyes shut. Thinking of that period in her life always made her so sad. Not so much because she'd lost T.J. . . . that pain had long dissipated into thankfulness, especially now that she'd seen the kind of man he'd become. It terrified her to think of what she'd nearly given up for one selfish boy who hadn't been willing to sacrifice anything for her.

Her mother may believe she was stronger, but Annie wasn't so sure. How could she know, when she hadn't been tested all this time? She couldn't take that chance. If she ended up a lonely old woman living with her cat and her bird, then so be it. At least she'd be living the life she chose.

By four o'clock they were on their way back to Kenton, carting three dozen farm fresh eggs, and plenty of leftovers. Drake inhaled loudly. "God, my mouth is already watering for another bowl of your mom's gumbo. Hey, Annie, can you cook that recipe as well as she does?"

She turned toward him. "Of course I can."

"What would it take to get you to cook that for me again? I'm willing to negotiate."

Annie sent him a sly grin. "All negotiations should be in writing and duly witnessed."

He nodded approvingly. "Smart girl."

"My daddy taught me always to protect myself in business."

"And your brothers goaded you into taking self-defense training to protect yourself physically." He threw a glance in her direction. "I guess I have good old T.J. to thank for you protecting your heart the way you do."

She stared out of the passenger window at the passing landscape. "That's none of your concern."

"It's only fair to warn you. I plan on tearing down that wall of resistance you've built—brick by brick, if I have to."

Her heart seized at his confession, though she didn't dare face him. "How do you propose to do that?"

"With my charm and devastatingly good looks, of course."

He spoke with such confidence that Annie couldn't help but stare at him. "Jesus, you're full of yourself."

"We've had this discussion before. I told you then it's called confidence."

"We have had this discussion. I told you then you were a pompous ass. It seems you're absolutely unparalleled at it."

Drake chuckled. "Unparalleled? I don't know about that. I think ole *Tom* should be in the running, don't you think?"

Annie smiled. "I guess I can't argue with you about that. I'd also have to add his fiancée, Britt, to the list, as well. If that's even her real name, since you insist nothing else about her is." A thought had her turning to face him again. "By the way, you just happened to notice she wasn't wearing a bra when we were standing in a church. Have you no sense of reverence?"

He shrugged. "If she didn't want people to notice, she would have worn a bra."

She made a face. "But you shouldn't have noticed in a church. It's downright sacrilegious."

"If she had introduced herself to your dad or the priest I bet they would have noticed too, Annie. It's a guy thing."

A surprised laugh burst through Annie's mouth before she could stop it. "Don't you *dare* bring my father into this conversation."

"Which father?" His mouth twisted into a grin.

"My dad, of course," she chuckled.

Drake laughed along with her. "Okay, then, your priest."

"Our priest would not have noticed that, I assure you."

"Your priest is just a guy under that robe. He's human—we *all* have our frailties and weaknesses."

Annie stared at his profile, helpless against her absolute attraction to this man, no matter how much she tried to deny it. Again, she found herself wondering how God could favor one man with such an excess of good genes. "Weaknesses? Is the great, confidant, Drake LeBlanc admitting he has one?" Annie caught her breath as he shot her another one of those sexy, crooked grins.

"Well, sure I do, hon. I thought you knew," he drawled. "You're my weakness, Annie Girl. You're my kryptonite."

They pulled into her driveway around five fifteen, after a quick stop at the grocery store for a few more perishables. Drake, being a total dairy food junkie, bought two containers of ice cream, along with a gallon of milk, and cheese cubes to snack on.

They unloaded the groceries and items they'd brought back from her parent's house, then stepped into the familiar routine of feeding the animals.

Drake leaned close to the bird's cage. "Hey Lewis, who's the man?"

"Drake! Drake's the man!" Lewis squawked excitedly.

Annie groaned. "That is so wrong."

Drake was eating it up. "He's such an intelligent creature, aren't you Lewis? Lewis is a smart bird, yes he is."

"Lewis! Sharp as a tack." The bird cocked his head to the side as the large yellow cat sauntered into the room. "Heeerree's Martin!"

"Yeah, there's our fat cat." Drake scooped up the animal. The cat placed both his paws on Drake's face softly, as he'd done to Annie the previous day.

Annie watched him, growing more upset by the minute. "He's not *our* cat. He's *my* cat, and you need to remember that." Something about seeing Martin being so affectionate with Drake made her nervous. Threatened her little bubble, somehow.

Drake placed the cat on the floor. "Well, I'm borrowing him for as long as I'm here. When I'm gone, you can have him back."

She took a deep breath. *When he's gone.* What if, when it was time for him to go, she didn't want him to leave? What then? The thought made her chest tighten. "I'm going to shower. There's something I want to watch on the tube tonight."

"Great, what is it?"

"I don't know the name of it, but it's on the Lifetime network."

Drake made a face. "Isn't that the one that shows all of those made for television chick flicks?"

She smiled. "That would be the one. But there's a television set in the guest room, so feel free to spend the remainder of the evening in that part of the house."

Drake frowned. "I've seen it. What is it, a twelve inch? Is it even color?"

"Yes, it's color," she sneered. "It's the one I had in my bedroom for ten years. We didn't all grow up with silver spoons in our mouths like you did."

He watched her through narrowed eyes. "I've just seen your family home, remember? You were hardly destitute, so don't even try to play the sympathy card. That's a great house and you have a great family. And *you*, being the baby of the family, no doubt got even more than your older siblings did, am I right?"

She made a face at him and turned to leave the room.

"Hey, hold off on that shower, would you? I'd like to go to my place and pick up a few more things I need."

She gave him a long, suffering look. "Just go, Drake. I'll be fine here."

He shook his head. "Hell no, I made a promise to Mr. Pete, and I'm not leaving you alone. I need to call Red to help me move something."

"What do you need moved here that's so big you need help?"

Drake grinned at her. "My flat screen television. It's too heavy to handle by myself."

Her curiosity got the better of her. "How big?"

"It's a fifty-two inch—the kind you can hang on the wall, but I have a stand for it."

"I can help you," Annie suggested.

He lowered his cell phone. "Are you sure you can handle it?"

"I can as long as you don't drop your end of it." She headed for the door, and left him staring after her.

Drake connected the last cable and slid the box into place. The credenza, holding the flat screen as well as his blue ray player and folder of discs, took up an entire corner of the spare bedroom. He watched Annie's departure, noting the look of envy she gave the set-up on her way out of the guest room. He turned toward the too-short bed for a man of his size, promising himself to take the time to purchase a king-size mattress tomorrow. Drake smiled to himself, thinking maybe he could use it to his advantage. A large screen television hooked up with blue-ray . . . he'd seen her admiring his collection of movies. Maybe he could entice her to watch a few with him in his new bed. It might be the first time he'd get her into bed, but if he was patient, it may not be the last.

He smiled to himself, supposing he should be ashamed of his thoughts. But then, again, this was Annie and he wasn't above a little materialistic bribery to get the woman he wanted. It's not like he only wanted her in his bed—he wanted a hell of a lot more than that from his little spitfire.

He walked into the kitchen still wearing a grin, stopped to appreciate the sight of her standing at the stove stirring the pot of reheated gumbo.

She pulled two bowls from the cabinet and turned to catch him watching her. "It's heated if you're ready for supper."

"I'm ready." He kept the rest of the thought to himself. I'm ready for that—and a hell of a lot more.

Chapter Eleven

"I'm hungry."

Chad's gaze settled on his teenaged son, standing in the bathroom door of their shared hotel room. "You must have gone through two family sized bags of chips and a six pack of cold drinks on the drive over here. Where the hell are you putting all that food?"

"I can't help it if I have an overactive metabolism. Grandpa Pete says you can't fight DNA."

"Ah yeah, Grandpa Pete. The Sam Clemens of Gardiner, Louisiana."

"Who?"

"Samuel Clemens—you know, wrote under the pen name Mark Twain?"

"Never heard of him."

"Tom Sawyer and Huck Finn?" Chad prodded, hoping to open a window of understanding. What he got was an even more confused look from his son.

"What kind of name is Huck?"

"Short for Huckleberry, the character in the book was Huckleberry Finn." He breathed a sigh of relief when his son's face lit up.

"Oh, Huckleberry! He must have named the character after Brad Paisley's son."

"What? No!" Chad shook his head, feeling a cold dread wash over him. "Good God, I fear for your generation. What's your required reading in high school these days—the Twilight Saga and Harry Potter?" He held his hand up when his son started to answer. "Don't tell me, Jacob. I'm sure it'll only send me spiraling uncontrollably into a deep, dark depression I'll never be able to claw my way out of."

He picked up the room phone and called Julia's room. She answered, sounding tired. "Hey, your son is hungry again. I'll treat all of you to supper tonight. The hotel restaurant is excellent."

"I'm sure Miranda would enjoy it, but I'm not hungry, Chad. I'm still stuffed from Vivi's good cooking."

"I understand." He paused a moment, waited until Jacob closed the bathroom door behind him. "I want to tell you again, Jules, how sorry I am for—"

"Stop. I don't want to think about it, much less discuss it. I'll tell Miranda to meet you in your room."

"But, Jules—" A click and dead air space greeted him. He dropped his head back against the headboard, wondering if he'd ever get another chance with his wife.

Jacob patted his belly. "Dad, you were right about this place. That rib-eye was outstanding."

"Yep, good food." Miranda polished off her last fried shrimp. "Not quite as good as Maw Maw Vivi's cooking, but plenty good enough."

"Yeah Dad, you missed out on some primo grub today," Jacob said, before wiping his mouth with a napkin.

Chad groaned. "So your mother said." He pushed his empty plate away from him. "Maybe there'll still be leftovers when I get there tomorrow."

Miranda snorted daintily. "I wouldn't count on it. Drake ate like he hadn't had a decent meal in months, and I think Maw Maw sent the rest home with Aunt Annie."

Chad shrugged before placing his elbows on the table, hands clasped tightly. "So, how's your mom doing?"

"She looks great," Miranda commented. "I think she looks younger every year. That new hairstyle is perfect for her."

Chad's eyes grew misty. "She's more beautiful now than the day I married her." He blinked twice then looked at his son. "Jake, she's-she's not . . . I mean-is she . . ."

"Is she seeing anyone?" Jacob finished for him. "Not that I know of, although there *is* this guy at the office, I think his name is Douglas. He's always bugging her to go out with him. I heard her say once she was running out of excuses to turn him down."

Chad panicked momentarily. "But she does turn him down."

"Well, yeah . . . so far."

"What do you mean, so far?"

"If nothing else, Douglas is persistent, and if she decides to take the permanent position in London, he may have more opportunity to wear down her defenses."

Chad saw Miranda's gaze dart to her brother, as though trying to warn him. Too late. Damage done. He felt the blood drain from his face. "*What* permanent position?"

Jacob's gaze shifted quickly from his sister then back to his dad. "Well, I'm not sure, maybe I misunderstood—"

"Son! Was she, or was she not, offered a permanent position in London?"

Jacob took a deep breath and nodded, looking like he'd rather be anywhere than where he was at that particular moment.

"Son of a bitch!" Chad hissed under his breath. He threw his napkin on the table, called for the check, then turned to his kids. "You two go on up to the room. Miranda, not a word to your mother about this. I want you to get whatever you need for the night and go to Jacob's room. We're going to need some privacy—it's time she and I had a talk."

Miranda and Jacob looked at each other then turned to their father. "Actually, it's way past time, Dad," Miranda added. "I hope you didn't wait too long."

"Yeah, good luck," Chad added as the two of them left the table.

Jules released a groan of appreciation as she sank into hot water up to her chin in the oversized whirlpool tub. Her eyelids fluttered open at the knock on the bathroom door. "Yes?"

"Hey, Mom?"

Miranda. "Yeah, honey. I had to soak for a while. I'll be out in a minute then it's all yours."

"Take your time. I'm going to go visit at Jacob and Dad's room for a while, okay?"

She closed her eyes, glad for the extra time to herself. She'd need all the relaxation she could get before facing Chad again. "Sounds good."

Chad walked purposely toward his daughter, who exited the room carrying her purse, her laptop, and an overnight bag. He clenched his jaw tightly in anger, already planning his verbal rampage toward his wife. As he approached Miranda, she held out the room pass card.

"I'll trade you." She wore a smug look.

Unsmiling, he opened his wallet, handed her his card, and grabbed hers from her. "Did you warn her?" he asked gruffly.

"No. She's soaking in the tub."

He turned toward Julia's room, but Miranda grabbed his arm.

"Dad!"

He turned, irritation at his wife setting him on edge. "What, Miranda?"

"If you walk in there like that, you're going to blow it with her; you *do* know that, don't you? She's just about had enough of your attitude and ultimatums."

"Miranda, I think I can handle your mo—"

"Oh my God! You're going to do it, aren't you? You're going to walk in there, huffing and puffing, ordering her around, and you're going to blow it for all of us. It's been a *year,* and you haven't learned a damn thing, have you?"

Chad gave his daughter a stern look. "Little girl, you'd better think carefully before you talk to me like that again."

Clearly frustrated, Miranda shook her head slowly. She averted her gaze, laughing nervously before releasing a long sigh, as though accepting the inevitable. By the time her gaze returned to his, her eyes were brimming with tears.

"Never mind, Dad. You go right ahead and do it your way, just like you always do. Mom said you would do this. She knows you so well, and you don't know her at all. I'm beginning to think you don't deserve her after all." She turned her back on him and disappeared into the room where her brother was waiting.

Chad turned to study the closed door before him. His wife was behind that door…soaking in a tub. The mental image had him groaning, and within seconds, adjusting the painful tightening of his jeans. Instead of barging in, as he'd intended, he walked to the end of the hallway and stared out the window that looked out onto the city lights of Houston. He stood there for a good ten minutes, reflecting on everything Miranda had told him. Finally, he lifted his head, uttering a silent prayer for a little help from the man up above.

Much calmer now, he walked slowly back to the room, using the card key to open the door. The sound of a blow dryer reached him from the bathroom and he dropped himself onto the couch to wait her out.

Julia came out of the bathroom wearing an ice blue silk pajama set, her cheeks rosy pink from the relaxing soak in the tub. She folded her clothes and placed them neatly in her bag and removed another set, draped them over the desk chair. She grabbed a book from her purse and turned toward the king size bed just as he clicked on the lamp next to the couch in the darkened corner of the room. Her startled gaze whipped around to face him.

"You scared the life out of me, Chad! What are you doing here?"

He forced himself to smile and stay calm. God she was beautiful. "I didn't mean to scare you. I asked the kids to let us talk."

He could tell Julia felt somewhat at a disadvantage when she turned to her suitcase looking for something.

"Dammit," she swore barely loud enough for him to hear. "I left it in my large suitcase."

"What?" he asked.

"My robe." She crossed her arms before facing him.

"Please, Jules. Sit down and talk to me."

She sat on the opposite end of the sofa, holding one of its pillows in front of her. "What do you want to talk about?"

He forced himself not to blurt out the one question bouncing around in his head. "How's your job going?"

She looked at him, warily. "It's fabulous."

He nodded. "That was to be expected, of course; you've always done everything well."

She frowned. "Did you hope I would go all the way over there just to fall flat on my face?"

"I only meant that everything you've done, you've excelled at. It's called a *compliment*."

She flushed, seeming to regret the jibe. "Not everything, obviously. Just look at us."

He smiled sadly at her. "We're just going through a rough patch, hon."

Julia studied her husband. He looked good. Too damn good for as bad as she wanted him. She shook herself out of her husband-induced state of sexual desire. "That's easy to say, but it doesn't fix anything."

"I know, Jules. But, I love you so damn much. That's gotta count for something, doesn't it?"

She sent him an accusing glare. "It would, if you were willing to give an inch, but I know you're not." She nearly gasped at the look of absolute hunger he sent her way.

"It hasn't been so long that you've forgotten, has it, babe? Because I could sure as hell give you a lot more than an inch right now."

"Stop." She refused to give in to her dire need for him. "Are you saying you're willing to move to England?"

"If I said yes, would you have me?"

"What kind of question is that?"

"You're the one who left me, Julia."

"You hurt me. I wanted you to come with me. Two years, Chad. Half of it is over already. It flew by, and you never came, never even considered it. Do you know how . . ." Her voice trailed off as she searched for words. "How insignificant you've made me feel? Insignificant and unworthy of you being inconvenienced the slightest for something so important to me."

"You're neither insignificant, nor unworthy, Julia. You're my life, but you've always been my life here. Our home is here, not in London, England. I'm in strange places three weeks out of four. If I can't lay my head on my own pillow, on my own bed, in my own home, for at least one week out of the month, I'll go insane."

"A year goes by so fast, and before you know it, we'll be home." She wouldn't beg him.

His light blue eyes seemed to search hers. "Would we? What if they offered you a permanent position?"

She stiffened, biting down on her bottom lip as she saw the glint of victory in his eyes. *He knows.*

"When were you going to tell me, Jules?"

"I haven't accepted it." She stopped suddenly.

He cocked his head, narrowing his eyes. "Yet. You haven't accepted it, yet. That's what you were going to say, wasn't it?"

"I haven't decided what I'm going to do, yet," she said, defensively.

"Dammit, Julia Anne, don't play games with me!" His voice rose, angrily.

Julia rose to her feet to glare down at him. "Don't you raise your voice to me, Chad Michael."

He stood suddenly, towering over her. "What were you going to do, Jules? Wait until I got over there, *then* break the news to me? 'Oh, by the way, we're not going home in a year. We're not going home, ever!'"

"If you'd come with me in the first place, I'd never have even considered it."

"How do I know that?"

She lifted her chin. "Are you calling me a liar?"

"I'm calling you sneaky as hell. I'm saying you'd wait and get me over there, and then spring it on me."

"You have no right to accuse me of that."

"I have every right. How many people knew about this before I did, Jules?"

"You have the nerve to ask me that after you filed for a legal separation without even speaking to me?" She took a step closer. Here it came, that old familiar build-up of anger and resentment. "You arrogant, selfish, inconsiderate—"

"Here we go with the name calling!"

"—Childish—"

"Come on Baby! You can do better than that."

"Foolish—"

"Bring it, Jules. I know you're dying to get a couple of good ones in," he taunted.

"You self-centered asshole!" she snarled.

"*There* it is. Come on, baby, what else do you have for me, huh?"

"You're a bastard, you know that?" She glared at him through tear-filled eyes.

"Yeah, yeah, but at least I'm not sneaky," he countered, giving her a smug look.

"Oh, you!" She pushed at his chest with all her might.

As though he'd been waiting for this moment, Chad pulled her close, and locked her in his long-armed embrace.

"Let go." She struggled to pull away from him.

He shook his head and chuckled, obviously amused at her predicament. "So you can swing at me? I don't think so, Babe. My co-pilot just quit ribbing me about the last black eye you gave me. That was five years ago, and for a lot less than this."

"It wasn't a black eye. It was a tiny little bruise on the corner or your eye, and you would not stop egging me on, just like now. Let *go* of me, dammit."

"Sorry, I'm not about to be a punching bag for that hot little Irish temper of yours."

Julia struggled for a little while longer, mumbling profanities under her breath then gave up the fight and gazed up at him. "*Why* do you always do this to me? Why do you do whatever you can to make me so angry?" The look he gave her was full of need. Heated, longing, *promising* need.

"Because when you quit fighting, just for a moment, you're vulnerable. And when you're vulnerable, I can do this." He lowered his mouth to hers and kissed her softly.

She froze in his arms at first then began to struggle against him, but he didn't let up on her. He lengthened the kiss until she began to relax in his arms. When she moaned into his mouth he finally loosened his grip, seeming to know the battle was over. He lowered his mouth to her neck, just below her left ear, causing her to release a guttural growl of approval.

"God, I missed holding you, Jules; I missed kissing you. I'm lost, baby—I'm lost without you," he murmured.

"Chad, this won't fix anything. We have to talk, without arguing." Her mind clouded as he nibbled at her neck, causing goose flesh to rise on her skin. "We have to resolve our differences—this won't help us."

"I think it'll help us a lot." He slipped his hand under her silk pajama top to cup her breast.

She moaned low in her throat, saw the satisfied smile slip over his face just before she turned her own mouth to his bare neck.

She tasted the slight saltiness of his skin with her open mouth, and breathed in the scent she'd always found so enticing. It was pure Chad. Julia took her turn by lightly nipping at his neck with her teeth.

His mouth met hers again, more frantically this time, and all unaddressed issues disappeared as quickly as their clothing. Chad picked her up easily and fell into the bed with her.

Neither of them asked permission. Neither made demands. Their urgency, their need took precedence over everything else. They automatically fell into the easy ways they'd developed with each other over their twenty-one year marriage. Each knew exactly what to do to please the other.

His fingers found her, worked her skillfully before withdrawing, and refilling the space, settling himself into the spot that fit him like a custom made glove. They moved together, danced to the rhythm they'd created for themselves over the lifetime of their marriage. The rhythm drove them both closer to that precipice of no return. As Julia's low moan of pleasure began to crescendo, Chad used a mouth covering kiss to muffle the sounds of her release. Moments later, when he could no longer hold back his own tide of pleasure, he surrendered with what would have been a roar, had Julia not stifled it with another kiss.

Julia lay curled up against his side, her fingers making feather soft movements on his chest.

"I love you, Jules."

She lifted her hand to her husband's light auburn hair, trimmed neatly, as per the airline's guidelines. She toyed with the short side burns then ran her finger over his smooth lips. He took it into his mouth and she smiled. "I love you, too, Chad." She raised her arms over her head and stretched luxuriously in the large bed then curled her leg around her husband's. "I feel like I could sleep for two days."

Chad nestled his mouth in the soft curve of her neck. "Mmmm, Babe, was that as good for you as it was for me?"

Julia closed her eyes and smiled. "Oh, God—I really needed that. I've been so—"

"Horny?" A low chuckle accompanied his answer.

"I was going to try to find a more subtle term to use, like 'hungry for your touch' or 'sexually frustrated', but the truth is the truth, I guess." She searched his face and traced her finger along his chiseled jaw line. "No matter how angry I am at you, I always end up missing you . . . jerk."

"That's good for me," he snorted. "I'll take any breaks I can get." He placed his hands on both sides of her face and kissed her gently. Pulling her close for a hug, he nibbled at her lobe then whispered softly into her ear. "Babe, what are we going to do?"

She kept her eyes closed and sighed. "What do you mean?"

"I mean, London. Your work. What the hell are we going to do about it? I could try to arrange it so that I can take more flights to the U.K., but with your work schedule, I don't know how much time we'd have together."

"Chad, why don't you take a leave of absence for the next year? Come live with Jacob and I in London. We could take the weekends to get some real sight-seeing in."

"Come on, Babe," he sighed. "I can't just 'not work' for a year—I'm not made that way. *I'm* supposed to be the bread winner—I can't have you support me for an entire year."

"That's ridiculous. We have plenty of money in the savings. Savings that we have because you've supported us all these years. You could take one year off and really be an active part of Jacob's senior year. You're running out of time to do the dad thing with him, you know."

Chad stiffened. "I resent that, Jules. I've always been there for my children."

"But he's playing football, Chad, and he's really good at it. When's the last time you were able to attend one of his games?"

He sat up, swinging his legs off of the bed. "First of all, it's soccer, not football, and I guess it's been awhile since I've attended a game, but I've sat with him and watched the videos you recorded."

"They call it football there, and watching the video isn't the same as being there for the game. He wants his friends to see you there. He's got a girlfriend that you've never met. Isabella is a lovely girl. And if you can't do it for your son, do it for me."

Chad rose quickly from the bed and tunneled his fingers through his hair. "You just have to lay that guilt trip on me, don't you?"

Julia watched the tick in her husband's jaw that indicated just how angry he was. "I need you to be there, as well. I need your support, Chad. Do you realize how many dinner parties, barbeques, banquets, and award ceremonies I've attended with you? I had to put years of my life on hold for you. This is my chance to make an impact, make my mark in a career that I love. I have functions to attend that I really want you to be there for. All I'm asking for is *one year* of your life. You've already gotten out of the first year. If one year is too much for the airline to accept, I'd even take six months."

Chad shook his head in quick, jerky movements. "I'm sorry Jules, I can't do it. I can't walk away from my job. When I'm in London I'll make as many functions as I can." He leaned over and placed his hands on her face. "And I promise to do so with a smile and no complaining."

"So, what you're telling me is, you won't even consider it, for any length of time." She felt him brush his hand over her forehead, as though placating a fitful child.

"Babe, I just can't."

She pushed his hand away. "You mean you won't." She climbed out of her side of the bed. "I should have known." She pulled on her night clothes and spun toward him, furious with him and herself for letting him manipulate her . . . again. "We have nothing more to discuss. You need to leave now."

Chad closed his eyes and clenched his teeth. "Jules, you're angry now, but you'll get over this. You said yourself how quickly the first year went. I'll see you as much as I possibly can. It'll be fine, you'll see."

She threw her hands in the air. "You don't get it, Chad. You don't understand how badly it hurts to have you say that to me."

"Babe—"

"Get out." She pointed toward the door.

"Jules—"

"Get out, *now!*"

"You're being ridiculous, Julia." Chad bent over to step through his boxers.

As soon as he straightened, he got hit square in the face with his shirt.

"What the hell?" He pulled the shirt away from his face only to have his jeans, including his belt, wallet, and all, flung in his face. "Hey!" He pulled them away and grabbed his chin where the belt buckle had hit him.

"Get dressed and get out, you insensitive jerk!" She shook her head and blinked back angry tears. "You're still unwilling to sacrifice the least little bit for me. Just get the hell out of my sight. I don't want to see you again. Jacob and I will take the hotel shuttle to the airport in the morning." She opened her door and pointed to the hallway.

Chad slipped on his jeans, zipped them quickly, and pulled his shirt roughly over his head. He walked into the hallway. Julia slammed the door before he even had a chance to turn around. He stared at the room number plate and wondered how everything had gone to hell so quickly. A door opened down the hall. He turned to check it out, saw Miranda and Jacob's curious faces.

Jacob turned to his sister. "I told you he'd blow it."

"What did you do?" Miranda huffed, looking sorely disappointed.

He held up his hands in agitation. "Why do you assume it's always my fault? Your mother is the most stubborn woman in the world." Julia opened the door again to throw both his shoes out. He bent over to pick them up and when he straightened, he got two socks in his face before the door slammed shut again.

Chad took a deep breath and released it slowly, his shoulders drooping. He turned and walked dejectedly into the room where his two silent, teen-aged children waited. He collapsed onto the mattress, swearing lowly under his breath.

Jacob and Miranda each sat on a corner of the bed. "Well," Miranda said, "I'm going to assume that you guys reconciled, at least for a bit, anyway. So, what'd you do to screw that up?"

"Same old, same old," he told his daughter. "We're at the same stalemate we've been for an entire year. She can't accept that we could spend as much time together if I just see her between flights."

Jacob groaned, placing both hands on his head as his mouth fell open. "Dad, Mom doesn't want you visiting us in London; she wants you to live there for a year."

"Actually—" Chad said, pushing himself to a seated position on the bed, "—she said she'd be satisfied with six months, but it's still too long to be away from piloting."

"Six months?" Miranda's mouth dropped open. "You can't sacrifice six months for her? She only wants you to be there for her the way she's always been there for you. Don't you get it?"

"Why should I have to go through all the trouble of relocating, when it would work just as well if I commuted? It's only one more year—we've already been through the worst of it. If we could see each other several times a month, it wouldn't be nearly as bad as the first year was."

Miranda sighed and looked at her brother. "You talk to him, Jake. I can't deal with him anymore tonight. I'll see y'all in the morning." She reached into her pocket to pull out a card key and held it out to her father.

Chad handed hers over in silence, and accepted his own card back. He watched his daughter walk calmly out of the room then he turned to his son. "What do you think?"

Jacob shook his head slowly. "I tried to tell you, there's this guy over there that won't leave her alone. She's turned him down up until now, but after this . . ." He lifted his arms and dropped them. "She may consider taking the permanent job *and* good old persistent Douglas. And from what I can see, you'll have nobody to blame but yourself."

"I know your mother too well, Jake. She wouldn't do that. She wouldn't throw away twenty-one years of marriage over this. She'll calm down."

Jacob sat back against the headboard and grabbed the TV remote. "Whatever you say, Dad."

Chapter Twelve

The next week flew by for Annie and Drake as they settled into a comfortable routine. He dropped her off at her office in the mornings and picked her up every afternoon at the same time. On Monday, Wednesday, and Friday they drove back to the gym in Lake Coburn, where they worked out until seven o'clock. On Friday night, the last work day of their first week of cohabitation, Drake unlocked Annie's front door and let her walk in ahead of him.

Lewis greeted them with a raucous "Honey, I'm home!"

Annie walked up to the cage and stuck her face up to the bars. "Hello, Lewis, my love." She let the bird kiss her then walked away from him.

"I love you, Annie," the bird called.

"I love you, too, Lewis."

Drake approached the cage. "Hey, Lewis; who's the man?"

"Drake's the man!"

"Lewis is sharp as a tack," Drake returned. "We'll get your supper in a bit, buddy."

The bird fluttered his wings and began to screech at one of the toys in his cage.

Drake watched in amusement. "He sure gets excited with that thing."

She turned from the fridge where she was pouring herself a glass of orange juice. "You should have heard him when he was younger—I put one of those miniature sock monkey things in with him, and you could have sworn he was arguing with the darn thing. Dad got so sick of hearing him, he begged me to take it out." She sipped at her juice and pulled her sweat-dampened shirt away from her skin with a grimace. "I have to fix his supper, but I really need to take a shower first."

Drake turned to her. "Go ahead and take your shower. I'll tend to him."

"You sure?"

"Yeah, I always shower at the gym so I don't offend your delicate sense of smell inside the truck." He grinned at her.

She forced herself to keep a straight face as she walked to her bathroom. "Thanks."

Annie re-entered the kitchen fifteen minutes later, feeling fresh from her shampoo and shower. She paused in the doorway reveling in the sound of an older song blaring from her computer's sound system. "Oh, man, I haven't heard that in years." She closed her eyes and swayed to the music. "That brings back some good memories. Fifteen years old and not a care in the world. I saw that group in concert when that song made the charts."

Drake cracked a huge grin at her. "Big Head Todd and the Monsters; I saw them too, in Houston."

Annie nodded. "That's right! It was the closest they ever got, so a bunch of us drove to see them at some stadium over there."

"That's the only concert they played in Houston that year, so we must have seen them the same night. Strange we were there at the same time."

Annie started swaying again, as she listened to words and remembered how simple her life used to be. "Boy, if I could go back to those days and know even a tiny bit of what I know now."

Drake began to play air guitar, then turned to Annie, singing the chorus of "Bittersweet". He danced his way over to her and grabbed her by the waist with one hand, capturing her right hand in his other.

Caught up in the nostalgia of the moment, and somewhat relaxed after spending a week with him, Annie didn't resist. She let him lead her around the room, allowed the music to carry her troubles away for a short time. She timed the last notes to coincide with a pirouetting spin that ended in a graceful pose, wrapped it up with a burst of laughter that had Drake joining in.

"That was actually fun," she said, turning to answer the sudden ringing of her phone. "Hello." There was a slight pause on the line before she finally heard the caller speak.

"Is this Annie McAllister?"

"Hmm, it depends. Who's speaking, please?" She froze at the cackle of laughter on the other end of the phone.

"Oh yeah! I'd recognize that voice anywhere. You have a brother who owns a club in Lake Charles called Red's, don't you, sweet thang?"

Annie shot Drake a frantic look. "Who is this?" All hint of laughter suddenly gone from her voice.

"How's your headache, honey?"

"What?" Her heart pounded frantically.

Drake took a step toward her. "Who is that?"

"Who is this?" She tried to remain calm while pointing to the second handset. Drake picked it up and hit the talk button.

"Is your boyfriend there tonight, or are you all alone?"

"Who is this?" She struggled to keep her building panic from surfacing.

"Well, I'm hurt that you don't recognize the sound of my voice. Tell your boyfriend next time I see him I'll be ready."

"He's not my boyfriend." She heard her voice quaver, and hated it.

"He's not? Well that's even better, then, ain't it, sweet thang? I guarantee next time I see you, I'll be able to finish what I started the other night."

The self-assured cockiness pissed her off more than the words. "I guarantee next time you try that, I'll give you more than you bargained for. I won't be as easy as that girl in Magnolia—you low life, back woods, ignorant redneck." The chuckle he emitted sounded like pure evil.

"Next time, I won't be as gentle."

She replied with a caustic comeback. "Oh yeah, it takes a real big man to attack a girl half his size who's already in pain. Your daddy must be so proud."

"My daddy used to be a hard-ass, till I taught him a lesson. It looks like I'll have to do the same to you, little lady."

Suddenly Drake spoke from the other phone. "Why don't you bring it over here right now, you piece of shit, so I can finish you off this time."

Annie got chills from the sound of gleeful laughter erupting from the earpiece.

"Whoop, there he is! I got a big fat tire iron with your name on it fer the next time I see you, asshole. Nobody beats on me and gets away with it."

"You'd better bring some help then jerk wad, because I can do worse than that with one hand tied behind my back," Drake snarled.

"Oh, yeah? Wells 'all I can say is you better watch yer back, city boy."

"Thanks for the warning, J.B. I'll be waiting for you. Have you seen your picture on the tube, yet? It's plastered all over the local network. I think I drew an amazing likeness, don't you?"

The caller laughed wickedly. "You musta done that after I asked around to find out which sister of Red's was at the club that night. It didn't take long to find out that it was Annie McAllister I missed out on."

A chill ran down Drake's spine as he heard him speak Annie's name. "If you come near her, I'll kill you."

"Yeah? You're gonna have to catch me to do that, and nobody denies I'm a slippery sumbitch when I wanna be."

Annie heard the click of the receiver then the silence of the dead line.

"Annie, where's your phonebook? Do you know if you have a trace call feature with your phone company?"

Annie pointed to a drawer that held the phone book and shook her head, too upset to speak.

Drake found the phone book, and after a minute of searching, pried the phone from her hand. He punched in *57, listened for instructions then hung up the phone. He placed both hands firmly on her shoulders. "Annie, we need to call the police now, but I need to know if you're okay."

She shook her head slowly. "I'm so stupid, Drake. I have no one to blame but myself for this mess. Why did I tell him about Red owning the club? Only a complete imbecile would do something so stupid."

"You need to stop being so hard on yourself."

"Oh God, if he knows who Red and I are, he could find out about everyone in my family. I've put *everyone* in danger."

Drake shook his head. "Sweetie, the only one he wants is you. You're the one that can link him to the murder in Arkansas. You're the one who can testify at a trial about what he said to you. Granted, they probably have enough on him now, but you could certainly cement his guilty verdict."

She placed her hand on her queasy stomach. "I can handle anything, as long as my family is okay." Eventually she began to feel the touch of his hands running up and down her arms, as though to warm her. "Stop that, I'm okay now."

He did what she asked but leaned into her line of sight. "Listen to me, Annie. I'm not going to let anything happen to you. The first thing I need to do is call Captain Woodard in Lake Coburn to coordinate things with the Kenton Police." He paused to swear under his breath. "We may need to get you out of here."

His comment, more than anything else, spurred her to life. "You mean go into hiding for as long as he's running loose?"

"He called your land line, Annie. He knows where to find you."

"I'm not leaving my home. That animal is *not* going to chase me away from this place. Besides, if he knows where I live, he'll eventually find out where I work. I haven't been at the clinic long enough to take a leave of absence. I have a partner and patients depending on me." She could hear herself talking faster and faster, spinning out of control. She couldn't stop. "I c-can't do that! What about M-Martin and Lewis?" she stammered. "Who would take care of them? I'm n-not leaving here."

She felt Drake's arms go around her, heard him speak in a gentle, soothing tone. "Okay, Annie. It's okay. We'll figure something out. I promise, I won't let you face this alone."

She calmed in his embrace, wishing for a moment she could stay there forever. Common sense prevailed and she pushed gently away from him. "I don't want you thinking this is going to change anything between us."

He lifted her chin until their gazes locked. "Look, whether you like it or not, we're in this together. He's out to get me back for whipping his ass, and he knows the best way of doing that is to get to you. It's my job to make sure that doesn't happen."

"It's the police department's job, not yours. You can still walk away from this," she insisted. "He doesn't know who you are yet, and he doesn't know where you live."

"Exactly. Don't you think that's reason enough to move into my place for a while?"

She shook her head again. "I told you, he's not going to chase me away from here."

He sighed, obviously frustrated with her. "All right, but as long as you're here, I'm here too."

When she started to protest he raised his brows and pointed at her. "Don't you make me go to your parents with this, because I will. I don't have a damn thing to hide, and furthermore, as soon as I speak to the police, I'm going to call my father and see if he knows the names of any reputable bodyguards."

Annie's mouth dropped. "No way in hell do I want a bodyguard following my every move." She turned away from him.

He grabbed her hand and pulled her gently around to face him again. "You don't have a choice in the matter. Again, don't make me go to your parents."

Annie's chin lifted. "I think you're bluffing."

Drake pulled his cell phone from his pocket and pushed a couple of buttons. "Peter McAllister in Gardiner, Louisiana," he spoke into the phone. Within seconds he showed her the number to her parent's home flashing on the screen. "Still think I'm bluffing, or do I call it right now?"

She crossed her arms tightly across her chest. "Why are you doing this?"

He placed both hands on either side of her face. "Because your safety is all that matters, Annie."

"Why?" she asked.

Why? He'd tell her if he thought she trusted him enough to hear the truth. Her eyes glistened with unshed tears. "For now, let me be the one to keep you safe. Please, I need you to trust me enough to do that."

Annie pulled away from him and walked over to Lewis's cage. She rested her forehead against the bars. "How did this happen?"

Drake lowered his voice to answer, wishing like hell he could do things over. "Because I didn't kill the son of a bitch when I had the chance."

Annie cringed at his words, turned her head slightly as Lewis cocked his head to the side and flapped his wings.

"Aaa-nnie!" the bird cried.

"Annie's tired, Lewis." She walked over to the comfortably worn leather couch and plopped down on it, tucking her feet up under her. Martin chose that moment to make his appearance and jumped up next to her. The large cat crawled onto her lap, rubbed his head under her chin then gently touched each of her cheeks with his paws.

Drake dialed the number to the Lake Coburn Police station. He explained the situation with the phone call, and asked to have Captain Woodard call him back at that number immediately. His gaze fell on Annie as he called Red from his cell phone. "We have a problem," he said, before telling his brother-in-law about the call.

Obviously upset, and worried for his sister, Red released a string of expletives. "Damn, I'd hoped that guy would be long gone by now. I'll take care of the bodyguard on my end. Sydney Graske gave me the name of a guy in Texas who's the best. I know how Annie is about her privacy, but there's no help for it now. And Drake, thanks for being with her through this. I know she must be giving you flak about being there."

Drake paused in the security round he'd been making in the house to answer him. "I can't imagine myself anywhere else, Red. I'll take care of her whether she wants me to or not."

He ended the call, and continued his rounds, taking note of several items that got his attention. He punched in his dad's number, and played with a set of broken window locks while he brought his dad up to date. "I figured you could give me the name of a good security system installer."

"I can do a hell of a lot better than that, Son. I'll take care of that for her. I've grown quite fond of the members of that family. You've got enough on your plate. Just give me her physical address and home phone number. Someone will need to be home tomorrow for the install."

"You think they can get to it that quickly, Dad?"

"They will if they want any future business of mine," Daniel said. "You tell that little lady to keep her chin up. They'll catch that son of a bitch. When they do maybe they should let Pete McAllister have the first crack at him. I have a feeling that man could still put a whipping on a guy like that."

Drake loosened his tight jaw enough to answer through clenched teeth. "He'd have to stand in line." Drake walked back into the living room just in time to see Annie disappear into her bedroom and close the door. "I've already beaten him unconscious once; I'm almost afraid to think what I could do to him now."

"Drake, what exactly is going on between you and Annie?"

"Not a damn thing, but it's not for my lack of trying."

"Now look, Son, she's bound to be feeling emotionally unstable right now. I hope you don't intend to take advantage of her."

"No, Dad, I just want her to trust me enough to lower that barrier she's erected. It's like she's accepted that she'll always be alone because one *boy* hurt her in high school. She's created this safe haven for herself, Martin, and Lewis and there's no room in it for me or anyone else." He ran one hand through his hair. "It used to be safe, anyway."

"We'll get it safe again, but who the hell are Martin and Lewis?"

Drake chuckled. "Her pets. Picture a big yellow Garfield looking cat, and a huge African Grey Parrot with the vocabulary of a five year old kid." The trill of the house phone had him checking caller I.D. "Dad I need to take this call. It's Captain Woodard from Lake Coburn P.D.. I'll keep you informed, and we'll be here tomorrow." He disconnected and answered the phone. "Hello?"

"Drake, I heard Ms. McAllister's been contacted by J.B. Montgomery."

"That's correct. He called about twenty minutes ago. I placed a trace call on it with the phone company." He explained about the imminent security system installation as well as the bodyguard.

"Very good. I've already contacted the Kenton Police, so expect a visit from someone any minute now."

When the doorbell rang, Drake walked over and looked through the peep hole at the two men standing there. "They're here," he told Captain

Woodard, before opening the door for them.

One uniformed officer stepped forward. "We have a report of a threatening call to Miss Annie McAllister."

Drake turned as Annie re-entered the room and approached him.

"I'm Annie McAllister." She extended her hand to the officers.

An older officer, with detective B. LeBleu on his name tag touched his cap as he addressed her. "We've seen what this guy is capable of, Miss McAllister, and we want to assure you that we're not taking this matter lightly."

Annie nodded and sent him a grim look. "Thank you, I appreciate that. If it's okay, I'll go back in my room, I have some work to do."

The officers nodded and she went back into her bedroom, closing the door behind her.

The second officer shook his head in disgust. "It takes a real low life to target someone as tiny as she is. Ms. McAllister is my mom's physical therapist and has done wonders for her. Mom would have my head if anything happened to her *'petite fille'*, as she calls her, on my watch. She thinks the world of her."

The older officer added to the praise. "I've heard a lot of other folks in town talking good about her, too. She's a welcome asset to the medical community."

Drake smiled and nodded. "That's good to hear, guys. Maybe it'll lift her spirits."

The two men exited to begin their watch of the house.

Drake walked back to Annie's door and knocked again, entering when she gave the go ahead.

He walked over and sat on her bed. "You okay?"

"I'm peachy, Drake. I've got cops surrounding my house, a man living with me and corrupting my pets, and soon there'll be a complete stranger following my every move. All because a murderer is doing his damnedest to rape and probably kill or maim me the first chance he gets." Her brow rose dramatically. "Life doesn't get any better than this."

He reached out to place his hand over hers. "Annie, it'll be okay. None of this is going to last forever."

"Of course not. Nothing lasts forever." She closed her laptop with a snap and set it aside. "But it sure as hell is depressing for the moment." She crawled out of the bed and smoothed the bedspread after Martin jumped down and sauntered out of the room.

As she pivoted to face Drake, he gently took hold of her shoulders and gazed into her liquid blue eyes. "Please trust me, Annie girl."

She took a deep breath and closed her eyes. "Please stop calling me that. I've asked you countless times."

"Tell me why, and I'll consider it."

"I told you, it brings back bad memories for me."

"Tell me about them. What did he do that was so bad it turned you off all men?"

She laughed softly. "It's just like a *guy* to say something like that. He didn't turn me off men, but he did convince me there's no room in my life for a permanent relationship."

"What did he do to you, Annie?"

She took a deep breath and released it. "He didn't do anything to me, Drake. It's what *I* nearly did that scares the hell out of me."

"What? Tell me. Please, trust me," he pleaded with her. She tried to pull away, but he wouldn't let her. "Look at me," he urged.

"Let it go, Drake. It's too personal to talk about to anyone else besides my God and my shrink—in that order."

He lifted her chin with one hand. "All right, as long as you can accept that I'll do anything to keep you from being hurt again. I won't give up on getting you to trust me, though."

She studied him for several moments, as though contemplating his statement, but finally turned away. "I'm tired Drake, I think I want to go to sleep now."

He gave her a brief nod. "Don't lock your door. I'll be coming in to check on you."

"That's not necessary."

"Yes, it is. Until the security alarm is installed tomorrow, it's necessary for my own peace of mind."

Her face registered momentary confusion before acceptance, born through exhaustion, washed across her features. "Whatever. I'm going to bed now. I'd appreciate it if you give me at least an hour to get to sleep before you come barging into my bedroom."

"I'll be so quiet you won't even notice me." He left her room, closing the door behind him.

Drake checked the doors and windows in the rest of the house for the third time then cast an eye at the police cruiser parked in the front. "A lot of good that's going to do if that asshole tries to break in through the back of the house," he murmured. *I should have checked her windows again while I was in there.*

Just then, Martin rubbed up against his leg, meowing purposely and looking toward the hallway. "You want to go back in there, don't you, buddy?" He lifted him to eye level. "You let me know if anything is wrong, okay Martin? It's up to us to take care of her, you know."

The cat placed his paw on Drake's face, as if in understanding.

"I could swear you know exactly what I'm saying," he mumbled. If any of his former colleagues could see him now, they'd file a claim on his behalf for loss of mental faculties. He walked silently over to Annie's door and cracked it open just enough to drop Martin inside the room, then pulled the door closed again.

Annie felt her cat jump up on the bed and waited as he curled comfortably beside her. She pulled him closer, finally admitting that she was truly terrified. Someone could be lurking just outside her home. Someone who wanted to rape, torture, and murder her, and suddenly it was all too much to bear. In seconds, all of the emotions she'd been holding back the entire evening came bubbling up to the surface. She turned her head into her pillow in an attempt to muffle the sobs that came with no warning.

Martin jumped from the bed, as though he knew he was in over his head, and began scratching and meowing loudly at the door. Within seconds Drake was there, seated beside her.

"I know, Annie. I know you're scared."

Without turning her face from her pillow, she grabbed his arm and pulled it around her.

Drake lay down behind her and wrapped his muscled arm around her waist, pulling her close to him. She trembled, shaking with the sobs that wracked her body and soul. She heard murmurs of soft endearments and reassurances as he held her tightly. Her tears wouldn't stop, and she turned toward Drake. He held her closely with one arm while running his other hand gently through her hair.

"Let go of it, Annie. You don't have to be strong all the time. I'm here," he murmured.

Annie cried, even after realizing Drake's strong arms did much to ease her fears. She tried to tell herself she didn't want this, only needed it for the moment. Too exhausted to analyze it any further, the tears finally subsided to quiet sniffles. She needed to feel safe again, and if she knew nothing else about Drake, she knew this man would do whatever he could to make that happen. The thought eased her troubled mind—allowed her to relax in the solace of his embrace.

Drake lay there, listening to the sounds in the room. The tick of a clock, the purring of Martin, and the steady rhythm of Annie's breathing. Once she'd stopped crying, it only took a few minutes for her to fall into a peaceful sleep in his arms. He was happy that being in his arms had seemed to help her accomplish that feat, but he knew that until the security alarm was installed and doing its job properly, he wouldn't be able to fully rest.

For the first four hours he napped fitfully, waking at every creak the house made. The last thing he remembered was turning toward Annie and her snuggling closer to him in her sleep. Drake closed his eyes and asked God to keep her safe before falling into a deep sleep, with the love of his life cradled protectively in his arms, and Martin purring softly at his back.

Chapter Thirteen

Drake awoke slowly to the sounds of soft snoring coming from somewhere near his ear. He opened one eye, and then the other, in an attempt to find the culprit. Annie's soft, warm body pressed up against him. He turned his head gingerly toward the delicate face that rested on his chest, a face framed by a wild disarray of light auburn curls, barely visible in the dimness of the night light's glow. Her mouth formed a perfect little pout, but there were no lines of worry or stress on her face. She seemed to be resting quietly.

He frowned, still looking for the snorer, finally realized it came from above his head. He raised one arm, feeling the large ball of fur lying across the top of his pillow. He shook the cat gently until Martin awoke with a start, and stood, staring down at him accusingly. The cat yawned, baring his teeth as well as a remarkable resemblance to the MGM lion. He leapt easily off the bed and ran down the hallway.

Turning so that he could watch Annie in her sleep, Drake touched her soft curls, and let a long ringlet wind around his finger. He watched her sleep for several minutes, her perfectly shaped lips still pouting daintily. He longed to wake his sleeping beauty with a kiss, but knew her well enough to know that waking to this situation wouldn't please her. She'd see last night's loss of composure as a chink in her armor, a sign of weakness. Waking in his arms would only symbolize a result of that weakness.

Drake took one last look at her, slipped out of bed, and pulled the door softly shut behind him. He walked to the living room window to stare out at the police cruiser, still parked in the same spot. A quick glance at his watch told him it was six thirty on a Saturday morning. He'd slept much later than normal, even though it had taken him a few hours to get to sleep.

He pushed the brew button on the coffee pot before heading to the guest bath. By the time he stepped out, freshly showered and shaved, it was to the aroma of strongly brewed, Cajun coffee.

Drake peeked in on Annie, still sound asleep. Proof enough of how trying the previous evening had been for her. Hopefully, they'd both feel better once the alarm system was in place and working properly.

Drake looked in the fridge for something to eat. He found bacon and eggs and decided to try his hand at cooking breakfast. He'd never cooked before, but he'd watched Annie. He caught the reflection of his Harvard Alumni tee shirt in the immaculately polished surface of the wall oven door, and shrugged. "Hell yeah, Bubba. You're a Harvard graduate," he told his mirror image. "How difficult could it be?"

The faint sound of muffled cursing and the smell of burnt eggs woke her. She stretched and cracked opened her puffy eyes, feeling remarkably well-rested, despite last night's monumental tear fest. She wrinkled her nose, thinking Drake must be trying his hand at cooking breakfast, unsuccessfully if the strengthening smell of charred food was any indication. She'd better help before any permanent damage was done to her kitchen. She crawled out of bed and padded to her bathroom in an attempt to erase the ravages of the previous night.

A few minutes later, she entered the smoke-filled kitchen and paused, unseen by Drake, to watch the scene before her.

She swallowed at the sight of him, looking good in faded jeans and a tee, his hair slightly shower damp. It still shocked her a little to see him dressed down like this. Texan or no, he sprang from money and corporate law. He turned enough for her to get a look at the front of his shirt. Instantly, it reminded her that anyone who could afford to wear a Harvard alumni T-shirt had probably purchased the jeans appropriately pre-faded for effect. He stood in front of the sink, holding a smoking frying pan up to the open windows. The overcooked eggs were in a second frying pan still sitting on the smooth surface of the cook top. At least he'd thought to turn off the burner.

Lewis flapped his wings and shrieked. "Aaa-nnie, call 911!"

Drake muttered from the sink. "Shut it, Lewis. It's not that bad."

Annie walked over to the cook top and flipped a lever, switching on the vent. She grabbed a potholder and retrieved the pan from Drake, setting it on the stove. The vent's fan motor whirred and hummed, performing its job of removing the smoke and odors from the air.

"I didn't know you had a vent," he said sheepishly. "There's no hood."

"It's built in, don't worry about it."

Drake reached over to close the windows, but Annie stopped him. "Leave them open for a few minutes. Every little bit helps." She couldn't help but smile at his flush of embarrassment.

"You made it look so easy the other day, but your kitchen may never be the same."

She indicated the two frying pans. "The kitchen survived, but I'm not sure about the pans."

"Damn, did I ruin them? I'm sorry, I'll buy you a new set." Drake stepped forward to inspect the damage.

Annie laughed and shook her head. "I'm kidding, Drake. As much as I paid for this cookware it should be able to take a little burnt bacon and eggs. They'll be fine, you'll see." She walked over to the fridge and retrieved the remaining bacon and eggs. She placed the bacon in a new pan on medium heat. "Here, break the rest of these eggs into this bowl." She placed one in front of him.

Drake looked at her with a doubtful expression on his face. "Uh, that didn't go over so well the last time I tried." He nodded toward the pan of burnt eggs. "I think there were more shells than eggs in there."

Annie grabbed an egg and a bowl. "I'll show you how to do it properly. If you're going to use my kitchen, I'd rather you not burn it down the first week." She tapped an egg on the rim then emptied its contents into the bowl.

Drake looked at the egg, its yolk in one piece with absolutely no shells floating around. "It can't be that easy. You should have seen my mess."

"I do see your mess. You just need practice."

Drake turned pleading eyes toward her. "Wouldn't it be easier if you did it and I watched?"

"Come on Drake, I'm a firm believer in the old adage, 'Cook for a man and he eats for a day, teach him to cook and he eats for a lifetime'."

He rolled his eyes. "You made that up."

She chuckled. "Yeah, well I think the original was about teaching a man to fish, but I've never fished in my life."

"You're kidding, right? You're a southerner. Not even once?"

She shook her head. "I don't have to try something to know I'd stink at it. I'd never have the patience to sit still and be quiet for that long."

Drake grinned at her. "I never would have guessed."

"That's right, smart ass," she replied. "I can admit my own limitations. Too bad I can't say the same for you."

He puffed his chest out and flexed his arms. "I would, if I had any." He exuded his usual overabundance of attitude and male bravado.

Annie couldn't help but laugh. "Jesus, Drake, all you need is a set of tail feathers and you'd look like my dad's prize rooster."

"Oh, yeah? You did say *prize* rooster, which means I'll win the blue ribbon, eventually; the blue ribbon being you, in this case."

"You just keep telling yourself that, Rocky. Too much of that isn't always a good thing."

"Rocky, as in Balboa?"

She shook her head. "As in Rocky the rooster."

"I didn't see a rooster in your dad's chicken yard."

She lifted one eyebrow. "Exactly."

"What happened to him?"

"He got eaten."

"Like fried, or in a gumbo?"

"Nope. Rocky got a little too cocky with the neighbor's Labrador Retriever. By the time Dad got to him, all that was left was a handful of feathers."

Drake grimaced. "Oh, poor Rocky."

She nodded serenely. "You could learn a thing or two from 'Cocky Rocky's' demise."

He shook his head. "I told you before, there's a difference between being cocky and being confident. The difference is being able to back up the talk. "

"Well, counselor, you can talk the talk, I'll give you that."

He gave her that sexy, crooked grin and leaned in closer to murmur into her ear. "If you're interested, I can always show you that I'm fully capable of walking the walk, as well."

Annie tried to ignore the frisson of excitement his softly spoken words caused in her. She cleared her throat and pushed him away with both hands. "Are you ready to cook?"

His grin broadened. "I could ask the same of you."

The look she gave him conveyed that she was a little tired of his comebacks.

He released a low chuckle. "Okay, okay. But don't say I didn't warn you," he said. He took a deep breath then picked up an egg, tapped it too hard against the rim of the bowl, cursed as a flood of broken eggshells contaminated the bowl of eggs.

Annie giggled. "You have to separate the egg shell, Drake. Pull it apart, don't pulverize it. Use your thumbnails to catch the shell, if you have to. Watch." She performed the simple task once more for his benefit.

He tried it again and beamed as he got the whole egg into the bowl without a speck of shell. He cracked the remaining two into the bowl with the same result. "Hey, there's hope for me yet. Thanks, Annie Girl."

She handed him a fork to whisk the eggs. Remarkably, he seemed to excel at it. She cocked one eyebrow and glanced over at his smug look.

"I've got this part under control. It's all in the wrist," he said, with a grin as he met her gaze.

She bit her lower lip to keep from smiling. "Yeah, looks like you're quite adept at that wrist action. Practice much?"

His hand froze as he stared down at the bowl. "Oh-uh-that is not what I meant at all. I never, I mean, I hardly, I mean, I . . ."

Annie shrugged, quite amused at his discomfort. "You could always plead the Fifth—refuse to answer on the grounds that it may incriminate you."

Drake snorted then continued to whisk the eggs. "You'd love that, wouldn't you? I admit that although I got quite accomplished at it during my pubescent years, I haven't needed that particular for of relief in years." He gave the bowl of eggs several more swipes before pausing. "I've also taken an increasing amount of cold showers since meeting you."

Her hand came up. "Information overload! I didn't ask to be all up in your business." She grabbed the bowl of eggs from him. "Okay, that's enough." She handed him a frying pan and a can of non-stick spray. "Here, give the pan a shot of that and put it on a medium heat." With the occasional tip from her, Drake managed to whip up a passable meal of scrambled eggs, bacon, and whole wheat toast for the two of them.

They ate their breakfast and read the paper, as Lewis chattered from his cage. When Annie stood at the sink to load the dishwasher, Drake followed. As he reached for the bowl she held out to him, he let his fingers cover hers longer than necessary. She didn't dare meet his gaze, but couldn't ignore the zing his touch caused in the pit of her belly.

"How are you? After last night, I mean?"

She pulled her fingers from his and cleared her throat. "I'm over it."

"If you ever need to talk, I'm here."

"I said I'm over it." She hadn't meant it to sound so sharp, so abrupt. The truth was, she was embarrassed at falling apart last night. She hadn't intended for him or anyone else to see her that way. And he wouldn't have if he'd left her alone in her room. She tried to shrug it off.

"I-I wasn't prepared. That call took-it took me by surprise. I-I guess I'd begun to assume J.B. had left town with his tail between his legs."

He gave a low grunt, as though accepting her excuse.

It wasn't a lie. She had been shocked by the call. But the feeling of terror afterwards, when she was alone in her room had knocked her on her butt.

She continued to clean the kitchen in silence, keeping her thoughts to herself. Thoughts of how good it felt last night to have Drake around to comfort her. She'd awakened during the night, feeling safe and secure, wrapped in his embrace. Part of her treasured the feeling.

Another part of her saw it as a threat to her ability to stand on her own two feet. At the time, she considered pulling away. She told herself to inch herself over to the opposite side of the bed. Instead, she'd laid there, fully able to enjoy his closeness without him knowing.

She'd listened to his measured breathing, placed her palm on his chest to feel the rise and fall of his chest. Lured by the steady thud of his heart beneath her hand, she'd laid her head gently on his chest to see what it would feel like.

And it had been so good.

Before she found the willpower to move, he'd wrapped his arm around her shoulders to pull her closer. Even sound asleep he was trying to protect her. She hadn't wanted to move—so she stayed.

Her heart pounded, heat rose to her face and neck, just thinking about it. To date, it was the most indulgent act she'd ever allowed herself. Her own guilty little pleasure. A secret she could take to her grave.

She'd just poured herself another cup of coffee when the work crew arrived to install the alarm. After introductions, the foreman and his team scoped out the house, laying out a diagram of the system they would install.

After inspecting the doors and windows, the foreman approached Annie. "Ma'am, we've been instructed to place security bars on your windows as well, that is, if you want them."

Annie narrowed her eyes at him. "Instructed by whom?"

"Mr. LeBlanc, ma'am."

She aimed a curious look in Drake's direction.

The foreman added quickly. "A Mr. Daniel LeBlanc, ma'am."

She tensed, thinking that having a stalker was proving to be far too expensive. "Well, are the bars extra? I mean, how much will all this cost me?"

"That's been taken care of, ma'am. Mr. LeBlanc said you are not to worry about any of this. His only concern is that you are safe."

"Oh . . ." Her voice trailed off as she stared at Drake.

He gave her a one-shouldered shrug. "Let him do it, Annie. The cost is nothing for him and he can make sure it's done in record time."

"That's a fact ma'am," the foreman added. "Tonight, you'll be completely safe in your own home with the best security system money can buy."

Annie stared at him, then back at Drake. "I'll want to see the final bill. I make a decent living and I'd like to pay your father back."

Drake nodded. "I'll let him know. You two hard-heads can fight that one out. Don't even involve me."

"Ma'am, about the security bars; can we go ahead and install them on every window?"

Annie's chest tightened-imagining being imprisoned by all those bars. "Every window? But they'll work to keep me trapped inside as well as keep others out. What if there's a fire and the doors are blocked?"

"Every set of bars is hinged and has its own quick release latch that is easily accessible from the inside only." She studied the diagram he held out to her, looking up at Drake's approach.

"Annie, they're not permanent. This is just until this guy is caught. I'd feel a whole lot better knowing you're safe."

"But I'll feel like I'm the one in jail, Drake."

"Ma'am, we're here to serve you. Every window and door will have electronic sensors to detect any kind of attempted break in. Regardless of how many windows we bar, so you should be fine."

Drake reached for the diagram. "What about in case of a power loss?"

"Each of our systems comes with its own rechargeable battery back-up. It'll provide power for up to a week without recharging."

Annie made her decision. "All windows except for the kitchen windows over the sink. I have to have at least one view free of bars."

"Yes, ma'am."

By noon, the security system was in place, working properly, and bars had been installed on the designated doors and windows.

Annie thanked the crew as they left then sat down at the table to examine the paperwork. Wide-eyed, she whistled under her breath at the total installation cost. "I'll have to take out a loan Monday."

Drake sat across from her and reached for the receipt. "Dad's got more money than Midas. He doesn't want you to pay him back, so please let him do this. He's grateful that you've all accepted him and Leah through Red and Tiffany, made them feel like a part of your family. Think of him as a rich relative who's worried about your well-being."

"This is all so bizarre." Annie stood suddenly and paced the floor. "I'm angry. I'm pissed that I can't walk around in my own house by myself and feel safe. I'm upset that I can't sleep in my own bed without thinking about who's lurking outside my window. I can't even go to the movies, dammit!" She clasped her hands in front of her. "And I love going to the movies."

Drake approached her slowly. "What do you want to see, Annie? I'll take you to the movies. I'll take you anywhere you want to go."

She thought about it and gave her head a vigorous shake. "I couldn't do it. Sitting in a dark theater, knowing he's out there somewhere—or worse, inside the theater with me. I couldn't." She pushed away from Drake when he tried to hug her. "No! I've worked too hard and given up too much to become dependent on a man at this point in my life. This—" She pointed back and forth between the two of them. "This—*set up* between us—is what upsets me the most. The fact that I can't set foot outside of my house without *you* by my side."

Drake took a single step nearer. "Annie—"

"Stop, Drake! Just-just stop. Let me be angry about this for a while. Hell, it's no hardship for you, is it? You're getting all the perks. You've got me exactly where you want me, don't you?"

Drake lunged forward to grab her shoulders. "You think I *want* this?" His voice was tight, controlled. "You really believe I'd rather have you terrified than to feel safe enough to walk out of this house and away from me?"

"Don't you?"

"Hell no!" He released her, his face lined with what seemed to be a mixture of disappointment and anger, with a little insult throw in. He paced the floor, hands on hips. "I want you, Annie, but not like this. I want you to come to me of your own free will, not grudgingly, and sure as hell not because you're terrified."

He continued his pacing, as well as his rant. "As infuriating as you can be, I despise seeing you too damn scared to set foot out of your own home. And another thing—" His finger appeared, inches from her nose. "As much as I loved getting to hold you in my arms, I hated hearing you cry yourself to sleep. That's the second time I hear you cry and both times it nearly broke my heart."

Drake stepped away from her. "So, to answer your question," he continued, still sounding as though he was seconds away from blowing a gasket. "I am *not* enjoying this." He turned his back on her then.

She stared at him. Stiff-backed and tense, the man was still furious at her accusation. Wracked with guilt, she took a deep breath, and attempted to smooth things over. "I'm not sure if I—" He rounded on her in a flash, and the words froze in her throat.

"I swear to *God*, if that's another insult you're about to throw my way, I will put you over my knee, right here, right damn now!"

An indignant scowl accompanied her comeback. "I was *going* to say I wasn't sure if I'd thanked you. So, thank you, Drake. From the bottom of my heart, thank you!" She marched off to her bedroom, grumbling the entire distance. She stopped at her bedroom door to add one last sentiment. "Jerk!" She slammed the bedroom door behind her.

Annie had just finished re-cleaning her already tidy bathroom when she heard a tentative knock at her door. She opened it and stared hard at Drake. "What?"

"I was wondering if you'd like to accompany me to the theater."

She frowned. "I already told you I can't handle it."

He held out his hand to her and gave her a crooked grin. "We're not leaving the house." He jerked his head to one side. "Trust me, Annie Girl." His eyes sparkled with mischief and a touch of mystery.

Forgetting her anger, she reached out and took the arm he offered. She let him escort her to the guest room. Or it *was* the guest room before its amazing transformation. He'd put a brown blanket over the windows to block out all light and had moved two comfy chairs directly in front of his huge television set. Dozens of high definition, blue-ray movies were spread out on the bed for her perusal.

"If you tell me what you want from the concession stand, I'll get it for you, while you decide what you'd like to watch. I know we have popcorn and ice cream. Is there anything else you'd like?"

She gazed up into his eyes and said the first thing that popped into her mind. "Dark chocolate M&M's. An entire bowl full of them." *Preferably just the brown ones . . . .*

"Hmmm, I don't know if we have any, but we can go get some. Come on, let's go now."

She waved him off. "You go, and I'll stay here."

"Ah, I wouldn't feel comfortable with that, Annie. Just come with me."

"Look, this place is as safe as Fort Knox. I'll stay here and narrow down the movie choices while you go."

"If you're sure." He still looked doubtful, but she waved him off. "All right, but I'll be right back. I'll re-set the alarm when I walk out, so don't worry." He lifted up his cell. "I've got it with me. Call if you think of anything else you want."

Seconds after he pulled out of the drive, her landline rang. Annie answered, sure it was Drake with more questions. "Don't tell me you forgot already?" The answering chuckle had pinpricks of fear making the hair at the back of her neck stand at attention.

"No chance of that. You felt entirely too good in my arms on New Year's Eve to forget you anytime soon. Where'd lover boy run off to? You two have a spat? Cause you know I'm only a few seconds from your door."

Annie heard a pounding, realized it was her own heart beating frantically in her chest. Her gaze flew to the bars on the window—to the opened bedroom door. She slammed it shut—no lock on this one. She shoved the desk chair up under the door knob to keep him out. She turned again to the window, at the bars. How strong were they? Could he break through? Was she really safe? Why hadn't she had that crew install them on every damn window in her house? She already felt like a prisoner. Wouldn't she feel better as a safe one? *I'm so stupid.*

"I know you're still there, Lil' Bit. I hear you breathing hard, like you'd be if I was in there with you. I'd have you breathing real hard. A lot of things would be hard. Hell, I'm hard now, just thinkin' about it."

"Why don't you leave me alone?" She tried to get her breathing under control.

"That wouldn't be any fun at all, now would it? And I intend to have a lot of fun with you. I'll be there in a few seconds, Baby. You know, no security system will keep me out for long. I'm coming for you."

Annie slammed the phone down and sank to a corner of the room facing the window and the door. It rang again but the phone in this room didn't have caller I.D. She picked it up, hesitantly, hoping it was— "Drake?"

"I'm at the door, Annie McAllister. I'm coming for you."

She slammed it down then left the receiver off the hook. Her panicked gaze darted back and forth between the door and the window. It shifted to the phone as the automated operator gave the standard message: *"If you would like to make a call, please hang up and try your call again. If you need help please hang up and call your operator for assistance."* She nearly jumped out of her skin when the phone began its steady *beep-beep-beeping.* Too terrified to move from her spot on the floor, Annie pulled her knees up to her chin and wrapped her arms around them as tightly as she could—too tight to make a sound—too tight to do much more than breathe—just enough to keep from passing out.

He knocked on the locked bedroom door. "Annie? You want to let me in now?" He jiggled the handle, realized it wasn't locked, but barricaded from the inside by something. "Annie, it's me, hon, open the door." When she didn't answer after several more calls to her, he panicked. He pushed, shoved, tried to force the door open. He cursed loud and long, desperate to get to her, but terrified at what he might find.

"Annie! Dammit, open the door!" He kicked at the door a few times, heard something crack. Gave one final shove and finally, the barricade gave way. He pushed through, saw the splintered chair. Searched the room, found her huddled in the corner, her forehead down on her knees like a scared child.

Relief surged through him as he sank to his knees in front of her. "What happened?"

She lifted her tear-filled gaze to his. Her voice was tight, hoarse with terror. "He called, as soon as you left, he called. He s-saw you l-leave. He's watching the house and saw you l-leave. He said he was coming for me. He was at the front door and was coming for me."

Drake sat back on his heels, wiped his mouth. "I'm an idiot, Annie. I'm sorry I left you alone. It was a stupid thing to do." Of course the slimy bastard would watch the house.

He broke the grip she had on her knees and pulled her up from the floor. "Did you call the police?" The look of terror in her eyes sickened him.

She shook her head. "I never even thought about it, Drake. I'm so stupid. I thought I was strong, and I could take care of myself. But I can't!" she shrieked. "I'm s-supposed to be trained in self-defense. I can't remember a thing. I don't know what to do."

He rubbed his hands briskly over her arms. Hated seeing her like this, so close to full-blown hysteria.

"I couldn't even remember to dial 911. Even Lewis knows to dial 911. I c-couldn't do anything but sit there and wait for him to show up."

Drake pulled her close, held her trembling body tight to his chest.

"I don't know what's wrong with me. I'm not usually like this. I'm not normally afraid of anything or anyone. I-I don't know what's happening."

The rising level of panic in her voice scared the shit out of him. "Shhh . . . Calm down, Annie. I'm here. He's not. I'll make sure he doesn't get to you. I'll never leave you alone again, I promise you that. Please, forgive me."

Drake held her tight until the tension eased from her body, until her terrified trembling abated. He kissed her hair, then her forehead. She looped her arms around his neck and he reveled in the feel of it, the feel of her fingers sifting through his hair. God, it felt so good having her in his arms, regardless of the reason. Before he knew it her sweet mouth was on his, her lips molded to his, forceful, needy.

And it was good.

He tore his mouth from hers, immediately hard, wanting her. "Annie— oh God."

"Hold me, Drake." Her tortured whisper reached him.

He pulled her closer, wrapped his hands around her tiny waist. Her sweater rode up, baring her satiny skin to his touch. He touched is forehead to hers. "Annie . . ."

She kissed him again . . . hungrily, impatiently . . . ran her hands under his tee-shirt. In seconds, she had it up and over his head, baring his chest to her palms, her fingers, and her mouth. His ragged breath turned into a sharp hiss as she placed a moist, hot kiss on the center of his chest. When she scraped her nails along his abs, he thought he'd lose his mind.

"Oh, God. Annie . . . what the hell are you doing to me?"

"Don't talk, Drake, just make love to me," she whispered. "I need you to make love to me. I need to feel safe. I feel safe with you, but I need you closer."

Drake lowered his mouth to her neck, and placed soft kisses, scraping her skin lightly with his teeth. He nearly lost it when she took his earlobe between her teeth with a low moan, and nipped at it. He knew what she wanted, and by God, he was up for it. He was ready to dive head first into the deep end of the pool, ready to make her feel safe, wanted, loved.

Right up until phrases of his father's speech bubbled up, shoved themselves into the light of day.

Realization began deep in the pit of his belly. If only it drenched his need like an icy shower. But it didn't. He had to struggle back from the want, the need to give Annie what she seemed to crave at this moment.

But his dad's words hit home . . . unwelcome and irrevocable. He couldn't take it back—couldn't un-hear the words of caution once he'd heard them. *She'll be emotionally unstable. Don't take advantage of the situation.*

Shit.

This couldn't happen. Not tonight. Not like this.

Drake allowed himself one more kiss, one more touch of his forehead to hers. Then he held her away from him. "We can't Annie, not like this. Jesus, I want you so bad, you have to know that by now." He cupped her face, kissed her mouth gently. "But we can't do this. Not with you feeling as vulnerable as you do right now."

She ran her hands over his abs, brushing his chest hair lightly with her fingers, her voice husky with need. "I want this, Drake."

He shook his head slowly, held her at arm's length. "Right now, maybe. But not in the morning, Babe. I know you. You'll hate yourself for feeling weak, and then you'll blame me for not turning you down. And I'd hate myself for not being strong enough to take control of this situation. As much as I want this, I don't want to take advantage of you."

She took a step back, the anger in her voice hinting at an emotional about face. "Oh, I cannot believe this. You've been sniffing at me like a dog since Christmas, and now you're turning me away? I only *thought* my day couldn't get any worse." She turned away, her eyes filled with angry tears.

He grabbed her arm, stopping her retreat. "You're not going until you've heard me out."

She glared at him. "What else can you say, but that you obviously don't want me?"

"Annie, for God's sake. Look at me and tell me that."

Her left brow rose accusingly. "You don't want me."

"Look. At. Me. Tell me I don't want you." He spoke sharply, taking one step backward.

She finally caught his meaning, glanced down. Her eyes widened as she caught sight of the front of his jeans. Her delicate mouth rounded in a silent "Oh."

"Yeah. So don't you dare walk out of here sulking because you think I don't want you. Not when the truth is, I've never wanted anyone—*anyone*—as badly as I want you right now." He turned partially away from her. "This is the most difficult thing I've ever had to do in my life. But I'm doing it, and I'm doing it for us." He felt her gaze on him, suspected she followed his every move.

"What if there's never any us?"

Rounding on her again, he placed his hands on her shoulders. His deep bass dipped dangerously low as he stared into crystal blue eyes and spoke. "You can't run fast enough or far enough from me, Annie Girl. If it's the last thing I do, I'll make damn sure there's an us."

Chapter Fourteen

Annie blinked several times to clear the sleep from her eyes. Here it was, Sunday morning, and she was still shaky with residual effects of the previous day's emotional roller coaster. She forced herself to get up and get moving.

Several minutes later, she entered the kitchen. A platter of perfectly crisp bacon, soft scrambled eggs, and about the sexiest man alive greeted her at the kitchen table. Drake sat there, freshly shaven, his hair, still damp from a shower, curled enticingly at the ends. He wore a pair of grey jogging pants and a just snug enough black tee shirt.

Drake looked up from the Sunday paper. "Hey, sleepyhead. You able to get some rest?"

She nodded, heading straight for the coffee pot.

He rose from the table and filled a plate with slices of bacon and scrambled eggs. "You want toast this morning?"

Annie shook her head. She'd have a hard enough time swallowing her coffee. "Honestly, I don't think I can eat anything just yet." She turned from the coffee maker, her mug gripped tightly between two hands.

"How are you feeling?"

Somewhere in the vicinity of mortified and humiliated. "Just fine," she lied, before curling up on one end of the hand me down leather sofa. She sat, tucked her feet under her then pulled an afghan up to her neck. She cupped both hands around her mug and sipped, while staring at the closed blinds of the window, resenting like hell the fact that she didn't feel comfortable enough to open them. Thank goodness there was no lean toward claustrophobia in her DNA. The hem of Drake's shirt came into view.

"Annie, we need to talk."

"No, we don't."

He leaned until he was eye level to her. "Yes, we do. I want to make sure you're not nursing some kind of idiotic grudge against me for what happened yesterday."

"Nothing happened, and all I feel is thankful that it didn't."

"Look, I know you were scared and feeling vulnerable, but I also know that we have this . . . connection."

"I had a moment of weakness, it won't happen again."

"How could you possibly know that?"

She stared stonily into his dark eyes. "Trust me, on this. You should have taken it when it was offered. I'm over it." She couldn't keep from commenting when he cocked his head to the side. "You know, you look remarkably like Lewis when you do that."

He sent her a smug grin. "I guess it was bound to happen, sooner or later. I'm not sure how you meant that, but I'm taking it as a compliment."

"It wasn't meant as one."

"But Lewis is an extremely bright bird, aren't you Lewis?" Drake called over his shoulder.

"Drake's the man! *Brawck!*" Lewis cried.

"Extremely bright, for a bird," she agreed. "And it *would* be a compliment, if you were a toddler." She cocked her head to the side, mimicking Lewis. "Not so much for a man in his thirties."

He rested his hands loosely on his hips. "You want to do anything in particular today?"

"Nope."

"You want to go shopping? We could go to the mall later."

"Nope."

"How about the movies? There's probably some chick flick out that you'd want to sit through, right?"

"Nope."

"Thriller? Action film?" he asked, sounding hopeful.

"Nope, I'm staying here, but please feel free to go wherever you'd like. I'll be fine here."

She made her best attempt to sound convincing, all the while holding her breath as she awaited his answer. Silently, she prayed he wouldn't take her up on the offer. No matter how hard she tried to tell herself she was fine, she knew she wasn't. The thought of him leaving her alone in this house terrified her nearly as much as the thought of being out there, where *he* could watch her, unobserved.

"Not a chance, sweetheart. You can't get rid of me that easily, no matter how much you'd like to."

Drake walked over to the coffee pot for another cup. He caught Martin gearing up to cheat on his diet again and called him out. "Martin! Don't even think about it."

The oversized cat had been about to jump on the table for the bacon and eggs, but instead hunched down, giving him what looked like a disappointed stare.

"Annie, if you don't want to eat this right now, I'll cover it, so he can't get to it."

Annie rose from the sofa with a huff. "Christ, it's almost like living with my parents, again." She grabbed the plate and sat down at her computer before plugging in her earbuds.

Drake smiled down at the top of her head, amused that she was trying to ignore him. After last night's episode, he figured their temporary living arrangement would be strained under the best of circumstances. Damned near impossible under the worst. He went into his bedroom and threw on a pair of grey slacks and a long-sleeved black shirt. He re-entered the living room, watching as Annie sat, with eyes closed and swaying slightly to whatever song she listened to. Her tongue darted out to wet her parted lips, lips that curved upward on one side, in a hesitant smile. He inched forward, remaining out of her line of sight in case she opened her eyes. He inhaled sharply, seeing the title display showing the same Adele number they'd nearly had vertical sex to on the dance floor.

"Annie," he said, placing his hands softly on her shoulders.

She turned suddenly, pulling the earplugs out, her eyes wide and registering three emotions nearly simultaneously. First, curiosity that turned into unconcealed terror as she studied his clothes, soon covered by a false bravado that made his heart ache for her.

"Where are *you* going?"

"I thought you might want to go to Sunday mass this morning."

She pasted an artificial smile on her face. "No, but I can tell you how to get to the church, if you want to go without me."

Drake lowered himself before her. "Listen, J.B. Montgomery is not going to be out there twenty-four hours a day, and even if he is, I won't leave your side for a second."

She shook her head too quickly. "It's not that," she insisted. "I just don't feel like going today. I miss sometimes."

Drake nodded, choosing to ignore her obvious lie. Any girl who carried a rosary in her pocket to church wasn't going to feel comfortable with missing unless it was completely unavoidable. "Okay, then, if you're sure."

Annie shrugged. "Sorry."

"Don't apologize to me, Annie Girl. There's no need." He went into his room and changed into jeans and a Henley shirt. Annie's gaze never left the computer screen when he pulled up a chair next to her.

"What are you doing?"

She pulled out one earpiece and seemed to study his new attire. "I was downloading some music."

"What artist?" he asked curiously, as she showed him her playlist.

"Country mostly. I'm a huge James Otto and Jake Owen fan, but I love so many. George Strait tops the list, of course."

Drake nodded. "King George—the man's music is timeless. There are so many more good singers out there today and you haven't even touched on any of the groups. I bet you don't have any Pat Green. He hasn't put anything out there in a while but I liked his stuff."

She released a low chuckle. "This is too easy. I should have made you put some money up." She pulled up a list in her music library.

Drake looked over her shoulder. "There it is." He covered her right hand so he could manipulate the mouse. Within seconds, an older song called 'Let Me' started up. "That's one of his best." Music flowed through the high quality sound system. Drake straightened and pulled her to her feet. "Come on, dance with me."

He pulled her close and she gave him a hesitant reply. "I'm not dancing with you again . . . ever." Her words resisted, but she didn't seem all that eager to leave his embrace.

Overcome with the ache to protect her, to comfort her, he lowered his head until their foreheads touched. "Tell me then, Annie, what *do* you want to do with me?" She shook her head slowly as he placed a hand on her waist to keep her close.

She finally managed to speak, her voice tinged with irritability. "Let go, Drake. I told you before, I won't dance with you again, and I meant it."

He clung tightly to her waist as he lowered his mouth to her ear. "Before I do, I'd like to speak to you about something extremely important." Drake smiled as he felt her shiver in his arms.

"What?"

"A bed."

Annie pulled back and blinked once, twice, and again. "What?" she repeated, this time louder.

Drake laughed at the confusion on her face. "My bed, in particular."

Her brow creased in a frown. "What about it?"

He released her, satisfied for the moment that he'd peaked her curiosity. Even more pleased that she faltered when he released her. "It's too short for me. For that matter, so is the one at my place. I was going to buy a new king size mattress set, but hadn't gotten around to it yet."

"How long have you been sleeping on a 'too-short' mattress?"

"Since I moved into Tiffany's old place—she had a few months left on her lease and I have six months left on mine in Houston, so I just moved my personal belongings over there until I decided what to do. Her bed is the same size as the one in your guest room."

"It seems like you could have brought yours over from Houston," she commented.

Drake shrugged and reached out to brush a stray curl away from Annie's forehead. For some reason, he found it difficult to keep his hands off of her, today. "I didn't want to go through the trouble just yet. Besides, I've had my mattress set for ten years and it needed replacing anyway. I want one like Red and Tiff's with the memory foam."

Annie took a deep breath and pulled away from his touch. "Yeah, I have one of those. You'll be very pleased."

"I'm counting on it." He grinned at the irritated glare she shot him. "So, I was wondering if you'd mind if I bought a mattress set and had it delivered here. I may as well be comfortable for the duration, don't you think?"

Her eyes narrowed. "Seems like a lot of trouble to go through, but I don't see a problem with that, as long as you take it with you when you leave here."

"*If* I leave here."

"When you leave."

He shrugged one shoulder. "You never know. You might decide you like having me around and ask me to stay."

"It's imperative I don't."

"Imperative to what, or should I ask to *whom*?"

She met his gaze. "You're a major kink in my coil, Drake. You're not in my plan. It's nothing personal."

"Honey, regardless of what you say, it's very personal. Before this is all over with it'll get even more personal." He reached out and softly grazed his thumb over her forehead and down the side of her face. "But, for now, I'd be happy with a new bed. You have two choices in the matter. You can come with me to shop for one or you can hear me bitch about it for the duration of my stay here."

"You can go without—"

"No, I can't." He took a step closer, cupped her face in his hands. "I won't leave you behind, Annie Girl. I'll always be here to take care of you."

She swallowed hard, in an obvious attempt to calm herself. Finally, she released a long, shaky sigh. "Okay, as long as we're leaving the house today, we may as well attend mass. I'll get dressed."

Mass was nearly over, and Annie still hadn't settled down. She tried paying attention to Father Mitch's homily, but could feel herself fidgeting, inside and out. She tried to keep her gaze from darting around the interior of the church, but couldn't keep from checking for anyone that looked remotely suspicious. She wondered if he was out there among the parishioners, watching, waiting for some kind of encounter.

She sensed Drake's gaze on her, glanced over to see that her instincts were right on the money. Those chocolaty orbs were zeroed in on her. His effect on her psyche baffled her, made her feel at the same time, both comforted and unsettled. Was that even possible?

She caught a sudden chill and shivered, knowing immediately it wasn't from the cold. The hair at the back of her neck tingled and stood on end, alerting her, to what? Danger? Or the fact that she was paranoid as hell? She wrapped her arms around herself then ran one hand nervously up and down the opposite arm. Drake reached over and put a protective arm around her shoulder. As much as she hated to admit it, his action helped.

Mass ended and they met up with Jackson, Giselle, and their two girls at the front doors of the church.

Giselle gave Annie a hug. "We're going to lunch at the steakhouse. Y'all come with us."

Annie glanced from Giselle, just beginning to show a belly pooch from the twins she carried, to her two daughters, Mackenzie and Lexie. She glanced around, scanning the milling crowd of church attendees. "Thanks, but we'll have to pass," she said, avoiding Drake's perusal.

Annie turned sideways to let a group of four people edge past to get to the exit. A gentle scrape of something along her side and across her lower back had Annie tensing, spinning around to check out the four as they reached the exit. The men wore hooded jackets, but only one had his hood on. Both were built like brick houses. From the rear, either of them could have been J.B. Montgomery—or not. She relaxed, seeing that these two men seemed to be paired off with the women. J.B. wasn't from around here so he'd be alone, obviously, and it was doubtful he'd be in church.

The thought soothed and she shook it off, deciding it must have been one of the girl's purses that had brushed up against her.

"Is something wrong?"

Drake's inquiry caught her off-guard and she turned to face him. She gave him a half smile and shook her head, dismissing the non-incident as the product of an over-active imagination.

Just outside the door, J.B. peeled away from the trio of people he'd used as covers, congratulating himself on copping a feel right under her boyfriend's nose. In broad daylight, and in church. *Grounds for braggin' rights.*

It was almost as if she felt him there by the way she fidgeted and scanned the place, like a little lady fox sniffin' out a hound dog on her tail. Her eyes had been everywhere—except where they shoulda been. But, she'd never spot him unless he wanted her to. He'd spent many a night hidin' from his ol' man to avoid ass whippins. The sumbitch always came home kick-ass-drunk and mean as Satan.

J.B. watched them leave together in that pussified pimp mobile only a rich man would call a truck. "Shit. I bet it ain't even got four-wheel drive. How the hell you gonna go mud hogging in that, bro?" He gave his head a shake as he threw the black Dodge in gear, and pulled out. "I'm thinkin' it's about time to raise the game level, bubba. Let's up the ante, some." Alone in his truck, he chuckled at his accidental play on words. "Time to up the Annie all right . . ."

Chapter Fifteen

"Oh man, this feels good. You've got to try this, Annie." Drake released a low moan as he stretched out on the plush, king-size mattress set.

"Don't need to." She didn't bother to look up from a text she was reading. "I already told you I have one like that."

"Your bed's too damn small."

She shrugged and threw her phone into her purse. "It's just right for me and Martin."

He rolled on his side and propped his head on his elbow. "But there's no room for me."

Annie sent him, yet another, impatient glare. "You must be exhausted."

Drake sat up. "Why do you say that?"

"From lugging around that big old ego of yours."

Drake rolled off the bed and re-tucked his shirt. "You must have been too busy looking for J.D. in church to pay attention to Father Mitch's homily. It was all about having faith and trusting God to do what's best for you." He reached out and tweaked her chin. "As it happens he and I talk on a regular basis now and—"

"You and Father Mitch?"

"Me and God, Annie. He's sent me several signs, letting me know not to give up on you."

"Are they delivered by Bill Engvall during a comedy skit? There's your sign!"

He grinned at her. "Who's talking sacrilege, now? I'm telling Mom."

"Save it, Drake. You might have *my mom* fooled, but not me." She walked away from him.

"They're all there, you know," he called out to her. "If you had a little faith, you'd see them too."

Drake buckled his seat belt and checked his watch before turning to his passenger. "I need to pick up a few things from that electronics store on Ambassador Drive. How about after that we catch the two o'clock showing of that comedy you want to see? We can sit all the way at the back and in a corner so nobody's behind us."

Annie thought about it and finally decided she could handle that. "Okay, but only if you promise to replace that dinosaur you call a laptop. All the cussing in the world won't make it work any faster. It's just sad, and frankly, I'm tired of hearing it."

Drake made a face as he threw his truck in gear. "You know enough about computers to help me make a decent choice?"

"Sure do," she said, with some satisfaction.

"I'm in your hands." The look he sent her said the innocent sounding comment was loaded with multiple meanings.

She shoved back the urge to touch his face, or worse. "You wish."

He settled his Oakley's lower on the bridge of his nose and grinned. "If you only knew . . ."

Within thirty minutes of their arrival at the electronics superstore, Annie had helped Drake narrow his choices.

"What's it gonna be, Drake? The final decision should be yours. This one has the better features for your money." Annie indicated the touch-screen model. "Normally I'm all for high-dollar-high-quality for a longer life-span, but computers become outdated so quickly these days. I hate to see anyone pay too much for something, even if they *were* born with a silver spoon up their a—"

"Annie!" he cut in. "We just came from church, you think you could abstain from the insults for the rest of the day?"

She fluttered her eyelashes innocently. "But, then, what would I do for fun?"

"Oh, I'm sure you'll think of some other way to have fun at my expense. Like walk around the house in a bikini wearing a big sign that says LOOK, DON'T TOUCH . . . or something along those lines."

"Again, you wish." She snorted with laughter.

"Not a second goes by . . ." He winked at her before turning his attention back to the laptops and the returning sales rep. "I'll take this one with the extended warranty, please."

While Drake was occupied providing payment information, Annie took the opportunity to check out the movie section for a couple of new releases. After no more than a minute, she found the hair standing up on the nape of her neck. She spun around and checked both directions, and behind her, with no results.

"Stop it, Annie. You're being paranoid," she muttered, still unable to shake the feeling. Suddenly realizing how far she'd strayed from Drake, she grabbed the blu-rays and rushed off to meet him. She collided with someone just rounding the end of the aisle. Annie's breath left her in a rush as J.B. Montgomery stood there grinning down at her.

"You look good, Sunshine." A throaty growl accompanied his approval. "Not as good as you did in church this morning. I do like that little green dress you wore." He ran his hand familiarly along her spine and down to her butt.

Annie stiffened and tried to push him away, but J.B.'s arms encircled her like a steel belt, squeezing the breath from her. She finally sucked in enough air to scream Drake's name.

J.B. grinned evilly, passed a final, possessive hand over her breast before releasing her. As quickly as he appeared, he vanished around the corner.

She ran in the opposite direction, heading for Drake's frantic calls from three rows over.

"Dammit Annie, where are you?"

"Here!"

He came around the end display, relief momentarily flooding his features. "What happened?"

"He w-was here! He grabbed me and s-spoke to me." She despised the stammer J.B.'s terrifying presence brought out in her.

"Where?" Drake spun around for the exit.

Annie grabbed at his arm. "Don't leave me here! I want to go h-home."

He grabbed her shoulders firmly. "I thought you were standing right behind me while I was checking out. I turned and you were gone."

Her gaze hit the floor, knowing she'd screwed up—again. "I was looking at some movies."

"Annie, you can't—" He cut off the frustrated lecture, took a deep breath instead. "Just stay close to me. I need to ask someone if they have security cameras set up in here."

"C-can't we just go home?" She made another attempt to steady her shaky voice.

"No, not this time. We're not leaving this place until we've seen if there's anything we can do to help the police catch this guy."

She gripped his arm tightly, scanned the aisle in both directions. "But Drake . . ."

He placed both hands on either side of her face. "Listen to me, Annie. What we do *now* could swing this in your favor, do you understand? We can't let this bastard terrorize you this way. We're going to stop him."

She shifted her gaze from one aisle to another, scanning the area for the face she'd seen in her nightmares, feeling like a trapped animal. Releasing a long, shuddering sigh, she barely heard the whispered words from her own mouth. "I'm afraid."

Drake wrapped his arms protectively around her. "It's smart to be afraid at a time like this, but that doesn't mean you aren't strong enough to fight back. The Annie McAllister I know wouldn't let him get away with this. She'd be so pissed off she'd want to rip his balls off. Or at the very least hit him in the gut with her fist. I happen to know it's quite effective on a guy when he's not expecting it."

His last words really got her attention. Annie glanced up in time to see the crooked smile she'd come to expect. She stiffened her spine and nodded. "I hate when you're right."

"You say that like it's happened before." He put one hand up to his ear. "When was that, exactly?"

Annie clamped her lips tightly shut, irritated with his smugness. "Let's go talk to somebody so we can get outta here."

They sat in a top floor office watching the digital video playback, accompanied by the store's manager and head of security, along with Captain Woodard and Detective Manuel.

Drake leaned forward in his chair. "There he is walking in."

The camera caught him several times, checking out a nicely dressed woman, then a group of teenage girls.

Drake grunted beside Annie. "Looking for more victims, J.B.? You piece of crap."

Finally, he reappeared at the far end of the store where Annie stood in front of the movie section. He appeared to be observing her from an aisle over.

Annie tensed, as they watched the scene unfold, feeling violated all over again as everyone in the room saw J.B. put his hands on her, touch her breast possessively. Drake's hand clamped over hers, letting her know she wasn't alone.

During the drive home, Drake sat with both hands clenching the steering wheel, thinking about what he'd seen. How the hell he'd managed to stay calm, he couldn't possibly explain. While watching that video, all he'd wanted to do was kill the bastard. Seeing him with his hands on Annie brought back all the feelings of rage he'd felt for that animal on the night of her attack.

He'd wanted to scream, to throw a chair across the room. But at some point, instead of watching the computer screen during the many playbacks of the footage, he'd begun to watch Annie. Each time, she seemed to retreat further into herself, hold herself a little tighter, as though trying to make herself smaller.

As much as he hated seeing that footage, he could only imagine how much worse it had been for her. He'd reined in his rage for her sake and suggested he bring her home.

They pulled into her garage an hour and a half after the incident. Drake scanned the area as they entered the house together, waving to occupants of the Kenton PD cruiser that arrived as soon as they did. He ushered her inside, carrying the single box containing his new laptop and a bag containing his other purchases. After locking the door and setting the alarm behind them, he ran through a quick check of the house.

"It's all clear," he said, catching her staring out the windows over the sink, her hands resting on the countertop. He approached slowly, covered her hand with his own and squeezed.

She pulled her hand back and turned, wearing a tentative smile. "Thanks."

"You okay?"

She shrugged, crossing her arms tightly. "Not really."

"Anything you want to talk about? It may help to get it off your chest."

She paused a moment. "I still can't believe he saw me at mass this morning."

"Yeah, that's disturbing. He must have followed us from here, parked outside the church to wait it out, and followed us to Lake Coburn."

"I think it's worse than that."

He stared down at the diminutive woman, suspecting she was about to reveal something he wouldn't like. He placed a hand on her shoulder, encouragingly. "Tell me."

"Something or *someone* touched my back this morning when we were talking to Jackson and Giselle. It happened when a group of four people passed us, but one of the guys could have been J.B. The hooded jacket, the same build . . ."

Drake squeezed her hand. "Touched, how?"

She swallowed audibly. "I blew it off. Told myself I was being paranoid. That it was a purse or someone's elbow, but it felt more intimate than that."

Drake turned sideways. "Show me." He studied her face as she used her nails to scrape across his back and clear down to the waistband of his jeans. He sucked in his breath. Her touch, as soft as it was, made goose bumps appear on his skin, raised the hair on his arms and nape. How much more effective would it have been on a tiny woman wearing nothing but a thin dress instead of jeans and a cotton shirt?

"Well, hell. I feel about as useless as tits on a boar hog."

Annie frowned. "Why?"

"Because I stood right next to you, and he still managed—that." He couldn't bear to think how violated she must feel. Drake muttered a low string of curses—the kind he saved for occasions such as this, topped it off with one more, "Useless . . ."

"Tits on a boar hog!" Lewis cried.

They both turned to stare at the bird.

Annie shook her head. "Oh, that's lovely, Lewis."

Drake grimaced. "I'm sorry."

"Lovely! Lovely Lewis!" the bird cried.

Drake turned back as Annie's first unexpected giggle turned into a full blown burst of laughter. His initial smile faltered, then faded completely as her laughter evolved into something slightly more hysterical. Within seconds, a single sob tore through her body, then another. Soon, she stood there, her hands over her face, crying uncontrollably.

Drake drew her close, wrapping his arms around her but kept his silence. As tightly wound as Annie had been since the incident, she needed this release. The only thing he needed was to be here for her. God, he loved this tiny little woman who'd made such a huge impact on his life, his emotions, his heart. In his world, all roads led to Annie.

Then and there, he made himself a promise to do a better job of making her feel safe.

"Dad, we've got a big problem, here." Drake kept his voice low as he addressed his father over the phone.

"What's going on, Son? Leah and I have been worried sick about you and Annie."

Drake settled on one end of the sofa and tunneled the fingers of one hand through his hair. "He's stalking her, Dad. He's managed to put his hands on her twice today, once literally right under my nose."

Daniel LeBlanc released a long, low whistle after Drake had explained the day's events. "Where's Annie now?"

"She's sleeping. I'm worried about her. You saw her at Christmas; she's a spunky little thing. But this has shaken her up. Hell, I'd rather have her spouting insults at me than shed one tear."

"That happens when you care about someone."

Drake sucked in his breath and released it slowly. "I didn't think it was possible to care for a woman this much. The thought of losing her now, for any reason—" His jaw clenched at the thought.

"That won't happen."

"I don't want to keep this guy away temporarily. I want him gone—vanished off the face of the earth. I don't ever want her looking over her shoulder, or having to worry about this bastard again. I don't think having him imprisoned would satisfy me, even though I may have to settle for that." He paused for effect. "Do you know what I'm getting at?"

Daniel LeBlanc gave his son a sympathetic grunt. "I think I do. Did you see about getting a bodyguard for her yet? If you haven't, Travis Blood just gave me a list of reputable individuals."

"Red hired someone. He should be arriving within the hour. He's driving in from Lubbock. A guy named Liam Nash."

Daniel grunted in approval. "He's at the top of my list. Travis said he's retired Navy Seal—very skilled at keeping his clientele safe."

Drake nodded. "Good to know. I'm going to let you go now. I want to get my thoughts together before Mr. Nash gets here."

"Son, keep safe and keep us posted. Leah sends her love."

"I will, and give her mine too." He ended the call then walked down the hallway. He opened the door, and peered inside Annie's darkened room. Martin lifted his huge head from his mistress's stomach and stared at him with glowing eyes. Satisfied that the watch cat was doing his job to keep her safe, Drake pulled the door softly closed. He returned to the living room in time to answer the doorbell.

The man standing at the door was a little taller than he was, broader across the shoulders and chest, with dark brown hair and green eyes. He extended his hand. "Drake LeBlanc? I'm Liam Nash."

Drake took the man's hand in a firm handshake. "Great to meet you. I'm counting on you to keep a very special lady safe for me, Mr. Nash. Call me Drake, please."

"Only if you call me Nash." He wrinkled his brow. "The lady is special to whom?"

"Annie's special to a lot of people, actually, but more specifically to me."

"So, she's your girlfriend? Fiancée?"

Drake grinned out of one corner of his mouth as he closed the door behind them. "Eh, not yet. I'm still waiting for her to realize I'm the air that she breathes."

Nash released a low chuckle. "That's how it is, huh? Well, don't worry about me infringing on your territory. I make it a point never to mix business with pleasure."

Drake snorted. "You haven't seen Annie yet, have you?"

"I pulled up a picture of her driver's license. Those are never good likenesses and it was over three years ago. Is she still tiny? The license said she was a little under five foot and barely a hundred pounds."

"That sounds about right," Drake told the man. "The most gorgeous blue eyes you'll ever see in your life and a head full of auburn hair."

Nash cocked one eyebrow. "Are we talking Lucille Ball red out of a bottle?"

Drake's laughter rang out in the room. "Lord, don't ever let her hear you say that. Everything about Annie is natural. You'll see what I mean."

"Still, I'm not into women that small. I like a woman closer to my height. And they'd better have some meat on their bones."

Drake laughed. "I know what you mean. I've dated women I was afraid to break." He shook his head. "Models."

Nash groaned loudly. "Models are the worst, aren't they? I dated this one chick—a runway model for some fancy ass designer. She dumped me when I said I was tired of dishing out for steak and lobster dinners so she could go barf it up as soon as I brought her home. Good riddance."

Drake grimaced. "That must be a hell of a life, huh?" He turned toward Lewis's cage as the bird started up a ruckus. "Now you've done it, Nash. You've upset the bird."

"Stranger danger! Annie, get your gun!" Lewis squawked.

Drake approached his cage. "It's okay, buddy, he's one of the good guys."

Nash followed. "I didn't know she had an African Grey. He looks like a Timneh."

"He is. This is Lewis, and he's very intelligent."

Liam raised his hand slowly and touched the cage. "Hello, Lewis."

The bird cocked his head sideways, seeming to study the strange man. "Hello."

Drake stared at the bodyguard. "You're familiar with them?"

Nash gave him a brief nod. "Yes, I had one for twenty years, but I lost him in a house fire. It—uh—it happened while I was away."

Drake recognized the unmistakable sound of sadness in Nash's voice, tinged with a dread of talking about it. "I'm sorry to hear that."

Nash shrugged. "Shit happens sometimes, you know?"

A shuffling sound from Annie's room had both men turning in time to see her door open. Martin made his appearance first.

"Here's Martin. He's her watch cat, or 'attack cat' in some instances."

"Martin and Lewis?" Nash guffawed. "Somebody's got a sense of humor."

Drake grinned profusely. "Somebody definitely does. Lewis, say 'Hey Lady' for me."

"Hey Laa-dy!" the bird cried.

"Damn, he sounds just like Jerry, doesn't he?" Nash exclaimed.

"Annie loves those old comedies from the sixties. I'm sure she'll be out in a minute." He felt Nash's gaze on him, and wasn't surprised at his next comment.

"You know, you're a pretty big guy, Drake, and I'd guess that you can handle yourself in a bar room brawl, if you had to. Seeing as how you feel about the lady, I'm kind of wondering what you need me for."

Drake nodded. "I'm with her all weekend. On weekdays I have to drop her off at the clinic where she works here in Kenton and then I drive to the law practice I'm opening in Lake Coburn. During those eight hours or so that I'm away from her, I'm tempted to call her at least a couple dozen times. Somehow, I manage to hold it down to once per hour. She always *tries* to sound irritated that I'm calling so often, but she always answers her cell on the first ring."

Nash nodded. "That's a sure sign she's waiting for it."

"I know," Drake agreed. "She tries to act brave when she's over there without me, but I know she's terrified. By the time I pick her up in the afternoons we're both on edge from worrying. I've told her I'd put off opening my practice until this is all over with. That way I'd be able to stay with her all day long, but she won't hear of it."

"Too proud to admit she wants you there," Nash added.

Drake nodded. "Annie hates feeling vulnerable and afraid. The one time I left her alone in the house, the bastard was watching and called her. He followed us to church this morning, then all the way to Lake Coburn where he dared to put his hands on her." Drake shook his head in frustration. "I don't care if it takes a flippin' army, Nash. That shit can't happen again."

"He's watching the house, then," Nash stated.

"He is, and she can't be left alone for a second."

"She won't be. Between you and me, I guarantee we can handle this. I heard you banged him up pretty good the night of the attack."

"I gave him a hell of a beating, but apparently not good enough. Right about now, I'm wishing I'd left him dead instead of unconscious. Did you get the background on him?"

"I did, and he sounds like a sadistic S-O-B."

Both men turned as Annie's bedroom door opened and she walked over to meet them. Drake made the introductions.

Annie tried to wipe the traces of her nap from her eyes. "This is a mess, isn't it?"

"It's not so bad compared to some of the cases I've handled. That old boy from Arkansas only *thought* he got tore up from Drake, here. Won't he be surprised when he has two big ole Texans opening up a can of whoop-ass on him the next time he shows his face?" Nash flipped his brown felt cowboy hat. "Miss McAllister, you can rest easy. Between Drake and me, J.B. Montgomery will never get his hands on you again."

She nodded. "Thanks, Mr. Nash. I appreciate what both you and Drake have been doing. He and I are kind of in the same boat. We both have fairly new businesses that need our attention."

"I understand," he said. "I want you to sit right here and tell me what your schedule is like for the next week. Be sure to let me know if you have any functions to attend after work."

Annie explained the schedule they had worked out the previous week. When she was done, she ran her hands through her hair then sat back in the chair. "I feel trapped. All of my choices have been taken away from me. When I don't have choices I get nervous." Her eyes darted around the room as though searching for something. "Where's your luggage, Mr. Nash?"

"It's in my car. I'll get it if you tell me where you want me to sleep. I don't want to do anything that makes you feel more uncomfortable, but please call me Liam, or better yet, Nash. After twenty years in the military, that's what I'm used to."

Annie smiled at him, liking him already. "I will if you call me Annie. Believe me, if I can get used to having Drake share my house with me, I can get used to anything. Go get your luggage—I'll make sure the back bedroom is ready for you." She turned and walked down the hallway toward the spare room number two.

Nash looked at Drake. "Well, she didn't mention you leaving, so maybe she's thinking there's safety in numbers."

"I can only hope. But, I know Annie. It'll come up the next time I piss her off."

"Has a bit of an Irish temper, does she?"

Drake walked over to the fridge. "I think it's Scottish, and it's more than a bit. You'll have to butt heads with her on occasion, no doubt." He removed two waters from the fridge, and offered one to Nash.

Nash accepted the bottle and thanked him. "She wouldn't be the first client I've butted heads with, but you're right about one thing. She is about the prettiest client I've had so far. You're lucky I don't mix business with pleasure."

Drake waved him off. "I'm not worried about it. You weren't around to see the sparks fly when Annie and I met for the first time."

Nash cocked an eyebrow. "Was it that heated?"

Drake nodded. "Sizzling."

Chapter Sixteen

Julia & Chad

Julia

Julia McAllister sat entranced and staring, without really seeing, out at the view of the park from her London office window. She held a highlighter in one hand and a mechanical pencil in the other. She tapped the latter nervously on the desk surface.

She sighed and shifted her gaze to the set of plans in front of her—a design for a very large, upscale shopping center, complete with an art gallery, a bevy of fine dining restaurants to choose from, shops bearing names of dozens of well-known designers, as well as a multi-screened theater complex. She was reconfiguring a section to include her recent brainstorm, a child care facility. She had just talked the owners into the idea, convinced them that it would bring those parents into the shops on days they would normally have stayed home with the children. Too bad there hadn't been a place like that in the local mall when she'd had to drag her children shopping. She'd never had help with them because of Chad's schedules, both as a CPA, then as a pilot, not to mention the years between the two careers, as he juggled both to get in his flight hours.

Throughout their marriage, she had kept up with her architectural drafting skills by designing private house plans from her home. Even managed to sneak in a leisure learning class or two to keep her computer skills sharp, but she'd always had an interest in designing something bigger. Every shopping center or mall she'd ever entered had drawn her interest. She'd find herself looking around, thinking how she could have made it better.

When a company wanted to hire her because of a design she'd entered in a competition, she'd jumped at the chance. Three short years later, her design for this mall had been chosen over several dozen others, and here she was in London, England.

Her mind drifted painfully back to the night she had told her husband about her fantastic chance to work hand-in-hand with the owners in the UK. Chad had turned what should have been a joyous occasion into a dismal disappointment. That terrible, awful night had extended into a week, then two until she finally decided to go without him or his approval, taking their son with her.

A knock on her door jarred Julia back to the present. Douglas Statham walked in, and she groaned inwardly at the bouquet of fresh flowers he carried. The man wouldn't give up.

He placed the vase on her desk, raising his palms in self-defense. "Don't get mad, Jules. I saw them and thought of you."

"You know, Douglas, where I come from, no means no."

He flashed his blue eyes at her and ran a hand through his sandy blond waves. "Well, where I come from, a real man doesn't give up so easily on a beautiful woman."

She turned to her computer and began drafting the changes she'd just marked up on the plans. "Eventually you'll have to, you know. I'm busy. Did you have business you wanted to discuss?"

"Not particularly. Heard from your foolish husband lately?"

"My foolish husband is no concern of yours."

"Ah, but does he remain a concern of yours?"

Right on schedule, an alert popped up on her computer. "I've got a meeting with my client in two hours and I've got to make these changes and get them plotted out." She pointed at her door, thankful when he took the hint and left.

"Things would be perfect if he weren't here," Julia mumbled, trying to concentrate on her work. His question tugged at her. *Was* Chad still a concern? She was still livid at his selfishness, but she did love him. If she'd forgotten that during the past year, she'd been reminded during her recent trip. The last night in particular, vividly fresh in her mind as she recalled the joy of being in his arms. Oh hell, the satisfaction of having her husband inside her where he belonged. The year of sexual abstinence had caused a stand out, or rather *stand-up* performance she'd never forget; most unfortunately, considering the situation.

She let her head fall forward on the desk and groaned loudly, missing him, needing him . . .there, in the place only her husband had ever occupied. "Damn you, Chad."

She rose from her chair, determined to put him out of her mind. She'd actually believed the selfish bastard had come around to her way of thinking and would agree to give her at the very least six months of his life. *I should have known better.*

Julia paced her office, finally paused in front of the crystal vase full of her favorite fresh flowers. She fingered the delicate petal of a rose, then bent to smell a carnation and smiled. Douglas may be extremely annoying at times, but he was certainly persistent, and he admired her for her creative talent in cutting-edge-design. After living abroad for a year and having others cater to *her* for a change, she knew she couldn't go back to living with a man who didn't believe in her. She loved her husband, desperately, but also knew she couldn't abide his current attitude toward her career. As heart-breaking as it would be for her, she'd have to give him up.

Julia set her brief case on the entry table and kicked off her heels at the door of the two bed room flat she shared with Jacob. Her phone dinged and she pulled it from her coat pocket to check the voice message her son had just left.

"Hey, Mom. It's right at noon, and I'm calling to let you know my plans for tonight, just like you asked me to. Remember this when it's time for my allowance, would you? Isabella and I are going to the movies tonight with Derek and his new girlfriend, Katarina. The feature is at eight o'clock, but we're going to go shopping right after school. You said you were tired of seeing me in worn jeans and tee shirts, remember? We'll grab somethin' to eat and hang out until the movie starts. I'll be home by midnight. Later."

Julia sighed and dropped her head back. "Great, another Friday night at home, alone, with nothing to do." She went into her bedroom and changed into her favorite pair of faded jeans and a sweater. She entered the kitchen in time to answer her ringing telephone.

"Have you eaten yet?"

Douglas. "No, as a matter of fact, I haven't."

"Why don't you let me treat you to dinner? There's this great little restaurant just around the corner from your flat."

"I'm too tired to go out, Douglas. I think I'll just order in some pizza."

"Perfect! Open your door."

Julia walked over to her door and pulled it open. Douglas stood there with pale yellow carnations in one hand, a box of pizza in the other, and a bottle of wine tucked under his arm. Gazing into eyes that sparkled with amusement, she couldn't help but smile. "You can be a real pest when you want to be, you know that?"

"Ay well, I've always been a firm believer in the old squeaky wheel getting the grease analogy." His clipped, British accent sounded sharp and crisp to Julia's ears.

She took the carnations from his outstretched hand and buried her nose in them, letting her eyes drift closed. The smell of her favorite flowers always jogged memories of homecoming dances, wrist corsages, and huge pink and blue bouquets when her children were born. Not to mention dozens of birthday, anniversary, and apology bouquets over the years, always arriving in a vast assortment of vases. "I love carnations," she mused.

Douglas responded with a smug "I knew that."

"Well, you're here, and I'm hungry, so you may as well come in." Julia opened the door wide to allow him inside.

Douglas raised one brow cockily. "What a gracious and heartfelt invitation."

She shoved the flowers back at him. "Or not, and you can go home."

He stepped over the threshold. "A perfectly lovely invitation, Jules."

She closed the door and chuckled. "As long as you know that I'm not interested in you for anything other than the flowers and the pizza. I'm starved."

He pulled the bottle of wine out from under his arm. "Shall I drink this alone?"

Julia looked at the label and saw that it was a very fine brand of merlot. "No, I think I'd like a glass of that, if you don't mind. It's been a hectic end to a hectic week."

"Do you have to meet with any contractors tomorrow?" Douglas asked.

She reached onto a shelf for two wine glasses. "We took care of everything today."

"Excellent!" He reached into his pocket and pulled out a corkscrew.

"Do you always carry one of those around with you?"

Douglas smiled wickedly. "A man never knows when he'll get the chance to get a beautiful woman drunk and take advantage of her."

Julia laughed. "Good luck with that. I can probably drink you under the table."

Doug grinned devilishly down at her. "Would you like to wager on that?"

She shook her head. "No, thanks." She set the glasses on the table, adding plates and napkins. Doug poured the wine while Julia placed a slice of pizza on each plate.

She dropped into her chair, reaching for her pizza, but stopped when Douglas began searching the area as though looking for something. "What else do you need?"

"Silverware would be nice."

"No self-respecting person eats pizza with silverware."

"Excuse me, but I have plenty of self-respect and I use silverware to eat my pizza."

"Oh, come on, Doug. Pizza should be eaten with your hands, like this." She demonstrated by picking up her slice and taking a bite out of it.

"You Yanks can be so barbaric at times."

"You Brits are entirely too stuffy, and that's how we *Americans* won our independence from you boys well over two hundred years ago."

"By eating with your hands?" Douglas smirked.

"By our spirit of adventure, and by getting our hands dirty. By finding new and better ways to do things. Any man who is too fancy to eat pizza with his hands doesn't deserve to control a country as fine as the United States of America." She got up to get him a fork and knife.

Douglas accepted the utensils and thanked her. "That's just as well—you're all too high maintenance to be English citizens."

"Says the man who needs a knife and fork to eat finger food," Julia shot back at him. She gave him a hooded look. "Don't even think of putting down my people *or* my country."

Douglas met her gaze. "If you're so bloody proud of your country and your people, why are you in England?"

"Because I owed it to myself and my career to be here, that's why."

"Despite what your wanker of a husband thought?"

She sent him a glare from over the rim of her wine glass. "Douglas, my husband is off limits to you, do you understand?"

He gave her a mischievous look. "I don't have a problem with that. I have no desire to put my hands on your husband, anyway. You, however, are an entirely different matter. You are, without a doubt, one of the two most beautiful, and talented women I've ever known—even if you *are* slightly obnoxious."

Julia smiled and took another sip of wine. "Why thank you, Douglas. You know, you can be quite charming when you want to be. Today must not be one of those days."

Douglas threw back the rest of his wine and set the glass down. "You're right, Jules, and I apologize. My daughter's put me in a beast of a mood, I'm afraid. She's started dating the one young man on this earth that I cannot abide, and I don't know what to do about it."

Jules snorted and picked up another piece of pizza. "You'd be better off doing absolutely nothing. If you do something stupid like forbid her to see him, she won't be able to get enough of him. Take it from me, I know."

"Do you really think so? She's always been such a sensible girl. This behavior is really out of character for her."

"How old is she?"

"She only just turned seventeen, but she acts . . ." his voice trailed off.

"More like she's 27?" Julia guessed.

"Exactly! I don't mind telling you, Jules, I'm terrified. If Addie were here she'd know how to handle her. She was always so good in these situations."

Julia searched the man's countenance and truly felt sorry for him for the first time. "How long has Addie been gone, Douglas?" She refilled his wine glass.

The man put his fork down and raised his glass. "She died four years ago, on our sixteenth anniversary."

Julia groaned. "How awful for you."

He shrugged. "I didn't think I'd be able to survive it. I was crazy about her. We grew up together, you know. We were friends all our lives, and then one day I saw her dancing with another chap, and got insanely jealous. I went to her and told her I didn't want her to dance with anyone else but me."

Julia chuckled. "I can imagine how well that went over. What did she say to that?"

Douglas sighed. "I believe the words "bugger off" came into play. It took me another year to convince her that we belonged together."

"A year?" Julia asked, astonished.

He nodded. "That was just to convince her to date me, exclusively. We dated for two years and lived together another four before I finally got her to marry me."

"Douglas, I never would have thought you had it in you to wait for someone that long."

"Patience and perseverance, my dear Jules. Patience is the companion of wisdom."

"A wise statement by St. Augustine," Julia answered as he nodded. "I've got one for you. Perseverance is failing nineteen times and succeeding the twentieth."

"Hmmm—Margaret Thatcher?" Douglas guessed.

"Not even close. Julie Andrews."

"I was close. They're both Brits and both women."

"Oh please, one's a politician and the other is a singer and actress," Julia objected.

"What does that have to do with anything?" Douglas demanded. "Have you forgotten about Ronald Reagan?"

Julia dropped her head back. "How the hell did we get started on this, anyway?"

"I bloody well don't know. How about if we call it a draw?"

Julia opened her white napkin and waved it over her head, laughing as Douglas joined in.

Two hours later, the bottle of wine was gone, along with another half bottle from Julia's fridge. The pizza was all gone and Julia was feeling more relaxed than she had in over a year. They talked about everything from their work to what their children were like as babies. Julia finally got him to understand that there would be no future with her and he seemed to accept it. As a result, she'd let her guard down and was having fun with him.

After checking his watch, Douglas stood up. "Well, thanks for the chat, Jules, but it's time I headed home. Katarina and Derek should be returning home from the movies fairly soon."

Julia's brow creased in concentration. "Wait a minute, did she say they were going with another couple?"

"Yes, I believe she mentioned an Isabella and ah—let me see, what did she say that young man's name was?"

"Jacob. Isabella and Jacob," Julia said.

"Yes, that's it." He paused, meeting her gaze. "That's not *your* Jacob?"

She grinned. "And *your* Katarina. I didn't realize they were acquainted with each other."

"I don't think they were, until tonight. She's known Derek for years— I've never liked that young chap. He's cocky and far too randy for my Kat."

"Come on, Douglas. Like anyone would ever be good enough for Daddy's little girl."

He sighed. "I guess you're right. She told me I liked Derek perfectly well all these years until she started to date him."

"I know Derek, and he's a good kid," Julia volunteered. "Try not to worry."

Douglas cocked an eyebrow and pursed his lips.

She laughed, "I know, I know! Chad and I were constantly worried when Miranda was that age. It's not as bad with Jacob."

"Because he's a guy, and guys don't get pregnant?"

"Because we've been through it once already. If Kat wasn't an only child you'd see what I mean. Besides, I know my son, and if Jacob got a girl pregnant, he'd take responsibility for that child also. He knows his life, as well as the mother's, would change dramatically."

"Oh, God. The thought of my little Kat out there, and maybe experimenting with sex terrifies me, Jules. I look at her and I can still see how she looked with her two front teeth missing in nursery class."

Julia smiled and placed a comforting hand on his arm. "I know, but you have to remember that she's a beautiful young woman now. We've all made mistakes as teenagers, Doug. They weren't all life altering, but we did manage to learn something from each and every one of them. She'll be fine."

She was surprised to feel a bit closer to him now that she was seeing his more personal side; the parental side that worried over his little girl.

"Thank you, Julia. It's all much easier to digest if one has someone to talk to. I've been walking around for days with this feeling, as though an elephant were sitting on my chest."

She acted on the urge to put a hand to his cheek. When she did, his eyes turned a shade darker, more intense.

Hesitantly, he leaned down and kissed her gently on the lips.

Jules wasn't surprised by the fact that he kissed her, as much as the fact that she liked it so much. She reached up with her other hand on the opposite side of his face and caressed him. Then she pulled slowly away from him. "I'm sorry Douglas. That was lovely, but, I'm not available for this kind of thing just yet."

"Just yet? Does that mean you will be, eventually?" He sounded hopeful.

She shook her head. "No, it only means that I don't know how it's all going to turn out. I'm still hoping my husband comes to his senses, even though the odds are pretty strong he won't."

He gave her a smug grin. "You're waiting for him to come and sweep you up on his white horse and take you away from all of this?"

Julia's light hearted laughter rang out in the apartment. "You can't blame a girl for wanting the fairytale, Douglas. Everyone wants the happily ever after." She shrugged. "But, even though my name is Julia, my last name is McAllister, not Roberts, and this is not a Hollywood movie. Some endings are neither happy nor typical."

He nodded and gave her a gentle brush on the lips. "Thanks, Jules. It's helped to have you to talk to, even though I can finally see that you're out of reach. It's a shame though, I think we'd make a smashing couple, and I think Katarina would benefit greatly from having you in her life."

Jules reached up and brushed his tousled dark locks away from his hazel eyes then touched his face again. Slowly pulling the door open, she smiled as he chucked her chin affectionately. "Thanks for understanding, Douglas."

"How about you get your hands the hell off my wife!"

Chad

Chad stood there with his hand on the buzzer while his wife let a complete stranger touch her face intimately, the same way he'd touched her thousands of times. Hearing her call him by his name caused something inside him to snap. Good old, *persistent* Douglas. "She is still married, you know."

"Chad!" Julia chided, recovering quickly from the apparent shock of seeing him. "He's a friend, and he's just leaving. You're completely out of line."

"Am I?" He sent her an accusing glare.

"Yes, you bloody well are," she snapped.

Chad snorted. "Bloody? Are you so much a British citizen now that you've forgotten how to cuss like an *American*, Jules?"

Obviously deciding it was time to take his leave, Douglas finally spoke. "I'll see you Monday at the office, Jules. Don't be afraid to ring me if you need me." He held up his cell phone, and sent a glare in Chad's direction. "Or do you need me to stay?"

She gave his arm an affectionate pat. "I'll be fine, don't worry."

Chad exchanged glares with the guy as he brushed past and headed for the elevator. He turned back toward Julia, whose eyes sparkled with quiet anger.

"Did you only come over to insult me, Chad, or is there another purpose for this visit?"

"I came to ask your forgiveness," he said. "I came to tell you that I've been a fool, but now I see that I may have been another kind of fool. Are you having an affair with good, old Douglas?"

"You asshole!" she hissed. "How do you find the nerve to come here and accuse me of that?"

Judging by her reaction, and knowing her as well as he did, Chad knew immediately just how bad he'd screwed up, yet again. He closed his eyes and clenched his teeth. "Jules—"

She pushed him roughly back, and just before the door slammed in his face, he heard her string together a collection of curses that would make a Marine proud. And this time it was in good, old, S-O-B calling, F-bomb flying American style. Apparently, the only motivation his wife needed to remember her roots was . . . him.

Chad knew better than to attempt re-entry that night. He walked slowly toward the elevator, where Douglas stood, holding the door open.

"Care to share the lift, Mr. McAllister?"

Chad nodded then stepped into the box. Neither men spoke until it opened into the lobby of the apartment complex.

They stepped out and just as Douglas began to walk toward the exit, Chad stopped him with his comment. "I love my wife. I don't want to lose her."

Douglas

Douglas turned slowly to observe Julia's husband. He saw weariness in the man's face, along with a panic the man couldn't quite hide. Chad McAllister was definitely still in love with his wife.

Blast it all!

In the second it took to recognize that, his resentment toward Julia's husband turned to sympathy. Losing one's wife to divorce would probably be just as painful as losing her to death, maybe even worse. Addie hadn't chosen to leave him, but had been taken from this world unexpectedly. Douglas knew that if he'd lost Addie to something that had been his own fault, he wouldn't be able to live with himself.

"I can see you don't want to lose her, McAllister. But I also see a very foolish man standing before me, and if you don't find a way to rid yourself of that foolishness, you may lose her for good."

Chad's shoulders drooped as he stared down at his shoes. "Every time I open my mouth around her lately, I screw something up. I love her more now than I ever have, but I can't seem to stop this downhill slide we're in. We were fine until this whole England thing came up. I don't see why she had to take this position. It's changed everything."

Douglas studied the man before him and thought he was beginning to understand the problem. "Look, I must be insane for suggesting this, but how about if I buy you a cup of tea, or coffee as most of you Americans seem to prefer."

Chad shook his head. "I like my tea iced, and I've had enough caffeine today to make my skin crawl. How about if I buy you a beer, instead? It's the least I could do for being such a jerk."

Douglas nodded. "I only have time for one, but I think I can shed some light on this situation for you. It may even save your marriage if you're intelligent enough to take my advice."

The two men walked down the street to a nearby city Pub and sat at a table in a somewhat quieter corner where they could talk. They ordered to lagers. Chad gave their barmaid a ten pound note and told her to keep the change.

Douglas took a swig and turned toward the other man. "Have you any idea how talented your wife is at design?"

Chad nodded. "I've seen her sketches and floor plans. She seems to do well enough."

Douglas raised his brows, unable to cloak his shock at Chad's answer. "Well enough? Her designs are fresh and innovative, she has a knack for handling last minute changes with exceptional grace, and somehow she's managed to get every contractor out there eating out of her hand. She's bloody phenomenal, is what she is."

Chad shrugged. "She's always been phenomenal at whatever she did. Maybe I'm so used to her being wonderful at everything that it's stopped being big news to me."

Douglas took a long swig from his bottle and checked his watch. "Come on, McAllister. You can't fully appreciate Julia's work by looking at a sketch. It's time you realize what a genius she is." He rose from the table and started for the door.

Chad took one more drink of his lager and rose to follow. "Where are we going?"

"I'm going to show you what your wife's been working on during her time here. You won't be able to see much in the dark, so I advise you to go back there tomorrow in the daylight. I can give you a tour if you'd like."

Chad

An hour later, Chad was still awed by the magnitude of Julia's design. He shook his head as he made his way carefully around the construction site. "I had no idea. You say she has to work daily with the engineers and contractors to make sure they're following the plans?"

"Absolutely. The business partners chose hers over hundreds of other entries and want to ensure no one deviates from the design. She has to approve any change that could affect the final outcome."

Chad stood with arms outspread. "You have no idea how amazed I am at all of this."

Douglas shook his head. "You have no idea how amazed I am that it took you this long to be amazed at your own wife's remarkable talents."

Chad looked at his own feet, shamed to the core that it took a complete stranger to point out his ignorance toward Julia's abilities. "Point taken. I'll come back tomorrow morning to see the rest, but I see now why she has to be here." He looked over at Douglas. "She mentioned functions that she'd like me to attend with her. How many have I missed?"

"We've attended dozens since the beginning of this thing. It's all part of the PR for the mall. Her presence is required. Not only that, but the owners are family oriented people. They like to have the spouses attend all functions with their employees. So far, Jules has attended every one of them alone. I can tell it's made her feel very uncomfortable."

Chad ran a hand through his hair. "I told her I'd try to be in for as many as I can, but it would be impossible to attend all of them with my flight schedule the way it is." He looked out at the huge structure before him, encompassing a vast amount of acreage. "I sure miss my wife."

Douglas nodded. "I know how you feel." He continued when Chad turned a curious look in his direction. "My wife died four years ago in a car crash. It's been hard on us."

Chad took a mental step back at the confession. "Us? Do you have children?"

"I have one seventeen year old daughter, Katarina. She looks more like her mother every day. It's been rough on my poor Kat. Teenage girls need a mother, you know? I do what I can, but I'm afraid I don't measure up, on occasion."

Chad narrowed his gaze on the Englishman. "Are you hoping to provide her with a new one by stealing my wife away from me?"

"Look here, McAllister, in your case, it wouldn't be stealing. You've been doing a fine job of pushing her away all by yourself."

Chad sent the man a reluctant nod. "I guess I have at that. I just never thought of her as having this kind of talent."

Douglas turned toward Chad. "Excuse me for saying this, but I think what you've done all these years was take her for granted. Once you fall into that mind-set, it's difficult to pull yourself out of it."

"Are you speaking from experience?"

"The only thing I took for granted with Addie was that she would be here with me for the rest of my life. All it took was one drunk driver and a phone call to change everything."

Chad studied his solemn face before answering. "I'm sorry for your loss."

"Not as sorry as I am, but thanks anyway. She was a beautiful person, inside and out." He added in a low murmur. "She was the absolute love of my life."

"Yet you're ready to move on, and possibly with the absolute love of *my* life?"

"Is she?" Douglas sent him a stern gaze.

"Of course she is."

"Then why the blast don't you act like it? If you loved her, you'd be here with her. She's nearly ready to weed you out of the garden if you don't wise up, you know. She's tired of being alone, anyone can see that. She's told me in no uncertain terms that she's not interested *as of now*, but if you keep up this foolishness, she might change her mind. If she does, I'll be right here, waiting to sweep her off her feet."

No way could he misinterpret the Englishman's threat. "You'd do that, knowing how I feel about her?"

Douglas gave him a throaty laugh as he nodded. "Absolutely. I'm not the fool here, old boy. You are."

Chapter Seventeen

Nash folded the Lake Coburn American Press into neat quarters and set it on the end table. His stomach reminded him with a low growl that it was time for lunch, but he checked his watch anyway. 11:45. He stood to stretch his legs, waited for Annie to finish with her last patient before the noon break. He pulled his buzzing phone from his pocket, knowing it would be Drake checking up.

Anything?

Like clockwork. The man checked in at least once an hour. That's not accounting for however many times the son-of-a-gun messaged Annie directly. One thing for sure, the poor bastard had it bad for her. He figured the feeling was mutual, but the little spitfire was too stubborn to admit it. Drake had warned him he'd likely butt heads with his client, and he'd been right on the money. Annie hadn't taken kindly to having him as a constant companion all day at her clinic.

"You're coming to the office with me?"

"Yes," he'd told her.

"You'll be inside. All day. Every day."

"That's generally the way it goes."

She'd frowned. "Do you plan on being there during the sessions? Will you accompany me to the bathroom?"

"That'll cost you extra." His attempt at humor hadn't been received well.

She'd narrowed those ice blue eyes and sneered. "You're not funny."

"I wasn't hired to give you laughs. I'm here to keep your butt safe. It's what I do."

"Can't you stay in your truck? I don't want you in the office. You'll make our customers uncomfortable."

"I don't really care what you want. It's imperative I be in the same building with you, within calling distance."

She'd opened her mouth to say something, but Drake had walked by and shut her up without a single word. He'd simply ran his finger down her back. Annie had whipped around, eyes wide with terror, shoulders drawn up, skin covered with goose bumps.

With one simple act, he'd reminded her how close J.B. had gotten to her right under everyone's nose. He'd given her a serious look and spoke in a low growl. "Let the man do what he needs to do to keep you safe, Annie."

The subtle message had worked and Annie had kept any further comments about Nash's tactics to herself.

Drake hadn't seemed too thrilled at being the cause for her bent will, but he'd apparently seen it as a necessary, albeit regretful, means to an end.

Nash sent a reply.

Nash: *No sign of him. No phone calls. I talked her into going to lunch today. Should be leaving shortly.*

Drake: *Good.*

Nash stared out the glass door into the parking lot, his thoughts returning to what he'd learned about J.B. Montgomery. The bastard was more than an attempted rapist. He was a stalker, in the truest since of the word. He loved the thrill of the chase, as well as the enjoyment of toying with his victims before going in for the kill.

The roommate of one of his victims said there had been a steady barrage of phone calls, written messages on her car, in her mailbox, and even tacked to her apartment door. The poor girl had been terrified to leave her apartment. In every case, J.B's initial meeting with these women had simply been a matter of being in the wrong place at the wrong time. In Annie's case, it had been that, and a little more. He'd seen this girl nearly incapacitated by her migraine and obviously couldn't pass up the chance to have a little no-risk fun. He hadn't counted on getting an ass-kicking from the pissed-off-Texas-transplant lawyer in love with her.

He turned at Annie's approach, raised his hand before she could utter the excuse already forming on her lips. "No, I don't want a sandwich and chips. No I don't want to order a pizza or anything from the deli down the street. Get your purse. We're going out into civilization."

Her shoulders drooped, deflated at his insistence; she grabbed her purse and met him. "I don't like this, Nash."

He slung one arm over her shoulders and turned her toward the door. "It'll be fine. Don't worry."

The savory smells inside the local seafood restaurant had Nash's stomach growling. "I'll take the deluxe seafood platter, and I'll pay extra to have the deviled crab replaced with more oysters. And more sweet tea, please." He held up his nearly empty glass.

"I'll have the small broiled catfish imperial please, and extra lemon for my water, please." Annie handed the menu to the waitress and stood. "Come on, Nash. The salad bar is over there."

"Good, I'm starving." He followed her, swung around in full bodyguard mode when someone called out to Annie. Her pleased reaction eased his mind immediately. The sight of the woman standing before him did more than that.

"Angelique!" Annie squealed, obviously delighted at the woman's presence. "It's great to see you. What brings you to Kenton?"

"Business, of course, but I'm so glad I get to mix a little pleasure in with my meal by meeting up with you."

Nash stood a little taller as the woman turned her gaze his direction. The exotic looking beauty didn't even attempt to hide her appreciative ogling. Her smooth as velvet, throaty voice called to mind old-time blues houses of the past . . . smoke-filled rooms, sweat-covered bodies plastered against each other, all moving in a slow, seductive dance.

Her eyes wide with curiosity, she pursed her lips. "Who, may I ask, are you?"

Nash gave God a silent thumbs up for creating the gorgeously sexy, black-haired beauty standing majestically before him. Nearly as tall as himself, the woman boasted an exotically olive complexion, and a body built like a brick shit house. As if all that perfect packaging wasn't enough, her eyes sealed the deal. Vibrantly alive, full of mischief, and the most beautiful shade of green he'd ever seen on any human being, *ever.*

He tipped his hat to the lady and gave her what he hoped was his most seductive smile. "Liam Nash, Ma'am . . . and can I just say that it is a *real* pleasure to meet you."

"Angelique Baptiste, Mr. Nash." She extended her hand as she flashed him a brilliant smile. "Apparently, it's my lucky day. Who thought I'd meet such a fine specimen in a town this size?" She turned to Annie. "You must tell me now before I get too attached, is he your beau, ma chere amie?"

Annie laughed. "No to the beau, and yes to the bodyguard, Red's idea since I seem to have picked up a stalker on New Year's Eve."

"Chere de Bon Dieu!" Angelique whispered, reverently. "I heard about the attack of course, but I didn't know the man was stalking you! You must tell me everything. I'm by myself, so may I sit with you?"

"Absolutely," Nash answered before Annie could reply. "Let's get our salads and sit."

The three of them seated themselves and began to carry on the easy conversation that would last throughout the meal.

"So, your company wants to transfer you to Lubbock, Texas?" The prospect of having her in his hometown thrilled Nash as he hadn't been in quite some time.

Angelique wiped the condensation from her glass of iced tea. "Yes, but I turned them down, of course. That's why I'm here for a job interview."

Nash turned to her and cleared his throat. "Lubbock is my home, you know. Do you have a problem with that place in particular, or Texas, in general?"

"I have a problem with being so far away from my parents, Mr. Nash. They live in Lafayette, and I'm an only child."

"Maybe you could take them with you," he suggested

She gave her head an adamant shake. "My parents are old and extremely set in their ways. It would be futile to ask."

"But how do you know unless you do?"

"Mr. Nash, my parents are of Creole blood. They would die if they left all they were accustomed to. The old traditional ways run deep in them both."

He gazed into her eyes, thinking it could explain her unique coloring. "Creole. I've heard of it, but I've always been confused about what makes up Creole bloodline. How is Creole different from Cajun?"

"Modern day Cajuns are descendants of the French families that left France so they could be free to practice their religion of Catholicism. They ended up in Nova Scotia—"

"Which used to be called Acadia. I know that much," Nash interjected. "One of my Navy buddies was Cajun."

"That's right," Annie continued. "They built thriving communities, were hard-working, and very devout Catholics. Protestant English came along and wanted them to swear allegiance to the Crown of England and stop practicing Catholicism."

"So they left one country because of religious persecution and the same flipping thing happened in their new home?" Nash grunted in disgust. "That sucks."

"The big one," Annie said. "Of course there was a lot more to it than that, but that would take a lot longer than a lunch break."

Nash nodded in understanding. "So the name Cajun is derived from the word Acadian?"

"Ca c'est bon. Very good, Liam. Step to the front of the class!" The green-eyed temptation flashed him a brilliant smile.

He grinned at her. "How about you?"

She ran her crimson nail around the rim of her empty coffee cup. "Creoles can be descendants of Spanish, Native American, and Caribbean— any, or all of these, always mixed with French blood, but born here in this country."

"So, which descendants do you come from?"

"That would be the box labeled *All of the above*." She pinned him with her mesmerizing gaze. "I'm curious to know what you think of that, Mr. Nash."

He returned her gaze, only slightly surprised by her frankness. "I don't have a problem with your curiosity at all, Ms. Baptiste. I only asked out of my own curiosity. I wanted to know who to credit for your exquisitely beautiful features. Your eyes, hair, skin tone . . ." He paused and scanned her from the top of her head, to her lovely hands resting on the table. "All of it, the entire breathtaking package."

Angelique actually blushed as she cleared her throat. "Well, that is certainly sweet of you to say. Merci beaucoup—thank you, Mr. Nash."

"Please, call me Nash or Liam," he commented.

She nodded slowly and gave him a smile. "I like the sound of Liam, as long as you call me Angelique, or Angie if you prefer."

"I like the sound of Angelique. It fits a woman of your extraordinary beauty."

Angelique blinked several times. "My goodness. How long can you keep that up, Liam?"

He dipped his head for a long, slow perusal of her. "Oh, I can keep it up a long, *long* time, Angelique."

Annie studied the pair of aces in front of Nash and the three sevens in front of Drake. She lay down her cards with a grin. "Read 'em and weep, boys. Full house—kings over jacks."

Drake groaned. "Hell in a hand basket! I have *never* seen anyone so damned lucky."

Nash eyed her suspiciously. "I swear Annie, you'd better not let me catch you cheating."

Annie chortled gleefully, pulling the sizeable pot of M&M's toward her already considerably larger pile. "Fa-git about it, Nash. I don't cheat, and if I did, you'd never catch me at it."

Drake gathered the cards to shuffle for the next deal. "I guaran-damn-tee I'd be able to tell if she was cheating, Nash, but she's not. She's just lucky, that's all."

Annie chuckled, feeling more relaxed than she had since before New Year's Eve, partly thanks to the three bottles of Abita beer she'd already put away. "Sorry to bust your bubble, boys, but you're both wrong. If I was known for my luck, I wouldn't be stuck here with you two clowns. And Nash, I never cheat. I don't have to. I'm just that good." Her tone held no tinge of boastfulness, just fact.

Drake frowned at her. "Well, I'm wondering how you got so damn good."

Annie shrugged and smiled secretively. "It'll cost you M&M's to find out." She sent him a wink.

Drake snorted. "I don't need to know that bad. You already have nearly every flippin' M&M in the house. What are you going to do with all of those?" He eyed her pile of candy.

"Eat them, of course." She popped a handful in her mouth and munched noisily. She lifted a single brown candy and squinted, trying to align it with Drake's eyes. "Anyone ever tell you your eyes are the same color as brown M&M's?"

Drake grinned at her. "Not that I can recall."

"Well they are. The exact. Same. Color." She popped the candy in her mouth. "M&M's are heavenly, but the brown ones are my favorite. They always seem to taste better than the others."

Nash shook his head. "You are so drunk. They all taste exactly the same."

"Am not, and not to me, they don't." She held up another brown one. *Yep, same color.*

The ring of Annie's landline had Nash getting up to lower the country music blaring from the computer's surround sound. He leaned toward the phone. "Who is it?"

"It says unknown caller." She smiled and reached for the phone. "I'm sure it's Publisher's Clearing House asking where to mail my million dollars."

"Why don't you ask for it in M&M's—cut out the middle man all together?" Drake suggested.

Annie picked up her cordless phone, still laughing over the comment. "Hello?"

"Damn sweet thang, if I'd a known you'd be this happy to hear from me, I'd a called you sooner."

She sucked in her breath before signaling Nash to begin the trace he'd set up with the Sheriff's department. She heard J.B.'s sadistic cackle from the opposite end of the line.

"Yeah, go ahead and have those two ol' boys try to trace this call, sweetheart. I won't be on long enough for that. I just wanted to remind you that all the bodyguards in the world ain't gonna protect you from me.

Sooner or later, you'll get tired and let your guard down. When you do, I'll be there to let you know how bad you screwed up. I already got it all planned out—everything I'm gonna do to that sweet little body of yours."

"Too bad you never had anyone decent in your life to teach you to pick on people your own size." Annie's voice shook throughout her comment, even though she was more pissed off than afraid. It really irked her that he felt confident enough to do something like this. "I bet when you were in the third grade you were bullying kids in kindergarten. That's assuming you even made it to the third grade, you ignorant hillbilly." She splayed one hand to placate a wild-eyed Drake as J.B. guffawed, seeming to enjoy himself tremendously.

"That's right, little miss, you go right ahead and act all full of piss and vinegar. It'll be that much more fun to break you. It's always the best part— the look on their faces when they figger it out."

"Figure what out, J.B.? That you're just a pathetic little man who picks on women because he can't hold his own in a fight with a real man?"

"When they realize there ain't no way out. You'll figger it out too, just before I strangle the life out of you."

"You're an animal." Annie's skin crawled at J.B.'s sadistic laughter.

"Before you go to bed tonight, think about me and all the things I'm gonna do to you when I get my hands on you agin."

"You don't s-scare me." She bit down against the terror threatening to engulf her.

"Aw, now you'll have to go to confession. A good Catholic girl like you knows it's a sin to lie. You'll want that soul of yours lily white 'fore you die. Time's up, Annie. See ya soon."

Annie stared at the phone in her hand, the connection dead, before casting a glance in Liam's direction.

He shook his head. "We didn't get it."

She set the phone down then curled up on the end of the couch, wrapping herself in the afghan her grandmother crocheted for her sixteenth birthday. She pulled it tight against the chill that engulfed her, trying to minimize the uncontrollable chattering of her teeth, a simple nervous reaction.

She caught the looks Drake and Liam exchanged, both obviously concerned, both probably eager to hear the recorded end of that phone call. Neither seemed inclined to subject her to it again, and for that, she was grateful.

Annie's mood quieted immediately. Worse than that, she seemed to shrink before his eyes, turning within herself, as she scanned the windows in the living room—the ones with no bars. Drake leaned toward her. "Annie, would it help if you moved to one of the rooms with the bars on the windows?"

"I don't want to be alone."

"We'll all go." He extended his hand. "Come on, we can watch some flix on my mack-daddy-big-screen in my room. Anything you want." Nash and I will even rent you a chick flick from pay per view, how's that sound?"

She took his hand, keeping the afghan wrapped tightly around her shivering body. Her knees buckled upon standing, and Drake scooped her up before she hit the floor. "I've got you, Annie Girl." He held her protectively against him, worried, more than anything, that she didn't protest as he carried her to his bedroom.

He stopped just inside the doorway. "Turn on the light, would you, hon? My hands are kind of full." His comment got no rise from her, aside from doing what he asked. More cause for concern because it was totally out of character for her. He wanted the old Annie back—the hot little habanero who would never have let his comment slide without making some crack about him keeping his hands to himself, or else.

Drake deposited her gently on the king size bed he'd had delivered to her home several days earlier, urging her to crawl under the covers before he plumped pillows behind her head. He tucked her in securely then sat down next to her on the bed, leaning up against the wall. The big shock came when she curled up on her side and rested her head on his thigh.

His heart ached as her hands clutched the afghan in a white-knuckled grip. Drake grabbed the remote control in his left hand while rubbing her back with his opposite. He pulled up the pay per view guide to scan through the choice of movies. The wind picked up outside as the winter storm-front pushed through the area. Annie jumped with every bump and scrape of tree limb against the exterior of the house. She jolted to a sitting position at a loud racket outside, her eyes large and fixed on the blinds.

"It's just the trash can outside, hon. The wind knocked it over, that's all." Drake touched her arm, hoping to soothe her frazzled nerves. He intercepted a look from Nash at his approach. He didn't need to read minds to see how disturbed the man was. Must have been one hell of a conversation between Annie and that bastard, Montgomery.

Nash wiped the worry from his face. "Hey, can I crash this party?"

Annie edged over to make room for her bodyguard, who stretched out his long legs on the soft bed.

"Oh, yeah, now we're talking," he groaned. "This makes me homesick for my California King."

"I guess your feet hang off the edge of your bed too, huh Nash."

Liam shrugged. "Even when I lay down diagonally. I think maybe I'll just camp out on the sofa from now on."

Annie covered her face and groaned. "Oh, Liam. I'm so sorry. I never even thought about how uncomfortable you must be. I've been meaning to buy a new bed for that room, anyway—how about if we go pick one out for you tomorrow?"

Nash's low rumble of laughter filled the room. "All I need is to have my old Navy Seal buddies find out I whined about a soft bed with a real roof over my head. I'd never hear the end of it."

Drake watched as Annie bit her lip in contemplation, scanning his bed from one corner to the other. "This bed is huge. I bet there's plenty enough room for the two of you."

Drake exchanged a look with Nash, who was equally horrified by the suggestion. They simultaneously turned to Annie and shook their heads.

Annie looked perplexed. "Why not?"

"We're grown men," Nash said.

"Heterosexual men," Drake added.

"And we sure as *hell* aren't sharing the same bed," Nash insisted.

"It's out of the question." Drake agreed, whole heartedly.

Annie shook her head. "Guys are so stupid. Two women wouldn't have a problem with that at all."

"Yeah, well—we do, so get over it," Drake admitted.

Nash grinned as he ruffled Annie's hair. "Don't worry about it, kiddo. I've slept in a lot worse places, I assure you. It doesn't take long to work the kinks out in the morning." He twisted and bent his back at the waist. "Now, what are we watching tonight? I hear it's ladies choice."

"What's on?"

Drake went through the menu and Annie made him stop at an older Vin Diesel movie about street racing. "Oh, I missed this one at the theaters. I was too busy studying for finals to see it when it came out."

Drake gave her a perplexed look. "Are you sure? Don't think you have to watch this on our account."

"I'm not. Contrary to what you have Lewis believing, I think *Vin* is the man."

"Whatever you want is fine by me," Nash said.

"Me . . . too," Drake gasped, pulling an imaginary dagger from his heart, until she laughed. He gave her a big smile. "You can think what you want about Vin. I guess it's only fair."

"Sure it is. What's not fair is the two of you being inconvenienced and overburdened with worrying about me all the time."

Nash guffawed. "As much as I enjoy having you as a client, Short-Shit, this is my job. I'm paid well to be inconvenienced, and I'm *not* overburdened. Now Drake, on the other hand . . ." He paused to give her a wink. "He may be here for an entirely different reason."

Drake met Annie's gaze without the barest hint of a smile. "She knows why I'm here, and I'm not going anywhere, unless she makes me." He reached out and chucked her chin gently as she swallowed and turned away from whatever it was she thought she saw in his eyes.

"You have a new business, Drake. I feel guilty because you're taking so much time away. It hasn't been that long for me, so I remember how difficult it is starting up with new clientele in a new location." Her fingers twisted the threads of the afghan into knots. "Nash is here now, and it's not necessary for you to stay. If you-If you feel you need to go."

Drake's heart beat like a jack hammer in his chest as she continued. Terror gripped his insides at the thought of leaving her home. Something told him she felt the same way, but knowing Annie as he did, she'd die before admitting it. She held her breath, waiting for his answer.

He sent Nash 'the look'—the unspoken man-language look—a throwback from ancient cave dwellers that. translated loosely, said "get the hell out" for one reason or another.

Nash cleared his throat and rose from the bed. "Think I'll go fix us some of that popcorn I saw in the pantry. Do we want kettle corn or regular with extra butter?" When neither of them answered, he cleared his throat again. "Kettle corn it is." He left the room, closing the door behind him.

Drake waited through several moments of uncomfortable silence before trusting himself to speak to the woman who sat with her head bowed and her eyes tightly shut. "Annie, look at me," he commanded. When she made no move to do so, he reached out, gently lifting her chin. He smiled, seeing that her eyes remained stubbornly closed. "Open your eyes please."

She did finally—blinking several times to clear the tears from them.

Drake ran his thumb along her lower lip as he spoke to her in a voice husky with emotion. "If you make me leave, I'll camp out on the street, right in front of this place. I'll never get a moment of rest, because I won't be satisfied unless I know you're safe. I'll patrol around the house several times a night, and I may even trip the alarm a time or two just to make sure you're okay."

He placed his hands on either side of her face, leaned in to place a feather-soft kiss upon her forehead before pulling her into his embrace. He released a long sigh as he rested his chin on her crown and made one final plea. "Please don't send me away."

Annie wrapped her arms tightly around his waist and released a shaky sigh.

"Does that mean I can stay?"

She answered in a small voice. "Yes, please."

Chapter Eighteen

As nice as it was, it didn't last nearly long enough. Annie pulled away, mumbling under her breath as she headed for the bathroom. She was barely out of sight when Drake hurried into the kitchen where Nash had the recording equipment set up on the end of the cabinet.

He picked up the headphones. "Okay, how do I make this thing play back?"

"It's already at the correct location. Just put 'em on and hit the red button."

Drake clamped and unclamped his jaw time and again while listening to the sadistic bastard's threats. He pulled the headphones off at the end of the recording and turned to Nash. "That son of a bitch *cannot* get his hands on her," he growled.

Nash shifted a big bowl of popcorn in his arms and replied in a low drawl. "I concur. That sadistic prick is enjoying this entirely too much. I don't like it. I don't like him scaring my client like that."

"Especially if he can do it right under our noses." Drake swore under his breath, stopping when he heard Annie's bathroom door opening. He turned as she entered the kitchen. "You ready to start the movie?"

She stopped to stare at her bodyguard's haul. "Hey Nash, I don't think that's enough popcorn."

Nash chuckled. "Yeah, I guess I got carried away."

Her brow furrowed. "No, I really don't think that's enough popcorn."

His tone turned sedate. "Seriously? I popped three bags."

Annie clucked her tongue as she pulled out another extra butter pack of popcorn. "You have completely underestimated my ability to put away some kernels." She placed the pack in the microwave and pushed the button.

Arms crossed, she leaned against the lower cabinet and stared at the recorder. "So, what did you boys think about this last call?"

Drake didn't hesitate before answering. "I think I should have killed the bastard when I had the chance."

"You don't really mean that, do you?" Her eyes widened with surprise.

Drake knew full well what he'd meant. He knew, without a shred of doubt, if he'd had the slightest inkling of what this guy was capable of that New Year's Eve night, he could easily have taken his life.

He also knew that, as an attorney, an upstanding American, and a Christian, that knowledge *should* scare the hell out of him.

It didn't.

The thought of J.B. putting his hands on Annie, or any other woman, and doing any of the things he mentioned in the call sickened him. The fact that this animal had the chance because of Drake's inaction on New Year's Eve . . . well, that was an even harder pill to swallow.

He made a show of checking his watch. "The movie will be starting up in five minutes."

"Popcorn will be another minute." Annie pulled a gallon of milk from the fridge.

Nash made a face. "You drink milk with popcorn?"

"Yup." Annie poured herself a huge glass. "There's something about the taste of them together. I swear I could eat it in a bowl of milk, just like cereal."

Drake's shoulders shook with laughter. "You're unique, Annie Girl. There's no denying that."

Annie poured her bag of popcorn into a separate bowl and grabbed her glass of milk. "Don't knock it till you try it, boys." She turned her back on them and headed for the bedroom.

"That's kinda weird, isn't it?" Nash whispered to Drake as he passed him a beer from the fridge.

Drake shrugged at the man. "Who's to say, buddy? You're talking to a guy who likes grape soda with chocolate cake." He laughed again as Nash shook off a frisson of pure disgust.

Within ten minutes of the opening credits, Annie was moaning at the leading man's bare chested appearance in front of the camera. "God, just look at that washboard stomach. His pecs are perfect, and those highly developed oblique muscles. Mmm-mm-mm. Now *that's* what I call love handles . . ."

Nash gave a disgusted snort. "He ain't so great. I have a nice pair of those, too, and I don't mind sayin' so."

"I do too, and we got ours without having our own personal trainer." Drake rose from the bed to strike a pose for her.

In seconds, Nash joined him and Annie had the sublime pleasure of watching her two buff-as-hell house mates alternate poses to showcase their own muscled physiques. She sat back on her pillow, wondering what she'd done so right today to deserve this display. She finally shook herself out of her reverie. "You two are just jealous, and there's no reason for it. I can appreciate how gorgeous *she* is." She indicated the leading lady gracing the large screen. "There's no way I could compete with her looks."

"Now see, that's a matter of opinion," Drake admitted. "I happen to think you compete very nicely."

Liam grinned. "Besides, we've seen what you look like first thing in the morning, all fresh faced, with no makeup. Your beauty is natural. We have no idea what those women look like without a makeup artist working on them for hours at a time."

Annie shrugged and settled back on the pillows they'd piled up.

The two men, obviously determined to make her forget her problems for the night, worked together to keep her in stitches throughout the feature. She managed to keep them amused as well. The fact that she knew a crankshaft, from a camshaft, from a piston, as well as her recognition of the makes and models of various muscle cars used in the movie, had them scratching their heads.

Drake asked her about it once the movie ended. "Okay, Annie, how the hell is it you know so much about cars?"

"I had older brothers whom I adored," she explained. "Chad was already off at college when I was about six or so, but Kenneth and Red were always working on some car. When I started bugging them with too many questions, they told me the only way I could stick around was if I made myself useful by handing tools to them. After years of watching and listening, I turned into a decent shade tree mechanic on the older models. Nobody can work on the newer ones without a diagnostic computer program."

Nash snorted, "And it costs an arm and a leg to fix anything."

"Yep," Drake agreed. "They completely took all the fun out of it."

Annie rolled her eyes at him. "Oh, please. You have never gotten grease under those fingernails. I bet you got your first car the day you turned fifteen and got your license. It was probably a Porsche or a BMW, or something straight off the showroom floor." The look he sent her made her want to sigh out loud, like he was certain he was about to say something that would absolutely rock her world.

"I probably could have, if that's what I wanted. But I asked for a '66 Mustang. Dad used to have one and I was hoping to get something we could work on together."

She studied him for a moment. "Did it work? Did the two of you work on it together?" She held her breath, waiting for his answer, and hoping it was yes. He shook his head, and the look he gave her made her want to cry.

"Nah, but I learned a hell of a lot about cars that summer. I loved that damn car," he said, wistfully.

"What color was it?" Annie asked.

"It was a black GT 350 with gold LeMans striping."

"Oh . . ." Annie breathed. "You had a Hertz. I never would have taken you for a 'muscle car' guy."

His mouth formed a crooked grin, giving him that boyishly sexy-as-hell look. "I never would have taken you for a girl who knew a muscle car from a VW Beetle, so I guess we're even."

Annie fought the strongest urge to reach out and run her fingers over his lips. Damn, but the man looked good enough to eat tonight, with his rumpled hair and shadow of a beard. Her gaze wandered down to his T-shirt; just right tight, and white, stretched over his sculpted chest like he was poured into it. He probably could give Vin Diesel a run for his money.

She let her gaze trail down to his legs, covered in jeans that fit snugly at the waist and thighs, down his calves to his socked feet, crossed casually at the ankles. Her perusal migrated back to his muscular thighs, and a little further up where her gaze froze on the bulge in his jeans.

Annie jerked her head forward. Heat, started at the base of her skull and flooded her face with an immediate flush of embarrassment.

Drake cleared his throat quietly while pulling a pillow over himself.

Annie excused herself for the privacy of her own bathroom. She splashed cold water on her flushed cheeks, patted her face dry. Her guilty reflection stared back at her from the mirror. "For God's sake, Annie. Pull. Yourself. Together."

She suddenly froze, overwhelmed with the certainty that she was falling for Drake LeBlanc. Fast and hard.

No. She had to stop this foolishness. This couldn't happen. She had to get this man out of her house before it was too late. She knew this. So why did the thought of him leaving send her into full-blown, anxiety ridden, panic mode?

If only there was some way to speed up this process of catching J.B. Montgomery. She wanted him behind bars so her life would go back to normal. She wanted things back the way they were. With her, comfortable in her own home . . . safe, relaxed, with no Nash, and definitely *no Drake*.

A tightness in her chest told her that time was running out. If she gave in to the temptation of caring about Drake, she knew from experience it would cost her more than she was able to give.

The gears in her mind clicked and spun at a rapid rate, grabbing at a scene from the movie they'd just watched. In minutes, she'd formed a solid plan that just might work.

Nash cleared his throat as he collected dirty dishes from the room. "I'm going to hit the sack now, if it's okay by you."

Drake nodded. "Fine by me, but you may want to clear that with Annie. As scared and antsy as she's been, she might want you to sleep in her room tonight." Nash's chuckle caught him by surprise.

"No denying she's antsy, and she might even be scared. It's not so much of old J.B. as the fact she's fighting a losing battle. Good job, LeBlanc." Nash sent him a wink before walking back to the kitchen.

Drake waited for Annie's return, stopping to consider Nash's comment. Was it possible? Was she starting to have the same feelings for him as he did for her?

He stood tall when Annie exited her room, determined to speak to her about it, bit back his disappointment when she bypassed his room for the kitchen. The hushed tone of Annie's conversation to her bodyguard caused his curiosity to peak. He entered the kitchen quietly, just in time to hear the tail end of her last comment.

"—but he knows not to come around when I'm constantly surrounded, and he knows not to stay on the phone too long. I think setting him up would work."

Setting him up? What the hell was she talking about? "Like how?" His question obviously surprised her, judging by the way she jumped at the sound of his voice.

"I'm not sure, but I think we need to lure him out somehow."

Drake pinned her with an angry glare. "Lure him? And what would we use as bait, Annie?" He saw the angry, but determined lift of her chin and braced himself to hear the words he didn't want to hear.

"I'll be the bait."

Drake got nose to nose with her and growled his reply. "Like hell you will."

She raised a hand. "Hear me out, Dra—"

"No. You will not put yourself at risk, Annie. I won't have it." She nearly gave in, nearly took a step back from his justified anger. But *nearly* didn't hold much clout in Annie's world.

He recognized the instant she got her nerve back. She wasn't about to back down from this. She stood her ground, her nostrils flaring angrily as she seemed to bow-up before his eyes. He likened Annie getting pissed to a bantam weight fighter pumping himself up for a prize match.

"You won't have it?"

Her tone was a hell of a lot more serene than he'd expected. More than likely, it meant he was about to witness a level of determination in the little lady he'd yet to experience.

"Who the hell are you to have any say in how I decide to handle this?"

Drake clamped his jaw shut before taking hold of her arms. "I'm the man who—" He stopped short, searching out Nash, who stood there wearing a shit-eating grin, and looking like he had a front row seat at afore-mentioned prize match. Drake hit the doorway, pulling Annie behind him. "I want to talk to you, *now!*"

She tried to pull away from him. "Let go of me, dammit!"

He didn't let go, but pulled her into his room, slammed the door behind him.

She turned on him, her eyes sparking with fury. "What the hell do you think you're doing? You're not my father, and I don't take orders from you."

Drake pulled her close "I'm sure as hell *not* your father. And no, you don't have to take orders from me. I will tell you who I am, though. I'm the man who loves you more than my own life." He barely recognized his own voice, hoarse with a disturbing combination of passion, terror, and determination. "I'm the man who could easily kill anyone who threatens to physically hurt you. And I will not stand for you putting yourself in danger."

He took several deep breaths to calm himself before he continued. "You can fight me on this all you want, but I'm telling you again, you'd do better to accept this now, because I'm not changing my mind, and I'm sure as hell not going anywhere."

Her reaction startled him. Her eyes widened with surprise just before her lids drooped. Judging by the way she'd previously ogled him, he knew she was sexually attracted to him. Based on her quickened pulse, and the slight pant in her breathing, it was kicking in.

Drake leaned in slowly, brushed her lips with a soft kiss, amazed at his own self-control. God knew he was already so damn close to the edge. He pulled back enough to stare into startled blue eyes—swore he could see the faces of their children in those eyes. He passed his hand through her auburn curls and caught her beautiful face between his two hands.

"Whether you're willing to admit this or not, I'm your future, Annie." He kissed her, molding his mouth to fit the satiny contours of her lips.

They fit, melded so perfectly that he hated to end it. He did, eventually, giving her several soft nibbles on her lower lip before finally pulling away. His breath caught at the sight of her, eyes closed, long lashes resting on the fairness of her peachy cream cheeks. Her lashes fluttered once, then again as her lids opened drowsily to peer up at him.

Just when he thought he'd won the battle, she seemed to awaken to the war within herself. She focused and pulled away, wiping her mouth with trembling fingers.

She stepped back, distancing herself. "I don't know who my future is, Drake. But, it's not you. It can't be you."

"I am. I've never wanted this before, not with any woman. From the moment I saw you, I felt the pull. Something linking the two of us. Something that made me stay and wait for your return.

I wasn't the type of man who needed to wait on a woman, Annie. But I sensed you were worth waiting for. And you were. You *are*. So. Worth. The wait."

He leaned in, kissed her softly, despite wanting nothing more than to lose control with her in his arms. This situation was different. She was different. He had to make her see.

Once more, she pushed away from him. "Stop. I can't do this, Drake." She looked up, her eyes brimming with tears. Pleading without words— wanting him to understand something he couldn't possibly understand. To accept something he couldn't possibly accept. "I swear to you, I have good reason."

Drake held on to her, determined to hear it all this time. "What reason? Tell me so I can reassure you there's no reason to fear loving me."

She shook her head frantically, still trying to pull away, looking as though she would turn inside out if she could to keep her secret hidden away within herself.

He gave her a gentle shake, until she met his gaze. "Trust me, Annie. That's all I'm asking for tonight. Only your trust."

"It's too much to ask of me, Drake. I did that once before and it nearly—" She gulped, gasped for air. "I-I came so close to-to losing everything." She pulled away from him.

He shook his head, refusing to move from his spot in front of the door. "I'm not letting you out of here until you tell me what happened. Whatever that *boy* did to you is not enough to keep yourself closed off from the man standing before you now."

She covered her face and groaned. "It's nothing to do with what he did to me. It only has to do with what I nearly did. That's what haunts me." She lifted her tear-filled gaze to meet his. "I've never spoken to anyone about this, Drake. Not even my parents . . . especially not my parents. And I can't talk to you about it now."

Drake ached for her. He could see how badly it haunted her, this past she kept locked away. He nearly decided to let it go, again, until he remembered something her father said.

"Are you sure your parents don't already know? Your dad mentioned a letter." The immediate transformation of her facial expression, from haunted to horrified, revealed he'd stumbled onto the key.

"What was in it, Annie?" He approached slowly, pulling her into his arms. "I'm begging you to trust me with this."

"Oh, dear God. M-my parents knew about the letter?"

He nodded, waiting several moments until she had time to let it soak in before continuing. "Your dad went home one day and found your mother sitting in the middle of your bedroom floor, crying over a letter she'd found. You were already in college. Who wrote you that letter, Annie? Was it T.J.?"

"D-dad didn't tell you?"

Her face paled to a shade he'd never seen on anyone with a pulse. "No, hon. He said it wasn't his place to tell me." He reached out and captured her face gently between his hands. "Please, Annie. I want *you* to tell me. I'm begging you to trust me with this, to help me to understand."

Her eyelids drifted shut. Her head fell forward against his chest. He heard the shakiness of her sigh, prayed she'd soften. By the time she lifted her gaze to meet his, he knew he'd won this particular battle.

"It was a bad time for me, Drake. I'd known T.J. all my life and we were best friends when we started dating. After the first year, everyone sort of took it for granted that we'd marry. I know I did, but looking back on it now, maybe he never did want me."

"He was an idiot if he thought he could ever do better than you." Drake hovered somewhere between being thankful to the asshole and wanting to smash his face in. "I know he chose UCLA over LSU, where you wanted to go."

Annie crossed her arms tightly. "He didn't choose UCLA over LSU, Drake. He chose California over me, and I told him to go. I was young and still believed in the fairytale ending back then. I believed with all my heart that he'd come back to me. Especially after . . ."

She had to pause, take another breath before she continued. "After two long years of dating him and holding on to my virginity, I finally let go of it after senior prom." She glanced up when Drake grunted in disapproval, quickly added to her comment. "He didn't force me, or give me an ultimatum, or anything. I chose to do it."

She looked away from him then. "I thought if I made that sacrifice, then surely, he wouldn't want to leave me." She shrugged, as though she were embarrassed by the whole thing. "I thought it was very nice, but he obviously didn't enjoy it, because the very next day is when he told me we should split up. It seems our first sexual encounter was his driving influence to choose California over me."

"Hello, Mr. Sensitivity," Drake snorted, unable to hide his disgust. "And if all you can say about it is 'it was very nice', I guaran-damn-tee he enjoyed it a hell of a lot more than you did." His jaw clenched at another thought. "Was he aware ahead of time? I mean, your plans for prom night— or did you just kind of spring it on him after the dance?"

"Oh no, we'd discussed it. He'd made reservations at a hotel in a nearby town and everything. We'd planned for it, taken precautions. But the worst part for me was after he left for California a few weeks later. It's like he cut me out of his life. No letters, no calls, nothing. I lost my best friend and my boyfriend at the same time."

"So, he waited until you put out on prom night then broke it off with you. Is that the letter your mom found? Is that how he did it? In a crappy letter?"

Her head fell forward. "T.J. didn't write that letter, Drake. I did." She faced him again, her cheeks now streaked with tears. "I wrote the letter to my parents."

Drake shook his head. "Am I missing something? Were you planning to leave town?"

She shook her head. "My dad was right," she whispered. "I was clinically depressed. T.J. left for California a few weeks after graduation and for two months I couldn't function. I couldn't eat, I couldn't talk to anyone about it. What was I going to say? Hey Mom and Dad, I lost my virginity to T.J. and he left me anyway? I couldn't talk about it."

Annie shook her head slowly. "I just . . . shut down. My parents finally had enough. They came to me one day and said how worried they were. I remember it was a Sunday and it was just after lunch. They said if I didn't snap out of it soon, they'd bring me to a doctor for the help I needed. I asked them to leave me alone for the rest of the day. I promised them I'd be fine by that night."

She squeezed her eyes shut and took a deep breath before releasing it slowly. "I went into my room and wrote that letter to them. I asked them to forgive me. I put it on my desk where'd they'd be sure to find it, and then locked myself in my bathroom."

Dread sucked the breath right out of Drake. It washed over him, left him too terrified to utter a single word. All he could do was wait for her to gather her courage and continue. She finally did, her voice low, calm, the only sound in the room.

"I filled a tub with hot water and got inside. I covered myself with a towel so they wouldn't have to find me completely naked." She stared down at her hands and continued in a quiet voice. "I stayed in that tub with a razorblade clenched in my fingers. When the water got cold I refilled it with hot water."

She stood there, twisting the birthstone ring on her finger. Drake thanked God that she hadn't gone through with taking her own life a dozen years ago. He reached out to cover her hands, stilling them, hoping his touch would give her the strength to continue. He wanted her to put an end to the story, to put all her demons to rest.

"I lost count of how many times I did that," she whispered. "But once I realized I couldn't do it, I looked at my watch and it was nearly eight p.m. A fog seemed to suddenly lift from my mind, and I knew I'd be fine. I only cried once more, and not because of T.J. It was when I finally realized what it would have done to my parents if I'd gone through with it. How it would have devastated them to find me like that."

She placed her hands on her abdomen as though she were nauseous. "All these years later and I still get sick inside thinking about it, Drake. That's why I hate you calling me Annie Girl. T.J. called me that, so it reminds me of that time in my life." She met his gaze then. "And now you're telling me my parents have known all this time."

He reached out, brushed his hand over her silken curls. "Why'd you keep the letter? Was there was a part of you that wanted them to find it?"

She shook her head. "I should have destroyed it. I only kept it to remind myself of what I was capable of doing. To remind myself not to let anyone ever get that close to me again."

"But you weren't capable of it, Annie. You didn't even attempt it."

"I did attempt it. I tried my damnedest to do it."

He reached out for her wrists. "Show me the scars, Babe." He examined first one wrist, then the other, passing his fingers over the soft, smooth area of her inner wrists. "You can't show me any scars, because you couldn't do it. You grieved over your loss for two months, but you finally decided he wasn't worth taking your own life over. Don't you see that?"

"I have scars, Drake. Maybe not on my wrists, but they exist." She pulled her hands from his and placed them over her heart. "Here." Annie's gaze clashed with his, the look in her eyes hard with certainty. "And you're right, Drake. T.J. wasn't worth it. But I'm afraid you would be. If I could come so close over a high school fling, imagine what I could if I lost you."

Drake pulled her into his arms and hugged her tightly. "You wouldn't lose me, Annie. I swear you wouldn't. God, if you would just give me one chance to show you how much I love you." He kissed her eyes, tasting the warm saltiness of fresh tears. "So does that mean you love me?"

Annie's chest heaved with the sobs she tried to hold back. With a final surge of will power, she pushed away from him. "I couldn't survive losing you, for any reason. I can't risk it."

"How do you feel about me, Annie? I need to hear it."

She shook her head. "You know how I feel. Don't make me say it."

"No chance. I need to hear it from your own beautiful lips." He leaned in to place a gentle kiss on her lips, smiled at the low, sensual moan that escaped her.

She pushed away from him and tried to turn away. "It won't do any good to admit anything because nothing can become of it."

He put both hands on her shoulders, keeping her in place. "So, you'd let something that happened a dozen years ago keep you from being happy for the rest of your life?"

"We might have six good months, maybe a year before you'd realize we're just too different to be together. Then, once you left, I'd be miserable for the rest of my life."

"But, you're miserable now."

"Only because you're *here*. Always in my face, and in my head. That's why I need to get this situation with J.B. resolved, so that we can both go back to living our lives normally. These feelings are only the results of two people being thrown together. They won't last."

"How the hell do you know that? Your parents lasted."

She lifted her chin. "My parents are a special case. They were meant to be together."

"So are we."

"Sexual attraction isn't love, Drake. You, of all people, should know that."

"I'm not denying we have the sexual attraction. I'm only denying that's all it is. I'm in love with you, Annie. I want to marry you, live the rest of my life with you, and raise babies together. I want it all with you."

"Don't you think I've made those plans before?" Her eyes were wild with frustration. "I had it all planned out with T.J. We'd marry and live in married housing at LSU. In this order," she said, holding up five fingers and counting them off. "We would get our degrees, set up practices next to each other, build a two story home complete with four bedrooms and white picket fence, child number one, a boy, we'd name Thomas Jared the 3rd after his father and grandfather and finally—child two, a daughter, named Jeri Nicole. They would have been perfect children, and we'd have been the perfect family. I made all those plans, Drake. I dreamed all those dreams, for all the good it did."

Drake shook his head. "You just dreamed and planned with a boy, hon. Let me show you how to plan a life with a real man."

"A real man, a real love. All that means is that I'll lose myself then have a real broken heart when it doesn't work out."

Drake lifted her hand and rubbed it gently against his face. "We'll work out, Annie. I swear it on my life."

"You don't know that, and I can't take the chance." She pulled her hand back. "That's my final answer." She retreated a few steps, obviously to put distance between them.

"I want to work with the police and Nash to set up J.B., to lure him out into the open. I'm tired of hiding away like some scared animal. It's time for me to go on the offensive and help the cops put him away. As soon as that's done, you'll have to leave here, and other than family functions, I don't want to see you again."

Drake grabbed at her hand when she turned to walk out. "Annie, you don't mean that."

All four foot, eleven or so inches of her pivoted to meet his gaze. "I damn sure do." She pulled away and walked out, leaving him alone in the room.

Drake stood in the space he called his own for the time being, sick with disappointment, though far from ready to give in and accept defeat. One glance at his king-size bed made him more determined than ever to make her see how good they would be together. He'd settle for no less than a lifetime with her.

He entered the kitchen just in time to catch another snippet of Nash and Annie's conversation.

"—it should happen at Red's club. We could make J.B. believe that you and I have had a falling out. I could walk outside alone and he'd probably follow me out there."

"Or be waiting for you already," Drake said, his voice icy.

She turned to look at him. "Yes, maybe he'd be waiting for me. Either way, Nash would be there to protect me."

"Where would I be?" he asked.

"You wouldn't be around, Drake. You're not a part of this."

He smiled and gave her a slow nod. "Like anything you say could keep me away from you."

Nash cleared his throat, sounding uncomfortable being caught up in their war of wills. "If you're sure this is what you want to do, I'll contact the Lake Coburn police to work with us. I think we should plan this for a week or so."

Drake recognized the look of determination on her face.

"I think we should plan it for this weekend. The sooner we get this over with," she met Drake's gaze head on. "The better."

Chapter Nineteen

Drake sat with Annie and Nash at the table the next morning, discussing strategies. This plan was getting too real, too damn close for comfort. Any minute, Red would be there with a set of his club's floor plans. The sweet aroma of cookies baking in the oven should have been a comfort. It would have been if he didn't know that Annie only baked when she was nervous.

Liam tapped a felt tipped pen on the pad in front of him. "The Lake Coburn PD, as well as the Sheriff's office are willing to work with us, but they all agree we should wait a week."

Drake gave a grunt of minor satisfaction at the delay, already planning a week's worth of strategies to convince Annie they belonged together. He kept his gaze on her, trying to gauge her tension level. If her constant fidgeting and refusal to make eye contact with him was any indication, it was off the damn charts. When the oven timer went off, she practically dove out of her chair, and then nearly dropped the pan of cookies when the doorbell rang soon after.

Nash answered the door, returning with Red McAllister. As soon as Annie's big brother entered the room, Lewis began to squawk his name until Red opened the cage door and let him climb onto his shoulder.

"Hey Lewis, old buddy, how's life treating you?"

"Red's home!" Lewis cried.

"Yeah, you missed me didn't you? Who's the man, Lewis?"

"Drake's the man."

"The hell you say!" Red looked at Drake and laughed. "I guess I've been replaced."

Drake grinned at his brother in law. "I had to do it, man. My fragile self-esteem was taking a beating with that whole 'prick' thing."

Annie snorted from her seat at the table. "Your male ego, you mean."

Red grinned again. "Same thing, ain't it?" He leaned over to give her a hug. "Hang in there, Sis." He straightened, and turned to Drake again. "But, really. You haven't been here that long. Big bird must really approve of you, if you trained him that quickly."

"We have an understanding, and it helps that I feed him and fat boy, here." Drake leaned over to pet Martin, who sat at his feet purring loudly.

Annie spoke from her chair. "He cheats, bribes them with food."

Red grinned at his sister. "Ah, there's the truth."

"Yep. He gives them food I don't allow them to have."

"I gave Lewis pistachios, once. That does not constitute cheating," Drake said, on his own behalf.

Red's brow furrowed, as though he were confused. "I thought Lewis could eat pistachios."

"He can have plain ones, but Drake sneaks him salted pistachios every chance he gets, when he *thinks* I'm not watching," Annie said. "Lewis loves them but the salt isn't good for him and now he won't eat them any other way." She glared at the offender. "You've ruined my bird."

"Jealous, Annie? I'd spoil you too if you let me." Drake beamed, pleased at the resulting blush he'd gotten out of her. "Besides, I'm going to miss them when you chase me out of here . . . *if* you chase me out of here." His gaze locked on Annie as she moved around the room making minor adjustments to her never-ending collection of photos.

Red grunted, an amused smirk breaking out over his face. "That's not all you'll miss, I bet."

Drake met his brother-in-law's gaze. "How's my sister doing?"

Read beamed at mention of his wife. "She's doing great, other than the mood swings and morning sickness, which seems to be worse in the evenings. My poor girl is thankful for all those saltines and bottles of ginger-ale I hoarded for her. But, man, she is growing absolutely more beautiful every day."

Nash's gaze softened inexplicably. "How far along is she?"

"Barely two months, and I'm looking forward to every minute of it."

The bodyguard paused, seemed to retreat to some other time, then shook himself out of it. "Your first?"

Red nodded. "Hopefully not the last, though. She's thirty-six and we want to try for at least one more after this one. The health risks are higher for older women, you know, but she's healthy and is fanatical about eating right and taking her supplements."

"It doesn't hurt that she's a doctor, either," Annie added. "Want some coffee and home-made cookies, big brother? I just took a batch out of the oven."

"Hell yeah." He examined the plate of cookies that Annie placed on the table. "These aren't Lewis's cookies, are they?"

Drake leaned in closer. "No, but his aren't bad either."

"Dude! You ate his cookies?"

"I didn't know they were his cookies at the time. They smelled great and I was hungry. She never did tell me what she puts in them."

"Don't you put roaches or grasshoppers in those things?" Red asked, obviously struggling to keep a straight face.

Drake swung around to face Annie. "No—huh?"

Annie giggled. "Of course not. Roaches spread disease, and grasshoppers—well, Lewis refuses to eat them fresh, freeze-dried, or otherwise."

Drake finally released the breath he'd been holding.

"But he adores crickets," she added.

Drake groaned and held his belly.

Red laughter finally died off, and he faced his sister. "Do the three of you have any plans for the day? Tiffany wants y'all over for lunch. She misses you two and she'd like to meet Liam."

Annie sobered immediately. "I'm not going over there. It'll only put Tiff in danger of becoming J.B.'s next target."

Red looked from Annie, back to Drake, who sent him a nod. "He's not above it, Red. He seems to thrive on risking confrontation."

Red put Lewis back in his cage and placed his hand on Annie's lower back. "Excuse me guys, but I need a word alone with my little sister." Without another word, he led her down the hallway into her bedroom.

Annie's bedroom door shut with a soft click, signaling the all clear to walk with head bowed into Red's open arms. It may well be a mistake to give in to her frustration and fear, but she couldn't help but break down in the comfort of her big brother's embrace.

He let her cry, waiting until her sobs turned to sniffles to speak. "I can totally relate to this, you know. Hell it was barely a month ago that Tiff and I were going through the same thing."

"It's all so awful, Red. I can't even go to church without having someone spy on me and feel me up. I'd love to visit with you and Tiff, but I'm afraid to get anyone else involved in this mess." She took the Kleenex he handed her from the box on her dresser and wiped her eyes. "And Drake—oh God, I don't know what the hell to do about Drake." She frowned, a little annoyed at her brother's I-know-all-about-it grin.

"Has he been staking his claim?"

She made a face. "How archaic. *Gold-rush* talk for him coming on to me?"

"Don't get all touchy with me, you know what I'm talking about. Has he been pushing you to—you know." He pulled uncomfortably at the collar of his shirt.

Annie gave a hysterical laugh and punched him on the arm. "Jesus, Red. We're both adults, here, aren't we? And no, he skipped right past asking to have sex and jumped straight to 'I want to marry you', 'I'm your future and you're mine' . . . that kind of sappy stuff." She frowned at her brother's smug look, like he'd been privy to a handful of deep, dark secrets.

"Hon, I know how he feels about you, so I guess I'm not seeing what the problem is. Are you trying to tell me you don't love him?"

She sucked in her breath. There it was. *That* word again. She shivered with what her mom called 'the frissons' as her brother burst into loud, bawdy laughter.

"I can't tell, Sis." He gasped, trying to catch his breath. "Coming from you, that reaction could either mean you're crazy about him, or you want to wring his neck."

She groaned, furious at being put in this situation. "What if I let him get too close? What happens when, one day, he realizes he gave up six-foot-tall models for this?" She used her hands to indicate her own body. "I'd be humiliated all over again."

Red's countenance turned seriously sober. "Is it the humiliation you're afraid of, or the heartbreak?"

She didn't answer, didn't even want to look at him.

Red stepped closer and put both hands on her shoulders. "Hon, you can't hide out for the rest of your life. You're not giving yourself much credit. You're older, stronger than you were back then. It's okay to let yourself be happy, Annie."

"No, it's not. You don't know." She shook her head, feeling more miserable by the second.

"I know."

"No, you don't." She squeezed her eyes shut against the memories.

Red used one hand to lift her chin. "Annie, look at me."

She did, saw by the look in his eyes that he did know. He knew everything. Once it sunk in, she pushed away from him. "Oh hell, what did Mom and Dad do? Call a family conference and tell everyone?"

He shook his head. "No, it wasn't anything like that. Other than them, I'm the only one who knows. A couple of years ago, I was on their asses to make you move out on your own. I called Mom an enabler and she broke down and ran off in tears."

"You made Mom cry? Was Dad around?" She struggled to remember if her brother had sported any broken bones around that time.

Red chuckled. "Yep. Not too smart, huh?"

"You'd think the Summa cum Laude graduate would know better," she snorted.

"The old man got in my face." He ran one hand through his hair, and grimaced. "Man, I hadn't seen Dad that pissed since Chad got caught target practicing on mailboxes."

"Chad . . ." She shook her head. "Now *there's* a dumb-ass."

"No shit." Red shook his head. "Anyway, he ended up blurting out the whole story."

Annie crooked her brow, still confused. "Yet for the nearly two years after that, you've stayed on my butt for still being at home."

One side of his mouth turned up at the corner in a crooked grin. "I've always stayed on your butt. It's the youngest siblings thing. If I'd started treating you differently, wouldn't you have suspected something was up?"

Annie thought about it before nodding. "Absolutely." She shook her head and laughed. "I never thought I'd be saying this, but thanks for being an asshole, Red."

Red grinned and drew her to him for a hug. "Anytime, shit-head. But seriously, don't let what happened in the past stop you from being happy now. It's okay to reach out for it."

She shook her head sadly. "I don't know, Red. I don't think I can right now. Maybe in a few years I'll feel differently."

"Maybe in a few years, so will Drake."

Annie shrugged. "He only met me two months ago. If he can't wait for me, then he definitely doesn't deserve me."

"Now *that* sounds more like the pain-in-the-ass-Annie I know and love." He pushed her playfully.

Annie sobered suddenly. "I told Drake everything, you know."

"You did?"

She nodded. "He's the one that told me Mom and Dad knew about the letter. Dad mentioned it to him without letting him know what was in it. Sometimes, I think my entire family is conspiring to throw us together."

Red nodded and gave her the barest hint of a smile. "What did you tell him, Sis?"

Annie's gaze locked with her brother's. "Everything. I told him everything. Things that weren't even in the letter." She smiled at the look of concern on his face. "I'm okay, Red. As long as I keep my heart protected."

Red cocked his head to the side and exhaled slowly. "I'll have to trust your judgment. You're the one that should know."

"Thanks for the confidence, and the shoulder." She reached up on her tiptoes and pulled him down the rest of the way until she could reach his cheek to give him a kiss. "You're my favorite brother, you know."

Red grinned then cracked open the door to call out to the other house guests. "Okay guys, we're coming out." He looked down at his sister. "I'm everyone's favorite."

Annie put all her weight into the shove she gave him. "Ugh, you are so full of yourself."

"Hey, little sister, don't start something you have no hope of winning." He gave her a one-handed shove back and sent her flying helplessly toward the open door. She lost her footing and the last thing she saw was him trying to catch her before she went sprawling backwards.

Annie would have landed with a thud on the hallway floor if Drake hadn't been there to catch her at the last second. She caught her breath as she looked up into his eyes, which had darkened with some unknown emotion. "Oh, thank you."

He leaned in close, as though to kiss her but stopped just short of her lips. "I'll always be here to save you from a rough landing, Annie. Always. You remember that." He straightened and righted her so she could stand on her own two feet. He faced his brother-in-law, extending one long finger in Red's direction. "You do that again and you'll have to answer to me."

Red raised both hands. "I hear you." He headed toward the front door. "Well, I'll go on home to tell my wife you three aren't coming for barbeque. I hate having to disappoint her, though."

"Better she be disappointed and safe than the alternative," Drake said. "That's my sister you're married to, don't forget."

Red looked back and nodded. "And don't you forget I'd give up my life to protect both the woman I love and our child." He glanced over at his youngest sister then back at Drake. "You'll see, one day."

Drake nodded. "I already do."

"Wait 'til there's a baby thrown into the mix." Red reached out to give Drake a reassuring pat on the back.

Drake turned slowly to face Annie. "From your mouth to God's ears, brother-in-law."

Annie's breath caught at the look of stark longing on Drake's face. She managed to clear her throat before slipping quietly from the room. She caught up with Nash in the kitchen and pulled him to a stop.

"What's up, Lil Bit?"

"We have to catch J.B. soon, Nash." She turned to watch Drake as he closed the front door and swiveled, a sexy smile plastered on that kissable mouth of his. His gaze seared her with its intensity, awakening her body to all kinds of wants and needs. She groaned and turned away from Mr.Sexy Texas transplant, knowing damn well she could only say no for so long.

"Please Nash. We have to."

Drake spent the next week, sitting for hours with Nash, their heads bent over the club's floor plans, memorizing every nook and cranny of the building. By the end of the week they had worked out a plan that even Drake believed was fool-proof enough to keep him from spinning off into full-blown-panic-mode.

When Annie's phone rang on Saturday morning, the label of unknown caller had her nodding at Nash, who immediately began the trace. She picked up the receiver, pushed the speaker button and took a deep breath before speaking, her face a mixture of trepidation and determination.

"Hello asshole."

"If it ain't little Annie McAllister."

"Yep. That's me," she replied, drawing out her speech, slowing it down as much as possible. "What happened, J.B.? Did you run out of kittens to drown? Or maybe you couldn't find a puppy to torture this morning? Or an old person to kick? Or is it that you enjoy having people laugh about your ineffective, red-neck threats to a woman less than half your size?"

For once, Drake prayed it *was* J.B. and not some poor salesman over the phone. Said asshole's evil chuckle had him tensing.

"Full of piss and vinegar mighty early this morning, aren't you, bitch? I like that. Like I said, it'll be way more fun to see the look on your face when you know you're gonna die."

At her first cringe, Drake approached her, hoping his presence would ground her, give her strength.

"I've been making plans all week long, coming up with new ways to play with my little bitch in heat. I've even decided to keep you alive a while longer so we can play some more. How many ways have you been fu—"

"You're a sick bastard." Drake's snarled reply cut off the vile question.

"Well, if it ain't old lover boy, there to protect the bitch's virgin ears. I'll bet that's the only thing virginal about that little tease."

"I sure as hell wish you'd come over here and fight like a real man so I can rid the world of you, you son of a bitch. I promise you, if I ever get my hands on you again, I won't stop until you're good and dead."

Nash pointed at his watch and nodded, encouraging him to keep going, to draw him in to the conversation as long as possible.

"You know, I read this study once while I was still in law school, J.B. There are tons of statistics proving that sexual predators, just like you, have usually been molested when they were kids by an older male. Who was it that molested you, J.B.? Was it a preacher? A teacher? A Boy Scout leader, maybe? Or an older kid down the street? Was it an uncle or some other relative? Or did somebody just make you their bitch in one of your prison stays?"

"You don't know what the hell you're talking about you mother fu—"

"Bingo!" Drake cut him off loudly. "We've got a winner! That's it, isn't it, Montgomery? I bet some big guy named 'Bubba' made you his bitch during a lock-up. I bet you liked it too, didn't you, J.B.?" J.B.'s furious roar sounded from the speaker. Nash grinned as he gave Drake the thumbs up sign, telling him he'd succeeded in keeping him on the line long enough to trace the call.

"You're both gonna die now, asshole! As a matter of fact, I'm gonna play with your little bitch girlfriend and kill her real slow-like while I make you watch. And there ain't gonna be a damn thing you'll be able to do about it."

Drake's voice hardened as he growled into the base of the phone. "Bring it on you ignorant piece of shit. I'm waiting for you. I can't wait to put the pointed toe of my size thirteen boot right up your ass. Of course, it'll probably get lost up in there, what with all the action you got from 'Big Bubba'. Who's the bitch now, J.B.?"

The air filled with a strangled yell of fury, then a long string of profanities before he stopped cold. The call cut off in the middle of one last angry roar.

Nash jumped up, punching the air in triumph. "Whoo-ee! You did good, Son! The Lake Coburn police are probably swarming the place right this second. With any luck at all, we won't have to go through with the plan tonight."

Drake kept his gaze on Annie. "That was the goal." He approached her, lowering his voice. "You okay?"

She nodded—too pale, too shaky. "God, I hope they pick him up."

He nodded. "Me too. I'm not looking forward to seeing you in any kind of danger tonight. Especially after I riled him up that way." Drake reached for her.

Before he could make contact, she lifted her chin and turned to face Nash. "How long before we know?"

An ear-splitting, satisfied grin covered Nash's face. "We should hear something within the next five or ten minutes."

Annie walked over to the couch and curled up on one end of it. Martin jumped up and laid protectively across her as she curled her fingers into his thick fur.

Drake was on his way to wearing a path in the carpet with steady pacing. He felt her gaze on him as he shoved his hands deep into the pockets of his jeans. He looked at his watch, passed a hand through his hair. By the time Nash's phone rang, he was ready to explode. He faced him, praying for good news.

Nash hit the button on his cell. "Nash here." He listened for a few seconds, then let loose with a Texas style holler. "They got the bastard!"

Drake rushed to Annie's side. She covered her face, trying to hide the onslaught of emotional tears. He pulled her close before she had a chance to resist.

"Shh . . ." He smoothed her hair. "It's okay now, Annie Girl." He closed his eyes, his voice husky with emotion and relief. "Thank you, God. I owe you one."

Nash watched the two people he'd come to respect, and hoped this would be the catalyst to bring them together at long last. Drake was right. Everyone could see they were perfect for each other. Everyone but Annie.

Annie McAllister. The tiny little woman who'd put both he and Drake in their places on more than one occasion. There would be a lot of passionate arguments between those two, no doubt. But, he knew from experience that the making-up would make everything worthwhile.

He smiled sadly as the thought brought to mind a memory he'd pushed to the far corners of his mind. *Kimberly.* It had been too damn long since he'd allowed himself to think about her, much less say her name out loud.

Annie spent the rest of the afternoon making phone calls to her relieved parents and siblings, telling them the danger was over. Drake called his dad and step-mom while Nash talked at length to Captain Woodard of the Lake Coburn police department, as well as the Kenton PD.

Nash ended his call and sent Annie a glorified grin. "Well, hell, little lady. I feel like celebrating. How about I take you both out for a meal at a fancy restaurant tonight?"

Annie had an inkling she'd miss the company of her two roommates. "I've got a better idea. How about if I cook one last meal for us then we can all go to Red's club to celebrate? It's got the coldest beer in town and the best country band around."

"Along with the prettiest girls in the south," Drake added, smiling at Annie.

Nash gave her a one-armed hug. "Sounds good to me, Lil Bit."

She craned her neck to look up at him. "Can you dance, Nash? Or are both of those huge feet of yours lefties?"

"Oh hell, honey." Nash gave her a wink and a smile. "Might be I could teach you a thing or two."

She laughed, feeling lighter, more carefree than she had in months. "I doubt it seriously, but don't let that stop you from giving it your best shot, Tex."

Chapter Twenty

By eight p.m. Drake had seated himself with Tiffany, Red, and some friends of theirs in the club filled to capacity. He nursed the same beer he'd started with, sipping as he kept his eyes glued to the doorway for Annie and Nash.

Earlier that afternoon, he'd loaded his truck with all his belongings except for the bed, and returned to his rental in Lake Coburn. As nice as Tiffany's old place was, he couldn't help but notice the place felt colder, bleaker, emptier than it ever had before.

No Martin to rub up against his leg, begging him for a scratch behind the ears. No Lewis belting out songs and calling him 'the man'. No Nash to watch boxing or any other sports with. Worst of all, no Annie. No beautiful blue eyes to sparkle when she was happy, or flash in anger when he'd said something to set her off.

Gone were the acidic comments in her frisky moments; the sweet smiles when she was feeling generous. God almighty, he was going to miss seeing Annie every day. He'd spent nearly every minute since then, praying that their separation would have the same effect on her.

"Hasn't anyone ever told you a watched pot never boils?"

Drake turned to answer the woman he recognized as a friend of Red and Tiffany's. "Sorry, I'm a little preoccupied."

"Looks as though you've grown accustomed to worrying about her."

He nodded. "I'm warning you. I'll be lousy company until they get here." He fidgeted under Angelique Baptiste's studious gaze.

"I think you must care about her a great deal."

"Does it show?"

Her head tilted in amusement. "*Absolument!* So why are you here instead of there with her?"

"I'd like to be. It's not what she wants. Not now, anyway."

"Ah, yes." Angelique gave him a knowing smile. "She's been hurt before. She's afraid you'll hurt her, too. Would you, Drake?"

Drake shifted his gaze to the door, this time to be rewarded by the sight of Annie walking in, followed closely by Nash. His broad smile covered his face, transforming his mood instantly. "Not for anything in the world."

"*Bon Dieu*, you're definitely in love with her."

Drake stood as Annie made a bee line for their table. "That, I am."

Angelique turned toward the door and gave a startled gasp. "Holy Mother, *he* is with her."

Drake grinned, recognizing blatant sexual attraction when he saw it. "You mean Nash? Have you met?"

She nodded. "I certainly have. *Cher bon Dieu*, let him be a dancer, *sil vous plait!*"

Annie and Nash began the long walk from the door to the table where Drake sat. Her heart skipped a beat when he stood, then again when he started walking to meet them halfway. She tried not to think about how good he looked in his contemporary cowboy attire. Jeans, a tailored navy blue shirt, western in cut, wearing a pair of high-end boots, and carrying a black Stetson. She'd tried to tell herself she wasn't dressing to please him tonight. He was only one of many men who would be at the club. He was one of a few men who may want to dance with her, or who may want to take her home with them. He, along with any others, would be disappointed when she told him no.

But her outfit tonight consisted of a short skirt, made of brown suede material, paired with knee-high stacked-heel-boots, and a form-fitting tan sweater. It was almost exactly the same outfit she'd worn the night she met him, and she'd worn it purposely. Call her a glutton for punishment, but she was curious to see if he'd remember what she'd worn that night. The tan sweater didn't show yet because she'd also thrown on her brown suede jacket that matched the skirt.

Drake met her with a smile and a quick hug before shaking her ex-bodyguard's hand. "Glad to see the both of you here. Nash, our table's over there in that corner."

Nash looked in the direction Drake had pointed and released a low whistle of admiration. "Holy crap. Angelique's here."

Drake grinned at him. "Yeah, she seemed damned glad to see you, too, for some reason. I didn't realize you two had met."

"Once in person, but several times in my dreams since then." Nash winked at his two former housemates. "Things are definitely looking up."

They made their way to the table, where Nash stopped in front of Angelique.

"Hello gorgeous, you interested in dancing with this old boy?"

She cast a glance down at his boots. "You're not going to step on my feet with those things are you, Liam? I'm not sure I'd recover."

Nash shook his head. "No ma'am, I won't. My Mom always said I learned to dance before I learned to walk, but you won't find out by sittin' on that pretty little butt of yours."

Angelique flashed him a brilliant smile as he helped her from the chair.

Annie watched them walk off. "He doesn't waste time, does he?"

"No reason to, once you know what you want, Annie Girl."

She tried to avoid his gaze in order to retain some semblance of a normal speech pattern. Even then it didn't stop her cheeks from heating under his perusal. She cleared her throat. "Are you settled in at your place?"

"Yes, and I hate it. The house is too damn quiet. No pets, no Nash—" He reached out to brush back a lock of her hair. "No you."

His outstretched hand came into her field of vision.

"Dance with me?"

Annie scanned the dance floor. Nash and Angelique were there, already wrapped in each other's presence, swaying to the slow belly-rubber from the country band. "Not to this. Ask me again when they play something less—"

"Tempting?" he finished for her.

"I was going to say slow."

"Coward."

"Absolutely." She headed off toward the bar without a backward glance.

Carrying their drinks, he followed her to the table as though there was a magic cord connecting them. She stopped to remove her jacket. He set the drinks on the table to help her out of it.

He lowered his head to her neck as he slid the suede slowly down her arms, breathing in the heady scent of her that turned him into a single minded man with a mission. God, if he could just get her alone for five minutes.

He draped the jacket over the back of her chair and pulled it out for her. She seated herself and scooted the chair closer to the table. He pulled out the chair next to her. "Nice threads," he said, pausing at the flash of disappointment registering on her face. He waited for her to give him a polite thank you before leaning in close so she could hear him. "I liked that outfit better with the tall heels you wore with it the night we met. Those boots cover up entirely too much of your gorgeous legs."

She turned to face him, obviously surprised at his confession. Drake lowered his head for a moment, trying to hide his satisfaction at her *wanting* him to recognize what she'd worn at their first meeting.

"You know, Annie, after meeting you, that night, I'd wake up wanting you so bad I couldn't stand it. Almost every damned night. I'd get out of bed and roam my apartment like a mad man. On the few nights I didn't dream about you, I got a full night's sleep, but would have gladly given it up for one more sight of you. One more glimpse of you in *that* skirt, *that* sweater, and a pair of stiletto heels that accentuated the most perfectly shaped calves I've ever seen on any woman before, or since." He dropped his gaze, perusing her from head to toe.

Time to put the next step of *Operation Annie* into action.

Annie struggled for breath, her heart pounding frantically. Heat started at her neck, rose to cover her cheeks. Drake's blatant proclamation succeeded in heating her through and through.

She nodded at something he asked her, without hearing the question.

"Are you sure?"

She blinked. "What?"

"I asked if you were all right. You look kind of shook up."

She nodded, focusing on his eyes. She saw a flash of it first. A smug, self-satisfied look because he'd rendered her speechless, however temporary the situation. She pulled her shoulders back and lifted her chin. Hell if she'd come this far and gone through this much to let him get the upper hand. She closed her eyes, took a deep breath to steel herself against his attack on her independence. She reopened them, staring at the empty spot he'd previously occupied. *What the hell?* She looked around, only to find him leaning over Angelique and speaking to her. Both Angelique and Nash laughed at something Drake said before the gorgeous woman placed her long, graceful hand into his as he led her onto the dance floor.

Annie watched, feeling hopelessly abandoned, as the two beautiful people swayed together gracefully to a sultry, slow, country ballad. She tried to pull her gaze from them, tried not to succumb to the surge of hurt and jealousy as she watched Drake lean closer to his partner and whisper something into her ear. Something that had her throwing her head back in laughter.

"Is she watching us?"

"Oh yes, and it's eating her up. She wants you Drake. She wants you badly."

"Are you sure she's not just pissed at me? She's got a pretty bad temper, you know. I only want her to realize she wants me, not to hate either of us in the process."

"Oh, she'll hate you all right, sha, but only because you make her want you so much. That lady is *certainment* in *amour* with you."

"I don't parlay the fran-say, Angie, so let me have it again in East Texan if you can."

Angelique chuckled. "I said she is certainly in love with you, *mon ami.* Oops, that would be my friend in East Texan."

Drake was so shocked by her presumption, that he missed a step in the dance. He picked it up again and shook his head. "Are you sure?"

"I've never been so sure of anything in my life. Are you sure this is the right way to handle her?"

Drake nodded. "Absolutely. I've told her how I feel; I've chased her, pleaded with her, and insisted how good we would be together. I just told her how I used to wake up every night wanting her, and when I walked away from her she was bracing herself to turn me down, *again*, because she's afraid to let herself care too much."

He shook his head, frustrated as hell at the situation. "I don't know what else to do to convince her, so I decided to handle it differently this time." He sent her a hopeful look. "I'm throwing it all out there on this one, so wish me luck."

Angelique gave him a nod. *"Bon chance,* Monsieur LeBlanc."

Drake's brow furrowed. "Thank you. I think."

Angelique's laughter rang out. "Good luck, silly man!"

Annie finally tore her gaze from Drake and Angelique. What the hell did she care if he danced with another woman? She told him she wouldn't dance anymore slow ones with him, so he had every right to make love with a near stranger on the middle of the dance floor. "Son of a *bitch*," she whispered under her breath.

"I hope you're not talking about me."

She turned as Red sat beside her, and forced herself to smile. "Hey big brother. Nice turn out. You have a knack for making a place successful."

"Thanks. Who were you cussing like that?"

"Nobody. I just realized I was getting another migraine." She made a show of rubbing her temples.

"Did you bring your medicine this time?" he asked, as always, concerned for her.

She nodded. "Yes, I put one in the glove compartment of my car before I left the house. I'd better go before it gets too bad to drive home."

"Are you sure you don't want somebody to bring you? I can't leave but I'll bet Nash or Drake wouldn't mind. Let me go get Drake for you."

"No!" She made a grab for Red's arm. "I can make it just fine."

"All right, but call me if you get too sick to make it all the way."

She nodded, grabbed her jacket and purse, and started making her way to the exit. As soon as she broke free from the edge of the crowd she felt a hand grab her arm. She swung around to face Drake.

"Red told me you may be getting another migraine. Need any help?"

"All the signs—blurry vision—flashes of light," she lied, thinking if she kept this up she'd have a lot to confess to Father Mitch next time around. "I'll be fine, but I have an injection in my car."

"How about Nash? Did he ride with you?"

"Separate vehicles. He's in the Holiday Inn down the street for tonight."

Drake nodded. "Annie, if you need me at all . . . for anything . . . I hope you know you can call. That's what friends are for, right?"

She blinked several times, not knowing why she suddenly felt like crying. "Friends." She managed a nod, biting her bottom lip to keep from blubbering.

"You don't seem to want anything else, so I've decided to stop pestering you. We can both go on about our lives, and when we see each other we'll say hi, and be able to talk like friends . . . right?"

"Right." She smiled too broadly. Nodded too animatedly. Made a big show of agreeing with him.

"Good!" He took a step closer. "Take care, Annie."

She stood there as he leaned over to give her a *friendly* peck on the cheek, as well as a *friendly* pat on the arm. He started to walk away.

Just when Annie was about to turn for the door, he called to her again. She looked hopefully back at him.

"Hey, if you change your mind, just let me know. You know, about needing any help getting home . . . because of the migraine and all." He smiled, gave her a little wink, and turned to walk away. Within seconds, he'd disappeared into the throng of people. Out of her sight.

She turned toward the door and suddenly froze. An irrational wave of anxiety gripped her insides. She told herself there was no reason to be terrified to walk out there alone. There was no J.B. Montgomery out there waiting for her. No would-be-rapists, or murderers, or monsters hiding in the dark.

So why couldn't she take a step?

Drake watched Annie from the inner edge of the crowd. She faced the door and froze, and he knew as sure as he knew his own name, she was terrified to walk out there. Terrified of meeting J.B. out there, or someone else just like him.

She turned back to the crowd of dancers, scanned the area, as if she was searching for him. "Me? Are you looking for me, Annie?"

He physically ached to go to her, but knew she needed to do this for herself. He wanted her, but he wanted all of her. Every volatile, beautiful, self-sufficient, independent, moody, sarcastic, lovable, funny, sexy inch of her. Most of all, he wanted her willing, coming to him freely, and not because she needed a protector. He wanted her brave enough to face the world alone, but *still* willing to have him be a part of it.

His heart surged when she turned back toward the exit. He felt the struggle within her. Saw her take one step toward the door, then another, then a third. Drake's chest puffed with pride as the beautiful, strong woman he loved straightened her spine, lifted her chin in determination, and walked out the door. He smiled, nodding to himself. "That's my girl."

He returned to the table, resisting the urge to run after her, or at the very least, call her. He danced with several members of their party, trying to make the best of an evening without Annie present. Several dances later, Drake thanked Tiffany for the dance and brought her back to Red. He'd just sat down when Nash pulled his phone from his pocket. He watched him answer, his heart tight with panic as Nash's horrified gaze locked onto his.

He was already out of his chair before Nash uttered those dreaded words.

"Montgomery escaped."

Drake barreled his way to the nearest exit, knowing in his gut where the sadistic bastard would go first. Annie had been gone for over thirty minutes already. He prayed she would be able to lock herself up safely by the time J.B. got there. He pictured her as he'd found her that day, curled up in a ball on the floor of his room. The image made him physically sick but he shook it off. No time for that now—he had to get to her.

Within seconds of reaching his truck, he'd peeled out of the parking lot, and was on his way to Annie.

Chapter Twenty-One

Annie made the drive home at a leisurely pace, using the time to think—to wonder why she felt at odds with herself tonight. She finally pulled into her drive and let herself inside through the kitchen door off the carport. Lewis called to her loudly with his typical "Annie's home!" Preoccupied, she passed his cage, nearly tripped over Martin as she stepped inside. The cat wove himself around her legs then looked toward the door, as though expecting someone else. Annie bent to pick him up and rubbed her chin on the scruff of his neck before setting him back down.

"Sorry to disappoint you gentlemen, but it's back to just me, tonight and every night. Get used to it." She locked up, but disarmed the alarm system, wanting to prove to herself there was no reason to fear being alone in her own home. She could do this—without a bodyguard, or any other man, for that matter.

She went to her bedroom, her mind muddled with thoughts of Drake, and changed into her flannel pajamas. Afterward, she went into the bathroom and washed the make-up from her face.

Annie had just pulled the comforter back on her bed, ready to climb in when she heard the sound of a door opening in the other part of the house. Drake hadn't returned her keys. It had to be him. She smiled, had just started for the door when Lewis began to squawk frantically.

"Stranger danger! Annie—get your gun!"

Annie froze in terror as Martin came running into the bedroom to meet her. The sound of footsteps in the hallway had her lunging for the door. She slammed it shut just as a hand with a disturbingly familiar tattoo reached for the knob. She turned the lock the instant it was closed then shoved her chair under the knob. A flashback of Drake forcing the door of the guest room open even with the chair shoved under it.

The last thing she needed was to get stuck in that room with J.B. She ran to the window and opened it as quietly as she could. She fumbled with the key until she heard the locking mechanism open, but the iron grill wouldn't budge. She jiggled it, panicked bile rising in her throat at a sudden realization. She was a prisoner in her own bedroom. Annie reached for the bedroom phone to call for help. Nothing—completely dead. She slammed the phone down, made a futile attempt to find her purse. Her shoulders sagged as she pictured it, hanging on the hook by the door, her phone securely snapped into its side pocket. Damn! Damn! Triple damn! She froze at the sound of J.B.'s evil chuckle through the door.

"Yeah, I cut the phone line," J.B. crowed. "That alarm system won't work without it. Not only that, but I made damn sure you couldn't escape through the window. Kind of ass-chappin', ain't it sweet cheeks? All this security and now you're a prisoner in your own home."

He must have heard her soft curse because his sadistic, blood-chilling laughter reached her from the hallway.

"I bet you didn't think you'd hear from me again, did you, sweet thang?" J.B. issued another evil chuckle. "You know, it was easy enough getting away from that stupid cop, and if I was a smart man, I'd be halfway to Arkansas by now, but ain't nobody ever accused me a'bein' too damn smart."

Annie tore through her closet looking for anything she could use as a weapon. Nothing. Not a damn thing. She finally found the biggest, deepest purse she could find and began loading it down with anything with a little weight to it. She zipped it shut then swung it a few times to test it out. Satisfied that she wouldn't have to face him completely empty handed, she made a mental note to keep a baseball bat in her closet from now on, or better yet, a gun. She'd always said she didn't want to live in a house with guns. Funny how a girl's perspective changed when a murdering rapist had her trapped in her own bedroom. She closed her eyes, uttering a prayer for help as J.B. continued his terrifying ode to himself.

"I had too many nights of thinking about all the things I was gonna do to you to walk away without a sample, so here I am."

"I guess I should feel honored." Annie kept scanning her room for something to use as a weapon.

"You'll feel a lot of things in a few minutes," he told her, "but honored ain't exactly gonna be one of them."

Annie cringed at his words, and then spied the heavy iron curtain rod over her window. It had solid, blunt tipped fleur de lis finials on both ends, and should make an effective weapon. She set the purse down, then climbed on her bed to get to the rod. After struggling for a few seconds, she finally reached it, freed it from the filmy curtains. She swung it several times to adjust to the weight of it then prepared herself mentally for what she had to do. Within seconds, J.B. was pounding at the door, then shoving at the chair she'd jammed under the knob.

Drake wove his truck dangerously in and out of traffic, his cell phone in hand. He'd been trying to call Annie's house phone and kept getting a busy signal. He knew in his gut what that meant. Montgomery was already there. The first thing he'd do would be to cut the phone lines—disable the alarm.

Oh God. He called her cell phone and groaned when her sweet voice asked him to leave a message. He pictured the hook just inside the door where she hung her purse, sure she'd left her phone inside. He swore and hit a speed dial button. "Nash! That son of a bitch is there, I know he is."

"I know, Drake. The phone is inoperable. I've already called the Kenton Police Department as well as the Sheriff's Office. They know what they're dealing with. Just stay calm."

"I can't be calm." When he spoke again, his voice held a sharp edge of steely determination. "I'll kill him. I swear it on my life. If he touches one hair on her head, I'll kill the bastard."

"You'll have to stand in line, buddy. Where are you?"

"I'll be there in ten minutes."

Nash cursed loudly. "You just left from here five damn minutes ago. You'll get yourself killed before you get there."

"Not a chance, but I do need to let you go. Get there as soon as you can." He snapped the phone shut and tried to call Annie's cell again. He'd nearly disconnected when he heard someone answer.

"Hey man, glad you could join the party," J.B. drawled.

"You're a dead man, do you hear me?" He cringed as J.B.'s maniacal laugh reached him.

"Not before I taste me a little bit of that sweet lil redhead in that room she's got herself holed up in. Not fer long, though. I got a gun here, sweet cheeks—you get outta the way, you hear? I don't want you shot before I get to play with you."

Drake jumped as the sound of gunshots rang out over the speaker. "Dammit, Montogomery! I'll kill you, you son of a bitch!"

"Move sweet cheeks, I'm firing the gun again. I ain't got all night to play, and I'm sure the cops 'er on the way by now."

Drake swore loudly as he heard another pop of gunfire.

"Coming through."

Drake heard a crash then J.B. howled with glee.

"Whoo-ee! What is that, honey? You gonna knock my ass out with that little old curtain rod? Your gal has quite a swing there, lover boy. She's just a mite slow."

"Drake?"

Annie's screech filled him with dread. "I'm nearly there, Annie. Hold on Baby!"

"Drake! He's in my bedroom!"

The last thing he heard was her terrified scream. Drake cursed and sped past a parish sheriff's vehicle. The lights came on and began to follow him. He never slowed down.

"I gotta put this phone down now, cuz I need both my hands to do what I want to do," J.B. said, "but I'll put it on speaker so you can listen in. Too bad you can't watch as well as hear what's happenin'."

Annie's skin crawled as she watched him place the phone on the dresser so Drake could be an active participant. She tightened her grip on the curtain rod and braced herself as J.B. turned to rush her. She managed to side swipe his head with the curtain rod on her second swing.

He grabbed the side of his head and snarled. "You bitch!" He lunged for her as she swung it again and caught the rod an inch from his face. She let go of it and kicked him in the knee. He grunted and let go of the rod to lunge at her again. This time he caught her by the neck and squeezed with both hands.

Annie brought her knee up with a sharp jab in his groin area. His breath released with a whoosh as he fell to his knees. She made a run for the door but he caught her foot and tripped her. Annie screeched as she fell with a thud, but a year's worth of self-defense training kicked in, along with a tremendous surge of terror driven adrenaline. She turned and kicked him in the nose with the heel of her foot.

J.B. howled in pain as he grabbed his nose and scrambled to his feet. He pulled his gun out and crowed, "Your bitch is about to die, lover boy!" He aimed the gun at her, totally unprepared for the giant yellow fur-ball of growling, hissing, scratching, biting attack-cat landing on his face.

In one fraction of a second, Annie went from a quick prayer before dying to watching, in a sort of fascinated horror, as Martin literally flew onto the man's face. Her cat's front paws were declawed, but it didn't stop him from digging his rear claws into J.B.'s shoulders in order to get a better grip on his skull with his teeth. The sound of little girl screams coming from a grown man filled the room as his gun carrying arm swung wildly through the air. She hit the bedroom doorway, praying she wouldn't be hit by any stray bullets.

The last thing Drake heard were screams mixed with gunshots before a loud crash made the line go dead. He dropped his cell phone and entered Kenton's city limits at a hundred plus miles per hour, with the sheriff's car in hot pursuit. He slammed on his brakes and made the first turn on two wheels, praying he wasn't too late. By the time he screeched to a halt in front of Annie's house seconds later, red and blue lights were flashing all over the front lawn and driveway. He ran to the door only to be stopped by a police officer.

"Sir, this is a crime scene, you can't go in there."

"Annie!" He scanned the area, desperate to find her, trying to push past the officer.

"Sir, you can't go in there." The officer's voice grew sterner with the second warning.

"Annie McAllister lives here. Is she all right? Was she hurt? Where's that son of a bitch, J.B.?"

"Sir, you'll have to calm down!"

Drake grabbed the officer by the collar, pushed him through the door and up against the wall. "*You* calm the hell down!" he roared. "I need to know, is Annie all right?" He heard a click by his ear and realized the officer had a pistol pointed at his head. All motion and noise ceased in the room as more than a dozen officers joined in by aiming their Glocks at him. He released the officer's collar and raised his hands. "Please," he pleaded, trying to control the pounding of his heart. "Just tell me. Where is Annie? Is she all right?"

His peripheral vision caught a slight movement in the crowd of light blue and khaki colored shirts. Kenton's police chief stepped up to the front. "Stand down everyone—now!" His tone demanded compliance. "He's with Miss McAllister. Let her through."

Drake turned slowly to his left as the sea of uniforms parted to let Annie pass. She was wrapped in her afghan and clinging to Martin but seemed physically unharmed. She got to the edge of the crowd and stopped.

Drake's breath came out in a rush of relief when he saw her. "You're okay . . ."

She nodded, gave him a smile. "I'm okay."

He took a step toward her. "I heard that gunshot and you screamed, and then-then the phone went dead." He shook his head. "I thought . . . oh God . . . I was afraid you were . . ."

She met him the rest of the way, stopping just in front of him. "I probably would be if Martin hadn't jumped on him. I guess it's kind of hard to aim with twelve plus pounds of furious feline in attack-cat mode attached to your face."

Drake emitted something that sounded like a cross between a laugh and a sob as he reached out to take Martin from her. "So, what you're telling me is that fat-boy here, saved your life?"

She nodded. "Yep, and Lewis did his part, too."

"Oh, yeah? What did Lewis do?"

"He warned me when J.B. broke in."

Drake reached out with his cat-free hand to brush the hair back from her face. "Stranger danger?" He sent her a crooked grin.

She nodded. "And 'Annie get your gun'." Her eyes crinkled with laughter. "And Martin ran in my bedroom like The Flash. I had just enough time to lock and barricade my door." She shrugged, "It didn't keep him out for good, but it bought me some time."

He opened up the afghan, gasping at her blood covered clothes. "Jesus, I thought you said you weren't hurt."

She shook her head. "It's not my blood, it's his, and some of this is from Martin's teeth, but not all."

"What'd you do to him?" he asked, amazed at the amount of blood on her.

She cocked her head to the side and counted off on her fingers. "I hit him in the head with a curtain rod, kicked him in the knee—that one really seemed to hurt him, then I put my knee in his groin—that hurt him even more, and after he tripped me I kicked him in the nose with my heel. I may have fractured his arm, and I'm pretty sure I broke his nose. The last thing I saw before I hit the door running was J.B. trying to pull Martin off of his face." She bit her bottom lip. "You missed all the fun."

"So all that high-pitched, muffled screaming I heard . . ."

"That was all J.B."

He stepped closer to her. "I see. But, tell me something. How does a 'harmless', *de-clawed* cat like Martin, manage to keep such a good grip on poor old J.B.'s head?"

Annie grinned as several of the officers heard the question and began to snicker amongst themselves.

"That cat had his teeth buried so deep in that guy's skull I thought we'd have to use a crow bar to pry him off," one officer admitted.

"Man you should have seen it," another added. "There was blood everywhere."

Drake shook his head, filled with a mixture of relief and amusement. Officer LeBleu walked over to meet him and extended his hand. "That cat did a hell of a number on him. He'll need several dozen stitches. The first guys on the scene said it looked like a re-enactment of that old "Alien" movie." He placed his hand over his face.

Drake scratched the cat affectionately behind the ears but didn't take his gaze from Annie. "The next time we eat pizza, Martin gets to eat his fill, okay?"

"I think that could be arranged." Her pixie grin spread across her face.

He reached out one hand to pull her head close to him. He spoke softly into her ear. "Are you sure you're okay?"

"I'm fine."

He closed his eyes, gently touching his forehead to hers. "God, I'm proud of you, Annie Girl."

They stood, relatively isolated in the center of the room as it started to clear out, totally absorbed in each other. So much so, that neither of them paid much heed when an officer led a bloody and battered J.B. into the room, one arm in an awkward sling with his hands cuffed in front of him. A sarcastic comment from the prisoner jarred them both to attention.

"Oh, ain't that sweet? Look at the two lovebirds," J.B. taunted.

As a lawyer, Drake definitely knew better than to strike an unarmed prisoner. "You're so damned lucky you didn't hurt her, J.B. Now you get to live."

"I shoulda snapped that pretty lil' neck as soon as I got my hands on it a while ago," J.B. sneered.

Drake frowned and checked Annie's neck. "Son of a bitch," he hissed, seeing the beginning of what would surely be ugly bruising. He turned and took a step toward J.B. while keeping dangerously silent.

J.B. cackled loudly and rattled his cuffs. "Come on over here if you want a piece of me, fancy man. I kin still whip your ass, even loaded down with a little jailhouse bling."

"Don't do it," Officer LeBleu warned. "That's the quickest way to see that S-O-B walk."

Drake turned his head so that only the officer and Annie could hear what he said next. "Just let me have two minutes alone with him. I swear I won't kill him."

Officer LeBleu shook his head.

"One minute, then. Hell, I'd take thirty seconds. You can be in the room with me. Just un-cuff the bastard and look away for thirty seconds, please."

"Maybe they do that kind of thing in Houston, but not here—"

"—Too bad, sounds entertaining as hell to me," Nash said from the door. Drake pivoted to face the man as Annie met him for a huge, Texas style hug.

"Houston?" J.B. drawled. "I didn't know you was from Texas. I hate Texas! The only thing comes from Texas is steers and queers, and I don't see no horns on you, asshole." When the officer pushed him to move forward again he leered at Annie and licked his lips disgustingly. "Too bad, sweet cheeks, I'd a been the best you ever had. Right up until the moment I squeezed the life right outta you."

Drake vibrated with fury, his hands clenched at his sides as an angry murmur began to spread throughout the room of remaining policemen. "Shut up. You aren't fit to speak to her, you sadistic bastard."

"Oh, you called me a name. My feelings are so hurt." J.B. put his head back and laughed loudly. One of the officers standing on the side shook his head and turned his back to speak to someone behind him. J.B. lunged for the officer's holster, grabbed his gun, and had it turned on Annie before anyone knew what was happening. "You're dead, bitch!"

Drake had just enough time to throw himself in front of Annie as Nash came around with a lightning fast kick to J.B.'s arm the instant a shot was fired. Another kick to his gut had him bent forward so that Nash's third kick to the man's nose ended it for good, shoving already shattered bones into spaces they didn't belong. Everyone watched as J.B. crumpled to the floor.

Officer LeBleu leaned over to check him out and the roomful of people held its' collective breath as he felt for a pulse. He shook his head and stood up slowly. "Well, I know the ambulance is on its way, but by the time it arrives, we'll only need a hearse." The man looked around at his fellow officers. "Him being from Arkansas and all, I guess he never heard that slogan, 'Don't Mess With Texas'. "

Annie released a sob as Drake tried to comfort her. "Shh, babe—it's over now."

"Oh, God. I hope so. I don't think I can take anymore today," she blubbered, fast approaching hysteria. She tore her gaze from the man on the floor to stare up at Drake. In that instant she finally saw what he'd claimed to see all along. She saw her future . . . with Drake LeBlanc. She smiled, suddenly overwhelmed by a complete and utter acceptance of being where she belonged. With him. A second later, she saw something else. Something terribly, terribly wrong.

"Drake? Are you-are you bleeding? Oh God." She screamed as he crumpled to the floor, still holding tightly to Martin with one hand.

Chapter Twenty-Two

Annie stood over his body, tissue in hand, her heart aching with sadness over her loss. Red stood on one side of her, trying to comfort an inconsolable Tiffany, while Liam Nash stood on the other, his head bowed reverently as he tried to hide the fact that he was crying.

Men. She'd never understand why they were so ashamed to shed a tear in front of others. Especially Nash, who'd gotten to know him so well in the last two weeks. Did he believe she'd think less of him for being upset enough to cry?

She leaned over to press a gentle kiss to his head. "Thank you for saving my life. I've loved you since the second I laid eyes on you." Annie straightened, wiping at her tears. She turned away from the gurney, knowing that whatever was left to do, only she could handle. Halfway to her car, Nash caught up with her.

"Annie Girl, do you need some help with anything, or just to talk?"

She gave him a sad smile. Annie Girl—Drake's nickname for her. Why had she given him so much flak over it? Oh yeah, T.J. That felt like a lifetime ago. She shook her head. Two lifetimes ago. She reached out to Liam, brushed his arm softly. "No, but thanks. This is something I need to do by myself. Just one more step to earning my big girl panties, know what I mean?" She smiled through tears at the man who'd earned her everlasting friendship.

He nodded, tight lipped with grief. "I'm sorry, Annie. I've replayed it in my mind a hundred times over. If I'd only been quicker, all this could have been prevented. He wouldn't have had to die." He covered his eyes with one hand to hide his tears.

"He'd understand, Nash. He gave up his life for me, and none of this is your fault. It's J.B. Montgomery's fault, and thanks to you, I'll never have to worry about him again. So stop blaming yourself, do you hear me?"

He choked back a sob and tried to cover it up with a cough. "Okay. You sure you don't want some company?"

She smiled again but shook her head. "I can handle it, and thanks again. For everything." Silently, she climbed into her car and started it. She paused several seconds to blow Nash a kiss and drove off, thinking how badly she dreaded the next hour or so.

Annie pushed open the door with one hand and stood there, trying to accustom her eyes to the dim light of the room. Where the hell was he?

"Boo!"

She jumped at the sound from behind her, accompanied by a sharp jab to each side.

"Gotcha!" He wrapped his arms around her waist before she had a chance to fuss at him.

Annie sighed and leaned back against him. "Jerk!" She turned in his arms. "Drake, are you feeling well enough for some bad news?" She smiled at the face he made, all scrunched up, looking like a little boy who wouldn't eat his oatmeal.

"Oh man. What now?" he groaned.

She paused, bracing herself for his reaction. "Martin's gone." Drake paled noticeably and she struggled to get him to the bed without touching the gauze on his upper chest wound. "Sit, so I can explain."

"Explain what? Your cat's dead because of me. I thought the wound was superficial. Aw man." He hung his head. "Dammit, if I hadn't taken him from your arms he'd be alive now."

"And you'd be dead, remember? He's the only thing that prevented that gunshot from doing any serious damage to you. I think, no, I *know* he would have chosen this if he could have. Especially under the circumstances."

He eyed her curiously. "What circumstances?"

"He was dying, Drake." She tried to control the quaver in her voice. "I just came from the vet and she told me he had cancer, a fast growing type. There was no sign of it for his last physical just under a year ago. It was already in his bones and she said he must have been in unbearable pain."

"He didn't act like he was in pain," Drake whispered. "I'm so sorry, Babe." He pulled her as close as he could with one arm. "When did it happen?"

She grabbed a tissue from the bedside table and wiped her eyes, sniffing loudly. "I came straight here from the vet's office. The wound was serious enough, but she said he probably would have made a full recovery if not for his condition. When she checked on him this morning, he'd passed away in his sleep." She reached up to smooth the frown lines on his forehead. "He was old, Drake, and he went to sleep and just didn't wake up. That's what his chart shows. No spikes. No drastic drops in any readings. He just faded away in his sleep. We should all be so lucky to go that peacefully." She pulled her shoulders back and dabbed at her eyes again. "Besides, he's in kitty heaven now . . ."

Drake kissed her forehead. "Where he can eat all the pizza he wants."

She lifted her finger to add, "And never gain an ounce."

"Not to mention kick all the bad-guy-ass he wants. I think going all 'Alien' on J.B. was probably the most fun he'd had since—"

"Since scaring the crap out of you on New Year's Eve," she added, wearing a somber smile.

"That's likely." Drake released a big sigh. "I'm sure gonna miss him. Can I get you another one?"

Annie raised her hand. "Oh no—Martin can't be replaced just like that. He was too special. He showed up on the doorstep, and as soon as I saw him, I knew, I just *knew* he was meant to be a part of our family. God had a hand in it, and if he wants me to have another pet, he'll send one that needs a family." She looked around the hospital room, saw his suitcase already packed and on the bed. "If you're ready to go, I'm your ride home."

"Sure, but before you bring me home, you think we could swing by Kenton first? I'd kind of like to say goodbye to Martin, unless—it's not too late, is it?" he asked.

"I'll call her and let her know we're on our way," she said, touched by the fact that he even wanted to.

The nurse entered the room with the wheelchair. "Mr. LeBlanc, here's your horse and buggy," she said, winking at Annie. "We usually call it a chariot, but I'm makin' an exception for Tex, here."

"Well, ma'am, you are right on time," Annie said. "I left my own wagon double parked downstairs, and the last thing I need to deal with right now is a ticket from the sheriff o' this here town."

Drake sat in the wheel chair. "Aw, don't you fret none, little lady. All it takes is one good attorney to get you out of that," he said.

"Hmph. Looks like I'm in a heap a trouble then, mister—seeing as how those are pert near non-existent," Annie said.

"Yes'm," the nurse drawled, playing along. "Right up there with Santy Claus and that there Easter Bunny." The two women burst into laughter as Drake grumbled something about not getting any respect.

Annie pulled up under her garage and cut the engine. She sat listening to the sound of silence, mixed with clicks and ticks of the cooling engine, and something else. Steady, rhythmic breathing, not her own, but that of her sleeping passenger. He'd had a difficult time at the vet's office saying goodbye to Martin. More difficult than she, or even he, had imagined. Seeing him bent over her cat, whispering his thanks, his regrets, his gratitude over the part Martin had played in saving his own life and hers— she'd never forget that moment. That was the do or die moment for her. The No-U-Turn experience that led to the here and now.

She turned in her seat to study the man next to her; every glorious feature of his handsome face. Chiseled jaw with its three day growth of beard, perfect brow, straight nose, slightly cleft chin and kissable lips. She loved his looks, but it *so* wasn't the best part of him. The goodness in him topped her list of pros, followed by his intelligence, talent, wit, ability to understand her, his patience with her . . . all of it topped off by the fact that he loved her. His looks? Well, hell, that was *lagniappe*. A little bit extra, the icing on the sexy, delectable Drake cake.

Annie reached over and touched his face, ran the back of her hand down his cheek. "Drake . . ." She spoke in a gentle tone so she wouldn't startle him. The ride from the hospital had been hard physically on him even with the pain pill he'd taken just before departing. Getting out at the vet's office, one town over had nearly done him in, and she'd been glad to see him fall asleep in his seat. She touched him lightly on the arm. "Drake, we're home."

He woke with a start, wincing at the sudden movement. "We'n Lake Coburn already?" he said, sounding a little sleep and a lot drugged up. "Musta passed out." He fiddled with the electric seat adjuster until he was sitting upright. "This isn't—ma house." He squinted through the windshield.

"You're staying with me." She unbuckled her seatbelt then reached over to free him from his.

"I yam?"

She smiled, amused at the sound of Drake on drugs, completely vulnerable, completely out of it. "You certainly yam. I want you here with me."

"Y'do?"

Annie slipped out of the driver's seat and walked around to meet him. "Uh huh, so I can take care of you. It's the least I can do." She got him out of the car and onto her couch with no more questions asked. She brought his suitcase in on the next trip and sat beside him. "Do you need anything?"

He turned his drugged, adoring eyes on her. "I need-ju."

"That's nice, but how do you feel?"

He reached over to grab her hand and placed it on his groin area. "I dunno—you tell me," he slurred. His mouth twisted in an adorable, grin.

Annie laughed as she pulled her hand away. "You feel just fine Tex, now how about you rein in that pony? At least until those stitches come out."

He grunted. "Tha's not a pony. Tha's a stallion." He managed to sound slightly insulted even as he slurred syllables and dropped t's in his drug-induced state.

"Whatever you say, stud." She couldn't stop grinning. "You want to go to bed now?"

"Thought you'd nevuh ashk." He sounded even more drugged, if that was possible.

She helped him off the sofa and walked him down the hallway and into his bedroom.

Once he'd settled, Drake patted the mattress next to him.

She sent him a suspicious look before lying next to him. "Are you in any pain?"

"Mm'fine." He closed his eyes, looking as though he was about to attend a *fais-do-do* as the guest of honor.

Annie curled up on her side against him, her head resting on his left arm and listened as his breathing became even and relaxed. She lay quietly, playing with the hair on his bare chest then lightly tracing the perimeter of gauze covered wound. What if he hadn't been holding Martin? What if that bullet hadn't stopped a fraction of an inch short of causing major damage to his heart? Yes, she loved the pet she'd had for twelve years, but...but what? She loved Drake, that's what. He snorted loudly in his sleep and turned slightly, pulling her closer.

She lifted her finger to trace his eyes, his nose, his lips, and stopped on the dimple in his chin. "I love you." She whispered the words softly, first, as though she were dipping her toe into a tub of warm water to test if the temperature was right. It felt good saying it out loud. It felt right. "I love you, Drake." She spoke louder, letting the warmth envelop her fully, pretending he could hear her.

Then she saw it. The miniscule twitch at the corner of his mouth. And there it was again, almost as though he was trying . . . not . . . to . . .

"Took long nuff," he slurred.

"Son of a . . . you were awake the entire time, weren't you?" She was amused enough not to be angry.

He cracked one eyelid opened, and grinned. "Could'n help m'shelf."

"At least the slur is real."

"Wha shlurr?"

She laughed, and sat up. "Never mind, sleepy head. We'll talk when you wake up."

"Don' leaf." He reached out for her arm. "Say't agin."

She leaned in closer. "I love you, Drake."

He gave her a lopsided smile. "Luff you, Annie Girl." He groaned as she kissed him full on the lips.

"Now go to sleep."

He looped one arm around her neck, pulled her closer. "Mmmm...wanna make love t'you..."

"No strenuous activity for two full weeks. Doctor's orders."

"You c'ld be on top." He clutched at her breast, couldn't quite manage to hold on.

Annie chuckled as his hand fell feebly to the bed. She climbed out and grabbed a quilt from her rocker. By the time she'd finished tucking it in around him, he was breathing deeply and snoring—asleep for real this time. She kissed him soundly on the lips to make sure, and turned away, muttering softly to herself.

"It's gonna be a long two weeks."

Drake finished drying himself and stepped out of the shower onto the tiled floor of Annie's guest bath. He leaned in close to the mirror to examine the stitch free scar on his chest. Not too bad, and other than a slight itchy feeling, it didn't bother him a bit. As of today, he was finally released. They'd celebrated by going to their favorite Mexican restaurant for supper. Annie had a mango margarita and he'd limited himself to one beer, anticipating getting to drive home for the first time in two weeks. It turned out to be a good idea, since they ran to the truck in the middle of a torrential rain that soaked them both to the bone. He pulled on his briefs and jeans, remembering how delectable Annie had looked during the ride home, with her blouse soaked through and clinging to wet skin.

He groaned at the image, feeling the all too familiar tightening in his lower midsection. Living with Annie without touching her had been torture, almost to the point of him packing up and moving back to his rental on more than one occasion. She'd asked him to stay, but suggested they cease and desist on all physical contact until later. When he'd asked how much later, she'd given him a non-committal shrug.

Drake looked around for his shirt, realizing he'd forgotten to pull his clothes from the dryer before showering. He sighed, gathered his rain soaked clothes and headed down the hallway to the laundry room. He was just thinking how good his bare feet felt on the plush carpeting when he rounded the corner and froze in the doorway.

Annie's delectable bottom, covered in faded jeans, bobbed up and down enticingly as she bent over to place her own rain-soaked clothes into the front-loading washer. He took it for as long as he could. Finally, he cleared his throat then adjusted his armload of damp clothes to hide his all too frequent affliction of late. She turned at the sound and straightened. If the rear view was enticing, the front was down-right decadent. The front of her scoop-necked knit shirt dipped dangerously low to reveal a bit of cleavage, while her damp hair curled delicately around her dewy face, still pink from her hot shower. He closed his eyes, biting back another groan.

"Hey." She finally managed to speak, as she forced her gaze from his glorious bared chest. She reached for his laundry, immediately feeling her jump in body temperature. "I'll take those. I'm washing a batch of colored laundry right now."

"I can do it," he said, leaning against the door. "Go ahead and finish what you were doing."

She added a couple more items into the machine and stepped back. "It's all yours," she said, waving her hand at the washer. She squeezed to the side so he could pass and couldn't help but close her eyes to breathe in his masculine scent. She watched him load the washer, then the pre-packaged laundry detergent before starting the cycle, just as she'd taught him.

She was all ready to tell him job well done, but once he faced her, all she could do was stare at the towel dried tufts of hair falling across his forehead. Her line of sight dropped lower, to the mouth she adored kissing, and lower yet, to encompass an overabundance of well-sculpted pecs and planed abs. The few glimpses she'd caught of him without a shirt had never been in such close proximity.

His scar was at eye level and she found it strangely alluring. Her fingers itched to touch him. Her palms ached to examine the silken mat of golden brown hair feathering his broad chest. She pictured herself showering soft kisses across his broad chest. Tasting him, getting her fill of touching him.

Eventually, she became aware that he'd spoken. "Did you say something?" She looked up, found his gaze locked on her. Annie blinked several times to clear her head and bring him into focus. She moistened her parched lips with her tongue. The urge to taste him grew stronger. "What?" she asked again, slightly breathless.

"I asked if you'd warmed up. Your teeth were still chattering when we got home. Are you feeling all right?"

Annie nodded. Fact was, if she made the one move she was dying to make, the walls of this invisible barrier she'd erected would come tumbling down, bundles of bricks at a time. She took one deep breath and forged ahead by placing her palm on his chest at eye level. Curving her fingers, she molded her hand to the shape of him before sliding it slowly along his ribcage and onto his ripped abdomen. Other than his sharp gasp at her initial touch, he hadn't moved. Hadn't made a sound. Assuming she hadn't affected him, she chanced a look up and nearly lost her breath at the searing heat emanating from those chocolaty brown irises. "I've never felt better."

His wove his fingers through her hair, crunching handfuls as he stepped closer, forcing her back against the wall.

Annie landed with a soft thud against the sheet rock and brought her hands to his biceps, marveling at the strength rippling through them.

"Annie . . ." Drake's voice came out in a hoarse croak.

"Oh. God." An instant later their mouths met in a tidal wave of want. Drake smothered her moan with a mind-blowing kiss. He lowered his hands to her butt, lifted her easily from the floor. One thrust of his hips and she was vividly aware of his mutually blatant desire. She wrapped her legs around his hips as he pushed firmly against her with a grunt.

She broke free from the kiss. "That sounded painful, Drake. Are you in pain?" she gasped, concerned for his wound.

"The only pain I'm in is this." He pressed against her. "I'm sorry, Babe, but if I don't get some kind of relief soon . . ." His voice trailed off in a tortured groan.

His predicament thrilled her. Annie rewarded herself with a quick taste of his neck with her mouth and tongue.

"Annie . . ." He pressed harder against her.

Annie nipped him lightly with her teeth, smiling at every shudder and groan he released. This is what she wanted. Complete control of the situation. With Drake completely out of it, unable to think straight because he wanted her so badly. She gloated for a full thirty seconds before he buried his mouth on her neck and soon had her writhing in the slow, sweet torture of sexual frustration.

He lifted his mouth from her neck. "Annie, we need to talk first." He spoke in a low, hoarse murmur before planting another searing kiss on her lips. He pulled away and she nearly cried out from the loss. She wanted him so badly, but forced herself into some semblance of control long enough to speak close to his ear.

"Drake, listen to me," she whispered, but couldn't resist the temptation of catching his earlobe between her two teeth. She smiled when she heard Drake's hybrid groan of pleasure and frustration. "Are you listening to me?"

"Uh huh—God, yeah—I'm listening Annie, I swear."

"Good. I want to tell you . . ." Nip. "How much . . ." Tickle. "I love you, Drake." Nip-nip-bite-nip. "I really, really, love you."

He found her mouth and kissed her gently. "I love you, Annie. I love you so much." He tightened his arms around her bottom, and carried her carefully down the hallway.

"Drake, put me down. I don't want you hurting yourself."

"Don't worry about me, Babe. I'm fine."

"Where are we going?" She continued to nip playfully at his neck, smiled at his shudder.

"Anywhere but the laundry room." He finally made it to his king-size bed in the room he'd occupied for nearly six weeks.

"Are you sure you don't want to go back? Melissa and Bailey have both raved about washing machine spin-cycles. Something about good vibrations."

Drake grinned as he dropped her onto the huge, soft mattress. "By the time I'm done with you, you won't be missing any spin-cycle, I can promise you that."

Judging from the way he was looking at her, she didn't doubt it for second.

"Marry me, Annie." He'd meant to have this conversation before their first time. Things being what they were, it didn't happen that way.

Annie lay at a ninety degree angle to him with her head on his chest. She gave him a sweet smile before shaking her head. "No."

"You said you loved me." With his head supported by two pillows, he stared at the woman he adored.

She smiled again. "I do love you."

He tightened his arm around her. "Then marry me. I love you."

"No Drake. This is all so new to both of us. Let's just be happy that we're together for now. There's no rush, is there? Let's make sure we're right for each other and enjoy this time, for however long it lasts."

Determined to end this night with a resounding 'yes', Drake rolled her to her back and leaned over, his face mere inches from hers. "From the moment I met you, I knew you were the one for me. I took one look at you and my heart knew it. I want to grow old with you, Annie Girl."

"Is that an old pick-up line?" she asked, one eyebrow arched playfully.

Drake shook his head and laughed. "I've never needed pick-up lines. *You're* the only one who's ever been this obstinate."

"So, how do you know it's not just 'the chase' you find so appealing? How do you know now that you've had me, the wanting won't make a run for the border?"

He played with her hair, letting the silky, auburn tresses loop and curl around his fingers, loving the feel of it. "Because, Ms. McAllister. That 'chase' you're talking about usually ended in bed, not with me imagining what our children would look like."

"You do that?"

"Absolutely. When I picture my children, I see them with this gorgeous red hair and your crystal-blue eyes." He kissed the tip of her nose. "And when I see myself as an older man, I see you beside me, also older, but still the most beautiful woman I've ever known." He placed his hand gently along the side of her face and hovered over her.

"There's no one else for me. I'll never leave you, I'll never break your heart, and I'll never stop asking. I love you, Annie Nicole McAllister. Will you please put me out of my miserable bachelor existence? Please make me the happiest man alive, and marry me?"

"Oh." She released a long slow breath. "Oh, Drake . . . " She blinked back tears.

"Yes?" His eyebrow lifted in question.

"Yes."

Chapter Twenty-Three

"What are we waiting for?" Drake pulled at the collar of his black designer tux. He stood, lined-up with the rest of the wedding party just outside the door of Red's Club. The day had dawned with gorgeous spring weather, clear as fine crystal and cool, despite the warming rays of the sun. Drake groaned. "I'm dying to get out of this thing."

Tiffany clucked her tongue. "Poor baby brother, you want some cheese with that whine?"

Drake regarded his sister, well into her fifth month of pregnancy. "I'm taking under consideration the fact that you're hormonal and two months away from looking like a beached whale, and I'll let that one slide."

Annie slapped playfully at the hand still tugging at his collar. "Leave that alone and stop picking on your pregnant sister."

"She started it!" He froze as Annie's right eye brow arched dangerously. "Okay, but why are we waiting out here when everyone else is inside?"

"We're waiting for the traditional Cajun wedding march to begin. We had this discussion with Mom, remember?"

"Yeah, something about walking in a circle to somebody playing a Cajun song, and then everyone pins money on us?" His face lit up, suddenly.

Annie laughed. "You and I walk the circle alone first while the march is being played, then the wedding party joins in. The 'money dances' come in a little later when the D.J. announces it, but you've got the gist of it."

Red slapped his brother-in-law on the back and laughed. "We'll make a Cajun out of you yet, boy."

Drake gave Red a thumbs-up. "Any tradition that has people pinning money on me and my bride is one I want to be a part of. Besides, Tiff and I have Cajun roots already, remember?"

"Yeah," Tiffany offered. "They've just been buried pretty deep for four decades, that's all. And I lost my Texas accent years ago. You will too, eventually, little brother."

"Oh, I hope not." Annie gazed up at her new husband. "I like having my big, strong cowboy with his east Texas twang. It's kind of hot."

Drake gave his new wife a pained expression. "For God's sake, Annie. Don't say that when I've been without it for two long months."

"You mean *hot*?" She giggled at his strained expression.

"Keep it up, Annie," he groaned. "We'll see how funny you think it is when I drag you into the nearest storeroom in this place and have my way with you. In my condition, all I need is a sturdy wall, about six square feet of floor space, and two minutes . . . tops."

"Don't you dare! You'll mess up this masterpiece." She touched her hair up-do with its artfully arranged curls.

Drake gave her a dangerous look. "Annie, I can get in and out of there without touching a hair on your head. You've been warned."

Red snorted with laughter as the doors opened and they entered the club to the sound of an accordion playing Cajun music.

Annie and Drake entered first to applause then walked slowly in a large circle on the dance floor, as required by the old Cajun tradition. The rest of the wedding party joined in until all four couples, along with the miniature bride and groom, circled the dance floor three more times by the end of the song.

Vivienne McAllister approached them with hugs. "I want to thank you both for including that in the reception. Lots of younger couples don't care to include that in their ceremonies. We're losing our culture." She grabbed each of their hands and beamed, "It mean a lot to me that you did. Thank you again."

"It's a family tradition, Mom. Of course I'd want to include it in my wedding. Drake understands." Annie nodded at her new husband.

"Sure do, Ms. Vivi," Drake added. "It was kinda fun; like being the grand marshal in our own little parade or something."

Vivi laughed. "I guess it would feel a little like that, except it's over a lot sooner. Are you going to include the money dances too?"

Drake's face lit up like a kid with his first bike. "Absolutely! First we get to lead our very own parade, and then we get paid to dance with people. This day's gettin' better all the time."

Annie braced herself as the DJ called for the father-daughter dance, fully prepared to shed a few tears. Her dad joined her for the band's beautiful rendition of *Stealing Cinderella*.

Pete McAllister led his youngest daughter, hand in hand, to the dance floor and gave her a hug. "Are you happy, baby girl?"

Annie hand to lean far back to smile up at the gentle giant of a man she called her father. "I am, Dad." She glanced over at her husband, who stood watching from the sidelines. "I found a good one, didn't I?"

"I believe you did, honey." He glanced over to where Drake stood next to Red and Tiffany, who were providing him with another grandchild in four months. "We got two great in-laws out of your marriages, as well as two wonderful new friends in Daniel and Leah. I wish we could see them more often."

"We will. The property down the road from Red's ranch came up for sale and Mr. Daniel snatched it up. They have some updating to do to the house on the spot but they should be moved in before their first grandchild is born at the end of August. It'll be nice to have them around here."

"Well, hell that is good news! They're going to love being close to their kids and grandchildren," the big man said. "And speaking of grandchildren, when do you two plan on starting a family?"

"We'd discussed waiting a couple of years, but you never know." She caught her breath when her dad's eyes misted over suddenly. If he was about to have a meltdown in the middle of their father-daughter dance, she wouldn't be far behind him. "You okay, Dad?"

He nodded, blinking rapidly. "Annie, if I haven't told you this recently, it needs to be said. You have been an absolute joy to your mother and me."

Annie sniffed and nodded. "Thanks, but you don't have to sugar coat it. I know I was a royal pain in the butt for you and Mom."

He shook his head. "No more than any of the others and less than most of them."

"Except that I was home longer," she added.

"You want to hear a secret? I didn't mind for the most part. I wasn't ready to see our baby leave the nest."

"Speaking of secrets—" She paused, wondering how to approach the subject of what happened twelve years earlier. "I know you and Mom found the letter."

Her father gave his head a quick shake. "We don't have to talk about that, baby girl."

"I do. I'm sorry Mom had to find it like she did. I kept the letter to remind myself how weak I'd been. It ended up being more of a reminder of how strong I was, instead. It kept me from letting anyone get too close."

Her dad gave her an indulgent smile. "And did it work?"

Annie glanced over at her new husband, standing with some members of her family. "Long enough for the right guy to come along." She watched as Drake reached out for her five month old niece and seemed to struggle for a comfortable hold on the infant. The slightly awkward, but totally adorable "daddy look" worked for him.

She found herself wondering how he'd feel about ditching the plans to start a family later, rather than sooner. He looked up unexpectedly to meet her gaze, lifted the child in his arms and nodded. Then he gave her a sexy smile and a wink. She laughed, suspecting she wouldn't hear much resistance on his part if she broached the subject.

Several songs later, Drake tugged Annie onto the dance floor for a belly rubbing oldie. She kissed him once, and a second time, suddenly felt the need to nibble on his lower lip, then his ear lobe, then his neck.

Drake pulled away with a groan and craned his neck as though searching for something.

"What are you looking for, Babe?"

"Six square feet of unoccupied space," he growled. "You were warned."

She smiled mischievously at him. "I know the last two months of abstinence have been difficult, but I think Father Mitch was right when he said it would strengthen our relationship. It's proven to both of us that our feelings for each other are about more than just sex."

He leaned in and nipped her on the neck. "Yep, it's about having someone to share the rest of my life with. But damn, I'm ready for the honeymoon to start."

"We need to show our faces around here for another hour or so, at the very least. Besides—" She lifted Drake's watch to check the time. "The band should be making an announcement any minute now."

Within seconds of ending their dance, the house band's guitarist announced that their drummer, a stand-in for the night, had written a song for his wife and wanted to sing it for her.

Annie's eyes sparkled with excitement. "This is about to get interesting. Let's get closer."

On the way to the area edging the bandstand, she spotted Julia speaking to her parents. Annie grabbed her hand and pulled her along with them to the front of the crowd, where Tiffany and Red already stood.

Julia arrived at the area in front of the bandstand, feeling a distinct undercurrent of excitement rippling through her in-laws. She turned to Annie. "What's going on?"

"Some guy in the band is about to sing a song he wrote for his wife."

"Oh, how utterly romantic." Julia began to search the crowd. "Is she here? Where is she?"

"I don't know," Annie said. "He's about to start…shh…"

Julia searched the shadows of the bandstand. The area around the drummer seemed to be darker than the rest of the stage. The man cleared his throat nervously.

"I apologize for interrupting the reception, folks, but the bride and groom have graciously allowed me to use this moment as a chance to get my life back."

Julia strained to see into the darkness. The drummer sounded kind of like Chad, although slightly muffled by the microphone. But for some reason, Chad wasn't here. He was supposed to be, but nobody seemed to know where he was. She couldn't believe he'd *choose* to miss his sister's wedding. One more reason to be disappointed in her husband.

"Annie and Drake," the man continued. "I'll always be grateful for this opportunity to tell my beautiful wife how much she means to me. Tiffany and Red, I want to thank you for helping me put to music, the words I wrote for her. I only pray that it works. It's called *Heaven in Your Eyes,* and this is for you, Jules."

The words had Julia's breath rushing out in a shocked gasp. Frozen in place, she felt herself being nudged gently forward as the spotlight fell upon the drummer. "Oh my God," she murmured softly, as the band began to play a hauntingly beautiful melody. A few bars later, her husband's beautiful tenor voice began singing the lyrics he claimed to have written . . . for her.

> *When I look into—those vivid eyes of blue,*
> *I can't imagine life without your love.*
> *Hold me in your arms—keep me safe and warm*
> *You're it for me, fit me like a glove.*
>
> *Each day I see heaven in your eyes…*
> *Our love will stand the test the time.*
> *You see it too, it's no surprise.*
> *When I saw you, the love I saw was mine.*

Her heart melted as her husband sang for her for the first time in years.

> *I can't forget the day—can't forget the way,*
> *I failed you, the love I held true.*
> *Your love betrayed—I should have stayed.*
> *Instead I walked away from you.*
>
> *I caused you pain—I put a strain*
> *On our love. The good Lord above*
> *Helped me to see through the rain.*
> *The only thing important is our love.*
>
> *I'd done my part, to break your heart*
> *I let you go—but now I know*
> *I'll do my part, for a brand new start.*
> *Now I know, I can't let your love go.*

He'd quit the band he loved because he'd begun to panic singing in front of crowds, even if it was just his family. Knowing this must be torture for her husband, she took a step closer so she could watch as he sang to her of love. Everlasting, ever growing, ever faithful, temporarily betraying but ever forgiving, resounding love.

> *I can't go on without heaven in your eyes . . .*
> *I want our love to stand the test the time.*

You see it too, it's no surprise.
When I saw you, the love I saw was mine.

I'll follow you to heaven and above.
You're my home, wherever you roam
You're my heart—take me back my love.
Wherever you are is where I'll call my home.
Where my sweet love is . . .
that's where I'll call my home.

The last haunting notes reverberated then drifted off into silence as Chad stood and walked to the edge of the band stand. "I've been a fool, Julia, and I'm so sorry. If you'll have me back, I'll follow you anywhere. I understand now what I didn't fifteen months ago. It makes no difference which continent I call home, as long as I lay my head next to the woman I love." Chad climbed off the stage and walked over to his wife.

Julia wiped the tears she'd cried throughout her husband's performance, as well as his speech.

"Please, please forgive me Julia. I promise I will spend the rest of my life making up for the time we lost. I love you, Babe."

The crowd had dissipated around them until the two of them stood alone.

"Chad, you sang for me . . ." Tears clogged her whispered reply.

"I tried Jules. I tried my best."

"It used to terrify you."

He picked up his shaking, sweaty palms to show her. "It still does, but not nearly as much as the thought of losing you."

Julia tried to stem the tears, unsuccessfully. "How—when did you do all this?"

"I wrote the song after I left you in London and begged Red to compose the melody for me. I didn't know how I'd get you to hear it, but another wedding in the family was the perfect way to get you over to play it for you." He placed his hands gently on her face and stepped closer. "Julia, tell me it worked. Please tell me it's not too late."

"You . . . wrote that song . . . for me?"

He nodded. "It's far from perfect, I know. But it's from the heart."

Julia covered her face, sobbing quietly into both hands as she shook her head from side to side.

"Julia . . ." The word came out in a brokenhearted whisper. He released a single, drawn-out sigh as he released her, one filled with regrets and missed opportunities. "I'll always love you, Babe. Always, no matter what." He turned slowly, began to walk away.

"Chad."

He stopped and turned, a glimmer of hope touching his eyes.

"It's not."

"Not what?"

"Too late," she said. "It's not too late. Loving you has never been the problem. I've always loved you."

He retraced his steps until he stood before her. "Are you giving me another chance?"

"Come back with us to England, Chad. Just nine more months, and then we can all come home for good."

He cupped her face in both hands, touched his forehead to hers. "For longer than that, if you need to be there. And thank you, Baby. You won't regret it, I promise." He kissed her softly, then wrapped her in his arms, rocking her gently.

Julia released a long, luxurious sigh, knowing this was where she belonged, in her husband's arms, no matter the geographic location.

A throat cleared loudly behind them.

Chad released her and the two of them turned to see Red standing there, his face covered in a satisfied grin. He gave her a quick hug, then extended his hand to Chad, who grasped it immediately. When Red pulled back his hand, Chad stared at the key his brother had left in his palm.

"My office is at the end of that hallway if you two want to, you know, talk things over. Nobody will bother you, just lock the door." He turned, paused, and turned back to face them. "Oh . . . it's sound proof. Just in case you were wondering." He winked.

Julia glanced at her husband.

His face broke into that sexy grin every McAllister male seemed to have mastered. "Say the word, Babe."

She grabbed his hand and headed for the hallway. Hearing Red's chuckle and a call out of "You're welcome," she stopped short. "Chad, wait."

She rushed back to her brother-in-law and threw her arms around his waist for a big hug. "Thanks, Red. You know you'll always be my favorite." She gave him a kiss on the cheek then grabbed her husband's hand again as they hurried to the end of the hallway.

Annie approached Red from behind, followed by other curious family members. "Did it work?"

"I believe so." He beamed, looking rather pleased with the outcome.

Annie clapped her hands and turned to her husband for a hug. "Now I feel as though we can go on our honeymoon and not stress over anything." She beamed at her mother, who suddenly looked as though she had something important to say. "Are you okay, Mom?"

Vivienne smiled, placing a hand on either side of Annie's face. "I want you to be so happy, Annie Nicole."

Annie nodded. "I am, Mom. You've always set a wonderful example for us and if my marriage is half as happy as yours and Daddy's turned out, it'll be a success."

Vivienne hugged her tightly, then turned to her newest son-in-law. "Welcome to the family, Son."

"Thanks, Mom. Does that mean I'm privy to when you bake one of those coconut cakes again?"

Vivienne placed her hand on his cheek. "Anytime you want one, sweetie, you just say the word."

He barely managed a quick "Will do," before Annie pulled her husband onto the dance floor for another slow song, this time the country band's own rendition of an old Lionel Ritchie song, *Stuck on You*. She practically purred with satisfaction as he wrapped his arms around her.

Drake gave her a soft, lingering kiss before speaking. "It's like I told you on Christmas Day at Red and Tiffany's ranch. You're stuck with me, Annie Girl. Come hell or high water."

Annie beamed at her new husband. "You should have put money on it, counselor."

"You're right, I should've."

"And now, I've got you exactly where I want you." She looped her arms around his neck, rose on her tiptoes for another heated kiss from the man who'd convinced her to take one last gamble on love. She'd bet her entire pile of M&M's on one hand, and walked away a winner.

Annie pulled back far enough to get a good look at Drake's chocolate brown eyes.

Mm-mm. Her kind of heaven . . . for sure.

ABOUT THE AUTHOR

Lori Leger is a wife, mother, doting grandmother, and Mistress of Procrastination. She lives in Louisiana with the love of her life, her very own Studley-do-Right. He's earned his spot in the Keeper Husband's Hall of Fame by allowing her to walk away from an eighteen year career as an Engineering Technician in Road Design to stay home and write.

She adores writing stories set in her beloved south Louisiana, where good Cajun cooking, helping your neighbors, and saying y'all is as normal as hurricanes, heat, and humidity. She figures as long as she's not tunneling through ten feet of snow to get to her car, it's a perfectly acceptable trade-off.

Lori has nine novels published in two series: La Fleur de Love and its spin-off, Halos & Horns series. She has also contributed to, as well as published, short stories in each of the five Seasons of Love anthologies, an author collaboration series. She's contributed to the Sweet & Savory Cookbook of Amazon Authors, published by Top Ten Press. Lori also has an article published in the non-fiction book Writing After Retirement: Tips From Retired Writers, published by Rowman and Littlefield Publishers, and edited and compiled by Carol Smallwood and Christine Redman-Waldeyer.

Her latest book, Running Out of Rain is the first book in her Prime of Love Series, novels dedicated to mature characters finding love and laughter through the everyday twists and turns of growing older. She has a second planned for a fall 2015 release date, and a third set for the summer of 2016.

Lori Leger
P.O. Box 641
Kinder, LA 70648
cajunflair@lorilegerauthor.com
www.lorilegerauthor.com
www.facebook.com/lorilegerauthor
www.facebook.com/llegerauthor
www.facebook.com/CajunflairPublishing
Twitter: @LoriLegerAuthor

OTHER WORK BY LORI LEGER

Fleur de Love
(Series set in southwest Louisiana)
Book 1: SOME DAY SOMEBODY
Book 2: LAST FIRST KISS
Book 2.5: HART'S DESIRE - A Novella
Book 3: BROWN EYED GIRL
Book 4: HEAVEN IN YOUR EYES

Halos & Horns
(Spinoff series: Where residents of Louisiana and Texas cross the state line to find romance.)
Book 1: GREEN EYED TEMPTATION
Book 2: SARAH SMILE
Book 3: MEAGAN'S MARINE
Book 4: ONE YEAR TO FOREVER

Seasons of Love
(Multi-authored Seasonal series by Cajunflair Publishing)
Book 1: HEARTS, HEARTHS & HOLIDAYS
("Bells Will be Ringing" by Lori Leger)
Book 2: SPRING PROMISE
("Loving Cat" by Lori Leger)
Book 3: SWEET SUMMERTIME LOVE
("Still Loving Cat" by Lori Leger)
Book 4: CHRISTMAS BY CANDLELIGHT
("Baby Blues Christmas" by Lori Leger)
Book 5: IT'S A SUMMER THING
("Full Circle Summer" by Lori Leger)

FULL CIRCLE LOVE
Cat & Zach Stories
(The last four stories from the Seasons of Love Series in one book)

Prime of Love
(A Mature Love Series)
Book1: RUNNING OUT OF RAIN

Non-Fiction article in the book:
WRITING AFTER RETIREMENT
Published by: Rowman and Littlefield Publishers

www.ingramcontent.com/pod-product-compliance
Lightning Source LLC
Chambersburg PA
CBHW051948220626
47052CB00004B/845